THE BERLIN WARNING

THE BERLIN WARNING

NICHOLAS GUILD

G. P. PUTNAM'S SONS / NEW YORK

Library of Congress Cataloging in Publication Data

Guild, Nicholas.
  The Berlin warning.

  1. World War, 1939–1945—Fiction. I. Title.
PS3557.U357B4 1984 813'.54 83-19195
ISBN 0-399-12914-6

Printed in the United States of America

This book is for Joanie,

Οἰ μὲν ἰππήων στρότον, οἰ δὲ πέσδων,
οἰ δὲ νάων φαῖο᾽ ἐπὶ γᾶν μέ λαιναν
᾽ἐμμεναι κάλλιστον, ᾽ἐγω δὲ κῆν᾽ ὄτ-
τω τις ᾽ἐραται . . .

Sappho, 16, 1–4

THE BERLIN WARNING

I

OCTOBER 24, 1941

Hauptmann Egon Weinschenk of the Security Department of the SS fidgeted nervously on the back seat of his staff car, waiting for his aide to return with sweetrolls and a thermos of coffee from the bakery around the corner. It would be the only chance they had all morning for any breakfast, but somehow it struck him as slightly undignified, almost ludicrous, that Max, in his uniform and his polished black storm-trooper's boots, should be standing around in a cake shop, waiting meekly to be served.

Outside there was a faint breeze stirring; he rolled down his window to avail himself of a little fresh air. It was autumn, the season when, to Weinschenk's mind, Berlin looked the prettiest. The leaves on the linden trees were just beginning to change color, and the morning sky was characteristically a pale, pearly gray. People could still go out-of-doors without their overcoats, and somehow the city seemed cleaner. Wein-schenk was a Swabian and detested Berlin, with its vulgar official buildings and its hateful modernity, but in the autumn he could just tolerate it.

The Hauptmann took off his soft civilian hat and ran a hand over his dark brown thinning hair. At thirty-four, the slowly accumulating signs of age were beginning to depress him. The bluish shadows in the corners of his eyes, which had been with him since boyhood, had seemed deeper of late, as if the eyes themselves had started to sink farther back into their sockets, and his whole countenance struck him as more angular, especially around the lower half of his face.

Of course, most of the people he knew were making the same complaint. His friends in the SS, the men with whom he had attended university, it seemed that everyone was feeling it. One could hardly hold a friendly conversation anymore without hearing that life was becoming leaden and hopeless. Possibly it was just the war, or possibly this was simply something that happened at his time of life, but, in his own case at least, Weinschenk thought not. The grievances were more specific than that. As imperceptibly as the wind wears away stone, failure had settled over him like a shadow.

What hadn't seemed possible after his first tour in Spain? He had volunteered for duty in the Condor Legion and had come home covered in glory. He had distinguished himself in combat when not half a hundred SS officers had ever even heard a shot fired in anger, and the Führer himself had signed the order promoting him to Hauptmann. He could have stayed in Berlin then and risen effortlessly up through the command structure; he was a young man people had noticed. He could have had everything, but he had asked for a new posting to Madrid. It had struck him as the only thing possible. It was in Spain that the battle had been joined, and life wasn't about fashioning a career. Life was the sacred honor of German arms and the final victory for a New Europe. Life was the romance of the spirit. How very distant all of that seemed now.

They had assigned him to counterintelligence. He was a staff officer now and could hardly expect to spend his time clambering over battlefields. He would protect secrets. Madrid, as everyone knew, was full of spies; he would find plenty to keep himself occupied.

He had been on his way to distinguishing himself all over again, until his one great and dramatic failure.

When the war had ended and he had come home for the last time, there had been no parade review in front of the Reichskanzlei and no order for promotion. It was 1939, and war, this time the real war, was inevitable—they would need him. Spain had become something of an embarrassment. Men who had hardly finished their officer training classes when he was a hardened veteran were colonels today, having won promotion commanding the *Einsatzgruppen* in the Eastern Territories. That was what the SS had become, a brotherhood of file clerks and murderers in which one rose to glory by shooting Jewish children with a pistol.

Hauptmann Weinschenk would remain Hauptmann Weinschenk, perhaps forever. His immediate superior disliked him and intrigued against him, and there was very little opportunity of being noticed for the sort of routine work that had fallen his way. There were always the *Einsatzgruppen*, but since he did not choose to follow the butcher's trade he was stymied.

Perhaps he wouldn't have minded so very much if things had been better at home. Other men were able to console themselves in their domestic happiness, but Magda . . .

He turned his head slightly and saw Max coming around the corner, carrying a white cardboard parcel done up with string, balancing it with ridiculous delicacy in his huge hand. His black military tunic seemed stretched to the bursting point—somehow it was impossible ever to find him a uniform that didn't look too small—and the corporal's stripes on the sleeves gleamed luridly in the sunshine. With his cap pitched to one side of his massive, carefully cropped head, he gave the impression of a dangerous animal tamed to service.

The heavy scar across his throat, a souvenir, like Max himself, of the time in Madrid, showed where a knife slash had cut his vocal cords, rendering him speechless, but Weinschenk, whose memories of him preceded the incident, was of the opinion that it had made remarkably little difference. Max was a useful assistant in all practical matters, rather like a well-trained dog, but his intellect was not of a very high order and he had never been particularly chatty. A growl and a gesture served most of his needs quite eloquently.

They had wanted to invalid him out after his wounding—they had felt that a mute beast could hardly do the SS much credit—but Weinschenk had managed to prevent them. What would have become of Max if they had taken away his stripes and abandoned him to the great mad world? He would have ended in the gutter, or on the gallows, within half a year. That too would hardly have done the SS much credit. Besides, Max was his comrade in arms, almost his only friend. One must be able to trust someone. No—to desert him would have been unthinkable.

Max opened the door on the driver's side, climbed in, and handed back the thermos and the cardboard parcel with a narrowing of his eyelids and a low, atavistic grunt—one gathered the bakery had been out of *Berliner Pfannkuchen*.

"Never mind, Max. Another day. I'm sure you made your disappointment known to them."

The Hauptmann smiled and made a gesture with the fingers of his right hand, as if to say, "*get on with it*," and Max twisted back to the windscreen and turned the key in the ignition. The car jumped forward a few inches and edged its way into the sparse traffic of the Möckenstrasse. Weinschenk had a call to pay.

Gruppenführer Nebe had been extremely vague. "It concerns one of the Foreign Minister's little projects," he had said, raising his eyebrows contemptuously. "He wishes us to investigate someone in his office, to discover if he has been in treasonous contact with the enemy. You will establish that—and only that. Needless to say, Reichsführer Himmler will not be excessively distressed if Herr von Ribbentrop's intrigue comes to nothing."

There was a large polished window behind the Gruppenführer's desk; the light streaming in formed a kind of halo around his head and made it impossible to read his expression. Weinschenk hardly minded—it wouldn't do to react to Nebe's obvious hostility. If it could have been managed, he would have preferred to receive his orders from behind a screen, like absolution in a confessional.

Above a certain level, the SS was more like a harem than the army it parodied—everyone was competing for the Master's attention. If one was ambitious—and Weinschenk was perceived to be half mad with ambition; why else would anyone have volunteered for a second tour in Spain?—the wisest policy was to disguise the fact, to play the humble acolyte, to appear ready to bask in the reflected power of others. Men like Gruppenführer Nebe had not the slightest intention of allowing a subordinate to develop into a rival and, unfortunately, returning to Berlin with the dust of war still clinging to his boots, Weinschenk hadn't learned quite fast enough that the former upholstery salesman from Lübeck had no taste for heroics.

At any rate, the Hauptmann gained the distinct impression that he was being ordered to look the other way while that "treasonous contact" was being made.

"Here is the man's dossier," Nebe went on, sliding a heavy manila envelope across his desk. Weinschenk picked it up and clamped it under his arm; any display of curiosity just then might have been interpreted as a breach of military etiquette. "When you have discovered what he's been up to, shoot him. No one is interested in the embarrassment of a trial."

"And if he hasn't been up to anything, Herr Gruppenführer?"

"Shoot him in any case. It will flatter von Ribbentrop's vanity."

That was clear enough. The SS had no real interest in this matter beyond undermining the position of the Foreign Minister, which was one of Reichsführer Himmler's favorite projects. Did von Ribbentrop even know that the Security Department was investigating one of his people? It seemed unlikely, but there was no shortage of SS spies at the Wilhelmstrasse to ferret out such lapses of vigilance. Hauptmann Weinschenk was assigned to commit what amounted to a judicial murder. The facts of the case were irrelevant; a man was to die as part of some obscure bureaucratic struggle in which neither he nor his executioner had any share. Weinschenk hoped that the "treasonous contact" didn't turn out to be merely another invention in the continuing unreality into which life had descended. He hoped the little worm was guilty. He didn't like to think what would become of them both if he weren't.

"My regards to your wife, Weinschenk."

Even in the glare from his polished window, the expression on Nebe's face was recognizably a sneer. As he stood at attention, the Hauptmann could feel the shame and anger turning his bowels into ice water.

The next morning, sitting in the back of a police van that had been painted over to look like a newspaper delivery truck, Weinschenk caught his first glimpse of the pawn in this chess game of ministerial rivalries. Klaus von Abeken was a small, spare, bleached-out little man in his mid-fifties who walked with his elbows bent and turned away from his body. He wore a black jacket, gray trousers with a thin white stripe, and wing collars on his shirt—a costume which had by then become slightly obsolete even in the diplomatic corps. His gray hair was swept back from his thin, dissatisfied face, and he carried a black hat, possibly a bowler, in his right hand. He looked English. He had been stationed in London for several years during the twenties, and apparently it had taken hold with him. He was suspected of being a British spy.

But that was conjecture. All that was known for certain was that he hated the foreign minister, which was neither surprising nor unusual. The foreign minister was a bully, something of a fool, and, by von Abeken's standards, a parvenu as well.

Everyone hated von Ribbentrop, but not everyone was a traitor.

However, there appeared to be more. Certain radio transmissions had been intercepted, carrying coded information about a matter referred to cryptically in the dossier as "the American project." It had not been difficult to trace the probable source.

Herr von Abeken's head was well and truly on the chopping block. His friends in London should have employed a higher clearance of code.

Hauptmann Weinschenk set to work. He assigned teams to keep Herr von Abeken under surveillance every moment he wasn't at home or at the Wilhelmstrasse, and to watch his door while he slept at night. He had his telephones tapped. He arranged to have his mail intercepted and read. The apartment directly below von Abeken's happened to belong to an employee of the Ministry of Information; Weinschenk arranged to have him transferred to Salzburg on twelve hours' notice and put one of his own people in to man the best listening equipment the SS had to offer. Von Abeken couldn't shave in the morning without someone from the Security Department listening to the razor scratch his face.

Weinschenk had decided he would like to make a personal inspection of the suspect's quarters. Now, dressed in civilian clothes, he waited in his car until he received word from his watchdogs that von Abeken was away for the morning, and then he left Max to finish breakfast alone.

The apartment was up two flights of stairs which were covered with a thin runner of carpet that was almost worn away in the middle. The hallways were painted a depressing sandy brown, but the sconces for the light fixtures were made out of brass and rather well done. Possibly, at the end of the previous century, this had been an agreeable place to live, a little corner of upper-middle-class luxury of the kind bachelor gentlemen would favor, but things had obviously been allowed to run down. Weinschenk took out his skeleton key and inserted it in the lock; the mechanism clicked into place and then turned soundlessly.

The front door opened onto the sitting room, which was furnished with incongruously massive oak furniture—a divan, two chairs, a low, rather awkward table, and a handsome, well-made armoire decorated with scrollwork and carved cameo heads of medieval German knights with full mustaches and fierce expressions. There was an expensive Turkish carpet on the floor. The two small windows that faced the street were tall and narrow and let in very little light; through them one had a view of a restaurant, a bicycle repair shop, and a vacant lot. The neighborhood was not what it had been.

The kitchen had a tiny wooden table. Weinschenk passed through quickly and went into the bedroom.

The bed was narrow and set into a corner of the room—clearly von Abeken didn't entertain much. On the chest of drawers was a set of hairbrushes with yellowed ivory backs and a hinged picture frame holding a pair of oval portraits, done in brown tint, of a ferociously respectable couple in their mid-forties. The photographs had obviously been taken well before the 1914–18 War; it seemed unlikely that these people could still be alive. Probably it was from them that von Abeken had inherited most of the furniture.

Weinschenk opened the drawer of a marble-topped night table and was surprised to find a small nickel-plated automatic pistol—seven millimeters, he guessed—clearly well taken care of. He took it out and removed the magazine; it was full, and there was a round in the chamber. The cartridges had shiny brass casings that gave the impression they had been purchased recently.

Evidently the little diplomat was expecting trouble. Had it occurred to him yet that he was under suspicion? After a week or two, a sensitive man will usually know he is being followed, but it had been only three days since Weinschenk had undertaken his surveillance, and his team were all experienced men.

As he strolled back down the sidewalk to where he had left Max listening to the soccer scores on the car radio, he discovered within himself an unpleasant if not unfamiliar confusion of feeling. On the one hand there was a certain satisfaction, almost amounting to relief. Klaus von Abeken was a traitor, which meant that Weinschenk could order his execution without any crisis of conscience, and even the motives for his treason were now detectably clearer.

After all, why not? Here was a man with remarkably few reasons to treasure his existence—a limited income, no career expectations, no visible sexual interests. His early life and family background had led him to expect that by now he would be in charge of his own mission in one of the smaller capitals—say, Athens or Belgrade. The von Abekens were a respected family within the narrow world of official Berlin, but the economic collapse of 1919 and the caprice of Joachim von Ribbentrop had put an end to all that. Now the man had nothing to nurse except his resentments.

But competing with the pride of the policeman was a distinct surge of unmeditated sympathy for one who, after all, was not so different from himself. If the SS was a harem, the Foreign Office was the court around an aging, vain, jealous dowager. Ribbentrop hated pedigrees, just as Nebe hated anyone who had ventured closer to danger than the filing cabinets of the Hohenzollerndamm. It was inevitable that von Abeken's career should come to grief.

And all of this the man had had to face in the isolation of his withered private life, without friends or family or lovers to let him see himself as something more than a casualty and a stale joke. Failure and solitude, the two ultimate disasters.

Weinschenk had been married for twelve years, but that hadn't saved him. Silence had become a precondition of their continuing together— it was impossible to talk to Magda about certain subjects. Sometimes love must wrap itself in reserve, and one can be as alone in a marriage bed as anywhere on earth. So Weinschenk had more than an inkling of von Abeken's plight.

But the Hauptmann could regard himself as fortunate. He had never been tempted into treason. He was one of the new men, who belonged to a new world, and von Abeken was a relic. His world was gone, that world of aristocratic privilege which it was one of the Führer's greatest accomplishments to have swept away, and von Abeken had simply grown reckless with despair.

When Weinschenk got back to the car, Max pointed to the radiophone, which took up half of the back seat. The harsh rumble that came from between his clenched teeth, like the sound of a grindstone, indicated that the message had been important. Weinschenk picked up the receiver.

"Herr Hauptmann, Von Abeken's made a telephone call—from a booth on the Friedrichstrasse. He left his office in the middle of working hours, walked to the booth, and made the call. What are your orders?"

"Has he returned to the ministry?"

"No, Herr Hauptmann. He's across the street from me now, waiting for a tramcar."

"Which line?"

"The Unter den Linden, Herr Hauptmann."

Weinschenk stared at the leaves that were drifting over the sidewalk outside his car window. The Unter den Linden line meant that von Abeken was probably on his way back to his apartment.

"Stay with him," he said, and hung up the telephone receiver. He couldn't have offered any conclusive reasons, but he had a sense that they were coming to the final moves of the game.

"Max, he's coming home—and in the middle of the morning. Doesn't that strike you as out of character?"

The yellow glint in Max's eye could have meant almost anything.

The tramcar pulled into sight and stopped. When it had pulled away again, von Abeken was already making his brisk way down the sidewalk toward them. Weinschenk had played his hunch and gathered most of the team around the immediate area; they were in their cars, peeking out of the sidestreets like children waiting to play a prank.

"He came here directly?" Weinschenk asked, leaning out through his open window to talk to the corporal in the blue civilian suit who was supporting himself against the car roof, panting like a dog—the man had just had a long run the back way from the tram stop.

"Yes, Herr Hauptmann." The corporal pulled himself up to attention. "I stayed behind him the whole distance. He never got off until just now."

"Could he have met someone on the tram?"

"I don't think so, Herr Hauptmann. There wouldn't have been time after he placed the call."

They were parked on the opposite side of the street, just around a corner, so they had the very best view of von Abeken's progress home and ran a negligible risk of being seen themselves. Von Abeken gave the impression of a man who knew what he was about; there was something almost grim in the way he was stalking over the sidewalk, with his head down and his hands thrust deep into the pockets of his overcoat.

And then, suddenly, he did something unexpected. He crossed the street and entered the restaurant that was almost the first thing one saw looking out through his living room window. Weinschenk got out of his car and walked around to the sound truck that was parked about twenty yards farther back on the side street.

"Can you get a microphone in there?" he asked, calling the sergeant in charge outside and pointing to the back door, just visible behind a barricade of trash cans at the end of a narrow little alley. "Our friend is having his lunch. If anyone should happen to join him, it might be instructive to hear what they have to say to one another. Can you manage it?"

The sergeant seemed to consider the matter for a moment. He was a small, precise man with rimless glasses and hair so blond it actually seemed to be white. He stood there, examining the backs of his narrow, clever-looking hands, and then looked up with a grin. He couldn't have been more than twenty-two.

"*Jawohl*, Herr Hauptmann. It can be done."

"So that he won't suspect? We don't want him to break cover now."

"If the restaurant is not too crowded, it should work. We have directional microphones that are disguised as briefcases—it's the latest thing. We send in two men. They sit at different ends of the room so that they and von Abeken form three points of a triangle. They rest their briefcases on the chairs opposite from where they are sitting, lined up on von Abeken, and go ahead and enjoy their lunch. The fact that we will have two microphones will screen out some of the background noise, so we should get a good, clear signal. The men will be equipped with battery packs and transmitters; you will be able to sit right here in the truck and hear every word."

"Very good. Then do it."

Now there was nothing left to do except to wait. Weinschenk sat on the rear seat of his car, smoking a cigarette and watching the back of Max's head. If anyone of any interest should show up, Max would be the first to spot him. Having a brute for an aide sometimes had its little advantages.

It was twenty-five minutes after twelve when Max's ears began to crawl up into his short, bristly hair. He turned around and made a noise as if to clear his throat. He was very excited.

"Yes—I see him. It's Lupescu, isn't it?"

Max growled and nodded; he didn't much like it either.

Weinschenk tried to look unconcerned, but he found it advisable to keep his hands folded together on his lap. This was the worst possible calamity, as direct a threat as someone pointing a pistol at his head. Lupescu happened to be a particular friend of his. Nebe would be delighted.

Weinschenk stepped out of the car and into the shadow of a shop awning, the scalloped edge of which was just low enough to brush the top of his head. Standing there, watching this man in his loud checkered overcoat cross the street, was one of the most uncomfortable moments of his life.

It was most unfortunate. It would require the most delicate handling or the consequences could be extremely dangerous. Already, in imagination, Weinschenk could feel the piano wire tightening around his neck.

Ion Lupescu was some sort of third secretary in the Rumanian delegation, a few years younger than Weinschenk, a great favorite of Magda's. He seemed a charming, thoughtless, harmless sort of person, interested in his own pleasure and without any marked political opinions. If one had troubled to ask him how he managed his yellow five-liter Daimler and his vulgar but expensive wardrobe on the salary of a minor diplomat, he probably would have grinned—he had a way of grinning so that his upper lip seemed almost to disappear—and made some sort of tasteless joke about his many feminine admirers. Somehow he succeeded in creating the impression that his family had money, that he was the sort to whom success came without effort, and that the principal attraction of the foreign service was that it allowed him to escape from Bucharest. He was entertaining company and he knew a great deal about French literature. And he was a great favorite of Magda's.

And now, it seemed, he was a British agent. Weinschenk had to admit it did make a certain amount of sense. If one was a spy, failed Foreign Office careerists and dissatisfied officers in the Security Department of the SS would be precisely the sorts of persons one would cultivate.

Weinschenk wondered if Lupescu might not also be one of his wife's lovers, and what sort of things Magda could have told him as they lay together in the twilight darkness of some hotel room. If Lupescu's role in this matter became known, and if he should chance to be arrested and interrogated in a prison basement, what secrets would his torturers wring from him before they consigned his broken body to a bomb crater in Weissensee?

Magda's whispered confidences, the stuff a woman says to justify her betrayal of her husband, must not find their way into one of Nebe's thick personnel files.

"Well, Max," Weinschenk murmured, surprised at the strained, unreal quality of his own voice, "at least we don't have to wonder anymore if Herr von Abeken is here just because he likes the desserts. This is the real thing."

But Max merely glanced down at the pavement, as if embarrassed.

As soon as Lupescu was out of sight, the Hauptmann went back to the sound truck, where he tapped on the rear door with the joint of his middle finger and was helped inside by the sergeant with the pale hair.

"Is it working?"

"Yes, Herr Hauptmann, it's working." The sergeant took off the earphones that had been clamped over his head and flipped a switch on the massive control panel that took up almost one whole wall of the interior compartment. Instantly Weinschenk could hear the clatter of dishes and the faint hum of a dozen different conversations—and then, with shocking clarity, the voice of Klaus von Abeken.

"*Were you followed?*"

There was a little pause. The sound of something being set down on the table—perhaps a water glass. The clicking of silverware. It was as if one were at the table with them. It was a miracle.

"*How should I know?*" There was no difficulty in imagining the sly smile that went with those words. "*Who can be bothered to notice? Besides, you ask me that same question every time.*"

"*One day there will be someone, and then it will be your neck. Wait and see.*"

"It's all going on the tapes," the sergeant announced quietly, pointing to the big spools that were slowly turning just over his head. Weinschenk nodded.

"*I haven't seen you since your return from Obersalzberg,*" Lupescu said after a silence of perhaps a quarter of a minute. "*How was the great man when last you saw him? Any new plans of conquering the world yet? Hah!*"

It was a joke. The two men in the back of the sound truck regarded each other with embarrassed silence.

"*Our employers are very well pleased with your reports. I think they would not be averse to an increase in your basic salary scale—if this last thing of yours proves out, there should be a sizable bonus involved. For both of us.*"

"*Really?*" Von Abeken didn't sound very convinced. He wasn't a fool, and doubtless he knew that in all probability Lupescu had already been collecting the money for weeks, committing robbery at both ends of the transaction.

"Where are they sitting that they can dare to talk like this?" Weinschenk asked. It was astonishing to hear even Lupescu speaking so carelessly. The sergeant shrugged his shoulders.

"They have a table in the corner near the front," he said. "It couldn't be better for our purposes, but there is no one near them."

"They wonder, in fact, if you have heard any more of that little matter which you mentioned as pending."

There was a faint sound, like the chair creaking. Weinschenk could imagine Lupescu leaning forward confidentially.

"You recall—Ribbentrop's little coup? You can imagine what they would be willing to pay for that!"

"Oh, yes. It seems to me that I heard something." It was merely a game now. One could tell as much from von Abeken's voice—didn't the man care about anything? *"And I expect to exact a high price for it."*

"I don't think we'll have a problem there. I'm sure they'll pay whatever you ask."

There was another long pause. Weinschenk felt the sweat running down his back and wished he had another cigarette.

"Oh, don't worry. It won't be the British who pay." Another pause. One hoped that von Abeken was enjoying this as much as he seemed to be.

"You will send a signal," he went on finally. *"The signal will consist of one word:* Kungsholm. *They'll understand—they're waiting."*

It took a few seconds. Lupescu seemed to have the instincts of a petty criminal, and finally he grasped the situation. Weinschenk would have given a great deal to have seen the expression on von Abeken's face at that moment.

"Yes—did you imagine the British wouldn't provide me with an alternative contact? I sent a coded letter to an address in a neutral city. I never had the slightest intention of delivering anything of this importance into your hands. Why should you be allowed to barter with them over the outcome of the war?"

"Is it as important as that?"

"Yes—it's as important as that."

For fifteen or perhaps twenty seconds there was silence. The loudest sound was the faint crackle of static from the radio transmitters. The sergeant's face looked as if it had been modeled out of wax, and Weinschenk couldn't blame him in the least. It was like waiting to hear the death sentence pronounced.

"*You will send the signal,*" von Abeken continued, his tone almost consoling. "*You will get out your little shortwave radio and you will send the signal. They're waiting for it, and if you don't send it you will have more than simply the Gestapo to worry about.*"

"*And I suppose you've worked out your own deal with them. What did they promise you—fifteen thousand? Fifty?*" The Balkan's voice was heavy with longing, as if the only pleasure left to him would be to hear the figure named.

"*Nothing. No money. My price is my revenge, and the Nazis will pay me that when they lose the war.*"

There was the sound of a chair scraping. It had the heavy quality one associates with the movements of the very old.

"*And now you will wait here.*" It was von Abeken—it must have been he who stood up. "*Send the message. Just one word:* Kungsholm. *Send it. When I have been gone for five minutes, go and send it.*"

Weinschenk made a gesture that he had heard enough, and the sergeant reached up to switch off the speaker.

"You will have him arrested now, Herr Hauptmann?"

"No."

He climbed out of the rear of the truck and began walking back to his car. By the time he reached it, he could see von Abeken standing in the doorway of his apartment building. Weinschenk was remembering his orders. He was in the business of proving that von Abeken was a traitor.

You will establish that—and only that. Needless to say, Reichsführer Himmler will not be excessively distressed if Herr von Ribbentrop's intrigue comes to nothing.

He would not interfere. The apartment was being watched—von Abeken wasn't going anywhere. He would wait until Lupescu was safely away, and could send his signal in peace, and then he would move in and tidy up all the awkward little details.

When you've discovered what he's been up to, shoot him. No one is interested in the embarrassment of a trial.

He would have to remember to tell the sergeant to erase that tape. The sergeant was a good man and would know enough to keep his mouth shut without having to be told.

Finally Lupescu emerged from the restaurant. Only now he really was frightened; he almost ran across the street to his car, glancing back over his shoulder as if he imagined the police were everywhere—and they were. The yellow Daimler jumped forward as he popped it into gear.

Good. Let him go. There was nothing in Weinschenk's orders about stopping any conspiracies, and he did not intend to precipitate the disaster that would come down upon him if he arrested Lupescu. There would be no mention of Lupescu in the report he would write. Lupescu didn't exist.

When you've discovered what he's been up to, shoot him.

Weinschenk stood on the corner, looking up at von Abeken's apartment window, wondering what was going on behind it, wondering what thoughts could be filling the mind of that strange little man.

"Do you suppose, Max, that there is even the slightest possibility this matter could be as important as our friend up there would have us believe? Wouldn't that be a plum for us, wouldn't it just? Perhaps we might be justified in putting a few questions to him before we carry out our orders—no point in being overly scrupulous, is there?"

He turned around and was a little startled to see that his aide had been standing almost directly behind him. Max bared his teeth. He enjoyed that sort of thing. It was virtually his only pleasure.

"But we still have to get him down from that apartment, hey, Max? A little finesse might be in order, don't you think? It wouldn't do to go in there with guns blazing—no point in needlessly upsetting the civilian population—and we don't want him to have any advance warning. It's impossible to predict what he might do. Mustn't have our own people getting killed out of sheer carelessness."

Weinschenk realized, with an uncomfortable start of surprise, that he was talking too much. It was nerves, of course. He would have to watch himself.

He tried to focus his mind on the purely technical problem. He phoned across to the apartment where one of his listeners was still on duty, and determined that von Abeken was in fact upstairs, and then he and Max walked back to the car and drove around to park on a side street behind the building.

They entered through the basement door, where the man on duty there saluted, and made their way quietly up to the second floor. Weinschenk had considered a number of alternatives and thought perhaps he might just stage a good, smoky fire under one of the stairwells, perhaps even ordering in a fire truck for authenticity. He could catch von Abeken on the landing while the apartment house was being evacuated. It wasn't the sort of thing he would care to try on a real professional, but von Abeken wasn't that. He expected it would work like a charm.

After that, a few quiet hours somewhere, just he and von Abeken and Max. He might even discover what was going on—or at least the name of von Abeken's alternate British contact.

Kungsholm. He wondered what it could mean. Perhaps, if it was really as important as all that, it might go a long way toward solving a number of problems.

"Herr Hauptmann, I think something's gone wrong." The listener stood in the apartment doorway. The collar of his shirt was undone, and his adam's apple worked its way up and down in his throat. He pointed toward the ceiling. "I think I heard a shot."

"That damned pistol—I should have known!"

They ran the rest of the way, not caring how much noise they made. All Weinschenk could hear was his heart pounding, but as they reached the door, and he put his hand on the knob, he felt himself being pushed violently against the wall. Max's hand was against his chest, holding him pinned there; he might as well have been nailed in place.

Max shook his head—no, this wasn't going to be a case where he would listen to orders—and unsnapped his holster flap. He held his Luger up as if he were showing it off, gently lifted his other hand away from Weinschenk's chest, and kicked in the door, throwing himself through the opening like a man diving into the sea.

There wasn't any shooting. There wasn't anything. After a few seconds Max rose up on one knee, looked sullenly back at his officer, and gestured him inside. No one had anything more to worry about. Von Abeken was sitting propped in a corner of the great oak divan with his brains leaking down the side of his face. It would seem, god damn him, that he had decided to save the SS the trouble.

"*Kungsholm*," Weinschenk murmured, almost to himself. He stepped over to von Abeken's body, took the little nickel-plated automatic out of the dead hand, examined it for a moment, quite as if he had never seen anything like it before, and then threw it onto the cushions of the divan. Von Abeken's eyes were still wide open, and his face was twisted into a sneer that somehow reminded the Hauptmann of Gruppenführer Nebe. Weinschenk felt an oppressive and, of course, irrational anger welling up inside his chest. It was almost as if von Abeken had cheated him of something more precious than anyone except the two of them could possibly imagine.

"*Kungsholm*," he repeated, as if the word itself might have some calming effect on him. "What do you think of that, Max? He died over a single word."

II

OCTOBER 27, 1941

It was one of those lovely, clear autumn mornings when it almost seemed a crime against nature to take the bus to work; Karen Windermere decided she would walk instead. It was only a trace more than two miles from her flat in Brompton to Whitehall, a distance any fit person could cover in forty minutes, and the shift change at the ministry wasn't until seven-thirty. There hadn't been any air raids last night—or, at least, she hadn't heard the flak guns in Hyde Park, and there wasn't any smoke on the horizon. She had slept like a stone.

Along Birdcage Walk, with the park on one side and the Wellington Barracks on the other, she thought how very prewar everything looked, as if the Nazis were great respecters of persons and had deliberately refrained from blowing up the King's own neighborhood. That was hardly fair to His Majesty, of course, since, as everybody knew, Buckingham Palace had been bombed several times; but just here, with the grass and the iron palings and the careful rows of red and yellow tulips, it was easy to imagine it was still 1936, the year she had been presented to King Edward and the King had sat sulking on his throne the whole time and they had all gotten rained on out in the palace gardens.

The following June she had married Bertie Windermere, and Hitler had been a figure of low comedy, and nobody had worried about where it was all going to end. Now Bertie was lost to her and half of London was in ruins, but the tulips still bloomed in St. James's Park. She could walk along the gravel pathways and feel something almost like happiness. She wondered if that meant she was beginning to recover.

She came to the corner of the Parade and stopped while she waited for the traffic to ease. After a moment she happened to glance across the street, to the mouth of an underground shelter in Storey's Gate; people were filing up into the sunshine, people with anxious, haggard faces who blinked and squinted as they looked into the light. Thousands of people still did that, every night. The worst of the Blitz had been over for months, but the shelters were still full. She turned her eyes away, and the familiar feeling of constriction returned to her throat.

No, it wasn't over. She was still a resident in the city of the dead, and the past had not returned. There was only the futureless present—the broken buildings, the bad food, and the drudgery of confusion and struggle. She was a staff assistant in Military Intelligence, and her husband was a shadow, hardly more than a memory now, but strong enough to darken the rest of her life.

She wrapped her coat more tightly around her and trudged on, crossing the Parade and heading up toward Downing Street. There would be a small crowd around Number Ten—there always was, anytime of the day—but Churchill wouldn't be there. He would still be asleep in his bunkered headquarters, a hundred and fifty feet beneath Whitehall.

The military policeman at the checkpoint outside the War Ministry looked at her pass, frowned, and waved her through, just as he had done almost every day for the past year.

The vast corridors were choked with uniforms. Even the women—and they were mostly women one saw—were in uniform. Even after a year, Karen could not come here without feeling out of place. For some reason, the staff of Operational Sector Three persisted in remaining relentlessly civilian.

Everywhere women. Every day she was bumping into one or another of the girls she had gone to school with, smiling and wearing a trace too much lipstick and tucked inside a WRENS uniform. Half of them were widows who had joined up to serve king and country, or to have something to do, or out of some vague desire to get even. They seemed cheerful enough, as if they had learned their lesson and the world would never touch them again. It was even possible to envy them.

Was she like that—all fresh paint on the outside and nothing showing?

She hoped so. Probably they were all just alike, all the young women of that generation whose husbands had sacrificed themselves in Norway or France or Africa or in the air war over the Channel. It was considered bad form to let the wounds show.

As usual in the morning, her desk was covered with untidy piles of manila file folders. Karen's impression was that none of the women working there had any clear idea just exactly what Sector Three was in business to do. One wasn't encouraged to talk about one's work.

They had little cubicles constructed from some sort of composition board that was supposed to keep the noise down, and there was just room for a desk and a chair. Probably thirty women were working in that one room, bumping into one another in the canteen or the powder room, but for the rest as separated from one another as prisoners in their cells. There wasn't even any tapping on the walls.

She fetched herself a cup of coffee from the urn—that was one of the small advantages of working for the War Ministry; it was one of the last places in London where it was still possible to procure a cup of real coffee—and sat down at her desk to begin picking her way through that morning's allotment of personnel records.

The dossiers were full of short biographies, psychological profiles, and test scores—IQ, shortwave transmission, language facility, marksmanship, stress management. In her bottom drawer she kept a small ring binder containing all the current job descriptions from all the nameless little bureaus serviced by the Sector, and her work was to find the right people to fill those slots. The dossiers contained no names or photographs, merely identifying numbers, and the job descriptions were nothing more than lists of desired qualifications. The whole process was kept deliberately abstract, but it didn't take a mental giant to deduce that these bright and interesting young men and women were being slated for duty in occupied Europe. "Radio man, knowledge of Polish, knowledge of chemical engineering, height between 5'5" and 5'10"." Karen merely made her recommendations, and the matter was closed. Probably half a dozen other women were recommending half a dozen other candidates for the same assignment. Who was finally chosen, and whether they succeeded, and whether they ever came back, was not something she would ever know. She had a feeling she was better off not knowing.

It wasn't what she had expected. After it had finally sunk in that Bertie wasn't coming back to her, she had wanted to burn up the whole world. When she had begun to understand that she would have to do something or she would end up strangling on her own bitterness she went around to see a few people and arranged to have a few strings pulled—the sort of thing that was so easy to manage within her own particular set—and had fetched up in a wine bar in Holborn, sitting at a booth across the table from one of her husband's old messmates.

Brian Horton wasn't more than thirty, but the huge, prawnlike mustache he affected made him look already faintly middle-aged, as if, along with that emblem of the military caste, he had acquired in advance the cynicism of a whole career. His sandy hair and moist, pale blue eyes helped to further the impression of careless, unsought authority.

Five years ago, on a balcony in Mayfair, at a ball at which the Duke of Kent had been present, Brian had proposed to her. He had brought her out a glass of champagne and asked her to marry him, just like that. By then she had already met Bertie, but her first season wasn't more than a month old and she had been flattered. She had let him down gently, and ever since, even after she had become Lady Windermere and the happiest of wedded women, he had still looked at her with the same sad, entreating expression, as if he found unrequited passion somehow congenial.

They had never spoken about it again, but his eyes told her that she had lost none of her power over him. She was trading on that now, and she knew it. She just didn't care.

"You probably see yourself as another Mata Hari," he had said to her, absentmindedly running the tip of a finger along the fringe of his mustache. "There's not so much of that, thank God. You'll find it isn't the least romantic."

She had squirmed in her seat, stared down at her gloved hands, and mumbled something about not expecting romance.

"Yes, well—perhaps we could find you something."

The interview was over. Brian had waited until she was finished with her sherry and had handed her into a taxi, and that had been that. They had taken her up, it appeared. She had spent the rest of the afternoon wandering around the Regent Street shops in a trance of excitement. She had fully expected to be parachuted into France within the next day or two.

But it hadn't happened that way.

First, there had been a training camp in Oxfordshire—a cross between a ladies' academy and the Girl Guides, where, by the end of seven weeks, she had learned to shoot a pistol, lie, crawl under barbed wire, tap out gibberish on a Morse key, and run a mile in under six and a half minutes. And then back to London, with her orders in a sealed brown envelope.

But the orders had directed her to a desk in the War Ministry. No explanations, just a pay booklet and a copy of the Official Secrets Act.

That had been in October, 1940—she had returned just in time for the worst part of the Blitz.

Her mother had been horrified. "Oh, my dear, you simply *must* come down to me in the country. It must be *ghastly* for you—a person probably comes in contact with all *sorts* of unsavory types in those air-raid shelters."

Karen wouldn't have known because she never used the shelters, so her mother needn't have worried. For her mother, an encounter with a cockney greengrocer seventy feet underground was a danger far more real and terrifying than being blown to pieces by a thousand-kilogram bomb.

Karen had lain in her bed in the flat she and Bertie had kept for the three years of their marriage, and she had waited for the crash that would bring down the walls.

It had been something like a fearful dare at first—if they wouldn't take her for service overseas, she would stand her risk here in her bedroom in Brompton—but one can grow accustomed to anything. After a month, the bombs hardly even woke her up anymore.

"Karen? Could I have a word?"

Standing directly behind her chair, in the doorway of the cubicle, was Brian Horton—her boss. He hadn't told her that that was the way things would work themselves out; he had kept that part a secret while they had sat sipping sherry in that dreadful little saloon, or perhaps he hadn't made up his mind yet.

Like everyone else in the Sector, he wore no uniform, but he had been a major in the regular army as recently as February of 1940. She turned around and smiled. Why shouldn't she smile? Brian was in the nature of a family friend.

"Not here. In my office, please."

She followed him down a short corridor to a large, bare room, where he invited her to occupy a chair that seemed to have been designed for maximum discomfort—the armrests were strategically placed to catch one's elbows with every movement. Brian took his place behind the huge, modern, intensely cluttered desk, laced his fingers together under his chin, and smiled.

"I have a problem," he said suddenly, after a silence that seemed ready to last until luncheon. "A certain object will be transported out of a certain neutral country, and the War Ministry would very much like to be assured that it never arrives at its destination."

"I suppose somebody should steal it."

Karen laughed soundlessly, out of pure embarrassment—it seemed like such a stupidly obvious thing for her to have said.

"Yes, precisely. But who?"

"I'm sure I don't know. Who?"

Brian Horton looked as if that were the last answer he had expected. And then he allowed his hands slowly to sink down to the surface of the desk, where they seemed to spread out slightly, like putty.

"That's our problem. You see, it would cause no end of grief if Britain were seen to be involved in the disappearance of this—object. And since, in the nature of the thing, the chances of our agent being apprehended are fairly high . . ."

"Then you want someone who isn't British." She smiled, shrugging her shoulders. "What could be easier? Look in the files—we've got Poles, Czechs, even a couple of . . ."

"What we need is an American."

It was like an order. Abrupt, almost impatient. He must have realized the impression he was creating, because the hands came back from the desktop and turned palm up in a gesture apparently intended to convey a certain amused helplessness.

"You and Bertie used to run with a pretty trans-Atlantic crowd, if I remember," he went on finally. "And Bertie cut a pretty wide dash in his day. You must have known someone with the proper criminal instincts. The files are no help at all."

"Well, I'm afraid we never knew anyone like that."

She stood up to leave, vexed and slightly offended and not at all minding how obvious she was about it. What a tactless, thoughtless thing to suggest.

But if he saw that she was annoyed, he certainly did nothing to betray it. He merely rose from his chair and smiled, obviously glad to be getting rid of her if she couldn't provide him with his answer.

"But keep it in mind," he said, his voice expressionless. "If you think of anyone who would do, let me know. It's not the sort of thing that can wait."

On her way home, after the bus had dropped her off in the Cromwell Road so she could take her chances with everyone else at what there was left of fresh fruit and vegetables—meat, of course, was unobtainable unless one was prepared to sell one's white body to the butcher—she wondered if perhaps she hadn't been unfair with Brian. It was perfectly true that Bertie had collected some pretty odd friends.

The late-afternoon sun smoldered in the plate-glass show windows, almost covering the criss-cross patterns of air-raid tape with its glare. Shadows hung around the craggy stonework of the buildings, and the pace of life began to rise as everyone hurried to finish their shopping before the beginning of darkness. It was a holdover from the Blitz—people couldn't bring themselves to believe that Hitler's bombers wouldn't be back with all their old ferocity. A woman with a shopping basket full of tomatoes nearly knocked Karen down in her rush to catch up with the last of the glistening, pale light.

Karen hardly noticed. She was too busy looking around her, trying to remember what these streets had been like in the old days, during that first winter when she and Bertie had come up from Kent for the London season.

Yes, Bertie had cut a pretty wide dash. She wondered why now, over a year after the crash that seemed to have finished everything, that description of him had so much power to offend her; hadn't that kind of glamour had a lot to do with why she had married him?

Bertie belonged to the time before the war. Chasing Jerry fighters back across the Channel had been great sport, and he had loved his Hurricane the way he had loved his hunting dogs or the bird gun his father had given him for Christmas in 1934. If he ever woke up from the dream in which he had wrapped himself, he wouldn't like what had become of England. He would never understand clothes rationing coupons or the lack of eggs; she couldn't imagine him shivering in an Underground station while the water from some shattered main gathered around his ankles. He had never had any use for causes.

Perhaps that, as much as the cold and the fear of death, was what had unhinged him after they fished him out of the water after thirty-six hours off the Belgian coast. So near occupied Europe, he was lucky the search planes had found him at all. But plenty of men had been shot down that summer, and the ones who lived hadn't all come unstuck like kitchen wallpaper. It hadn't been only that.

"You must understand that his plane seems to have exploded as he was climbing out of it," the medical officer had told her, smiling serenely from behind his hooded eyes. "The effects of the concussion are unpredictable. We have no way of knowing how much damage to the nervous system he may have sustained."

That was his explanation, but it seemed to Karen that what had undone her husband was the belated recognition that those German pilots had been trying to kill him—*really* trying to kill him—that it wasn't a game after all. Bertie had awakened to the seriousness of life, and he couldn't deal with it.

So, after he got out of the hospital, he had retired to the house in Kent and shut everyone out of his life. He had a medical discharge from the RAF; his war was over. He had made it pointedly clear that he no longer had any need for the disturbance of a wife.

She hadn't even seen him in nearly eight months.

Had that woman actually had tomatoes?

Her flat was on the third floor of a building that faced onto Bulls Gardens, and in a fit of patriotic enthusiasm at the announcement that the British Expeditionary Force was on its way to France the tenants had elected to turn the elevator off until after the victory celebrations. It had only been recently that Karen had discovered that climbing stairs had lost its magic for her.

The corridor was dark, and she had trouble finding her latchkey in her handbag. The net shopping bag that was half full of tomatoes, along with a quarter pound of grated cheese and ninepence worth of forced greengages, was balanced against her knee as the drawstring sawed a line through the middle of her forearm. And even after she had found her key, the lock was sticky. Everything, the simplest domestic operation, even opening her own front door, seemed to have taken on the complexity of a problem in the infinitesimal calculus.

When she got inside, she locked the door behind her and threw the bolt, then kicked off her shoes and started padding noiselessly toward the kitchen, which was just off the entrance hall.

The door to the sitting room was open, and as she passed by, and happened to glance inside, she saw something that almost caused her to fall down in sheer stark astonishment.

The sitting room was dark—she must have forgotten to pull up the blackout curtains—but the outlines of things were perfectly visible. Opposite the gas fireplace was the huge leather-upholstered chair that had been Bertie's favorite, where he had liked to sit after dinner, reading a copy of Country Life and drinking his brandy and water. From the doorway, only the back and left side were to be seen, and it was a great wingbacked thing that enclosed one like a telephone booth. She wouldn't have known anyone was there if she hadn't spotted his legs stretched out to the edge of the hearthstone.

For a moment—no longer than a second or two—there was no thought in her mind except to run away. Without her realizing it, her hand had stolen up to her throat. She took a step backward. She felt her rising panic not so much as an emotion as a purely physical excitement, a pain just under her heart and a giddiness that fluttered inside her chest like an animal trying to get out. She remembered the locked door behind her and thought it possible she might gag on the brassy taste in her mouth.

The light went on, the reading lamp next to the chair, and the man stood up and grinned at her like a schoolboy caught in a neighbor's orchard.

"David!" she cried, in a mixture of surprise and relief. "How did you get in here?"

"Through your back window. I came down from the roof—I didn't want to give you a bad name with your neighbors, and I'd forgotten your telephone number."

It was at least a seventy-foot drop from the roof, and no fire escape. It was appalling—he could have killed himself.

She wanted to say something. She wanted to tell him what a fool he was, but she couldn't seem to make a beginning. Perhaps that didn't matter, however, since he seemed to be able to read it all in her face.

Incredibly, he merely shrugged his shoulders, as if to dismiss her anxiety for his life the way one might the questions of a child, as unanswerable because they were incomprehensible. They both knew he could simply have waited for her across the street, or left a message in her mailbox, or inquired at the War Ministry. They both knew, in fact, that he also probably hadn't forgotten her telephone number, since he wasn't the forgetting sort.

"There was a drainpipe," he said finally, as if that explained everything. "One of those great, heavy iron jobs from before the last war—I could have hung an elephant on that thing."

He grinned again, looking very unlike an elephant in his pale brown suit that seemed a couple of sizes too large for him. His thin face, with its expression of incongruous, knowing innocence, looked haggard, as if he had been many days on the move, and his streaky blond hair needed cutting.

Yes, she thought. Given a choice, of course he would have come through my bedroom window on an iron drainpipe. He had been doing such things since reaching manhood—and probably long before that. Trying, it would seem, to provoke the gods into taking away his charmed life.

And trying, just possibly, to catch her attention as well. There was something there of the undergraduate stunt. Did he imagine that otherwise she would fail to notice him?

"I brought half a dozen veal chops—all the way from Lisbon, packed in dry ice." There was a certain shyness in his demeanor as he stood there, his left hand resting lightly on the top of the chair. "They're in the fridge. I was hoping I could talk you into cooking them."

The broiled tomatoes went down very well with the veal. There was even a bottle of wine, a luxurious item in these times, carried—along with the veal chops, a Portuguese rumcake, a change of clothes, and several small packages destined for Spanish refugee families living in England—in a canvas rucksack that David Steadman had balanced on his knees during one of the irregular and dangerous flights between Lisbon and London, to gain passage on which a civilian—and especially a citizen of a neutral country—had to be willing to pay a great deal of money.

That was no problem. David Steadman always seemed to have a great deal of money.

Karen set the tiny alcove table in her kitchen, and let him pour her glass after glass of the delicious, honey-colored wine, and listened to him evading a direct answer to her question about what he had been doing in Lisbon.

"I didn't spend much time in Portugal," he murmured, just a shade too glibly. "I had a little item of business to take care of in Madrid."

"Was that wise? I mean, I was under the impression that you were still on Franco's list."

For a moment, for reasons she herself did not fully understand, she found it difficult to meet his eyes. But she was aware that he was smiling at her in triumph.

"I am. All of us 'red mercenaries' are under death sentence if they catch us, but you're safe enough traveling under false papers—hell, what are the chances of running into some Fascist policeman who's going to know you by sight?" He made an apologetic gesture, as if he were trying to sweep away a cobweb from in front of his face. "They had a friend of mine on a chain gang—it was supposed to be twenty years in the sulfur mines, but who could live twenty years down there? What could I do? I owed him."

There was an anxiety that hovered around the corners of his mouth, a suggestion not so much of fear as of the pain of frustrated ambition. Spain—David Steadman's Spain—was a place where there was more to worry about than the remote possibility of an encounter with some old enemy; the inquiries about him, she knew, had reached as far as London. The Generalissimo's government wanted him back, so they could have the satisfaction of shooting him. It was the sort of honor they didn't pay to just anyone.

She wondered what sort of friend could be worth such risks. She wondered about the sort of man who, with his eyes open, would consent to take them. For David Steadman, as it was not in the case of Bertie Windermere, the war had never been a game.

"I can't get into uniform," he said. "I must've tried every recruiting post in the country, and nobody wants me. Franco is having his little joke on me after all—nobody is interested in having any 'red mercenaries' in their service. Besides, the minute I take my shirt off for the physical, they all tell me I'm too shot up inside anyway."

She watched him from the other side of the narrow table, marveling that there could be anyone left in this squalid and dangerous age who would feel ashamed because a bellyful of Fascist shrapnel was keeping him out of the military. But he was ashamed—it seemed to have colored his whole existence. So he had had himself smuggled into Spain to save a casual acquaintance from a slow death at hard labor, and he had dangled from a drainpipe seventy feet above the London pavements to get in through her bedroom window.

You must have known someone with the proper criminal instincts, Brian had said. *The files are no help at all.*

Could he have meant David? She experienced a great wave of protective feeling for him. She knew he loved her, and she didn't want anything to happen to him—she felt like wrapping him in her arms and guarding him against this war he seemed to long for so much, as if Brian Horton had suddenly become her rival for him. She knew that she had come to rely on him; she seemed to need to warm herself with his love.

She knew she was merely being selfish. David wouldn't thank her. David would see this business of Brian's as the answer to his prayers. But he would never need to know.

But no—that wouldn't do. This war was real.

"David," she said, rising slightly out of her chair while she smiled and laid a hand across his forearm, "would you excuse me for a moment? I have to make a telephone call."

OCTOBER 29, 1941

The airfield, such as it was, was probably about forty miles inland from the Baltic coast. The plane set down on a narrow strip of runway, hardly wider than a country lane, which someone had thoughtfully lined with kerosene lamps. Still, it had been a stylish bit of flying—on the north side, almost lapping against the weathered asphalt, lay what the map identified as Lake Hjälmaren, and on the south nothing except pine trees. From the air the landing area appeared to be nothing more than a mud flat. It looked as if it had been forgotten.

And that was fine—no one was interested in attracting a welcoming committee. The idea was to slink into Stockholm unobserved, and it was felt that a British Mosquito landing at Bromma Terminal might have been the sort of thing even the Nazis could be counted upon to notice.

When the plane finally shuddered to a stop, Karen and David climbed out through the bomb bay, still wrapped to the eyes in their thermal flying suits and stiff with cold. It had been freezing up there; the edges of one's face, where the mask hadn't reached, felt as if they no longer belonged to one. But at least it was nice not to be breathing canned air.

As soon as Karen had walked around enough to start the blood moving in her legs again, she went back to the plane and waited in the back draft from the propellers until the pilot opened his cockpit window, handed her down a thick envelope, about the size of one of her mother's letters, and gave her the thumbs-up sign for luck. There was too much noise for conversation, so they didn't try. She stepped away, and the plane swung its tail around and started back down the runway. In an instant it disappeared into the darkness. After perhaps half a minute one couldn't even hear the engines.

"I don't suppose they thought to put a gun in that thing," David Steadman said, staring contemptuously at the envelope she held in her hand. She was startled by his nearness. She hadn't heard him coming up behind her, but then perhaps she was still a little deaf from all those hours inside the Mosquito.

"There must be one in the car," she answered, smiling in embarrassment. "I'm sure they would have thought of that."

"Let's hope so."

He swooped down and picked up one of the kerosene lamps, holding it up to eye level in his gloved hand and glancing around at the trees, as if he expected someone to step out through that blank, impenetrable wall. He looked so odd in his heavy, hooded coveralls, like a khaki snowman. The only thing that restrained her from laughing was the saving thought that she must look just the same.

"Let's go find this car of yours. And keep your hood on—it's fortunate that everyone looks alike in these things."

She was about to say something—had he read her mind?—when she saw that he was already heading away, toward the thin wedge of cleared ground where the runway ended. He was carrying the lantern down by his knee now, letting it hang at the end of his arm. He seemed to know where he was heading. The light spread out on the ground, leaving him almost invisible.

There really was a car—she had begun to doubt its existence. On a dirt road that ran right up to the shore of the lake, only about twenty feet through the trees, there it was. A dark four-seater sedan of no make she recognized. David walked around it, staying off the road and holding the lantern out in front of him. He gave the impression that he had been through this sort of thing before.

"Either your friends brought an army along with them for the ride, or we've been visited." He stepped forward, took off his left glove, and laid the palm of his hand on the car's bonnet. "It's still a little warm. I don't suppose it's been here longer than an hour."

"David, what *are* you talking about?"

He pointed down at the gray, dusty roadway. "Footprints. Two sets—

see? How many people does it take to park a car? Somebody came around afterwards to have himself a look."

It wasn't something she could control. Her eyes darted around, and her hand came up to her mouth.

"Here?"

David looked at her and smiled tensely. He was very matter-of-fact— she could sense that that was for her sake, that he wanted her to stay calm—but he was very far from relaxed.

"No, not here," he said, making a short, almost leisurely gesture with his free hand. "They aren't that stupid. But I imagine they're around somewhere. Farther up this road, maybe. Somewhere they can catch us as we drive by. Probably they want to see where we're heading."

"Or kill us."

"No. If that was the plan, I imagine we'd already be dead."

He made a sign for her to step back a few paces, and then, with a sudden movement, as if he wanted to take it by surprise, he opened the car door. The interior light popped on, but there was nothing else. Karen wondered why she was disappointed that there hadn't been a bang.

Lit up from the inside by a single little yellow bulb, the car seemed a squalid object in the middle of this intense darkness. She looked straight up, trying to see the sky above the trees, but she couldn't make out where the one ended and the other began. There weren't even any stars. It was lonely and cold, and now, apparently, there was a crowd of Germans waiting for them somewhere out in these black woods. David was crawling around out of sight on the floorboards, like a man who has dropped his latchkey.

When he came back outside, he was holding a large revolver that glowed dully in the lantern light, like a lump of coal.

"Aren't the British wonderful?" He looked as if he were about to laugh. "They think of everything—I haven't seen a Smith & Wesson since I left the States. I wonder if it works."

He seemed to lose interest in the question and set the revolver down on the roof of the car.

"Are you cold? I'm afraid we're probably going to be here for a while."

"Am I allowed to know why?"

She was sorry almost at once for the edge in her voice—one assumed it was merely the combination of fear and cold. On top of it all, David was being so maddeningly mysterious.

He wasn't offended, damn him. He was amused. He stood there, looking at her across the car's bonnet, grinning.

"We're staying because the Germans are great ones for sticking to their orders," he said, like a sixth-form boy lecturing his fag—not unkindly, but with a certain amused superiority. "That was something I learned about them in Spain; they're always thinking about how their reports are going to read. These guys haven't wired the car with a bomb, and they didn't shoot us from ambush, so probably they plan to behave like good little boys in a neutral country and just find out what we're up to. But they're Germans and they have their orders, and after an hour or two, when we don't come driving out, they'll trot in here to see what's holding us up. I'm sure they must have heard the plane."

"I don't believe you—this is ridiculous." She stared at the revolver that rested like a huge spider on the car roof. "You're imagining all this; how could the Germans have discovered us already? We only just got here."

He didn't answer. He picked up the revolver, replaced it with the lantern he had been carrying, and came around the car to take her under the elbow and lead her back about a hundred feet into the trees.

"We've got to find you someplace to hide," he said casually. They made a frightful crashing racket through the undergrowth; she couldn't imagine how he could have seen where he was going.

"Here, this looks good. At least you'll have something to your back."

He put his hand on her shoulder, and they crouched down beside a tiny clump of trees, so dense even a child couldn't have reached inside. The only sound was the faint whisper of the wind overhead. She felt as if she had vanished from the surface of the earth.

"I think we ought to get in the car and drive to Stockholm," Karen murmured—for some reason she was afraid to raise her voice. "You can't really imagine that someone in our embassy here would betray us. Nobody knew except them. Be serious, David."

"Sweetheart, if you were told that a typist in the German embassy was sleeping with one of your people, would you be surprised?"

She couldn't see his face, but she could imagine what he looked like. She had heard that tone in his voice once or twice before, when he had allowed himself to forget that Bertie Windermere was his friend and called her "sweetheart." The other times it had always annoyed her, but it didn't annoy her now. In the darkness, his voice was like a comforting arm across her shoulders.

"No—no, I shouldn't be surprised." It was strange how the conversation seemed to be about something else.

"Then don't make the mistake of imagining that British typists are made of any sterner stuff. After all, we're all a long way from home."

She could feel him slipping the glove from her right hand, but instead of the touch of his fingers what she found pressing into her palm was the butt of a revolver. It was cold and heavy and final.

"Do you know how to use one of these things?"

"Of course," she answered tartly. "I learned all of that in the Girl Guides."

She couldn't imagine why she had said that.

"Good. I'm going to leave you in a little while—you see the light from the lantern?"

Yes. She nodded, knowing he wouldn't be able to see.

"Then, when you're alone, you know what to do if anybody comes near you. Don't wait to find out who it is. Just pull the trigger, and keep on pulling it until you hear it click empty. It's only a .38 and it's got a big frame, so it won't kick to speak of. Just empty the thing into the bastard's guts."

"Where will you be?"

"Out there trying to make sure none of them ever gets close enough that you need to bother."

For a long moment neither of them spoke. She could hear him breathing, but in the blackness there seemed to be nothing else to prove that he was still there. He never moved. She felt his eyes on her, but it was just as dark for him.

"I'd better climb out of this," he said suddenly. There was a tearing sound as he opened the front zipper of his flying suit. She could just make out the movement; he seemed to expand and struggle like a bogie in a bad dream. "Here—you can wrap your hands in it and keep warm, but get clear before you try shooting. You don't want to jam the hammer. Christ, it was hot in that thing. I'm soaking wet."

She put her hand on his arm, and she could feel the damp. For a moment she wasn't sure she would be able to let go.

"Don't you think this would be better with you?" she asked, holding the revolver up so that he could see it—if, indeed, he could see anything—on top of his discarded flying suit.

"No. Familiar weapons are best."

With an abrupt movement he reached down to the bottom of his trouser leg and pulled up what glistened in the faint, distant lamplight like the heavy blade of a hunting knife. He must have been carrying it strapped to his shin all this time.

"Then will you kiss me, David?"

"You've never asked me to do that before."

"I've never felt I needed it before."

His lips just brushed hers, so lightly that she wasn't even really sure it had happened until she felt his arm slip away from beneath her hand. In an instant he was gone, as silently as a breath of air.

It was the first time she had been alone since they had left the airfield

in Scotland. But she was quite at leisure, until the Germans came, to
sit here in this dark forest, with an American revolver clutched in her
hands, to feel afraid and alone and to consider just precisely what she
had allowed herself to be delivered up to.

"It really would be the most immense help, you know."

Brian had said it with conviction, sitting behind his desk, scratching
at the end of his mustache with the nail of his little finger, watching her
through his pale, watery blue eyes.

"This fellow is perfect for the job—you did remarkably well to find
him for us," he went on, crossing his arms over his chest with the air of
a defeated man. "The trouble is that we have to send someone along with
him—liaison, you know, that sort of thing—and he trusts you. It'd put
the whole business on so much more of a personal basis with him, don't
you see. He'll manage better—be more reliable—if he sees himself as
doing this little job not just for us but for you. I don't care how bloody
keen he is on fighting the Nazis; in the end it's only your friends you die
for. I say, you aren't sweet on him or anything, are you?"

"No."

"Well, there's a relief. We can't have it cutting both ways, now can
we?"

As she watched him digging around in the pockets of his jacket for a
cigarette and matches, Karen wished that somehow she could convey to
him just how offensive this proprietary tone of his was becoming. It had
started almost as soon as she had called him about David, the faint
implication that there was some sort of understanding between them,
that he had a claim on her which soon she would be called upon to
make good. It was almost as if, by denying that David Steadman was her
lover, she had acknowledged Brian's rights in his place.

But it was pointless to say anything, of course. And so Brian didn't
deserve more than the blunt end of something she didn't know herself.
Quite honestly, she hadn't allowed herself a chance to decide how she
felt about David, but that was her private affair.

"In any case, I think you're doing him an injustice," she had said,
perhaps in place of saying something else. "He was in Spain, you know.
I've met one or two of his friends from there, and I gather he didn't spend
his time cheering from the sidelines."

"Is that a thrust, Karen dear?"

He merely smiled—he wasn't taking offense. He opened his cigarette
case and held it out to her, putting it away again when she shook her
head, and then went through the complicated ritual of lighting up. All
the while, the silence was allowed to build.

"I know all about Mr. Steadman's record in Spain," he went on finally.

"I know that he seems to have irritated the Nationalists enough that we still find it necessary to explain to them every so often why we're not prepared to comply with their extradition requests. I know he was rather badly wounded—that was when you and Bertie first met him, if memory serves, while he was convalescing in Kent. Am I right?"

"He took a cottage near us, yes," she answered, her voice empty of everything except the neutral fact. "He said he didn't like hospitals, and the doctor there had been recommended to him. The first time he came to dinner he was hardly able to eat anything. He was more Bertie's friend than mine."

"Quite." The smile on his lips tightened slightly. "It isn't what one would have thought, but then the man seems to be full of contradictions. David Steadman was a bit of a playboy, wasn't he? And still it turns out that he's a Communist."

"He was never a Communist."

"No?" He shrugged his shoulders in faint compliance. "Very well, he was never a Communist. He served under Communist direction in Spain, but if you feel the distinction is worth drawing . . . Regardless, we still would feel better if he had a little discreet direction while he's over there— just something to remind him that he's working for His Majesty's Government, and not the solidarity of the international proletariat. It doesn't seem so very much to ask."

Oh, David, she thought to herself, sitting there in the piny woods with his flying suit folded neatly over her hands, what have I gotten you into? And what right had I to ask?

Because she knew, at least as well as Brian Horton, that David had signed on to please her.

Perhaps he would have anyway. But the fact of her involvement had been enough to make his decision automatic. And so, knowing that, she could hardly have refused herself. Brian needn't have worried—she hadn't wanted to refuse.

And what had there been to refuse? Neither of them even knew yet. *A certain object will be transported out of a certain neutral country*, Brian had said—he had used almost the identical words when he had spoken to David. Obviously, the neutral country was Sweden, but for the rest . . . ? The specifics were in the envelope the pilot had handed her upon landing. She hadn't even looked inside yet. There hadn't been time.

Should she hide it? Suppose David was right and the Germans were really coming back, and suppose they captured her . . . The idea itself made her feel colder than the black night air.

She unzipped the pocket over her right thigh and slipped out the envelope, measuring its thickness between middle finger and thumb.

What could she possibly do with it? It seemed foolish to get up and go looking for a hiding place—in this darkness, she might not even find her way back—and how would she even know where the thing was hidden? And how would she ever find it again if it was?

No, it seemed safer to keep it with her. After all, she hadn't received any instructions about keeping it out of enemy hands—maybe there was nothing there the Germans didn't know about already. She returned it to her pocket and tucked her hands back under David's flying suit. The night was cold and dark, and suddenly she was very frightened.

The lantern on the roof of their car was nothing more than a pale, flickering wash, enough to make visible the outlines of a few trees but not enough to see by. She had the impression even that was failing—it would have to run out of kerosene fairly quickly, and then there would be only this impenetrable blackness, like being in the belly of an animal. She didn't find the idea comforting.

She couldn't see, but she could listen. It had never dawned on her before how many sounds there could be in the emptiness of night—the wind, the branches of trees scraping against one another, the little clicks and pops and whispers that might be anything. A world of noise, terrifying in its indefiniteness.

Then, finally, there was something. An engine, the grind of automobile tires on an unpaved road—distant, but perfectly distinct. The closing of doors.

So David had been right after all. And the Germans had come back. How could it be anyone else?

As quietly as possible, she lifted David's flying suit from her lap and set it on the ground beside her. *You don't want to jam the hammer,* he had said. Her hands, she discovered, were so slick that she had to wipe them dry before she could hold the revolver steady.

Just empty the thing into the bastard's guts. She had told him that she knew how to use a pistol, but that was only true in a purely formal sense—paper targets at fifty feet hardly seemed to qualify. As far as she was aware, she had never killed a living creature in her entire life.

But it wouldn't be a man she would be shooting at—merely a shadow, a shape against the darkness. Perhaps, if she kept that in mind, it would be possible.

The dim glow of the lantern vanished—someone must have turned down the wick—and then, almost immediately, tiny points of light began to dart here and there, a nervous, insectlike probing, revealing little corners of yellow and black that then fell back into their shadowy incoherence. They had electric torches with them. She could hear them beginning to move about. They seemed ill at ease and clumsy—it was only an impression. Perhaps they were frightened as well.

Sometimes she felt as if she could hardly breathe, and she had to force herself to keep her hand from tightening on the pistol grip until the muscles in her arm ached. It seemed impossible that she could simply sit there, waiting for them to come.

She tried to concentrate, to take her mind off her fear. How many men were there? And where? There were no voices, only the flickerings of their torches and the soft sound, like the crumpling of tissue paper, of their movements through the undergrowth.

The patterns of light began to diverge, so there were two of them at least. Yes, there were two of them—she thought sometimes she could hear them, quite distinctly. Then, after about a minute, she was just as sure there was only one. Perhaps the second man had moved off in another direction, out of range.

But the one she could trace perfectly easily. A couple of times she almost thought she had caught a glimpse of him, a shadowy outline that disappeared at once. He was being very cautious, as if he hardly knew what he was looking for; he didn't seem to be heading in her direction— how far away was he? Sixty, or perhaps seventy feet. It struck her as a species of miracle that he hadn't seen her yet.

Where in God's name was David? She found it necessary to hold the pistol in both hands, just to keep it steady. Had they found him already? Had they killed him? She hadn't heard any sounds of struggle, but perhaps she wouldn't have. She wished he had told her how close she should let this fellow come before she began firing. By now, he might be no more than fifty feet away.

She could hear each footfall quite clearly now. She couldn't even hear her own breathing anymore, but she could hear the damp leaves crackling under his shoes. The torch was no longer just a glimmer in the trees, but a hard band of light. The man behind it was invisible, as if he were behind a curtain, but she could sense him there. He was real now, and in the next second or two he would shine his light toward her, where it would come to rest. And he would have discovered what he was looking for.

How close should he be? Her arms seemed to raise as if of their own accord, and she found herself trying to take aim on the light. If it touched her, she decided, she would shoot.

She wondered if he had a gun, too, if he would shoot back. She wondered what it would feel like to have a bullet pass through one's body.

Why hadn't he seen her yet? He wasn't more than ten yards away—the torchlight had once or twice come up the ground almost to her feet. She tried to hold the gun steady, but her arms felt as if they might break. Why hadn't he seen her?

The band of light contracted to a narrow circle, and she realized that it was pointed directly at her. It was still now, and so bright she was nearly blinded.

The gun was lined up on him. At that distance she couldn't have missed. She kept waiting for it to go off.

"*Fräulein?*" he said, his voice surprisingly faint in that stillness. "*Fräulein, kommen Sie. Was bedeutet . . . ?*"

Why hadn't the gun gone off? Hadn't she pulled the trigger? No, she hadn't. She had willed the action, but nothing had happened. The gun was simply a dead weight in her hand.

There was a tiny sound, like a gasp, and the torch fell from the German's hand. It hit the ground, bounced once, and was still. In the pale yellow light it threw up she could see . . .

It was the oddest thing. The German was standing there, his arms raised up above his shoulders; but were they all *his* arms? He seemed caught in a tangle of them—there was a hand clamped across his forehead, and the thin flash of what she knew instantly was a knife blade. There was a quick little motion, and the blade disappeared under the point of the German's chin.

He seemed to be not so much standing as hanging there. Hung up on the knife blade like a fish on a barbed hook.

He slumped forward, falling in sections. First down on his knees, then sliding over to the side until he was almost sitting, then straight forward, as limp as a cloth doll.

"Don't do anything rash. It's only me."

For a moment she didn't recognize the voice, and then she saw David kneel down beside the body, turn it over on its side, and pull the knife free from the dead German's throat. There was a sickening stream of blood that poured out of the wound, as well as out of the man's mouth. It looked black in the half-light, like pitch, but it was blood. David calmly wiped the blade off on the sleeve of the German's overcoat.

There was a terrible scream. It seemed to fill the inside of her head until she thought her ears would burst. It seemed to be coming from everywhere, to echo and come back again and build until it was unbearable.

It wasn't until she felt David's hands on her shoulders, felt him shaking her, making her head snap back and forth like the cracking of a whip, that she realized the screaming was her own.

IV

It was a long time before Steadman could get her to stop crying.

He crouched beside her in the darkness, letting her get it out of her system, his hands still clutching her shoulders as if he were afraid she might collapse completely if he let her go. It wasn't the first time he had seen this sort of thing happen to someone.

When she had hold of herself again, he let his hands slide down her arms and released her.

"I'm sorry," she said quietly, dabbing at her eyes with the handkerchief he had lent her. "I'm afraid I've made something of a spectacle of myself."

"Don't worry about it. It's the same with everybody. The first time I saw a man killed, I put my head down between my knees and puked like a baby."

"And does it ever get any easier?"

"I stopped throwing up, if that's what you mean."

At least she was able to smile. He could see that clearly enough, even in the faint, ghostly glow from the dead German's flashlight. It was better than nothing.

"Can you walk? I don't mean to rush you, but it might be a good idea if we got out of here."

"Yes—yes, I can walk."

He picked up the Smith & Wesson that was lying on the ground beside her and stuffed it into his pocket. There was nothing to be gained by making an issue of it now, but of course she hadn't fired. Strangely, he discovered that he was relieved.

The Germans had blocked off the narrow road with their own car—he had seen them do it; he had been crouched in the bushes, waiting for them, and they had come right to him. A search through this one's pockets didn't turn up the ignition key—so it had to be with his friend, who was every bit as dead and wouldn't mind being frisked. Steadman left Karen alone with one of the kerosene lamps from the runway. It would be her chance for a little privacy to change out of her flying suit.

The second German had gone off in the opposite direction, out near the clearing where the plane had landed. Steadman took the man's wallet, his passport, and his watch. Fortunately there was no ring, so he didn't have to cut off a finger to get it. He threw the watch out into the lake but kept everything else—if the Swedish authorities ever got near enough to turn his pockets inside out he'd be as good as dead anyway, and you never knew when a perfectly valid German diplomatic passport might come up useful. For the rest, nothing was lost by advancing the impression that two German embassy goons, out in this wilderness for reasons best known only to themselves, had been set upon and murdered by robbers. Nobody would be fooled, he supposed, but it would give everyone a good reason to let the matter die of old age on a police blotter.

Number Two had also had a knife stuffed up under his chin—they died quietly that way, and it wasn't nearly so messy as having to cut their throats. He had been only a kid, not much more than twenty. They always looked so startled, with their mouths wide open as if they had gone out screaming bloody murder. In fact, they hardly ever made a sound.

Steadman told himself what he had always told himself, that they were good Nazis and therefore fair game, that he didn't have any business feeling guilty about men who had thrown in their lot with the powers of darkness, but it never seemed to do very much good.

The car keys were in the German's overcoat pocket, along with a seven-millimeter Luger he apparently hadn't thought he would need in much of a hurry. You wondered what sorts of fairy tales the Reich Foreign Office could be telling its little boys.

"Would you like to let me know what's in that envelope the pilot gave you?" he asked as they turned off the dirt road onto a strip of pavement that theoretically was going to take them to Stockholm. He switched on the map light, which seemed to catch her by surprise. Her head jerked up, just as if she had been startled out of a profound sleep. She looked at him with what almost amounted to astonishment.

"Our marching orders." He took the envelope from where it was resting underneath her hand. "I assume that's what we've got here. I'd like to know, since we've come all this way, just what it is I'm supposed to steal."

There weren't any other cars on the road—at least, not so far. Probably gasoline was just as hard to come by in neutral Sweden these days as anywhere else. There was nothing to see except the forty or fifty feet of asphalt revealed by the headlights, and nothing to hear but the gravelly throb of the engine. They might as well have been sealed off from the rest of the universe.

Karen didn't even seem to be there. Probably she wasn't. Probably she was back in that forest, watching him kill that damned German.

"Maybe we should send you back home," he went on, putting an end to a silence that was growing increasingly awkward. "I really don't know what they were thinking of to involve you in this in the first place. I don't know what help you could possibly be."

"You think I should have shot that man."

"I didn't mean that," he answered, knowing that that was precisely what he had meant. "Everybody hesitates, at least the first time. That's why for most people the first time is all there is."

And then, of course, the silence was even worse.

"I won't freeze up next time."

"No?"

"No."

He glanced at her out of the corner of his eye and discovered that there were tears running down her face.

"Look, Karen, nobody thinks any the less of you because you couldn't find it in yourself to blow some poor clown's head off on half a second's notice. Why don't you just go home? When we get to Stockholm, you go straight to your embassy and let them worry about the details. If they get inquisitive, tell them I decided I didn't need the extra baggage. Tell them about our two dead friends—they'll understand. You don't owe it to anybody to let this war turn you into somebody you don't like."

"Is that what it's done to you?" She had turned to face him, and there was a smile on her lips that might have been intended as defiant or contemptuous or any number of things. Except that she couldn't control the trembling, so the effect was lost. "I didn't notice that you had any trouble."

"I'm not exactly a virgin at this."

"But does it bother you so much?"

"Yes—more and more. In some ways it gets worse."

All at once both of them seemed to have run out of things to say. In the awkward silence that followed, Steadman tried to concentrate on his driving. It didn't help very much, but it was better than nothing.

"I'm not going back."

"All right, you're not going back." He shrugged his shoulders—it wasn't exactly as if there was any way he could force her. "I don't know what Bertie would say about all this."

"I think the less you and I talk about Bertie, the better."

Steadman nodded, without taking his eyes from the road. It was going to be a long drive into Stockholm.

He kept wondering why on earth he had ever consented in the first place, why he hadn't made it a condition of his acceptance that Karen Windermere stayed in England. He hadn't believed a word that son of a bitch Horton had had to say.

Karen has a second cousin who works as a cipher clerk in our embassy there—it'll provide you with a channel for any logistic help you might need, don't you know. Besides, she has to get her feet wet sometime.

Bullshit. The oily bastard, with his silly-ass group captain's mustache and his "don't-you-know"s; they both understood why he wanted Karen along. In that respect the British were just like the Germans—they were so convinced of their own diabolical cleverness.

Doubtless, like the Germans, they kept files on their sensitive personnel. They had known all along about his association with the Windermeres—particularly with Lady Karen Windermere. Quite possibly that was why they had approached her in the first place. The only thing Steadman wondered about was whether they had figured out for themselves that he was in love with her, or if that could have been something Karen had told them. He wouldn't like to think that.

So Karen would be a kind of guarantee of his good intentions. The son of a bitch.

It was always the same—when they wanted you to do something really dreadful, they always made their pitch the same way. Love of country, love of cause, love of Karen Windermere. In Spain they had a proverb about it: *El corazón está una trampa.* The heart is a snare. In Spain they had a proverb about everything.

Was it so goddamned obvious? He had never said anything, not even to Karen, and yet it seemed to be public information. He wondered if Bertie could have guessed. Poor thickheaded old Bertie, who had been his friend—who was still his friend. It didn't seem very bloody likely.

Probably Bertie would think it the most natural thing in the world.

Splendid girl, you know, he would say. *Just what the doctor ordered.* Why shouldn't the whole world be in love with his wife?

And, of course, it would never have occurred to him that his friend would ever try to do him in behind his back. Bertie Windermere was a gentleman.

"Walk along home and meet the wife," he had said, that dusty August afternoon in 1939, after they had scraped up an acquaintance because his big black Labrador retriever, in an excess of sociability, had tried to trample Steadman to death with affection. After the usual exchange of assurances that, no, the dog wasn't the least little bit dangerous, just a big undisciplined brute of a puppy, and, yes, the muddy pawprints would certainly brush right out as soon as they had had a chance to dry, Windermere had pointed with his walking stick at the cane Steadman still used from time to time.

"Somebody told me you were mixed up in that Spanish fracas," he said, with faint disapproval. "Couldn't see it myself, but I expect we'll all be in the same soup before long."

He had issued his curiously offhand invitation, and Steadman, because he had nothing better to do and because he almost couldn't remember the last time he had had a purely social conversation in the English language—doctors, hotel managers, and real estate agents didn't count somehow—accepted. What the hell, even with the cane he was still good for half a mile or so, and he probably spent too much time alone as it was. The entire time Windermere had talked about hunting.

They had seemed an oddly assorted couple. The squire, with his solid heartiness and his brick-red complexion—his red mustache was almost invisible on his upper lip—and the lady of the manor, pretty, clever Karen, who seemed more suited to be the wife of a city intellectual. Still, they gave the impression of being happy enough together. Steadman could remember experiencing a pang of very real envy.

I think the less you and I talk about Bertie, the better. That was probably so.

Maybe that was why he hadn't resisted too hard when that desk soldier back at the War Ministry had insisted that Karen had to come along on this piece of business. Maybe, Steadman forced himself to realize, he just wanted to create an occasion when they would have something else to talk about besides Bertie Windermere. Now they could talk about the moral and psychological burdens of butchering Germans—it was a little something extra in their store of shared experiences.

The envelope was still lying on the car seat between them. He picked it up and dropped it into her lap.

"Once more I ask—what am I supposed to steal?"

She began working the flap loose with the nail of her little finger, with a concentration that made him suspect she was glad to have this little impersonal piece of business to attend to, and the cool precision of her whole manner made it difficult to remember that less than an hour ago she had been screaming her lungs out in revulsion and terror.

"There's a boat ticket here," she said. "Passage to New York aboard the *Kungsholm*, leaving on Saturday." She handed it across to him, and he stuffed it into his inside jacket pocket without bothering to look at it.

"Why should I go to New York? What's in New York?"

"I don't think New York is the point."

He glanced down at the small felt-lined tray beneath the instrument panel, where Karen had set a photograph to rest against the wooden dash. It showed the head and shoulders of a rather cadaverous-looking man in a bowler hat. His eyes were partially shaded and he didn't seem to have been looking into the camera; presumably the shot was unposed and taken covertly and at a considerable distance. This didn't give the impression of being anyone you would come to love like a brother.

"Who is the little maggot?"

" 'Subject's name is Jacob Protze,' " she answered, reading from a sheet of typing paper that she was holding awkwardly under the map light. " 'Subject is a German diplomatic courier who will be traveling under a Vichy passport aboard the liner *Kungsholm*, bound for New York. He will be carrying certain highly sensitive documents which are to be intercepted and destroyed, unopened and unread. Repeat: unopened and unread. It is recommended that this be accomplished in passage, since this will be the only period during which Protze will not be under Gestapo surveillance.' "

"Is there more?"

"No." She shook her head. "No—only a little note at the bottom, 'Read and Destroy.' " She refolded the sheet of paper and slipped it back inside the envelope. "There's one other thing—a reservation slip for the Hotel Berzelius, made out in the name of Mr. and Mrs. David Steadman."

"Mr. and Mrs.?"

"Mr. and Mrs."

"That isn't very subtle of them."

He had been under the impression that he was making a joke—a pretty thin joke perhaps, but a joke nevertheless. He didn't get much of a laugh, however. Karen, when he looked, was staring straight ahead, her face as empty as if she were alone and waiting for a bus.

"Don't fret yourself. We won't be using it."

She twisted around in her seat to face him and, curiously, there was something like resentment in the creases around her mouth.

"Why, Karen, were you looking forward to playing house?" he asked, smiling cruelly—somehow he was fresh out of patience. It was one of those moments when he felt the full humiliation of unrequited love. It passed away quickly enough. "It was very thoughtful of them, and probably they imagined it would be wonderful cover or something, but considering the way things have gone so far tonight, I haven't the least intention of walking into the Germans' arms. I'll just find my own accommodations, thanks, and so will you."

There was no response. She merely reopened the envelope and inserted the reservation slip. That left only the boat ticket and the photograph.

"I suppose they realize that their 'recommendation' involves murdering this guy." Steadman snapped the photograph with the tip of his middle finger, as if he were flicking away a speck of dirt. "Have you ever seen a diplomatic courier? They go around with their attaché cases handcuffed to their wrists—they even have to sleep that way because they aren't allowed to carry the keys. I'd probably have to lure him into a broom closet, kill him, and cut off his hand to get the case free. Or I suppose I could just chuck him and it over the side when nobody was looking."

"Is that a problem?"

The question wasn't kindly meant. Hell hath no fury like a woman scorned, especially, it seemed, when she had been looking forward to doing the scorning herself. It was astonishing how much his stock seemed to have dropped on this trip.

"Yes, that's a problem," he said. Karen could think anything she wanted to about him. "I keep wondering how I'm supposed to get away with it. You kill a man in a neutral country—or aboard a neutral ship—and it isn't combat, it's murder. Maybe your boss thinks I could fake a heart attack, but that might be a little unconvincing if the corpse is minus a hand."

"Maybe if he disappears altogether they'll assume he committed suicide."

"I wonder how I'd manage to do that without being seen. I don't particularly relish the idea of ending up in the electric chair, although it's possible they might ship me back to Sweden. They probably hang people in Sweden. No—I don't think I much like the War Ministry's plans for getting their hands on Herr Protze's little black bag."

"I suppose that means you won't do it."

She was studying his face with a tense curiosity, as if waiting to have her worst fears confirmed. In its way it was astonishing—all along she had been doing a pretty good job of making him feel like Jack the Ripper because she had seen him knife a German to death, and now she was ready to think him a coward if he didn't serve another the same way.

But it wasn't really as unfair as it seemed. She wasn't asking him if he was ready to kill, just if he was ready to die.

"That just means I won't do it their way."

Egon Weinschenk glanced down disapprovingly at his shoes, wondering if all this snow would leave them waterstained. In the distance he could hear the waves lapping against the shore of the lake. There was a damp chill in the air that made him hunch his shoulders inside his overcoat and wish he had thought to bring a hat. After so many years in uniform, he had lost the habit of civilian dress.

"The Swedes tend to be rather sensitive about the SS," Nebe had warned him. "They seem to have gotten the idea that we're not quite respectable, so you had better go in mufti. In any case, if there should chance to be a disaster we will have less trouble disowning you."

He smiled contemptuously as he said it, as if that termination to the affair was neither unlikely nor, for his part, particularly unwelcome.

"There won't be a disaster."

"Won't there? I seem to recall an episode to which that label might have been applied. Something involving the capture of a notorious Republican spy, whom you allowed to burn the Hotel Colón down around your ears." The smile took on a fixed quality, as if Nebe planned to wear it for the rest of the day, and then it collapsed. "Well—perhaps not this time. In any case, you are being sent because you have already been exposed to information which we wish to have as limited a currency as possible, but I must tell you I was not happy about making the assignment. Something of this importance is a little out of your depth, wouldn't you agree?"

"As I said, Herr Gruppenführer, there won't be a disaster."

"For your sake, I certainly hope not."

Weinschenk had gone straight back to his apartment to change and pack a bag—he would leave at once. Magda hadn't been there and, under the circumstances, he could hardly leave her a note explaining his absence, but he doubted that she would be much troubled. His comings and goings seemed to be a matter of indifference to her, as if he were just one more transient visitor to her bed.

He could remember the way she had looked that night in Madrid as they stood together in the street, watching the hotel where they had been celebrating their reunion burn to the ground. He could remember how the lurid, flickering light from the fire had lit her face as she turned her huge, frightened, questioning eyes to him—*How could you have let this happen to us?* they asked.

And what had he been able to answer? Nothing. Trembling with impotent rage, his hands and arms covered with Max's blood from helping to lift him into an ambulance, what could he possibly have said? *I was setting a trap, and the man against whom I set it has made a fool of me, walking straight through it as if it wasn't there. I never asked you to come to Spain—I wouldn't have dared. I didn't know you were coming tonight of all nights. I never expected anything like this.*

He hadn't said anything. The incident had gone into his record as a failure—a barrier had fallen between him and his wife because she had learned that there was no safety in his arms.

Now she looked for it in the arms of other men.

"Herr Hauptmann, we have found one of the bodies."

One of the embassy dogsbodies came clambering through the brush toward him, slipping on the icy undergrowth just like a man who has seen something unpleasant. He was like so many of them, slender and very Aryan, ignorant of the world outside the SS training academies that mass-produced them like belt buckles. This one had just missed being sent out to intercept the British agent who had been flown in the night before—oh, yes, the *Engländer* had come; the wheelmarks of his plane were still visible on the disused Swedish army tarmac hidden just beyond the line of trees—and the boy had hardly been able to catch his breath when Weinschenk had assured him, on the drive out this morning, that if he had been sent he would now almost certainly be dead.

Weinschenk turned around frostily and looked at him.

"Max!"

His aide appeared from behind a small clump of trees, still buttoning his fly. Max had thought to bring a hat, a green felt production with a badger brush sticking out of the black cord band. In fact, he looked quite human in his greenish-gray belted jacket, stretched even tighter than usual across his chest because of the pistol under his left armpit, and his brown striped plus fours. He wore a pair of heavy hiking shoes and tan leather gloves but no overcoat; he did not give the impression that he felt the cold.

The two men started down toward the lake, following the path left in the snow by SS corporal Meinhof, who showed no inclination to accompany them. What they discovered first, just beyond the break in the trees that marked the shoreline, was SS private Kistenmaker with his hands in his pockets and then, almost directly at his feet, the face-down body of a youth whose name Weinschenk had never troubled to learn—it seemed safe to assume that hereafter no one ever would again.

Weinschenk had arrived in Stockholm about four hours earlier, and it occurred to him that had he received his orders half a day sooner he might have prevented this, and it might have been the British agent whose nose was buried in the gravel. He had not inquired into the embassy's source of information and, of course, they would have had no way of knowing that their intended victim was anything more than perhaps some high-level diplomatic courier in transit to Russia. SS embassy personnel were generally very adequately trained thugs and doubtless could have handled something of the kind with no difficulty, but whoever had come off that plane was obviously a type quite beyond their experience. Whoever it had been, this one had clearly never known what hit him.

Half a day sooner, and it might have been . . .

But the stakes were too high now to indulge in morbid speculation. Weinschenk remembered the look in Nebe's eyes as he had said, *Something of this importance is a little out of your depth, wouldn't you agree?* The bastard thought he had finally found his opportunity to have him shipped off to concentration-camp duty in Poland.

"My regards to your wife, Weinschenk."

Perhaps Nebe had more than one motive for assigning him to this matter. Perhaps it was convenient that Frau Weinschenk's husband should be out of the country for a few days. After all, Hauptmann Weinschenk was not a man to be trusted with important duties. But that was what the SS was like—it was run as a private club for the convenience of its senior members. What should Gruppenführer Nebe care about the destiny of Europe?

"Max, see what you can find in his pockets."

With almost feminine tact, Max began searching the corpse, sliding his enormous hands along the outlines of the heavy clothing as if he feared waking this sleeper. He came up with a pocket handkerchief, neatly folded, a few silver coins, and a Luger—the arrogant fool probably hadn't even remembered he was carrying it.

"Anything else?"

Max frowned and shook his head.

Weinschenk crouched by the dead man and pulled back the right sleeve a few inches. There was a band of pale skin around his wrist but no watch; doubtless they could have found it if they mounted a thorough search—this had been no common robbery.

"He has the wallet, our Englishman, so he probably has the passport as well, wouldn't you say, Max? If we catch him with it, then at least we'll know we have the right one." Somehow he didn't think that a very promising possibility.

"Herr Hauptmann—the other one . . ."

It was SS corporal Meinhof again.

"We found him—Möllendorf is . . ."

They all waited while he struggled to continue his sentence. He bent over at the waist and struck himself on the thigh with his fist, like a stammerer trying to force out the next syllable—only the impediment was not the word but the thing itself.

"He's dead," he managed finally, a little calmer. "His throat was cut. There was blood all over him, like nothing you've ever seen!"

Some door seemed to open in Weinschenk's mind, a memory stirred as much by the expression on Meinhof's face as anything else. He had seen it before, on the faces of the men who had helped to carry Max, his throat cut and his life seeming already to have gushered out onto the paving stones of the Calle de Doña Maria. Important secrets had been at risk then, too—at least, that was the impression they had worked hard to create; actually the courier's briefcase had contained next to nothing— and a man whom Weinschenk had never seen but whom he had learned to hate and admire in almost equal proportions had taken them right out from under their hands, killed the courier and two guards, and left Max a heartbeat from death in a second-floor corridor. That night everyone's face had worn the same expression of horrified astonishment.

Weinschenk actually smiled, although the idea that was taking shape behind his slightly narrowed eyes was very far from amusing. For the first time since he had returned to Berlin in 1939, he felt that sickening, clammy sensation of fear that had been the constant companion of every German intelligence officer working in Madrid; it was the purely physical manifestation of the knowledge that his personal fate was something he could no longer control, that there was another tiger in the jungle besides himself.

"You think not, do you?" he asked evenly. With the point of his shoe he turned over the body that was lying on the pebbly shore in front of him. The dead man really was almost completely rigid, so there was no problem in shifting him on that slight declivity. The lower part of his face was smeared with heavy, clotted blood and, as Weinschenk had expected and dreaded, just underneath his jaw there was a small vertical slit.

"We've encountered such handiwork before, haven't we, Max."

Max's lips were pressed together in a thin white line as he growled in answer.

V

OCTOBER 30, 1941

The *Kungsholm* was due to arrive that morning, but David Steadman wasn't down at the docks to meet her. Instead, he was busy buying himself a new suit.

After his stomach wound, and four months of living on milk and rice pudding, he had lost about twenty-five pounds which, somehow, he had never managed to gain back. Your clothes don't fit terribly well after something like that, so about a year following his return from Spain, when he had become reasonably certain that this would be the way he was going to stay, he had taken the train into London and spent the better part of a week in conference with Bertie Windermere's tailor. The result had been half a dozen suits—very elegant, but hardly the thing for present purposes. If you wanted to be inconspicuous in a neutral city, you didn't manage it by walking around in an outfit that fairly bellowed Saville Row. You dressed like the natives.

Steadman had gone to a ready-made store and bought a hat, an overcoat the color of wet sand, and a dark cinnamon suit—those seemed to be the fashionable colors in Stockholm that year; you saw them everywhere. He tipped the salesman twenty kronor to have the suit ready by two o'clock that afternoon. His shoes were a pair he had picked up in Lisbon.

He had already found himself a place to sleep, and it wasn't the Hotel Berzelius. He couldn't imagine what the British could have been thinking of—he had taken a taxi by the front entrance, and the place was a regular palace. The Abwehr probably had a man on regular duty in the god-damned lobby.

He had engaged a room at a pension in the commercial district, the sort of place that catered to traveling salesmen and boys up from the country who needed a place to bring their girlfriends. You got breakfast if you were downstairs before eight-fifteen, and the landlady, who was a black-haired old harridan of at least sixty—but who still smiled at Stead-man as if she would enjoy making a meal out of him—didn't give the impression that she was the type to be overly curious about her guests. It was just the sort of arrangement he needed.

Outside there was hardly any snow on the ground, and the day was windstill and sunny. Steadman felt solid and healthy, better than he had felt in months, as if the cloud that had settled over him after Artesa de Segre had finally lifted. Maybe he hadn't lost his war after all. Maybe he had only misplaced it for a while.

Nearly three years later, he could still look back to that grubby little town, with its broken walls and garbage tips and smell of cordite and excrement, as if he had just left it. As if it had been his last stopover in solid reality before he lost his way among phantoms.

He had caught the best part of an Italian hand grenade just two days before the Fascists finally managed to overrun that part of the line. At first he couldn't feel a thing—nothing, not even surprise. He lay on the frozen mud at the bottom of a trench, trying not to look down at the hole in his side, hoping he could manage to die quietly before anybody had a chance to get to him. The mythology was that if you were hit in the appendages it was at least even money that you would get away with your life, but if you collected one in the body you could usually forget it.

He didn't really mind dying. For months he had known the Republican cause was lost; it wouldn't be the worst thing to fall in battle. The Na-tionalists, if they caught him, would shoot him out of hand, and there wasn't anything else to look forward to. It had never even entered his head to give up and go home.

Death with honor, he thought, lying there, trying to breathe. It was a phrase one heard more and more often as the heavy artillery fire rained in and the food rotted and the obvious and inevitable end approached. Death with honor.

But, once again, it was not to be. He led a charmed life, so they told him. Maybe it was even so.

From the beginning his Communist commanders had thought it was the funniest thing in the world to send him out on the most dangerous reconnaissance. He was the class enemy. Wasn't it right that the son of the great industrialist be sacrificed first in the anti-Fascist crusade? Because his father owned a manufacturing company—and because "Steadman Tool and Die" was a name they knew even in Catalonia—he was considered ideologically expendable. He seemed to have spent the whole war crawling under barbed wire, or walking around Seville and Madrid with his heart between his teeth, gathering intelligence. It wasn't the way you carried on if you wanted to live to reach eighty, but it was thought that the revolution would prosper just as well without him. Less work for the firing squads when the final reckoning came—one fewer bourgeois to be stood up against a wall.

He had defied all the odds and lived on through two years of the war. He was the Blessed One—*el Bendito*—the man no bullet could kill. Sometimes, before going into battle, men would touch him for luck.

On January 2, 1939, his luck still held, if you could call it that. At least, he didn't die.

Everybody knew that Artesa de Segre would be the beginning of the last battle. Republican Spain was squeezed down to a little sliver of land along the Mediterranean—there was nowhere left to retreat to. The driver of the truck onto which they loaded David Steadman and four other wounded men knew it too. He didn't bother to stop at the field hospital at Solsona; he drove right on across the border into France. Eighty miles, straight over the Pyrenees. By the time he parked his makeshift ambulance in front of the post office in Mont Louis and disappeared, three of his passengers were already dead, and Steadman was so close it was difficult to tell the difference.

Four hours after he had been wounded, they pumped him full of somebody else's blood and started to put him back together. They picked out as much of the shrapnel as they could find and tied off the severed arteries and sewed up the holes in his intestines. The doctor did the best he could, but his was only a small-town practice; the big stuff had to wait for the surgical clinic at Toulouse. There they took out about an eight-inch coil of Steadman's gut and told him he was very lucky he hadn't eaten anything the morning he was wounded and that he would certainly have died if he had had to wait any longer for treatment. Steadman had harbored a certain amount of ill will against the ambulance driver for not having taken them all directly to Solsona—if he had, then maybe nobody would have had to die—until he found out, nearly a month after the final collapse, that when the Nationalists had broken through his section of the line one of the first things they had done was to go through the military hospitals, shooting the patients in their beds.

He had been staying in Toulouse, learning how to walk again, when he heard that Negrín and the Republican government had fled into exile. He was still in considerable pain and could hardly cover the length of a city block without having to sit down and rest, but that evening he boarded the train to Paris. He had a private compartment—once outside of Spain, he was once more a rich man—and all night long he sat staring out through the window at the invisible French countryside, feeling the tears running down his face. The war was over and he was still alive. It struck him as a species of cowardice.

It was no good knowing that he had been saved purely as a matter of chance, that there was no one in the world who could think that he had run away. He had learned that shame could be as random and impersonal a misfortune as being struck by lightning.

But maybe all that was over now.

In Spain, in the filth and carnage of that cruel little war, it had been difficult not to imagine that they were fighting for the soul of Europe. If they lost there, so they had all believed—all of them except the Spaniards, who didn't give a damn about Europe—fascism would spread across the map like a bloody stain. There would be nothing to stop it. And that was just about the way it had happened.

But not quite. There was still England. Not everyone had quietly surrendered, and it was still possible to think that Hitler could be turned back. Perhaps they had all exaggerated the importance of Spain; perhaps all that had been nothing more than a preliminary skirmish. Then it might be worth something to have stayed alive to take a hand in the main action.

He had sent Karen off with a very specific list of instructions—if she really did have a cousin in the British embassy here, she might as well be put to some use. It was good to be back in the fight again. It put certain matters, like his relationship with Karen Windermere, into proper perspective.

It was a funny feeling to know that you were being held in reserve—not that Karen had ever said anything. Not that the subject of what was to happen between them had ever come up in the year since Bertie had gone down in flames. But a look and a nod were sometimes enough. *Don't make me make any choices now*, she had seemed to be telling him. *Just stick around, and when I've gotten myself free of this we'll work something out.*

There was a restaurant on Björklinge Street, at the end of the same block as the Royal Bank of Sweden. Steadman had chosen the place at random, but he liked it well enough when he stepped inside and looked around, unbuttoning his new overcoat and handing it to the neat little gray-haired woman who folded it over her arm, pressing it against her starched, blindingly white apron as she handed him a claim ticket. The walls were paneled in dark wood to within a yard of the ceiling, the heavy black rafters of which stuck out of the white plaster like the rib bones of a whale. It was nearly three-thirty in the afternoon, and the tables were crowded with people, mostly prosperous-looking women, sitting over coffee cups and plates of cake.

The actual dining room was four or five steps down from the entrance, railed off with a little wooden balustrade that somehow created the impression that you were standing on the foredeck of a ship. Steadman allowed his eyes to wander from table to table until he saw a slender, tentative arm raised in greeting. It belonged to Karen.

"I didn't recognize you at first," she said. Her hands were out of sight, presumably folded together in her lap, and the cup of coffee on the table in front of her looked as if it hadn't been touched.

"It's the suit. I bought it this morning. I bought everything new. If you don't want the Abwehr dogging you all over town, I suggest you do the same."

A waitress approached them, a blond farmgirl as silent as a ghost, and he ordered a pot of tea and a slice of the cheesecake that the woman at the next table was having. He ordered in German—it seemed to do the trick.

"I didn't know you could speak German."

"I lived in Zürich for years, until I was twenty-seven. I would have had my fun getting by without it. The Swiss don't like foreigners."

His tone, he realized, was harsher than he had intended, but their parting in the small hours of that morning hadn't been any too warm. If she wanted to come along and play the daring lady spy, that was fine with him, but she should leave her finer feelings parked back in Brompton, please. He didn't mind in the least if she realized that he resented being made the object of her moral squeamishness.

"Did you bring what I asked for?"

She nodded—that was something—and produced a handbag from somewhere beneath the table. She took out an envelope and handed it to him. He took it and put it out of sight in his inside jacket pocket.

She was wearing a mahogany-colored suit of a material that looked like the stuff they made gunny sacks out of but that had probably come right off the bolt at some Regent Street dressmaker's—Karen's sense of clothes was negligible and the stores robbed her blind; it was part of her charm. Her short, light brown hair looked as if she had washed it that morning.

She sat there in silence, watching him out of huge black eyes that seemed to go on forever, like caverns buried in shadow, and he realized, with a familiar twinge in the back of his throat, that there was nothing she could ever do or say that would make him feel any different about her than he had that first afternoon, when she had poured coffee for him on the terrace of her husband's house in Kent, that she would hold him prisoner that way for the rest of his life.

Anyway, he wasn't angry anymore.

"Did you find yourself somewhere to sleep?" he asked, smiling, but his order came before she could do more than nod. They sat there in uncomfortable silence, watching each other like enemies as the waitress arranged his cup and the silver teaspoon and a dessert plate with a huge slab of cheesecake on it, smothered in blueberries. He loathed blueberries—the lady next to him hadn't gotten blueberries—but this didn't seem like the moment to bring that up. The waitress made gracious little murmuring sounds while she did her work, as if she were attending to the comforts of an elderly invalid.

"I telephoned my cousin," Karen said when they were alone again. "I woke her up—she wasn't very pleased about it, but she took me in."

"Was she the one who got you all this?" He touched the slight bulge under his right lapel, as if he were pledging allegiance.

"Yes. She was very good about it—I never even had to leave the flat."

"Did you catch a little sack time?"

She peered at him for a moment, as if she hadn't recognized the expression, and then, when it clicked into place, her lips parted in a perfect spontaneous smile that made her look about seventeen.

"Yes—it was marvelous." Without actually moving, she gave the impression of stretching with luxurious, catlike slowness. "Five hours in a warm room. I'd almost forgotten what it could be like."

As Karen pushed along past the shopwindows on the Luntmarkargaten, letting the crowds of evening shoppers flow around her like a current of water, she kept remembering the expression on David's face as he talked about his stepfather's ducks on the Zürichsee.

They had had a house on the water, and every evening before dinner the three of them, David, his mother, and her second husband, would go down to the thin strip of pebbly shoreline and feed the ducks bread-crumbs from a paper bag. It was evident that David had been very fond of Herr Käselau, who seemed to have cultivated no career beyond that of being the sort of man to engage the affection of his adolescent stepson, and who had died of a heart attack in 1936, within a few months of his wife. Funnily, David had never before struck her as a man equipped with family memories; she had the sense of having learned more about his real character in the last twenty-four hours than in the whole previous time of their relationship. A tiny anecdote, related in half a dozen sentences over cake and tea, had disclosed the existence of unimagined worlds.

And now he wanted the floor plans for the German embassy and a camera with a long-range lens.

It was already pitch black out, although barely five-thirty in the afternoon. The streetlamps threw an intense white light over everything, revealing the lines in people's faces with pitiless clarity. Suddenly she missed London, where the Blitz had done away with that particular inconvenience. Stockholm was like being startled awake in a strange bed and not remembering how she had come to be there. She missed the familiarity of the war, the sense of life suspended for the duration.

David had killed a man last night—two men, unless she had made a mistake; and, yes, David had said "they"—he had knifed two men to death in the middle of an empty wilderness (Why did that seem to make it so much more . . . ? Yes, brutal), and this afternoon he had sat in a restaurant eating cheesecake and talking about his family. And it hadn't been anything like an act. Last night had just ceased to exist for him.

Bertie would come home on leave and not be able to talk about anything except his Hurricane and who had been killed and whether he had had a piece of downing this or that enemy plane. It had been an obsession, the way no serious thing could ever be. It was a game, and he and his mates—and even the Germans, on the other side—were all playing it together. He had been playing at war with the other boys.

Would David be the kind to tell stories when it was over? Would he be the kind, if he lived, to pass the port around the table after dinner, talking about how he had cut a couple of Germans' throats one night in Sweden? It didn't seem likely. He had had one war already, and in all those weeks in Kent he had hardly ever even mentioned Spain.

Once a friend of his had come down from London, a Belgian named Vidocq, a heavy, balding, middle-aged man with the thick hands of a laborer—David had said he was an engineer and had been his company commander during the Madrid fighting. Out of politeness, and perhaps a certain morbid curiosity, Bertie had promptly invited the two of them to dinner.

Vidocq was a talkative, entertaining guest, all the more so when he had had a little to drink.

"Look at him," he would say, leaning forward in his chair and gesturing toward David with the blunt point of his thumb. "Just look at him, madame—have you ever seen such a schoolboy, eh? An innocent! Do you know what they called him back there?" And he gave a sharp tilt to his chin, as if to suggest that Spain was just behind him, perhaps in the next room. "*El Cortador*—the Cutter! Hah! The cutter, that's what they called this harmless-looking little angel. The Spanish understand these questions, so when we were due to go out on patrol no one would look for our friend David. He would just disappear into the darkness, and we would never know where he was. Until we found the Fascist sentries, smiling from underneath their jawbones. A few more like him and Franco would still be back on the Canary Islands."

All the while, David had toyed with his brandy glass in closed, sullen silence.

"Come on, Arsène," he had said finally, "it's time to go home." No, there would be no war stories. David Steadman would not be one of those who would remember all this through a haze of gallantry.

He was right. What a boy Bertie seemed beside him, what an innocent.

As she stood gazing into a shopwindow, she could feel herself blushing with shame. Bertie had been her husband—was still her husband—and deserved better from her. What a disgraceful way to think about him, and only a year after he had lost everything short of his life fighting for king and country. She looked up, and the image she saw reflected in the bright, smeary glass seemed to belong to someone else. Was that used-up, cynical old jade really herself? Was that the way David had seen her this afternoon?

She thrust her hands deep into the pockets of her coat and walked on, looking neither right nor left. David didn't love her anymore—how could he? David looked at her and saw simply the wife of his friend, nothing more. Or, perhaps, someone who might be useful to him in doing his job.

She had covered perhaps as much as two blocks before she realized how much the thought distressed her—even when she knew it wasn't true.

It was important that David Steadman loved her. Lots of men had loved her, and some still did—Brian Horton, she was sure, would propose tomorrow if he thought there was any chance she would listen. She didn't care about Brian Horton, or anyone, except David. Why hadn't she grasped that simple fact before?

"There's my address," he had said, sliding the tiny scrap of paper across the table to her. "And the landlady's phone number. When you've got what we need . . ." He hadn't even looked her in the face while he said it, but could it have been an invitation just the same?

And what did David want with plans to the German embassy? It didn't seem to make any sense—what did it have to *do* with anything? He hadn't been at all in a humor to explain.

"Has it occurred to you to wonder," he had asked, as he used his fork to push the blueberries disdainfully from the surface of his slice of cheesecake, "just exactly why your Major Horton wants his little parcel picked up at this end of the line? Wouldn't it be easier to do something like that after Herr Protze has landed safely in New York?"

He squinted at the little pile of syrupy fruit lying to one side of his dish as if it represented some sort of moral contagion, holding his fork delicately between first finger and thumb. His entire attention, it seemed, was absorbed by his abhorrence of blueberries.

"The Germans don't even have a consulate over there anymore," he went on absentmindedly, as he appeared to steel himself for the ordeal of the first bite. "And everybody knows that Roosevelt is only waiting for a plausible excuse to declare war. I'm sure the police would be happy to look the other way while somebody shoves our friend under a taxi. So why does it have to be done here—or in mid-Atlantic, which is even a worse idea? Doesn't that strike you as a little fishy?"

When she thought about it, as she had to think about so many things now, from the very different perspective of a man like David Steadman, she had to admit that, yes, it was just a little fishy.

VI

Justus Boström was an unpleasant-looking man. His shoulders were bowed so that he hardly seemed capable of standing up straight, and his arms were too long and ended in white, delicately shaped, but extraordinarily hairy hands. There was something apelike about him—his hairline had retreated to the very top of his skull, and although his beard was carefully shaved up to the tops of his ears, his tiny face appeared to be swallowed up in dark, bristly shadow. He habitually breathed through his mouth, with his upper lip pulled back from a narrow row of teeth, giving him a jeering, dissatisfied expression.

He lived with his elderly sister in a small house on one of the narrow streets off the Österlanggaten, where the chilly, damp smell of the Baltic made your skin tingle like an outbreak of prickly heat. David Steadman had been waiting for him, about a block and a half away, in the shadow of a marine-supply warehouse, ever since five-fifteen, when the crew of the *Kungsholm*, on which he was chief engineer, had been dismissed for shore leave. Boström was home having his dinner, but it was to be hoped that after a week at sea, up to his armpits in grease and bilge water, he wouldn't be content to stay there. He really didn't give the impression of being a domestic character.

Sure enough, at about twenty minutes after eight, he slammed his

sister's front door behind him and appeared on the sidewalk, dressed up
like the village undertaker in a black suit that looked a little too large,
his remaining hair slicked back and shining in the dim light.

It was basically a problem of approach. Boström might or might not
be a man of sterling moral qualities—although, it had to be admitted,
his appearance told against him—but not many of us have the courage
to be a scoundrel in public. The trick would be to get him alone.

Steadman's heart sank as he watched the tidy sailor beginning to make
his way toward the wider streets and the glittering lights of the main part
of town. Visions of church socials plagued him, along with the gruesome
possibility that Boström might have a girlfriend somewhere—a nice,
respectable girlfriend, some slightly withered virgin waiting with her knees
pressed together to serve him tea and cookies and listen while he read to
her from the poetry of Karlfeldt. Blessed are the pure of heart, goddamn
them.

It was hard to tell. Steadman kept as close as he dared, which was
generally not more than a block or so. There weren't many cars, so he
stayed on the other side of the street. Boström wasn't very difficult to
follow; he loped along with a peculiar, ungainly stride, leaning out so
far on his left foot that he seemed almost ready to topple over, not
appearing to hurry. There was nothing to suggest that he even knew
where he was heading in any specific way. Apparently he was carrying
some candy or something because every once in a while he would reach
into his jacket pocket, take something out, and slip it into his mouth. It
seemed a perfectly mechanical operation.

There was no wind, thanks be to God, but it was cold. Steadman was
glad of his new hat and overcoat, and it was incomprehensible to him
how Boström could be comfortable in just a suit. He hoped this one
wasn't going to turn out to be one of those hardy Nordic types, with no
nerve endings and no imagination. It wasn't going to be a big help if he
had to deal with Popeye the Sailor.

They stopped in a tavern, not far from the main shipping yards, and
Steadman ordered a beer and watched his quarry sit by himself at a small
circular table, morosely hunched over a large glass of something that was
the same color as English stout. There was plenty of noise in the place—
somebody was playing a piano that sounded like a banjo, and the air was
thick with laughter and shouting and the occasional snatch of song.

Steadman stood by the bar, watching the man at the piano but keeping
a vague track of Boström out of the corner of his eye. The dandified little
clerk next to him, his occupation declared by the ink stains on his fingers,
addressed something to him that sounded like a question and he tried to

answer, first in English and then in French and German, but the clerk only shrugged his shoulders and the conversation came to an end. The bartender, who had heavy gray sideburns and looked as if his skin had been packed to the bursting point, was gasping with concentration as he washed glasses, his shirtsleeves rolled up over the elbows of his massive arms. The solitude was nearly perfect.

You wondered what Boström was doing there, what he could have been thinking about. He hardly moved, except once in a great while to take a tentative little swallow of his drink, which he didn't give the impression of enjoying very much. His upper lip kept creeping up over his gums, as if he were about to laugh unpleasantly, but he never did laugh. In the yellow light of the tavern the pallor of his skin, hardly surprising in someone who probably spent most of his life in the bowels of a ship, made him look almost deathlike.

But perhaps he wasn't so much of a mystery after all. The trick was to follow his eyes.

There were women there—not very many, and none of them precisely beauties. A couple of navvies had brought their girlfriends, who were not so much dancing as being mauled to the accompaniment of the piano. One of them was actually wearing a pair of tight black trousers, and her partner had his hand firmly planted on her left buttock as they swayed back and forth together like sleepwalkers.

Boström liked the one in trousers. He could hardly bear to look away, even when her boyfriend treated him to a pointed, almost threatening stare. His close-set, simian eyes glittered with envy as he watched the progress of that hand up and down that tight little ass.

Finally the dance ended, and the dancers went back to their table, and Boström finished off his drink with a couple of long swallows and got up to leave. At least there wasn't any doubt anymore what he was out looking for.

Steadman allowed him about a fifteen-second lead and then set out himself. Boström was walking faster now. Whatever had been in that glass had apparently helped him to make up his mind; the odd, topheavy amble had steadied up, and he paced along with the air of a man who knows where he is going. It took Steadman a couple of minutes before he could catch up.

There was an ugly little tangle of streets just off the main embankment, full of five-story walk-ups where the ground floor was apt to be occupied by an amusement arcade, or a grocery store, or maybe a bar where you could probably get stinking for the equivalent of about seventy-five cents. Sometimes you couldn't even count on a ground floor; sometimes there was only a narrow, unlit stairway, and you would have to go down into the basement to get whatever it was you were after. This was a terrible place.

There are certain conditions of life which don't allow for much refinement of feeling. Steadman had learned as much as that in Spain, where his first month in the trenches around Las Navas had cured him forever of any illusions that maggots and dirt and sleeplessness were other than the normal pattern.

In Madrid, the brothels that fell within the budget of the common soldier used to get so crowded that men would queue up outside to get to girls who worked them at a rate of about one every fifteen minutes. Steadman had drawn the line at that, but, then, he hadn't been born an authentic proletarian. His comrades, the men he had fought with, the slum boys for whom the war was something on the order of a personal quarrel, used to think such squeamishness was wonderfully funny, and he had been a little ashamed of it. He couldn't help himself; an hour alone with a razor and some hot running water and he returned, whether he liked it or not, to the arms of the middle class.

Maybe a sailor's life wasn't so very different, and maybe Justus Boström had spent his nights below decks, where he listened to the engines throb and his underwear stuck to him like wallpaper, dreaming of the dank little whores of these waterfront tenements. The chance to scrub his back and eat a hot, woman-cooked meal in his sister's neat little house hadn't done its magic—or perhaps he was one of those who only liked what he had to pay for. It was apparent that that was what he was down here to find.

There were girls around. It wasn't like Piccadilly Circus, where they practically blocked the traffic, but they were there. It was autumn in the north of Europe; peddling your ass had to be a fairly furtive business or you could come down with pneumonia. They stood in doorways, under the yellow entrance lights with the collars of their coats turned up, waiting. How long could they stand it out there before they had to turn back inside for a hot cup of tea and a few minutes with their feet up against the grate? It didn't seem like one of the easier ways to make a living.

Boström seemed to be a man of rather decided tastes. He took his time making up his mind, strolling down the sidewalks like a shopper at Harrod's. He seemed to enjoy the ritual—he would stop in front of one of the occupied doorways, take a sidewise glance that committed him to nothing, wait for the inevitable smile, and then move slowly on in all the state of an offended deacon. He wasn't ready to settle for just anything. He had his standards to maintain.

It wasn't difficult to keep track of him—he wasn't the only man out for a few laughs that night, and Steadman didn't have any trouble blending in with the other gentlemen with their shoulders hunched and their hands dug deep into their pockets. There seemed to be a kind of unspoken treaty in effect that nobody noticed anyone else's existence; Steadman was able to stay close while Boström conducted his survey over about four blocks of open invitations.

Finally the chief mechanic made his choice. In a country where tall blondes were ten to the yard, he had to have something exotic. The one he finally settled on was small and dark, not particularly pretty but with an almost Asiatic cast to her face, something she took care to point up with plenty of eye pencil. He stood there for a moment, watching her almost painful smile, and then mounted the three or four steps to the entrance of the apartment building, where she slipped her arm under his and led him inside.

The upper half of the door was a latticework of glass, and beyond it there was a narrow reception hall and then a stairway. Steadman stood outside until he was sure they had gained the first landing and then he tried the knob. It turned in his hand—the Swedes seemed to be a trusting race—and he pulled the door toward him and slipped inside.

He couldn't see them, but he could see their shadows through the slits in the balustrade, beyond which, if you pressed yourself against the wall, were just visible the tops of a line of doorways. But that was just on the second story, and the lady seemed to live a little higher up. Steadman tried the stairs and found that they didn't have any marked tendency to creak under him. He followed the shadows as they retreated up the balustrade like something moving behind the bars of a cage. Up another flight of stairs, and another. The little bitch would have to have her love nest all the way up on the top floor.

She had the corner room in the back. Steadman waited on the stairway and watched the patch of light on the ceiling overhead collapse as she closed her door behind her. He waited a moment—nothing was lost through a little caution; she might be the type to worry about her neighbors—and then continued up through a narrow hatchway to the roof.

It was cold up there. The snow, which no one had any reason to clear away, had thawed and refrozen often enough to cover the flat tar-paper roof with a treacherous patchwork of ice, and there was a wind tugging at the clotheslines that hadn't made itself felt on the ground. Steadman worked his way carefully, toe and heel, toe and heel, like a man walking a tightrope. There was plenty of time, and he didn't want anyone to hear him. Probably there hadn't been a soul up on this roof for two or three months. Toe and heel, toe and heel, right over to the edge, where he could support himself against the brick retaining ledge and slide along to the corner.

The light was still visible behind her window shades, and a small metal ladder led down to the fire escape. If he didn't slip and land with a crash that would wake up the whole building, the rest would be easy. Well—relatively easy. As long as no one got hysterical . . .

As he stood there at the edge of the roof, staring down at the fire-escape landing outside a whore's bedroom window, Steadman found himself wondering, and not for the first time, if he couldn't have thought of some simpler method. It seemed so theatrical, so unnecessarily complicated, to go to all this trouble just for the sake of a ten-minute conversation with a ship's mechanic. Maybe he was allowing himself to get carried away. Maybe he should go back downstairs and wait outside on the street for Boström to finish in his own good time. What the hell difference would it make?

But he couldn't do that—oddly enough, the risks were all the other way. He needed the psychological edge. On the street, where he would be a citizen again, a man with rights and dignity and a place in the world instead of a guilty little toad with his pants over the back of a chair, what was to keep Boström from just telling him to shove off? Steadman needed his undivided attention. He needed him naked and off guard and scared to death. Boström had to be ready to listen with both ears.

So it was down the fire escape and in through the window. The melodrama was just what the doctor ordered.

When he touched down on the landing, he pressed himself up against the outside wall and listened. There were no voices, and nobody raised the shade to see what all the racket was. There hadn't been any racket. There was nothing to hear but the wind. He looked at his watch—Boström had been in there about fourteen minutes now, which seemed about right. It would be worth something to catch him with his palms still sweating.

Steadman took a sidewise look at the window, and there was good news and bad news. The good news was that there was no outside storm window, so he didn't have to go through two panes of glass and risk cutting himself into long thin strips; the bad news was that the wire mesh screen hadn't been taken down from the summer.

He tried to pace the thing in his mind. One good pull and the screen would come right loose—there wasn't anything holding it except a couple of tiny metal runners at the top. Two seconds. Then you smash the window, reach inside to throw the latch, push it up, and climb inside.

Eight, maybe ten seconds. Call it twelve seconds, start to finish. In his whole life he had never been in the sack with a woman who didn't lock her bedroom door, and there didn't seem to be any reason to suppose that whores would constitute an exception. Rather the contrary. So how long does it take for someone to notice the noise, figure out that the bogeyman is trying to break in, get over the initial shock, get to the door, remember that it's bolted, throw the bolt . . . ? Partly, of course, it would depend on how busy they were up on that bed. The girl would be the first to catch on—probably, if all one heard about the profession was true, she wouldn't have as much to occupy her attention. It was to be hoped, then, that Boström favored the missionary position.

But how long? Twelve seconds? More? Less? It was going to be a nice call.

With great care, since he only had about a yard between the end of the fire-escape landing and the edge of the window—the blind wasn't all the way down, and somebody *might* notice something—Steadman began to work his arms free of his overcoat. When he was finished he took another look at his watch—sixteen minutes they had been at it in there, just about right assuming that Boström wasn't either painfully shy or the type who was always in a hurry—and then wrapped the overcoat around his left hand and arm.

It worked like a charm. The screen came away with hardly a whisper, and when Steadman hit the bottom pane of glass with his shielded fist the whole thing split right down the middle. He had the window up and one leg over the ledge, and Boström was still lying there, looking over his shoulder at him with the silliest expression he had ever seen on a grown man's face.

The girl *was* the first to react. Somehow she slipped out from underneath and had both feet on the floor when Steadman, in a single swift movement, whipped out the evil-looking hunting knife that he carried strapped to his leg and waved it at her, as if all he wanted was for her to see how the blade glittered in the light.

She stopped cold; she didn't even breathe, and her stare never left the point of Steadman's knife. Probably the fact that she was stark naked didn't make the prospect of getting carved up any more appealing. You could tell she was imagining how it would feel to have that thing dig a trench across her belly.

"Do you speak English?"

She nodded, very stiffly at first, as if the joints in her neck had frozen up. Her eyes, which turned out to be a pale blue and looked a little strange outlined so heavily with black pencil, were wide, almost gaping, and the flesh on her arms and breasts was covered with goose pimples. Whether that was fear or just the cold air from the broken window, there was no way of knowing.

"Then put on your clothes. My business isn't with you."

He made a small, impatient gesture with the point of his knife toward the pile of clothing that was spilling off the footboard of the bed, and slowly, without moving her feet or taking her eyes away from the knife, she reached out a hand toward the black skirt which happened to be on top.

"Go on," he said, his voice a little softer—what the hell, he didn't have anything against the girl. "Just get dressed. I won't hurt you."

And what of Boström? He was lying on his right side, his leg and arm out in front of him, clutching the bedsheet as if any second he expected to fall off onto the floor. He was so frightened that you could hear him breathing.

"Sit up!"

Boström scrambled into a sitting posture, pulling the sheet over his belly and legs like the veriest virgin. Fine—apparently everyone understood everyone else.

And then, as if by prior arrangement, both men turned to watch the girl getting dressed. She did it quickly, but without any appearance of hurry—it was wonderful the grace women could bring to things like that.

"Did this one pay you yet?"

She was almost finished by then, so she took a quarter step around toward Steadman while her hands worked to button up an unexpectedly starchy-looking white blouse. She shook her head, her gaze fixed sullenly on the floor—no, she hadn't been paid yet.

"How much do you usually rake in a night?"

The question seemed to surprise her. For an instant she looked almost offended, as if she thought he might be laughing at her. Her eyes went up to his face, and she could see that no one was kidding.

"I like fifty kronor," she said evenly. Was she lying? Did she think he was asking for himself? She even managed to smile at him. "Sometimes I have two or three gentlemen—sometimes not."

Steadman transferred the knife to his left hand and reached for the envelope in his inside jacket pocket. He took out five hundred-kronor notes and spread them out on a small table next to the door. Then he slipped the envelope back inside his coat.

"That should take care of the window and the inconvenience. I want a word with this 'gentleman'; if you come back in twenty minutes we'll both be gone, and there won't be any dead bodies in the closet. The only way you can get into any trouble will be if you call the police—do you understand that?"

"Yes, I understand."

"Good. Then get out of here."

He kept the door open a crack and watched her on her way down the stairs. She didn't seem to be in a hurry, which was a good sign. It didn't matter, however. Steadman didn't figure on hanging around long enough to get caught, even if she screamed her bloody lungs out the minute she hit the street. He closed the door and looked over at Boström, who was still keeping himself modestly covered with the bedsheet.

"May I put on my trousers at least?" he asked, in heavily accented but perfectly correct English.

"Please yourself."

Steadman replaced the knife in its sheath and brushed his trouser leg back into place with the flat of his hand. He tried not to look at Boström— he didn't want to seem as if he was waiting for what was bound to happen next.

Boström didn't disappoint him. As soon as he had his shirt and pants on he made a rush, grabbing Steadman around the chest and pinning his arms. He seemed to want to wrestle him to the floor, but Steadman never gave him the chance. Steadman kicked back and caught Boström's leg just above the ankle with the heel of his shoe. There was a grunt of pain, and the pressure around Steadman's chest slackened. It was all he needed. He swung his body a little to one side and drove an elbow into Boström's midsection. Boström had stopped even trying to fight. A short, sharp blow to the side of the head, and it was all over.

It was perhaps half a minute before Boström could do anything except hold his guts in and make funny noises. Finally, Steadman grabbed him by the shirt front and pulled him up into a sitting position. Playtime was over.

"I want to talk business," he said, crouching down so that his face was perhaps no more than a foot from Boström's. Boström looked up at him with pale, watery eyes, giving the impression that he had only the remotest idea what Steadman was talking about. "What do I have to do to get your attention, kill you?"

Boström swallowed hard—you could tell he was trying to concentrate. He watched very carefully as Steadman reached back into his jacket, took out the envelope, and extracted a thick wad of bank notes.

"This is five thousand kronor. It's a down payment. Five thousand kronor buys you a lot of fancy ladies—in five minutes you can be walking out of here with this in your pocket, and that's only the first half. Are you interested, or does this go back where it came from?"

He made a gesture as if to put the money away, and Boström made a feeble grab for it. Steadman grinned, not terribly kindly, and allowed him to take the notes from his hand.

"It's a lot," Boström murmured, with a kind of astonished reverence. "It must be something big that you want for it."

"Nothing you can't manage easily enough. Your ship, it's scheduled to sail the day after tomorrow—I want you to delay that by, say, forty-eight hours. I don't want the *Kungsholm* to keep its schedule."

Boström stared at him for a moment. The wind from the broken window was cold, but he didn't seem to feel it. He was too busy with his greed and his fear. And then his eyes fell back to the money. An astonishingly pink tongue worked its way across his lower lip.

"I can do that," he said finally, "if part of the drive linkage gets bent. A day to take the old shaft out, a day to put the new one in. Two days. Easy."

He smiled, a cunning smile that excited little trust. Steadman decided that he really didn't like Justus Boström very much.

"When do I get the other five thousand?"

You could tell from the way he said it that he liked the feel of the words on his tongue. *Five thousand.*

"The night after I know the sailing's been postponed, at, say, six o'clock, you tell your sister you're going to take a walk. You follow the same route you did tonight. By the time you get back home you'll be a lot richer."

"How do I know you won't forget?"

"I won't forget, pal." Steadman let his eyes narrow slightly. "We don't either of us want any trouble. You'll get your money and then we'll both forget."

Boström smiled again. The performance didn't improve with practice. "That's right," he said. "I trust you just like you trust me, right?"

"No, that's not right."

Steadman let his right hand drift down to the cuff of his trouser leg. In an instant the knife was back out, and he pressed the blade against the side of Boström's face, just below the eye, until the skin blanched white, daring him to move his head.

"I don't trust you one little bit, pal. If that ship doesn't stay in its berth until Monday morning, what do you think is going to happen to you? And where do you think you could run where I wouldn't find you?"

*   *   *

The wind followed Steadman home. Like a cold sigh, it seemed to pour down the back of his neck, making him feel chilled right through. There didn't seem to be a soul out any longer. Except for the streetlamps, you might as well have been back in London after blackout time.

He tried, as he always did when he had the hump, to remember that he had long since given up the idea that he had a right to think of himself as a private person with permission to worry about his comfort or his future. He was getting the job done. Boström was too scared and too greedy to do anything except what he was told, and everything was going very well. That ought to have been enough.

Except, of course, that it wasn't.

He walked along, listening to the sound of his footfalls against the concrete sidewalk, surrendering himself up to his misgivings. His plan was too convoluted—how the hell was he going to come out of it alive, let alone successful? Anyway, what was in Jacob Protze's diplomatic satchel that was worth so much trouble, and why couldn't he get over the idea that Karen's friend at the War Ministry was being less than candid with him? In a deal like this, no one had a right to expect the whole truth, but Steadman had the impression that somebody was playing him for a sucker.

What disturbed him most was the possibility that it might be Karen herself.

Except that some cold-hearted son of a bitch had decided she might be useful in ensuring his reliability, there wasn't any compelling reason why she had to be along; the boys at Whitehall must have had an inkling that there might be something about this business that wouldn't square with their honored American colleague. They had been so insistent that he enter Sweden carrying his own passport, when God knows they must have had drawerfuls of phony ones he could have used just as well. It made you wonder.

And what of Karen? How much of a hand had she had in delivering him up to his fate, and how much did she know that she was keeping to herself? He might love her—he was fool enough for that—but he was damned if he was going to trust her.

Karen. He must really have been some species of idiot, because anyone would have thought his experiences there enough to teach him not to expect too much from life. In every affair of the heart there was supposed to be a point where it was still possible simply to back out and no harm done; Steadman wondered how many months behind him that was, and if any part of him had recognized it when he had seen it. Bertie was still alive and still Karen's husband and still his friend.

Steadman had seen him two months ago. It had been one of the last fine days of the year, and Bertie was out on the huge lawn behind his house in Kent, practicing not very convincingly with a driving iron. They sat out on the terrace and drank lemonade—Bertie's doctors wouldn't allow him anything stronger. There hadn't been any marked improvement; he was in a state of extreme but carefully contained excitement, not much different from the day he was checked out of the military hospital at Horsham. Steadman noticed that he had fallen into the habit of picking at the tips of his fingers with his nails, so that they were covered with little scabs.

"You ought to have Karen down here with you."

"Oh, God, I couldn't stand that!" he had answered, his eyes taking on a strangely panicky expression. With the next sentence his whole manner changed abruptly, and you could have imagined they were talking about some remote acquaintance. "She's living in town now, you know."

And there it was.

By the time Steadman got back to his pension, everyone had long since gone to bed. The landlady had left the front door unlocked—maybe everyone did in this country. So he crept across the entrance hall and started making his cautious way up the stairs, thinking to himself what a cheerless business it was to come back to a house full of strangers, where there wasn't a soul awake to say hello and maybe make you a cup of coffee. Except for the trenches in Spain, it was just the way he had gotten through every night of his life since the morning of 1936 when he had told his father that he was quitting the family business and going off to fight with the Republicans—the first time he said it his father had thought little David was talking about the GOP, but he had gotten it right fast enough after that.

"Then you're quitting the family too, you know that, kid." That was just the way Frederick Steadman, chairman and principal stockholder of Steadman Tool and Die, expressed himself to his younger son. If you were Frederick Steadman's boy you didn't go off to fight in obscure foreign wars, and sure as hell not on the side of the godless Communist International.

Steadman fished his room key out of his pocket and was perhaps a third of the way up the creaking staircase when he noticed the band of light at the top of his door frame. Had he left the desklamp on? It didn't seem likely—he hadn't been near the place since eight-thirty that morning. Why in hell would anybody need to use a light at that hour?

Therefore it followed that somebody was up there waiting for him.

He slipped the knife out from under his trouser leg and slid it handle-first up the sleeve of his coat, letting his arm drop down. The point rested against his palm, just behind the joint of his middle knuckle, so that all he had to do was to straighten his fingers and the knife would fall down into his grasp. He was too tired to be frightened—his nervous system had undergone enough wear and tear. He was merely annoyed. He didn't like uninvited visitors; he didn't care who they were.

Of course, they were being awfully obvious about it. They could just as easily have waited outside.

Still, there was no harm in being prepared.

Assuming that they weren't deaf as well as stupid, by now they had to have heard him on the stairs, so there was no longer any point in being coy. He could either run for it or go right on up and march in. He rather thought he would let them have him—people were always so careless when they thought they had taken you flat-footed, and, besides, he was curious. Nobody ever found anything out by high-tailing it out into the black of night.

When he reached the door he inserted the key just as noisily as he could manage, even whistling a little tune as he did it and throwing in a faintly drunken slur for effect. Let them think the worst.

He gave it a little push, and the door swung open. He stayed on his side of the threshold, however, just for safety.

No guns went off, nobody tried to make a dive at him. There weren't any muscular men standing around with their hat brims pulled low over their eyes. There wasn't a thing to be seen except Karen, lying in his bed, covered up to her naked shoulders with a sheet.

"Hello," she said, smiling a little uncertainly. "I hope you don't mind, but I bribed your landlady. I've decided I'm tired of being a widow."

VII

OCTOBER 31, 1941

Brian Horton regarded himself as an amiable man—in the army one needed to be able to get along with all sorts—but he had nonetheless taken an instant dislike to this fellow Steadman. It was difficult to explain. On the face of it, Steadman wasn't a bad chap. He was brave and quiet; he had all the virtues which, as a soldier, Horton had always believed himself to admire in other men. But he had a way of smiling and seeming to look right through one, as if he knew the heart's secrets and hidden longings. And he was in love with Karen Windermere.

They had sat down across from each other at a bare little table in an airplane hangar in Surrey, waiting to start the first leg of the trip to Sweden, and Horton had explained to him the facts of life—that he would be expected to use his own passport, that the British government would know nothing about him if he were captured, that the mission would be outlined for him in detail once he reached his landing point at Hjälmaren, the whole sad story. Steadman had merely smiled, as if to say, *Is it ever any different?* A man shouldn't be so casual about risking his life. Somehow it wasn't quite decent.

Then there was the way his eyes would follow Karen's movements as she paced about, waiting for the plane to be ready. Horton wondered if he hadn't made a terrible mistake there.

He had no illusions about himself. He was a desk soldier, no figure of romance. He had seen a little action in India when he was fresh out of Sandhurst—Gandhi and all that, putting down mobs of half-naked rioters, bloody and dangerous in its way but no proper work for one of His Majesty's fusiliers—but since then he had been confined to administrative duties, which on the whole he preferred. He wasn't the type to stir a maiden's soul, not if she went for the blood-and-thunder boys. The record on Karen Windermere rather suggested that she did.

It had all seemed so obvious that afternoon when he had promised her over a couple of glasses of sherry that he would find her something to do to take her mind off what had happened to Bertie. She had been in such a state—and who could blame her, considering that her clod of a husband wouldn't even consent to be in the same room with her?—she had wanted taking in hand so badly that Horton had really imagined he might have a chance of pulling the thing off. Maybe she had had enough of heroics now that her tin god had come down with a more or less permanent case of the shakes, so maybe now she would be ready to listen to reason.

Over and over again, he had imagined how it would all come out. He had it rehearsed, like the lines of a play. The day would come when they would know they had finally turned the corner on these damned Germans, when the end would finally come into view, and on that day, out of, seemingly, nothing besides an excess of good feeling—the need to celebrate, of course, nothing more—they would leave the office early, just the two of them, old friends, to have a quiet drink. And then, over a couple of whiskeys, he would tell her, as something that had just popped into his head, that he had been in love with her for years. "I've been in love with you for years," he would say, just like that.

Well, naturally, under the circumstances, how many different results could there be?

He remembered exactly the way she had looked as a girl. She had been the prettiest deb coming out that year, the catch of the season. Horton had noticed her just too late, and she had gotten herself engaged to Bertie Windermere, his brother officer, who could wear a uniform as well as any man breathing, but perhaps not the soundest choice she could have made.

Any man could be happy with Karen—Bertie Windermere had been happy with her until he was chucked into the sea and came out with his spine turned into jelly. She was worth waiting for, worth planning for.

Then this fellow Steadman had come along.

There was something between them. One didn't have to spend more than a quarter of an hour in the same room with the two of them to sense that they had arrived at some sort of understanding, a kind of holding action against the inevitable. Now they were alone together in Stockholm, and Brian Horton had put them there.

It had been good strategy. Steadman was the right man for this job, and Karen was just what was needed to keep a leash on him. It had seemed like a good idea for other reasons as well—perhaps all Karen needed was a good, close brush with danger and she would see that that really wasn't what she wanted in a man. The theory had been sound enough.

But now Steadman had killed a couple of German thugs and he didn't want to play the War Ministry's game. Horton had it all in the cable that had come in that morning from the Stockholm embassy.

It was a proper mess. The Germans were sniffing around all over town, trying to find the British spy, which didn't bode particularly well for Steadman's chances of success—they must by now have deduced what he had come to steal. They would wrap that damned courier of theirs in hoops of steel, all the way to New York.

To top it off, now Steadman had decided to go all inventive. He didn't like the War Ministry's plan. He had asked for money and the floor plans to the German embassy—even a special camera. He was going to do this his own way, damn him.

Horton had approved the requests. There really hadn't been any choice, since it was a little late in the game to pull Steadman out.

Damn the man! God damn the arrogant American bastard, he seemed to think he could walk through walls. Well, we would all just see about that.

And now the Stockholm office was asking for instructions.

They had sent a man around to the apartment where Karen was staying with her cousin. He had been carrying the floor plans and the camera and his instructions had been to find out, without seeming to push the matter, as much as possible about what had happened to those two German hoods. Karen, however, hadn't been very communicative.

"I don't know anything about it," she had said, smiling and lying her pretty little head off. "Was anyone hurt?"

Brian Horton sat at his desk at the War Ministry, the cable from Stockholm spread out in front of him—it ran to three pages—wondering what sort of orders he should send in reply. There was a yellow notepad beside his right hand, and his pen was in his shirt pocket, but the task of writing out a few dozen words and carrying them into the coding station for transmission seemed as morally arduous as anything he could imagine.

Steadman was a security risk. Whatever his plan might turn out to be, if it worked it would put him in unsupervised possession of the contents of that courier's briefcase. They couldn't even put a tail on him for fear of alerting the Germans. If he came to suspect anything of that kind, God alone knew how he might react.

But they needed him. He was in place; he seemed to have a plan. No, Horton knew perfectly well that he couldn't afford to have Steadman taken out now.

It would have to wait until after he had made his snatch.

Once he had his hands on that briefcase he would know everything— at least, that would have to be the assumption; if he was his own man in everything else, why should he hesitate to disregard instructions about turning over the contents unexamined? No, once David Steadman had fulfilled his function, he became a liability, even a danger.

If he should reach Karen, if they should have even a moment together after he had completed his task, then the same line of reasoning would apply to her as well. That simply couldn't be permitted. A mishap would have to be arranged for Mr. Steadman. He would disappear so completely that no one would ever hear from him again.

Horton took the pen out of his shirt pocket, unscrewed the top, and began writing out his instructions to Stockholm. He couldn't deny to himself that it gave him a certain satisfaction to order David Steadman's death; the man both irritated and frightened him. The world would quickly return to normal as soon as there was that one less American in it.

He would cipher the message himself, he decided, with call letters at the beginning to indicate that it was to be decoded by the recipient only— the fewer clerks who knew about this matter the better. Safe was safe.

VIII

NOVEMBER 1, 1941

It happened much the way Steadman had expected. At a quarter past
eight on Saturday morning, which had to be just about the last possible
moment, the usual long black embassy limousine pulled up at the foot
of pier number five, and Jacob Protze, accompanied by a pair of enormous
goons who might as well have had "Gestapo" written across their backs
in letters four inches high, climbed out into the sunshine. One of the
goons opened the limousine trunk and took out a small suitcase—Protze
already had his attaché case chained to his wrist.

He was a sour-looking specimen of about forty-five, with his mouth
bracketed by deep folds and the expression of a man who suffers from
chronic stomach trouble, but apparently an old hand. He stood there,
studiously wiping the inside of his hatband with a handkerchief, glaring
at it as if it had insulted him mortally, like a city clerk waiting for the
bus. He wasn't even afraid of his guards.

In another few minutes all three of them would walk the hundred or
so yards down to where the *Kungsholm* was waiting at anchor, and there
they would be told by a ship's officer in a beautiful crisp white uniform
that, as much as he personally regretted it, they would not be able to

)oard, but that the company would be happy to arrange hotel accom-
nodations for them until Sunday afternoon, by which time certain unavoidable repairs would have been completed. Steadman knew all about
it, chapter and verse, because he had already been down there two hours
earlier and had heard the whole pitch.

Right at the moment, however, he was much more concerned with
getting his new camera to work.

It was an awkward affair, with a lens like a sea captain's telescope—
the British, who had supplied it through Karen's invaluable cousin, seemed
to have been under the impression he wanted something that would do
for photographing the outer reaches of the solar system. It must have
weighed ten or fifteen pounds; you couldn't even hold it steady without
a tripod, and they hadn't thought to include the tripod.

"Couldn't you rest it against the back of the rear seat and shoot through
the window?" Karen asked, smiling a peculiar, intimate smile that was
entirely new to Steadman and made him feel pleasantly uncomfortable.
They were parked up a side street in a car he had stolen for the occasion
just the night before. He twisted around in his seat, bumping his elbow
against the steering wheel, to have a look.

"I could try."

He did try, but it wouldn't do. There was just enough distortion in
the curve of the rear window, and it was just dirty enough, to throw
everything off. After all, when you were trying to photograph something
not much larger than a lady's handbag from a distance of perhaps two
hundred and fifty feet, how much does it take?

He tried something else. He waited until Protze and company had
started on their way down to the gangplank and then he circled around
until he found a place where he could park just at a corner, facing the
abandoned limousine. It was perhaps seventy-five feet closer, but that
couldn't be helped. He would crouch down on the front seat and brace
the camera against the open side window.

"Tell you what. I want you to stand there in front of the door so that
you can screen me—you never know; one of those lads might be farsighted
enough to notice the reflection off a lens from all the way over there."

"Now?"

"Now."

So she took up her position, sliding her hands into the pockets of her
charcoal-gray coat and leaning against the door of the car so that he
could slip the long camera lens in between her body and her right arm.
It was a cold morning and they were both frozen stiff.

"Shouldn't I be doing something out here?" she asked. "Maybe I could be smoking a cigarette or something, just to make it look more natural. What do you think?"

"I think you should just remember to hold still. You don't smoke, remember? You'd probably start coughing at precisely the critical moment—no thanks, I'll sacrifice a little verisimilitude for a steady shot."

"All right. *Okay*, it was just a thought."

She glanced back over her shoulder and smiled again, drawing in her elbow a little so that it pressed against his hand where he was cradling the camera lens against the edge of the open car window. Even the sound of her voice was like a caress; it seemed that lately she just couldn't be nice enough to him. Yesterday, while they waited for this morning, with nothing to do, they had strolled around the corridors of the Moderna Museet together, hardly noticing the pictures. They had even forgotten about lunch.

It was a funny way to feel. It wasn't the sort of thing that could last very long. Probably they would snap out of it in a day or two, when they both remembered that she was still Bertie Windermere's wife, but Steadman wasn't above settling for whatever he could get.

The Germans had parked about forty feet this side of the pier entrance, and Protze had the attaché case chained to his left wrist. So when they came back to their limousine they would be walking toward the camera, with the case on the street side. One of the two Gestapo thugs would hold the door open for Protze—they were all very correct about that sort of thing—and then Protze would turn, showing his left side, provided his wall of a bodyguard would just stay out of the way, and climb back inside. The only chance of success was to keep shooting every second, getting maybe ten or fifteen pictures in the time it would take them to cover that forty-foot distance, and hope they would show enough.

"Why?" Karen asked him. It was an obvious enough question. "Why do you want to take pictures of Protze—you know what he looks like, and he isn't even particularly pretty."

She had folded her gloved hands in a little tent over her nose and mouth to smother the laughter that still sparkled in her eyes. And right there in the museum, right in front of God and everybody, Steadman had put his arm around her shoulder and kissed her hair.

"Who said anything about Protze? We're going to photograph his attaché case."

He got precisely the reaction he had been hoping for. He had surprised the hell out of her. It was delicious.

"His *case?*"

"Yes."

"But why? We're supposed to *steal* it—what difference does it make what it looks like?"

"Silly girl. Hasn't it occurred to you that maybe one of the reasons your friends are so hot to have me snatch their little package out in the middle of the Atlantic is that they don't want the Germans to be in a position to do anything about it right away? I kill Protze and drop him and his luggage into the briny deep—it would be days before the Germans would even know. And then they'd have to cable back to Berlin. Ships don't leave Europe every day—not neutral ships, not ships that aren't being shot at—so it might take them weeks to make good the loss. Maybe the delay is important. Anyway, I think it would be fun if Protze got all the way to wherever he's bound before anyone figured out that the goods were missing. Isn't that a Munch over there? My mother used to have a lithograph of his hanging in her dining room of all places."

He raised his arm to point to a small monochrome of a dark, pathologically melancholy young man with deep-set eyes next to a blond girl who hardly seemed to realize he was in the same frame with her. It was a disturbing picture, the kind that commanded your uneasy attention, but Karen appeared not to have noticed it. She was still studying Steadman's face, as if she had never seen it before, and gradually there was a dawning of recognition.

"You're going to switch cases, aren't you. You're going to plant a duplicate on the Germans and let them carry that to New York while you keep the original."

"Give the lady a cigar," Steadman answered quietly, without taking his eyes from the picture. "But I can't get a duplicate until I know what the original looks like. Hence the camera."

Hence the camera. Hence the frantic click, click, click of the shutter as Protze and company emerged from the entrance to pier five and started briskly back toward their limousine. Steadman didn't even try to watch; he just worked the exposure button and hoped for the best. He thought Protze had shown him a full side view getting into the back seat—he thought so, but he didn't really know. He didn't have any clear idea what he had seen through the lens aperture.

At such a distance you couldn't hear the door slam. The impression of angry haste was purely visual. Steadman dropped the camera onto the seat beside him and slid across to the steering wheel.

"Get in. Let's see if our next guess was right."

Karen didn't say anything. She didn't make any jokes or ask any stupid questions. She just opened her door and climbed in. She was learning fast.

You didn't have to follow someone if you knew where he was going, and Steadman wouldn't have dared anyway. These guys were Gestapo. They were pros, and they would know to keep an eye on the back window. They might even take the long way home, just to check for tails—Steadman certainly hoped so. In the meantime, he thought he knew where he could catch them again.

It was Saturday morning and the streets were busy with delivery trucks and men coming into the office for half a day from the neat little houses out in the suburbs. Some probably had their wives along for lunch and a little shopping after business hours. It wasn't like New York or London or even Pittsburgh, but you had to weave around a lot if you wanted to make any time. That would be just as true for the Germans, and they had a bigger car.

Steadman pulled up at an intersection, let an elderly woman on a bicycle cross in front of him, and jumped the light. What the hell, it wasn't even his car, so let the Germans worry about the traffic laws. Karen sat very quietly, her hand through the strap above the doorpost and her feet wide apart and braced against the floor. They made it to the German embassy, a distance of some two and a half miles, in less than four minutes. There was no one in sight as they passed in front of the main gate, so they doubled back and parked in the next block.

"Are you so sure they'll come here?" she asked finally—after all, she was only human. Steadman reached across and settled his hand on her thigh, just above the knee, and she covered it with her own without looking at him.

"I'm never sure about anything, but I don't know where else they'd come. Not if the contents of that attaché case are as hot as everybody seems to imagine. They can't very well check it at a hotel luggage room."

"No. I suppose not."

After that they waited in perfect silence. Steadman lifted his hand away, but Karen wrapped her fingers around the base of the thumb, so they kept hold on each other. It was growing rather airless in the car, so he rolled down his window about three quarters of an inch.

After about five minutes the limousine, creeping along like a guilty secret, pulled into the short embassy driveway, sounded its horn, and passed through the gates. Perhaps someone had stopped along the way to telephone for instructions—that would be just like them—or perhaps they simply hadn't been in a hurry. In either case, they were back. Steadman took a deep breath and let it out slowly, savoring the relief.

For absolutely the first time he allowed himself to look around at the neighborhood. The trees were all bare, but he had to think that in the spring and summer—whenever those seasons arrived this far north—it was probably a very pleasant street. There wasn't much traffic and the houses, most of them only partly visible behind iron palings and walls of light gray stone, were large and expensive-looking. Somewhere in the middle distance he could hear a dog barking.

Of course, there wasn't any reason why the Nazis would put their embassy in a slum.

"Now we wait," he murmured, leaning back into his seat and half closing his eyes. Suddenly he felt very tired.

He must have dropped off to sleep, because when he became aware that Karen was pulling on the sleeve of his coat he had the unpleasant feeling of coming up out of a vague, warm emptiness, and his eyes felt sticky. He looked at the tiny clock on the instrument panel. It was nine twenty-seven.

"What is it?"

His voice sounded rusty from disuse and there was a dreadful taste in his mouth. Karen didn't answer—she was trained on a distant figure on the sidewalk opposite, someone too far away to be recognizable immediately but still someone disturbingly familiar.

Steadman reached into the back seat and retrieved the camera with its long, clumsy lens assembly. Picture time was over, but the thing could still serve as a telescope.

It was Protze, walking away from the embassy, swinging his arms like a man taking the air for the sake of his health and peace of mind. Only the back of him was visible, but it was Protze—the same walk, the same clothes, the same brisk, businesslike confidence—and the attaché was no longer chained to his wrist.

"So they've locked it away in their vault for safekeeping. Good for them."

Steadman laughed quietly to himself, out of fear as much as triumph. Because now he had closed the door on himself. Everything had worked out just as he had hoped. There was nothing left to do except the thing he had planned from the beginning. There was no way out anymore.

"What is this all about, David?" Once again Karen had him by the base of the thumb; he could feel the pressure of her sharp, pointed little fingernails. "You've maneuvered them into doing what you wanted, but why do you want it? What good is it to us that the Germans have our package in their safe?"

He looked at her and smiled. He thought it just possible that never again would life be so precious as it was that moment.

"I think probably tonight's as good a chance as any," he said evenly, still smiling. "I thought I'd break in there and steal it."

IX

Hauptmann Weinschenk sat in the small, virtually empty office that had been put at his disposal by Leutnant Aarenhold, the brainless young SS functionary who was in charge of security at the Stockholm embassy, staring unhappily at the dark brown attaché case that rested on top of the desk in front of him. He had thought, when he had left Berlin, that he would be back in time for the beginning of the workweek on Monday, but the difficulties seemed to be increasing almost from hour to hour, like a geometric progression. First the two men who had gotten themselves killed and now this peculiar delay.

Of course Nebe would be delighted if somehow the British managed to hijack this particular piece of diplomatic cargo—he would make the Reichsführer happy because von Ribbentrop would be embarrassed, and he would settle a score of his own by being provided with an excuse to ruin Weinschenk. Nebe had already distanced himself from the longed-for failure; he had actually gone so far as to write a letter to Obergruppenführer Heydrich, citing his reasons for objecting to Weinschenk's assignment. Aarenhold, as things turned out, was a protégé of Nebe's.

For not the first time since his return from Spain in 1939, Weinschenk told himself that he ought to resign from the SS and seek a commission in the regular army. The SS was no place anymore for an honest man.

As long as the attaché case was inside the embassy walls it was Aaren-
old's responsibility. All Weinschenk had to do was to get the courier
from the embassy to the ship next Monday morning, and this time he
and Max would accompany him themselves. Whatever the British had
in mind, they would need more than one or two agents to compass their
end. They would need something on the order of a battalion.

No, Nebe was about to be disappointed.

Perhaps, if whoever had killed those two embassy hooligans was really
the man from Spain—and if he could be induced to reveal himself—it
was possible that Weinschenk might at last have found a way to redeem
himself. The field of honor might turn out to be the back streets of
Stockholm after all.

Aarenhold had been furious, of course. He had somehow gotten it
into his head that because Weinschenk seemed to know who the assailant
might be it was all Weinschenk's fault that those men had ended the
night with their throats cut. It was simply the way his mind worked.

"If you continue to insist on keeping this office in the dark, I don't
suppose there's any way I can prevent you from allowing my entire
contingent to be murdered," he had said. He had stood there over the
shallow grave of two of his subordinates, watching the sandy soil being
shoveled over their faces.

"Really—I don't see why we have to do this. I don't see why we can't
just call in the police and let them run this man down. It's more their
affair than ours anyway."

Weinschenk had exchanged a glance with his aide, who was standing
at the foot of the trench, watching the gravediggers with sullen attention.
Max silently bared his teeth, as if it would have given him more than a
little satisfaction to take a bite out of the Leutnant's esophagus.

"I doubt that *this* man would be much impressed by the Stockholm
homicide squad," he answered dryly, allowing himself to smile at the
soft-looking young man whose receding chin was lost in the shadow of
his greatcoat collar, giving him rather the appearance of a plump, un-
intimidating death's-head. "They're only likely to get in the way—probably more to his advantage than ours."

"You make him sound quite formidable." The death's-head managed
a smirk. "I wasn't aware that the British had anyone of that caliber."

"He isn't British. He's an American, and that's one of the few things
I do know about him for certain."

"Quite the man of mystery it seems. How convenient."

The sky had by then resolved itself into a cold, unpitying gray, and
the dim sunlight only managed to make everything look pale and weary

and past hope. Weinschenk had been up all night, which, instead of making him irritable, only depressed him, so that Aarenhold's insolence to a superior officer seemed only one more unavoidable affliction in a world designed to plague him. Aarenhold was Nebe's man and therefore privileged, but perhaps Nebe would not always be such a support. Nebe had enemies too, and might one day fall.

"He is real enough," he went on, having resolved to be patient and to suffer all. "If it is the same man he will be extremely formidable. In Spain, he could come and go like a ghost. I myself never saw him, but Max has. Max is one of the few who have seen him and survived to tell about it—except that afterwards Max wasn't in a condition to tell anyone anything. He was left with his larynx slashed open; it was a miracle he didn't strangle in his own blood."

"If it *is* the same man."

Weinschenk continued to smile. He wondered how Aarenhold would ever have managed in Spain.

"That war was a brutal business," he had said finally. "I saw more than one poor soul with his throat cut, but never with such economy as this. I think I might venture to say that it's the same man."

And now Herr Protze's attaché case, instead of being safely out on the Baltic Sea, some twenty or thirty kilometers beyond the responsibility of the SS Department for the Suppression of Crime, was occupying space on a desk in the Stockholm embassy. Weinschenk watched it with resentful distrust, as if he expected the thing to disappear of its own volition. He would have it locked away in the vault so that he could stop worrying about it until Monday morning.

The significant question, in the meantime, was to what purpose this phantom American, this memory from the dust of Spain, had procured his two-day delay in the *Kungholm*'s sailing. To know that was to know everything else.

The embassy, of course, had its paid informers on board all the ships that regularly passed between Sweden and the United States—it would have been the grossest negligence to overlook so obvious a conduit between Europe and that most dangerous and belligerent of neutral powers. In a matter of a few hours Weinschenk would know how it had been done. Perhaps the distance from means to motive would not be so terribly great.

Weinschenk ate his lunch at a café on the Hamngaten. Through the large plate-glass windows that stretched almost from ceiling to floor along the front of the building, one could see the covered veranda where, during the short Scandinavian summer, the Swedes probably enjoyed taking their meals on the tables and chairs which now were stacked up and covered with canvas tarps. They made a lonely sight in November, though, and the café, at a quarter past three in the afternoon, was nearly empty.

The waiter—tall, stooped, and extremely ancient—had brought him a plate of grilled fish and a bottle of perfectly ghastly white wine. The fish, however, was excellent.

There had been places very like this in Munich, where Weinschenk had attended the university and fallen under the spell of the man who now ruled most of Europe. But in Munich, at least at first, he had been less interested in politics than in his work toward a degree in jurisprudence and the weekends when Magda would sometimes be able to come up by train to spend the day with him. They would sit together in places like this one—they both came from poor families, but it was always possible to scrape together a few marks for a couple of plates of sausage and some beer—and they would hold hands and plan the glorious future they would have when the Führer came to power and Weinschenk would be earning enough money to support a wife. Magda had been as pure as an angel then—it had never even occurred to him to take liberties.

Coffee and a small blackberry tart finished the meal. Weinschenk was smoking a cigarette and getting ready to pour himself a second cup of coffee from the silver urn in front of him when he saw Max glaring in through the glass door. He motioned for him to come inside, but Max shook his head.

"You've made a mistake, Max. You would have enjoyed the tart."

There was something like a flicker of remorse in the corporal's eyes, and his mouth tightened into a cruel, bloodless line—he was very fond of such things. And then he took his hand out of his overcoat pocket and pointed down the street to the car. Weinschenk didn't need to be encouraged; there was a brutal wind coming in from the bay.

They stopped the car behind a warehouse. It was a car Weinschenk had had procured against this evening, the sort of mud-spattered, dark blue sedan one tended to look at without seeing. And they left it a good quarter of a mile from their destination and got out to walk. If there was going to be trouble, Weinschenk didn't want anyone remembering a car.

It was the sort of fringe neighborhood where children play in the yards of breweries and men in leather aprons frequently have only to walk across the street to take their midday meal at home. The streets were wide to accommodate the ceaseless movement of trucks and heavy wagons, and the houses, dwarfed on every side by huge commercial buildings with painted-over windows, were narrow and obsessively well taken care of. Weinschenk, whose father had been the foreman in a plant that manufactured the equipment used in steam laundries, had grown up on such a street, living in the enforced intimacy of such a house. It represented everything he had made it the business of his life to escape, and now seeing row upon row of them made him feel profoundly uneasy.

When he reached the tiny house's front door, which was painted a bright, glistening blue, he waved Max back into the shadows and tapped lightly with his middle finger. The woman who answered looked surprisingly old, her reddish hair streaked with a yellowed white that reminded one of ivory. She smiled primly, displayed her jeweled fingers around the edge of the doorframe, and provided Weinschenk with his cue. He stepped back half a pace and bowed.

"Have I the honor of addressing Madame Boström?" he asked in carefully pronounced French. There was no answer, but the smile broadened slightly, suggesting that his instinct had been correct. He translated the question into English.

"Ja—yes. Can I help you?" The door opened no wider, but the hand crept a shade farther out onto the frame.

"I wonder if we might be permitted to speak to your brother."

There followed a tense second or two in which madame's eyes reflected uncertainty—or was it perhaps disappointment?—and Weinschenk showed his teeth like a department store ribbon clerk in the presence of his best customer.

"He is not here now," she answered, drawing out her o's to an unnatural length. It was clear she regarded them as having reached an impasse; the smile took on a certain quality of bewilderment.

Weinschenk had already satisfied himself that this was not someone who would ever risk making a scene, so he laid the palm of his hand flat against the door and frowned slightly. It would now amount to nothing more than a test of wills, and certainly the outcome was obvious to both of them.

"Then perhaps you would allow us to wait." It was not a question, and the pressure of his hand against the door increased gradually so that soon she would be forced either to resist or to submit. "Perhaps we might wait inside?"

As expected, she stepped out of the way, and Weinschenk was already across the threshold before Max stepped far enough out of the shadows for the elderly maiden to notice him. By then—and the moment was registered with great precision by the way her eyes widened and almost simultaneously clouded over with moisture—it was too late.

It really was a tiny house. The front door opened directly into the sitting room, where there was barely space for a gas fireplace, two small chairs upholstered in needlework, and a dark, highly polished wooden table, hardly more than half a meter square, where doubtless the chief engineer and his sister took all of their meals together. There was a door, probably leading to the kitchen, and a narrow circular staircase to the upper story, but those were the only other exits.

Max came in behind him, glared at Fräulein Boström, who by then had retreated the few steps to the center of the room, and had the good manners to remove his hat. He closed the door behind him and took up his position in front of it. It would have been obvious to anyone that no one was going anywhere without his approval.

"Oh! Please—sit down," Fräulein Boström gasped, smiling stupidly. She had not yet made the leap from uneasiness to fear, but she was clearly glad to have come upon this formula for retaining at least the appearance of normal courteousness. Weinschenk lowered himself gently into one of the two chairs, crossed his legs, and smiled. Max simply ignored her.

"You mustn't let my chauffeur alarm you," Weinschenk said evenly, allowing himself to relax. "He can't speak—the result of an accident— but he's under perfect control. Perhaps it would be best if you just forgot that he is there." He paused for a moment, glancing around him, creating the impression that he was about to pay a compliment. But, of course, he said nothing.

In fact, he was listening. The house was on a corner, so there was only one common wall—there wasn't a sound coming from next door, which might mean either that the wall was very thick or the neighbors very quiet. The silver clock over the mantel indicated that it was twenty minutes until five.

But in working-class quarters Saturday was often the evening when families would gather at a Hofbräu to eat sausages and hard rolls and drink beer. It was the weekly festival of freedom, when there would be money for sweets and when the oppression of tiny rooms was exchanged for tables set out-of-doors in warm, greenery-scented courtyards.

Of course, it was improbable enough that anyone would be out-of-doors in November, particularly at this latitude, but it was still possible that the family next door might not choose to stay at home. Weinschenk remembered the rings on Fräulein Boström's fingers, noted that there was no smell of cooking in the air, and thought it even likely that the lady had been waiting for her brother to return and take her out for dinner when his visitors had arrived.

He noted also that she had not moved from her position in the center of the room, that she was standing at what almost amounted to attention, and recalled that it might be some time before the chief mechanic returned. The poor woman, there was nothing to be gained by causing her to become alarmed. Certainly she looked innocent enough.

"We have some business with your brother." He smiled again. "It concerns an item we wish transported to America. Once he returns, we shan't detain him long."

The lie seemed to cost him nothing.

After a while she sat down in the other chair, and they all waited together in silence. It was shortly after six-thirty when Boström returned home.

Max, with his usual feral sensitivity, was the first to hear someone approaching from the street. Perhaps he had been listening, although there had been no indication of it, but suddenly he grew more alert. He seemed to draw himself up, and his right hand stole inside his jacket to rest on the butt of the Luger he carried under his armpit. He didn't look at Weinschenk. For something like this he required no instructions.

When she heard the key turning in the lock, Fräulein Boström began to rise out of her chair, but a glance from Weinschenk was enough to arrest the attempt. She sat down again, helpless, her eyes growing wide as she saw Max step to one side of the door and draw his pistol.

"*Sigrid, vad är . . . ?*"

Weinschenk smiled at him, and recrossed his legs. It was merely a diversion, something for the chief mechanic to stare at while Max closed the door behind him and touched his spine with the muzzle of the Luger. Boström started—he sprang up straight, as if he had been pulled by a string; his heels actually left the floor for an instant.

And then, oddly, nothing. No questions, no threats, nothing. He was frightened—one could see that from the way his eyes went shiny and his mouth kept opening and closing, as if he were a mechanical toy—but he almost seemed to have expected something like this.

"Herr Boström, I fear you have been dancing with the devil."

"Max, see that madame does not disturb us."

Weinschenk spoke in German, holding out his hand, palm up, until his aide placed the pistol in it. For a moment no one moved. Max waited with almost courtly patience until the chief mechanic's sister at last grasped what was expected of her and began feebly to stand up. Terror, which by then had taken complete possession of her, hardly even allowed her the will to do that.

"Yes, madame, go with him. He shan't hurt you."

Weinschenk comforted himself with the thought that it was probably perfectly true—Max had a knack for managing these things so quickly that doubtless one hardly felt a thing. He waited a moment, Fräulein Boström turned around to look at him in wordless supplication, and then Max took her gently by the arm and led her through the kitchen door. It swung closed behind them.

"Sit down, Herr Boström," Weinschenk said, his voice hardly above a murmur. "I have received information that you were the one who reported the *Kungsholm's* drive shaft out of commission. You have caused a great deal of trouble, and I want to know who bribed you to do it."

Boström hardly seemed to understand him. He glanced around at the floor, as if he expected to fall down and wished to be sure there was nothing in the way, and when Weinschenk motioned toward the other chair with the pistol barrel he managed a few shuffling steps in that direction but couldn't seem to summon up the decision actually to sit down. His mouth had never once ceased in its machinelike opening and closing.

At that moment Max returned from the kitchen, pulling the door shut with an almost inaudible click. There hadn't been a sound from that room.

With a few quick strides he was at Boström's side. He covered the man's shoulder with one of his enormous hands and thrust him down into the chair. If Boström entertained a thought about his sister, it never showed; he looked up into Max's cruel, impassive face with no idea of anything except his own peril. Weinschenk, whose profession had made him something of a connoisseur of men's behavior under duress, thought him rather a disgusting specimen.

"I will ask you again," he went on. "Who bribed you to delay your ship's sailing? You might as well tell me now."

"No one bribed me. The shaft was bent—it was bent."

Weinschenk merely smiled. After all, it was so obvious that he was lying. It was pleasant to have that last flicker of doubt removed, to know that he had guessed right and what had happened and was to happen that night was not all for nothing . . .

"Max, search him."

He wasn't gentle about it. He picked Boström up by the collar of his shirt, half strangling him while he turned the chief mechanic's pockets inside out. There were no weapons, of course—why should there have been any weapons? A comb, a handful of coins, several pieces of honey-colored candy wrapped in cellophane, the stub of a pencil, and a small keychain were scattered over the carpet. Max handed his officer the billfold, letting Boström drop back into his chair.

"You must have over nine thousand kronor here," Weinschenk said, riffling the contents of the billfold with the edge of his thumb. "Where would a little grease-wiper like you find that amount of money? And why would you still be carrying it on your person, except if you were afraid to let anyone know that you had it? Don't tell me again that you weren't bribed."

Boström gripped the arms of his chair, sweating and swallowing hard, unable to keep his eyes from wandering aimlessly, unable even to look at Weinschenk. Yes, he would have liked to say, once more, that no one had bribed him, that he was an honest man and this was all a terrible mistake, but he didn't have quite the courage for that. So he said nothing. He merely clung to the chair, as if afraid he would be torn out of it.

Weinschenk handed the Luger back to Max, who clicked off the safety and pressed the muzzle against Boström's right ear. There would be no lies now.

"Tell me about the man who gave you the money."

Boström opened his mouth and drew in a deep, ragged breath. His eyes squirmed in their sockets as he tried to catch sight of the Luger without moving his head.

"He was just a man," he whispered—he couldn't seem to catch his breath. "Tall, thin—very thin—with dark blond hair. He said he would kill me if I didn't fix the ship good. He had a knife."

Everywhere except over the trigger, Max's fingers tightened around the butt of his pistol. Weinschenk caught his eye, and he showed his teeth in a fierce grimace—they both knew all about the tall blond man with the knife.

"What was his name?" Weinschenk sounded almost bored, but in fact he was so excited that he felt as if his heart were twitching inside his chest. He ran a hand slowly down his trouser leg above the knee, just to wipe off the perspiration. "Why did he want you to sabotage your ship?"

"What have you done with my sister?"

"Your sister is in no danger. Tell us the truth and you will be with her shortly." Weinschenk smiled. He had the impression that Boström couldn't have cared less about his sister, that he was merely stalling for time. "Just tell us what he wanted, this man with the knife."

"I don't know—that I stop the ship. More than that, I don't know."

"What did he sound like?" Weinschenk asked, deciding to try a different tack.

"*Sound* like?"

"Yes—what language did he speak? Where do you think he came from?"

"America." Boström coughed in relief. "America. He was an American. I have been there many times—I know the accent." His lips quivered, as if he wanted to grin with pride.

"Why did he want you to stop the ship? He talked to you. He must have told you something. Why did he want you to stop the ship?"

"I don't know—I only saw him twice."

"When?"

"Two days ago. And again tonight, but he never said a word. He just gave me my money and was gone."

"But the first time, he must have let something slip."

"Nothing, I swear to you. Nothing!" Boström tried to twist away from where the Luger was still pressed up to his ear. "He just said, 'Do this.' I never heard his name. I never heard anything. He had a knife, I tell you. He said he would kill me!"

Well—perhaps there really was nothing more. Weinschenk was inclined to believe him; the little man was too frightened to lie. But of course there was always the possibility that he was more frightened of the man with the knife. Weinschenk could understand that. It would be necessary to find out for certain.

"Herr Boström, be so good as to remove your shoes."

"My what?"

"Your shoes." Weinschenk's mouth lengthened into something very unlike a smile. "And your stockings as well, if you please."

The chief mechanic complied, bending over heavily at the waist and undoing his laces, utterly baffled. When he was done he stared at his bare toes, quite like he had never seen them before.

"And give your belt to my aide."

Max grasped not the belt but the hand which held it, twisting it so that Boström gave an astonished little squeak of pain. Within a few seconds he had lashed the two arms together at the wrists.

Weinschenk nodded, seeming to suggest that both men had done their parts well. He peered into Boström's face for a long moment.

"Max," he said suddenly, quite as if he had just come back to himself with a start. "Break his feet."

When they left the little house, letting the door lock behind them, Weinschenk looked at his wristwatch and was surprised to discover how late it was. Possibly tomorrow, possibly the next day, someone would discover the bodies of Boström and his sister, the one in the kitchen with her neck broken and the other tied to a chair in the sitting room with a bullet hole in the side of his head. But time didn't matter. There was no danger of the police solving these murders—at least not until he and

Max were safely back in Berlin and out of reach. They had made no mistakes.

It had not been necessary to proceed on to the second foot. Just one, bent under until it snapped with a sound like a single hand clap, had been enough to reduce the chief mechanic to weeping, helpless submission. Max had stuffed his woolen stockings into his mouth to prevent his cries from being heard, had broken the foot, waited a moment for him to recover from his first agony of panic and pain, and had then removed the stockings. Then, when Weinschenk had asked if he had anything more he would like to add to his story, Boström had come apart in a way appalling to witness.

The whole business had been carried out with clinical efficiency, and the results had been textbook perfect. Now that it was over, Weinschenk simply wanted to forget that it had ever happened.

It was simply inconceivable that Boström could have been holding anything back—they had received a complete account, almost word for word, of that astonishing interview in the prostitute's bedroom. It simply wasn't the sort of story a man like Boström would be capable of inventing on the spur of the moment.

"It really is he, Max," the Hauptmann said as they walked slowly back to their car—there wasn't any reason to hurry; Weinschenk hadn't the faintest idea what to do next. "All the way from Spain, after all this time. I had rather hoped we got him at Solsona, but apparently not. The man seems to lead a charmed life."

X

The apartment belonging to Karen's cousin was in one of those modern buildings that looked more molded than built. There didn't seem to be a straight line anywhere, and the whole structure gave the impression of having been fashioned from a single piece, rather like a model carved out of a block of soap. David Steadman waited on the opposite sidewalk, looking up at it, thinking that was one of the advantages of having been born into the English gentry—you could work at a job that probably paid less than a good waiter might earn in tips and still afford to live in an architectural monstrosity.

He was reluctant to cross the street. Karen was waiting for him over there with the duplicate attaché case, the final few shreds of necessary information, and her own sweet body, but he felt a curious uneasiness about seeing her, although all that day he had thought he wanted nothing else in the world so much.

Probably it was nothing more than the effects of his encounter with Boström, whom he at once disliked and pitied and who somehow had struck him this evening as marked for disaster.

The little sailor had taken his money and rushed off like a thief—or a man who has just seen his own ghost. Probably by now that little whore with all the eye pencil . . .

It was cold out on the sidewalk. Steadman could feel it in his wound scars, a kind of giddy pain that was like an itch you couldn't bear the thought of touching. He wanted to be inside, where it was warm, where there was a woman to make him think the four walls of her bedroom compassed the whole world. But still . . .

In London, while he was between wars and had lots of time to think about such things, he had pictured to himself a thousand times what it would be like when Karen came around to the idea that it was his turn. It had seemed inevitable if he just stuck around long enough—she wasn't the type to slip contentedly into limbo, and, after all, Bertie had pretty emphatically taken himself out of play. Maybe Bertie would have snapped out of it, or maybe Karen would have found herself some other Prince Charming, but Steadman could at least hope that he might just be Prince Charming enough himself. And he had been right. She had ended up in his bed, whispering, *I'm tired of being a widow.*

Steadman looked up at the patchwork of illuminated windows and wondered which of them could be Karen's, and then it struck him as just as possible that her apartment might not face the front. So there was less point in standing out in the cold, wrapped in romantic melancholy, and he decided to go inside.

She opened the door for him and smiled.

"Have you had dinner?" she asked. "I've made something. I went shopping—they have everything in this country."

They stood there in the hallway, and she looked at him with such unselfconscious happiness. No, he hadn't had dinner. And, yes, it was wonderful to be able to buy lamb chops and apples and canned artichoke hearts. If she said it was wonderful, then it was wonderful.

"My cousin won't be back until tomorrow evening."

"I figure I'll hit the embassy about two this morning."

"We have until then."

"Yes. Did you manage everything?"

"Yes."

"Let's see."

Without a suggestion of hesitation she left him and went into another room to get her little housewarming presents. She knew without being told that all this between them was just a pleasant sideshow, that it could wait until business was finished. She was a good girl.

The attaché case she brought back with her looked enough like Protze's to Steadman's eyes, but he hadn't seen the photographs. He hefted it for an instant and was surprised to find it heavier than he had expected.

"What have you got in here?"

"About a dozen copies of this morning's *Svenska Dagbladet*. Protze might notice if the thing were entirely empty."

"And did you find out about the safe?"

"Yes, but the news isn't all good. It's a Grünlich Two-Sixty—it operates with a key and a regular combination lock, and you have to have both. Our people here seem to have had a duplicate of the key for some time, but they don't have a clue about the combination. Sorry."

She looked so genuinely distressed, standing there in front of him with her hands thrust into the pockets of the gauzy, light blue dress she must have bought just for this particular evening, that he felt sorry for her. She seemed to take it as some sort of personal failure.

"My stepfather had a Grünlich in his office," Steadman said quietly, smiling like a man about to tell a joke. "He didn't keep much in it, just his private papers and a couple of naughty novels from his university days and the household money. Sometimes, when I needed an advance on my allowance, I'd burgle the safe. There was a lever on the inside of the door that permitted you to change the combination, and my step-father was always changing the combination. It never did him a bit of good—I got so I could crack that thing open inside of a minute and a half."

It was odd, but Karen didn't look particularly reassured.

"There's something else inside the case," she said finally, after what gave the impression of being a prolonged interior struggle. "I think you'd better take a look."

The two keys to the attaché case were still tied to the handle by a short green ribbon, but the lock yielded at a touch to the release catch. The case sprang open about four inches, so great was the pressure from the folded-up newspapers inside, and buried in the midst of them Steadman found a small, flat automatic pistol with an extra section, about an inch long and shaped like a spool of thread, screwed into the end of the barrel. Probably, had you fired it, the pistol wouldn't have made any more noise than the click of a light switch.

"If someone should catch you, I thought that with a silencer you might have at least a fighting chance of getting away."

"If anybody catches me, then that'll mean I'm blown and it won't matter whether I get away or not."

"It'll matter to me," she said, with an expression in her eyes that seemed to say, *Do you see what you've done to me? Now I don't even care if you steal their stupid package for them, so long as you come back.*

"You can stay until two?" she asked. She was standing so close to him that he didn't need to move to put his arm around her. He drew her close and saw that there were tears welling up along the lower lids of her eyes.

"I can stay until then."

The house next to the German embassy belonged to somebody with a taste for shrubbery—or perhaps he just didn't like the looks of the seven-foot brick wall that divided his property from theirs. In either case, Steadman found he could stand right up against that wall and be completely concealed. He had been there for over three quarters of an hour. He was timing the sentries on the other side.

The wall was obviously of great age. Some of the bricks had been twisted out of shape by decades of baking summer heat, and all of them were discolored. There were places where tree roots or the movement of the earth had pushed it up enough to made substantial cracks in the mortar, and through one of these Steadman was able to catch the gleam from the sentries' flashlights as they made their rounds within the compound.

There were two of them, he had finally decided, moving in opposite directions. The first made his circuit around the embassy building in an average of three minutes and thirty-two seconds, and the second was about seven seconds faster. On Steadman's side of the compound, the place where their paths crossed had gradually been moving back from the front of the building until it was nearly parallel with where he was standing on the other side of the wall. Steadman calculated that when that happened he would have the longest period during which that section would remain unguarded—he figured on a minute and forty-five seconds. He would give them fifty seconds to separate and move out of sight around the corners of the building, and then he would have his chance. He would slip over the wall, get to one of the basement windows, jimmy it open with his knife, get inside, and close it behind him. Except for the locations of the basement windows, which he knew from the blueprints, he had no idea what he would find on the other side, and all he had was a minute and forty-five seconds.

And to make things even more interesting, it had been snowing for nearly two hours.

Steadman was wearing a heavy set of winter coveralls, and there were gloves on his hands, but it was still so cold that he couldn't be absolutely convinced his fingers would work properly when the moment came.

Finally the sentries completed their circle back to him—one of their flashlights played against the top of the wall. Steadman looked at his watch. It was two minutes and ten seconds after three in the morning. He simply couldn't risk waiting any longer.

At two minutes and thirty seconds past, when the sentries would at least have their backs to him, he tied a piece of clothesline around the attaché case, which was wrapped in oilcloth to protect it from the damp, and lowered it into the embassy garden. At two minutes and fifty-five seconds past, he took a short running start and hit the wall with a spring. He swung his legs up, balanced for a precarious moment, and then dropped down on the other side. He waited there for a few seconds, crouched and ready to run, but no one came. So far, so good.

There was shrubbery on the German side of the wall too, enough of it so that the ground for about fifteen feet all along that side was only patchily covered with snow. Then there was a lawn, about forty feet wide, and then more shrubbery around the house. The part that was going to be difficult to cross was the lawn, where the snow was now about an inch deep everywhere except where the sentries had left their footprints.

Men going round and round in a patrol like that will tend to follow the same paths. Only in this case you had two, so you had two paths, about seven feet apart and each about five feet wide. The only way to get across the lawn without leaving your own tracks behind was to follow those two paths, and that was going to take some doing.

One of the paths swung close to the shrubbery near the wall for about five feet. Steadman planned to enter it there, near the back of the compound, follow it until it drew in close to the other sentry's path, jump across, and then follow that until he could jump across to the shrubbery near the embassy building itself. If he slipped anywhere, and left a mark on the snow, he was as good as dead.

He picked up the attaché case and, staying close to the wall, started making his way as quickly and as quietly as he could back toward the point where the sentry's path came closest to the edge of the lawn. He had a flashlight in his back pocket but couldn't risk turning it on. When he reached the corner of the embassy building, he had to crouch down and wait because the sentry hadn't yet turned around to the other side and was still in sight. It was three minutes and twenty seconds past.

He had a bit of luck. There was a large tree just there, with a branch that hung out over the lawn. There was no wind and the snow was falling very gently; just under the tree branch there was a narrow spike of clear ground to within about six feet of the sentry's path. Steadman followed it out and jumped across, swinging the attaché case to give himself a little extra momentum—a little too much, as it turned out, because his feet skidded beneath him as he landed, nearly making him go flat on his face. The trampled snow was icy in places. It was necessary to be careful.

By the time he made it to the shrubbery border around the building, he was just about out of breath. He was cold, he was excited, and he was hurrying. That was a bad combination. His watch read four minutes and five seconds past. He had over thirty seconds—all the time in the world. He turned on his flashlight for an instant to try and locate the basement windows.

They were all precisely where they were supposed to be. The only small difficulty was that they were all barred.

It was one of the very worst moments of his life. He felt as if he had been led, step by step, into the center of some vast, crushing joke. They had him now. They had him cold. In less than half a minute German soldiers would come around from the front and back, find him there, and probably shoot him on the spot. After all, this was an embassy and therefore sovereign territory of the Reich—they could do anything they liked with him.

Unless, of course, he just turned tail and ran. He could simply drop everything and head for the wall. He could be over and on the other side before they ever even knew anyone had been there. It seemed his only chance.

There was the pistol in the attaché case. He could wait a moment and nail both the sentries before he took off. Maybe that way it wouldn't quite all have been for nothing.

But all the time his eyes were searching the shrubbery, looking for somewhere he could hide himself, because he knew he wasn't going anywhere. It was time he needed; there were no impassable obstacles. He could find a way around the bars if he just had a little time.

There was a short line of bushes, behind which were concealed a water faucet and a coil of garden hose that someone must have left out from the summer—it had been lying there all this time and nobody had thought to pick it up and put it away. That might be all the cover he needed.

He threw himself down, drawing his legs up toward his chest and struggling clumsily with his gloved hands to unwrap the oilcloth from the attaché case so he could get at Karen's pistol. *I thought with a silencer you might at least have a fighting chance . . . It'll matter to me.*

At least, if it came to that, he wouldn't be the only one to die.

He could hear the crunch of their boots on the crusted snow, and he stopped breathing. He just lay there, the pistol clutched in his hand, his thumb on the safety. It was just possible he might have left some trace of his passage back there on the snow, something they might notice. They might see something—that was their job, to see things.

When he opened his eyes he could see the tips of the shrubbery glittering in the flashlight beams over his head. Just let them come, he thought. Just let them come.

But they didn't come. They swept the ground with their flashlights, but they saw nothing. He could hardly believe it.

But why not? They had been out there for hours, those poor bastards, seeing nothing. They were used to it by now, numbed by round after round of emptiness and quiet, and there were only a few more hours until dawn. Boredom and cold could blind one to anything. The yellow tongues of light disappeared around the corners of the building and were gone.

Okay. That still left him with the bars on the basement windows. Steadman drew himself up onto his hands and knees and started crawling toward the embassy wall.

He had expected there would be unforeseen problems—there always were. The perfect plan, in which everything is known in advance, is known in advance to everyone. There wasn't an easier way in the world to guarantee failure than to insist that every possibility had to be anticipated, because you only purchased such knowledge at the cost of giving yourself away. Success consisted of the gift for improvisation.

And, of course, a little dumb luck never hurt.

The grillework was very elaborate, with wrought-iron ivy twining its way from bar to bar. It all looked sufficiently massive. But presumably the windows behind them had to be washed once in a while—in an embassy run by the Germans, it was probably more often than once in a while—and presumably to do that you had to take the grillework out. Steadman curled his fingers around one of the bars and gave it a tug. It didn't budge.

He crawled twenty or so feet down to the next window. The ground felt like cement, and his fingers were freezing.

The second window grille gave just a little, and Steadman snicked on his flashlight to have a look. The thing was merely screwed into its wooden frame, and the two top screws were missing. Perhaps they had gotten lost. Perhaps somebody just decided it was too much trouble to bother with them. Anyway, they were gone. Steadman grabbed the grille with both hands, as high up as he could find a purchase, braced his feet against the wall, and pulled. The two bottom screws pulled loose with what sounded to him like a terrific racket, and the grille came out.

The window behind was easy. The wood around it was crumbling with age; there was no difficulty about slipping the point of his knife in at the edge and slipping back the latch. There was a jointed metal arm to keep it from falling back too far; Steadman pried it loose and lowered the window all the way down to the inside basement wall. He was able to climb through feetfirst, pulling in the attaché case and setting it on the floor beside him, just as the first sentry's flashlight beam peeked around the front corner of the embassy. Steadman stuck his head and shoulders back outside, took hold of the grille with both hands, and lifted it back into place. He stood there, pulling it toward him, not daring to let go, until both of them had passed and were out of sight.

Squatting on the basement floor, he decided he would allow himself a few minutes of rest. He wiped his sweating hands against his chest, waiting for his heart to stop pounding. God alone knew what horrors waited for him just ahead—he didn't want to know. At that moment he wasn't ready to face them.

His mouth felt pasty. He would have given anything for a drink of water, but even if he could have found a tap he wouldn't have dared to turn it on.

Without moving, he turned on his flashlight and let it play over the floor of the crowded basement. The room was half filled with trunks and suitcases, stacked up almost to the ceiling. There were other things—what looked like a sofa, covered with a sheet that had been tied in place with rope; a shelf against one wall; filing cabinets; a carpenter's workbench; a furnace in one corner, roaring hoarsely. The floor looked as if it had just been mopped clean; there was no disorder and no dust.

And then there was David Steadman, late of Steadman Tool and Die and putative heir to one of the great industrial fortunes of America, crouched in a corner next to a stack of folded-up lounge chairs, shivering like a monkey. How the Founding Father would have laughed at that.

"David, you're going to wind up dead in some gutter," the old man had said, pouring himself a second cup of coffee at that memorable last breakfast back in Pittsburgh. He had said it just as calmly as if he had been describing how he would have the driveway resurfaced. "You've got an idea it's all going to be heroism and cavalry charges, but it won't be anything like that. These goddamned Bolsheviks play rough."

Steadman clicked off his flashlight and waited in the darkness for the sentries to pass by again outside. He had gotten so their rhythm was as natural to him as that of his own heartbeat. It wasn't even necessary for him to look at his watch.

He put on the flashlight again and started looking for the stairs. They were just to the other side of a support wall that ran about three quarters of the way through the middle of the basement, in effect dividing it into two rooms. There were no obstructions on the floor, so he wouldn't trip over anything and cause a racket. Everything was fine. He killed the light again.

But something was wrong. He had caught a glimpse of something, he wasn't sure of what. Something had simply registered on his brain, a meaningless image.

He directed the flashlight beam up to the ceiling, and there it was. A small metal cone attached to one of the floor supports; you might have imagined it to be a sprinkler head, except that it wasn't connected to a water pipe. This didn't have anything to do with fire safety.

This was a stress detector. The clever bastards, they had booby-trapped the floor.

XI

They were reasonably simple devices, basically the same sort of tremble switch Steadman had seen in certain types of land mines in Spain. A coil spring with a small weight at the top stands up in a metal cone; any small vibration will start the weight moving, and when it comes in contact with the side of the cone you have an electrical contact. Anyone walking across the upstairs floor would cause the support beams to flex enough to set the thing off. And there was more than just the one. They were spaced at intervals of about twenty-five feet. If a dog got loose upstairs, the whole house would know before the poor brute had run from one room to another.

Only about the rear third of the embassy was over the basement. There was a retaining wall and then, above that, a crawl space under the remainder of the building. Steadman looked in there, hoping without much conviction that the alarm system might not extend under the whole area of the floor, but it did. Front to back, the entire ground level of the embassy was trapped. That was all he needed.

It would be possible, he supposed, to jam the individual switches, to take a piece of paper or something and shove it down inside the cone so that the weight would be kept from moving, but anything of the kind would require hours. One mistake and the alarm would go off like the end of the world, so the greatest pains would be necessary. And Steadman only had until dawn. Perhaps not even that long.

And he hardly dared to interfere with the wiring. The Germans were certainly smart enough to have thought of that. Doubtless any break in the circuit would send it all up.

Steadman stripped off his coveralls and his shoes. There was only one way he could think of to evade such a system, and it would be like walking a tightrope. It would take forever, there would be no room for error, and if he were caught there would be nowhere to run and no way of defending himself. He hated the very idea of it, but there didn't seem to be any second choice.

He couldn't turn the alarm off, and he couldn't gag it. All that remained was to walk around it.

Once Herr Käselau had made a foredoomed attempt to interest his stepson in learning the violin. Steadman, to be agreeable, had gone for a few lessons, but at fourteen there had been lots of things that interested him more than scratching away on catgut in the name of high culture. He just couldn't seem to get the hang of it.

But the one thing he did remember was funny old Maestro Suvini, the long-suffering teacher of probably half the rich and untalented kids in Zürich, telling him that one should always "play to the center."

"Keep your bow away from the bridge, my boy. Give the string room to vibrate." It was the same with their precious alarm system.

The whole mechanism depended on the amount of play in the floorboards. Like an E string, if you pluck it near the center you get a nice tone; but if you try to play near the ends you get next to nothing. The tremble switches were all located well away from the interior supporting walls because it would only be near the centers of rooms that the floors would have enough give for them to work. So if he stayed right up against the walls, sliding along in his stocking feet so as not to jar anything, he might have a fighting chance.

It was a beautiful plan, except that it required him to leave his flashlight and pistol behind. He would need his hands free, and he didn't dare put the things in his pockets so that if he made a wrong move they would thump against the wall. And he couldn't put them in the attaché case because he didn't want that any heavier than necessary and, presuming he made it to the strongroom, he wouldn't be carrying it back with him anyway. Besides, what good would a flashlight and a pistol do him locked up in an attaché case?

As to the case itself, all he could think to do was to thread his belt through the handle and let it hang in front like a codpiece. It would be a trifle awkward, but not as awkward as trying to hold it with his hands.

He looked at his watch. It was three-twenty. There wasn't any point in hanging around in the basement.

He actually had his hand on the banister before it occurred to him to look under the basement stairwell to see whether they had trapped that as well.

They had. He took a sheet of newspaper from the attaché case and, holding the flashlight in his mouth so he would have both hands free to work, he slipped first one small piece and then another inside the tiny metal cone. It took him close to half an hour before he had packed it tight enough to be reasonably easy in his mind that it wouldn't go off.

He made his way cautiously up the stairs, fully expecting with each creak of the steps under his feet to hear the alarm bell.

The ground floor of the embassy was dark. Here and there a trace of gray light would come in through one of the heavily curtained windows, but not enough to see by. Steadman closed the basement door behind him, grateful that it swung so noiselessly on its hinges. He closed his eyes for a moment—they weren't of any use to him anyway—and tried to recall the details of the floor plan he had studied with such care all that afternoon, wondering what delightful surprises it had left out.

The strongroom was in a front corner of the building; half of it consisted of the vault itself and half of a small office where, presumably, a guard sat during the day, checking people in and out and making sure they wrote their names down in the registry book. To get there from the basement stairwell, which came up next to the kitchen and thus near the back, one had to cross through a hallway, two reception rooms, and a room that was simply marked *Büro* on the plans and probably housed the secretarial pool. The distance wasn't more than a hundred feet, but in the dark, crowded up against the wall, it seemed much longer.

The hallway floor, which was carpeted only with a runner, felt slick under his stocking feet. He worried that he might slip and fall, and the sound of his body brushing against the wall seemed loud enough to wake up the whole house. It was worse in the reception halls, where the floor near the wall was also bare—sticking out a foot, Steadman could feel the fringe of a Persian carpet with his toes—and where the first thing he did sliding around through the wide entranceway was to hit his head on the frame of a huge painting. As he stood there, his head ringing, listening to the awful noise the painting made swinging back and forth on its hook, he thought it perfectly possible he might die of fright.

But at least his theory seemed to be holding up. He had gone perhaps as far as twenty feet without tripping one of the floor switches.

And then there was the goddamned grand piano.

He didn't even know it was there until a corner of the lid caught him right under the rib cage. Suddenly he was just gasping, with the attaché case knocking wildly against his knees, wondering what the hell had happened, and then he reached out a hand and touched the keyboard and heard the low, murmuring growl of a single bass note.

They had the thing pushed right up into a corner, with no room to slip between it and the wall. To go around was almost certainly to set off the alarm.

Steadman undid his belt and set the attaché case on the piano, where he could easily reach it from the other side. He then crouched down and started to crawl on his elbows and knees around the massive legs, as slowly as he could manage. He tried to imagine he was carrying a pan of water on his back, that it was balanced right between his shoulder blades. He didn't want to spill a drop of it.

By the time he had reached the other side, and stood up, his legs were so tired he nearly stumbled.

The rest of the way to the strongroom was slow and tedious, but at least there weren't any more pianos.

The strongroom door, of course, was locked, but Steadman wasn't going to let that stand in his way. He had been able to see enough through the crawl space beyond the basement retaining wall to know that the floor of that room was reinforced with concrete blocks, doubtless to support the weight of the safe. He could hardly wait to get inside, where he could stop clinging to walls like a spider.

He had lifted a hairpin from the dressing table in Karen's cousin's bedroom, and it wasn't much of a lock. He was inside in about a quarter of a minute.

There were no windows in this room—you didn't have windows in a strongroom—so Steadman passed his hand down the wall to the left of the door until he made contact with a light switch. For the first few seconds it was nearly blinding. And then he looked around and saw a sofa against one wall and a desk with a wooden chair drawn up behind it. Beyond the desk was another locked door.

There wasn't more than about six feet of space between this inner door and the safe itself. A single light bulb hung down at the end of a naked cord—you pulled a string to turn it on. Steadman went back to the outer room and turned off the light there, locking the outside door behind him. It was nice to be able to walk in a straight line again, putting one foot in front of the other. He squatted down beside the combination lock on the safe door and started to work. The attaché case rested on the floor beside him.

There are three basic problems in opening a combination lock: (1) to establish the numbers themselves; (2) to establish the sequence of dial turns from left to right; and (3) to establish whether the lock operates on a three-, four-, or five-number combination. None of these is particularly difficult provided you have sufficient time and some means of listening for the sound of the tumblers falling into place. Many professionals used a doctor's stethoscope for that purpose, but Steadman had always found he was adequately served by an ordinary lead pencil with a very sharp point. He would put the blunt end as far into his ear as he could and then rest the point against the side of the lock—graphite was a wonderful conductor of sound.

And as for time . . . Well, that was in the hands of the embassy security officer.

The sequence was the usual left, right, left, right, but he kept assuming a three-number combination and the safe kept refusing to open. Then he went hunting for the fourth number, and finally the tumblers slid into place and he could feel the latch handle give against his palm and he knew he had it. He took out the key and it turned smoothly around in the lock. The door cracked open, sliding on its massive hinges without a sound. Steadman looked at his watch and discovered that it was nearly a quarter after four. He had been at this for slightly better than forty minutes.

Protze's attaché case was resting on a shelf in the back, at just about eye level. Steadman lifted it down and took it out into the light, where he could take a decent look at it.

Fortunately, it was nearly new. There were no scuff marks and no scratches. The only identifying mark was a small lead disk, about the size of a dime, with a number stamped into it. It was bent around the leather edge near a bottom corner, and there was no big deal about prying it loose and fastening it to the other case. You wondered why the Germans would even have gone to the trouble.

He held up both cases by the handles, balancing them against each other at the tips of his fingers. Protze's was lighter by a good deal—it felt almost as if it were empty; he opened his and took out all the folded newspapers except one and left the rest at the bottom of a deep metal drawer that was half full of account books. Then he placed the duplicate case on the shelf, precisely where Protze's had stood, and closed the safe door. The thing was done. Now all he had to worry about was the small matter of getting away.

The breath caught in his throat when he heard the sound of footsteps on a hardwood floor. Someone was outside the secretarial pool, and he wasn't alone. Steadman reached up to the light cord and pulled it off.

He was discovered. He was convinced of it. They had spotted him on his way in through the basement window and had only waited this long to find out what he had come to steal. He had set off one of the floor switches without realizing it, and the alarm had been silent. The safe door was trapped in some way he hadn't noticed. The possibilities flashed through his mind, one after the other, as quickly as a man might sort through a pack of cards looking for the right one. He reached down to slip the knife from under his trouser leg; he hadn't the slightest intention of selling his life cheap. He could hear the key turning in the lock of the outer office door.

"*Glaubst du, dass wir hier entdeckt werden?*"

It was a woman's voice, followed by a muffled little giggle. Her high-heeled shoes clicked against the floor like dice rattling in a cup. The man who was with her answered, but too low for Steadman to make out the individual words. When he laughed he sounded just a little drunk.

"Oh, well, if that's all . . ." Steadman thought, remembering the little sofa against the outside wall. He let the air out of his lungs in a long, silent sigh. There was nothing separating him from the lovers but the one door, which was standing open a few inches. He crouched down beside it, suddenly overwhelmed with a queer kind of weariness that made him feel as if he might never wish to stir again. But he kept the knife clutched tight in his hand.

He might as well have been in the same room with them—the rustle of garter belt and silk stockings was almost deafening. He hadn't realized that people could be that noisy about taking their clothes off. He could hear everything: the wet kisses, the sounds of breathing, the creak of the sofa springs, the muffled, incoherent snatches of talk. After all, it was Saturday night. It seemed that everybody was getting laid.

Involuntarily, even against his will, he thought of Karen. It seemed almost a kind of insult, but he couldn't help himself.

"Yes—God!—just that way. Oh, God . . ." It had surprised him to find out that she was such a talker. The whole time, with her mouth pressed up against his ear, she would whisper to him about what it was like for her. She made it seem, without actually being coarse enough to say so, that this was the best thing that had ever happened to her, that she could hardly believe in something so wonderful. It was very sexy.

Karen would be waiting for him back at her cousin's apartment. She wouldn't be able to sleep, but would wait until he returned. He tried to focus his whole mind on that, and have patience.

Finally they were done. The sofa springs groaned, and in his mind's eye Steadman could see the man sitting at one end, putting on his socks.

"Warst du damit zufrieden?"

The poor girl. All her coquettish, purring questions received the same answer, although the words might have varied a little. A few low monosyllables, a verbal shrug, as if all that he remembered now was that the strongroom might not be the best place for him at five o'clock in the morning. He just wanted to get out of there. So much for love.

It wasn't until they had left, and Steadman had heard the outer door lock behind them, that he remembered about the floor switches. Those two hadn't crept around trying to pretend they were wallpaper—they must have turned the goddamned alarm off.

And those two might just not think to turn it back on right away. If he could dodge around them on his way back to the basement door . . . It might just be worth a try.

He allowed them a quarter-of-a-minute head start and then opened the outer door, listened for a few seconds, satisfied himself that they weren't anywhere near, and started out. He held the attaché case in one hand and his knife in the other, keeping his eyes on the floor and trying not to run into any furniture. The alarm didn't sound.

By the time he had made his way down the stairs and could smell the safe, familiar dampness of the basement air, his heart was throbbing so hard inside his chest that it felt like a massive bruise. But he only waited by the window long enough to make sure that both sentries had passed by—their movements had long ceased to be synchronous on that side of the building; he would now have no more than a minute to get back over the wall—and then he scrambled out, leaving his coveralls neatly folded on top of a pile of suitcases. If he was out in that garden long enough to feel the cold, he would have enough other things to worry about that he probably wouldn't notice.

This trip there was no point in worrying about footprints; Steadman just made a straight dash across the snow-covered lawn. If the sentries noticed anything, they would be too late to do much about it. He got through the shrubbery, tossed the attaché case over the wall, and started climbing. At first his hand slipped and he scraped the palm rather badly, but then he found a foothold and made it over.

He was lying with his back against the brickwork, trying both to listen and to catch his breath, when the first sentry came back around. There were no shouts of alarm—the poor bastard was probably too frozen to bother about much of anything beyond keeping his feet moving.

His overcoat was rolled up and lodged in the crotch of a tree. He took it down and thrust his arms into the sleeves, marveling at how cold they felt. His gloves were in the pocket. He made his way out to the sidewalk and started back toward the center of the city, trying not to hurry, swinging the attaché case at his side like any citizen on his way to work. It was five-thirty in the morning.

Steadman had walked several blocks before he began to experience that giddy, almost panic-stricken euphoria that always came at the end of one of these operations. Part of him was sick with unfocused dread and a curious feeling of guilt—he wouldn't have been at all surprised if suddenly carloads of Gestapo thugs had started coming at him from every direction; it would have seemed to him perfectly reasonable, even fair—and part of him could scarcely be restrained from breaking out into uncontrolled laughter precisely because he knew that nothing of the sort was going to happen. There was a choking constriction in his throat and his pulse was something he could feel through his whole body, but these were only his nervous system taking its revenge and didn't matter. Once again, he had pulled it off. He was alive, and he had in his hands what he had been sent to get. It seemed a kind of miracle.

Karen was waiting for him back at her cousin's apartment, doubtless by now imagining that he must have been taken, but he couldn't go to her yet, not the way he was now. He wanted to wait until he had regained a decent composure, and he knew from experience that would be some time in coming. He was hungry. He would have some breakfast first and then go.

It was still dark outside—at this latitude the sun wouldn't be up for hours yet—but there were plenty of streetlamps to bathe everything in a cheerful, yellowish light. Already things were beginning to stir. Steadman witnessed a double-decker bus full of working-class men pulling past on the Karlavägen, and already a few businesses were beginning to open. He stepped inside the door of a tiny coffee shop, looked around for a moment, noticed the smell of freshly baked sweetrolls and sat down at a table out of sight of the street.

He set the attaché case down on the chair opposite. It was almost like another person invited to the feast. While he waited for someone to come out through the kitchen door and notice he was there, he sat staring at it, almost a little disappointed that the object of so much trouble should look so ordinary.

Its brown surface shone like shoe leather. The lock and other fittings were plated with chrome and extremely shiny—probably you could have picked up a duplicate in any luggage store between Lapland and the Pyrenees. Certainly that was just exactly what someone on the British embassy staff had done. Certainly there would be no very great problem about getting it open without recourse to a key.

It was something he hadn't allowed himself to think about until he had the thing safely in his possession, but all at once Steadman realized that he hadn't the slightest intention of following the War Ministry's orders. They had told him to destroy the case's contents without reading them. He wasn't going to destroy them; he was going to hand them over intact. But he was going to know what they were first.

Soldiers were supposed to do as they were told, but he wasn't a soldier and the British were being just a shade too cagey to inspire much confidence. What he didn't know might just hurt him, and, besides, he was curious to find out what they were so desperate to keep from him.

The trick, of course, was to keep them from ever catching on. If they knew that he knew, they weren't likely to content themselves with an expression of their disappointment. If it was a secret worth keeping, they would probably try to have him killed. And if it wasn't, why the big production? No—if he was going to have his peek, he would have to keep that a secret too.

He reached across the table and picked up the attaché case.

The lock was really childishly simple. Ten seconds with Karen's cousin's hairpin, and it snapped open. Inside there was nothing but a large manila envelope with a message written across the front in a heavy, jagged hand:

Thomsen! Den Inhalt persönlich in die Hände von Präsident Roosevelt ausliefern. Dies muss sofort und mit jeglicher Umsicht ausgeführt werden.

[Thomsen! Deliver the contents personally into the hands of President Roosevelt. This must be done at once and with all possible discretion.]

The British were intercepting mail to Roosevelt? No wonder they had been so close about it.

And no wonder they had chosen an American to do their work for them. The Germans would have had all sorts of fun if they had caught an Englishman breaking into their diplomatic pouches for this.

Steadman got up from his chair and went through the swinging door into the kitchen. A heavyset woman in a white apron that reached all the way to the floor looked up at him with astonishment through the wisps of honey-colored hair that had come loose from her complicated coiffure; she began unrolling a sleeve down over her heavy red forearm, as if he had caught her indecently exposed. Steadman smiled at her, trying to look harmless and trustworthy, and took a hundred-kronor note out of his jacket pocket.

"I'd like to use your teakettle," he said, offering her the money. "Why don't you go off somewhere and powder your nose."

Obviously she didn't understand a word he had said, but she understood the hundred kronor. Her fingers closed around the bill as she glanced about her at the counter top and stove, possibly wondering if it was worth the risk, if there could be anything there the loss of which wouldn't be covered by what was probably, for her, half a week's wages. Apparently there wasn't.

There was an old-fashioned pewter kettle on the stove which had just begun to boil. Steadman took the manila envelope by a corner and held the flap in the column of rising steam. After a few seconds the flap loosened. He opened the envelope and extracted another, smaller and almost perfectly square, of heavy white paper. There was nothing written on the outside of this one. He held it too in the steam until the flap came loose and popped up like something at the end of a spring.

There was a small platter of what looked like cinnamon pastries on a sideboard; Steadman took three, put them on a plate, made himself a cup of tea, gathered up his two envelopes, the glue on both of which was by then once again dry, and went back out to his table. He was aware that he had reached one of the great turning points in his life. He was calm, as if he already knew—had always known—the contents of the German Foreign Office's letter to President Roosevelt, and was conscious of nothing beyond a certain reluctance about proceeding to the next step. Suddenly the whole business struck him as faintly indelicate.

It was a type-written note, only two short paragraphs long. The first thing Steadman noticed was the signature, in the same thick, slanting hand as the instructions on the outside of the manila envelope. It was a signature everyone in Europe recognized: the first initial was simply a crooked, sawtooth line which could have represented anything, but the last name was clear enough.

Sehr geehrter Herr Präsident Roosevelt,
Das deutsche Reich hat sich immer in seiner Suche nach Frieden bemüht, auf dem besten Fusse mit anderen, nicht kriegführenden Regierungen, besonders mit der der U.S.A., deren rechtmässige Interessen in keiner Weise unseren Eigenen entgegengesetzt sind, zu bleiben. Deshalb, wegen diesem Wunsch, im Einklang mit einer

verbrüderten, germanischer Nation zu verbleiben, nehme ich diese Gelegenheit wahr, Sie vor einer grossen Gefahr, in welcher Sie und Ihre Nation ausgesetzt sind, zu warnen.

Ich habe unanfechtbare Kenntnis davon, dass die japanische Kriegsmarine beabsichtigt, Ihre Flotte, die sich in Hawaii im Stillen Ozean, vor Anker befindet, anzugreifen. Dieser Angriff wird nicht später als in der ersten Woche im Dezember stattfinden und mit der Beabsichtigung, mit gleichzeitigen Angriffen gegen englische Installationen im Fernen Osten zusammen zu treffen. Ich hoffe sehr, dass Sie mit zweckgemässiger Handlung solch eine Katastrophe vorbeugen können und, dass auf diese Weise der Krieg zwischen unseren zwei Ländern vermieden werden kann.

Mit vorzüglicher Hochachtung,

Führer und Reichskanzler

[Dear President Roosevelt,

The German Reich, in its quest for peace, has always strived to remain on the best of terms with other, nonbelligerent governments, particularly with that of the United States, whose legitimate interests are in no way opposed to our own. It is for this reason, our desire to remain at harmony with a brother Germanic nation, that I take this opportunity of warning you of a great danger to which you are exposed.

I have unimpeachable intelligence that the Japanese navy plans to attack your Pacific fleet at anchor in Hawaii. This attack will come no later than the first week in December and is intended to coincide with attacks against British installations in the Far East. It is my hope that you will take appropriate action to forestall such a catastrophe and that thus war between our two countries may be avoided.

Yours very truly,

Führer and Chancellor of the Reich]

Steadman sat peering at the carefully arranged blocks of letters until long after they had ceased to be anything for him except an unintelligible tangle of black lines. He felt as if time had been obliterated, as if everything had been arrested except for the meaningless progress of his own thoughts. After a while—which might as easily have been measured in hours as in seconds, for all he knew—he reached out and picked up his teacup, setting it down again almost instantly when he discovered, to his intense embarrassment, that his hand was shaking too violently to hold it. He wiped the tea from his fingers, noting that it had grown quite cold, and then refolded the letter, resealed it inside its envelope, and slipped it into his jacket pocket. There could be no thought now of handing anything over to the British.

Within five weeks, perhaps less, the Japanese navy was going to attack the American Pacific fleet. Hitler knew about it and was going behind the backs of his ally because he didn't want the United States to enter the war in Europe, which would be the inevitable consequence of such an attack, and Britain was trying to prevent him because she did. It was all so painfully obvious that Steadman had trouble accounting to himself for his own surprise. He was sitting on the secret that would decide the fates of thousands of men waiting in Hawaii like ducks in a pond, not to mention the outcome of the war, and all because he had burglarized a house in Sweden. He didn't have the faintest notion what he should do about it. All he knew for certain was that it had suddenly become very dangerous to be David Steadman.

Rising from his chair, he lurched against the table so hard that it nearly fell over. He dropped a handful of silver coins beside his plate, where the three cinnamon pastries remained untouched, and walked heavily out the door. Jacob Protze's attaché case lay disregarded on the floor, its lid open like the jaws of a trap.

XII

NOVEMBER 2, 1941

It was still dark out when the car came to take Hauptmann Weinschenk back to the embassy. He had been awake for hours, standing in his shirtsleeves, looking out through his hotel window at the empty street, trying to decide why he felt so sure that the American had outwitted him.

Down in the street he saw a black sedan, a shade too large to be inconspicuous, pull up to the curb in front of the hotel entrance. He did not recognize the man who got out—that would have been impossible since, from his window on the fourth floor, all he could see was a dark overcoat and the top of a black felt hat—but he knew well enough that he was one of Aarenhold's people. Weinschenk wished they wouldn't do such things; he had booked into a hotel because he had wanted to avoid calling attention to the official character of his presence in the city, and out of a vaguely defined sense that associating himself with the embassy building would somehow endanger him, but they would continually send around oversize black sedans and young men who couldn't seem to help looking and acting precisely like everyone's preconception of a Nazi policeman.

In the car, on the dark back seat, watching the streets slide by in the gray light, Weinschenk tried to see the problem from his enemy's vantage. It all came down to access to a locked briefcase chained to the arm of a government courier, and how that access would be increased by the fact that the *Kungsholm* would be sailing on one day rather than another. How did that shift the advantage toward the American?

Was it a question of time? There had been a forty-eight-hour delay, but how would that help him? The distance from the embassy to the dock remained the same; the security measures would be the same. Would something be different aboard the ship? The ship would be neither more nor less accessible for the passage of a few days.

Perhaps the American had simply wanted time to think of something. Perhaps the delay had been a measure of his desperation.

But the American was not a man who would be likely to give himself up to dangerous and time-consuming trifles. Weinschenk had felt the pressure of that cool intelligence before and could not bring himself to believe that so much ingenuity and daring had been thrown away on the corruption of Chief Mechanic Boström for no reason beyond the lack of any better plan. Such a thing was past imagining.

Perhaps it had not been merely a matter of capturing those forty-eight hours. Perhaps the American had been after something else.

Max was sitting far over on the other side of the seat, with his bowed head resting against the window glass. He was asleep. He wasn't used to the role of passenger and was enjoying the unaccustomed luxury. Probably he had spent the night in a chair in front of the door of his room waiting. Max seemed to imagine that the man who had cut his vocal cords three years ago in Madrid would be back to finish the job—he was taking the whole business quite personally.

Poor Max, he was probably the closest thing to a friend Weinschenk had on the broad earth. If he had been up all night it was doubtless only so that his officer could sleep in safety. Weinschenk decided he would have to do something for his aide, get him promoted to sergeant or buy him his weight in *Kirschtorte*, just to let him understand that his loyalty hadn't gone unnoticed.

The wrought-iron gates opened into the embassy driveway and they parked in the back, under a dark blue canvas awning that stretched all the way up to the rear entrance. Aarenhold was standing in front of the door, his hands clasped in front of him like a choirboy.

"I trust you slept well, Herr Hauptmann. No bad dreams?" He stood aside, allowing Weinschenk to pass in front of him and smiling blandly. "In a few hours—you will see—there will be no further cause for alarm."

"You really think so, Aarenhold?"

Weinschenk smiled pityingly and stepped inside, where the warm, moist air hit him with unpleasant force. They were like spiders in a terrarium, he thought to himself; what could they possibly know about the world beyond this Party hothouse, with its intrigues and its gaudy uniforms? He almost felt sorry for Aarenhold, who stood behind him, smirking and posing like an actor, who seemed to regard himself as the acme of civilization.

"Nevertheless, I think we shall go over the plans just once more."

This time they went into Aarenhold's office, which had a Turkish carpet on the floor and chairs upholstered in leather. On a small table near the window was a tea service on a silver tray, obviously more for display than use. Max, who followed the two officers inside, stood by the door, which he pushed closed behind him with the tips of his fingers. Weinschenk sank into the chair to which Aarenhold directed him. He felt done in, as if he hadn't slept in weeks.

"I thought to add another car," Aarenhold began, settling down behind his desk with a contented sigh. "It can follow behind with three men, and there will be a machine gun on the floor in back, covered with a blanket. The Swedes don't like our people to go about armed—and certainly not with anything like that—but since you seem to feel the risks might justify it . . ."

He didn't so much smile as allow the corners of his mouth to lengthen and become straight. It was almost as if he were embarrassed. One could imagine the report he would send back to Nebe.

"Let me tell you a story," Weinschenk began. He looked bored in advance, giving the impression that he knew he was wasting his breath. "It's something that happened in Spain. I wasn't there at the time; I was between tours and had taken three weeks off to visit my mother. But I'm not trying to excuse myself, because it would have happened just the same whether I had been there or not. I'm quite sure of that."

He stopped for a moment and began studying the cap of his left shoe, as if making sure it hadn't gotten muddy. And then he glanced up and frowned as he seemed to remember what he was about.

"There was a staff meeting in Avila, mostly junior men—hardly anyone there above the rank of major and most of them only recently arrived. There was an offensive planned for two days hence, and it was something in the nature of a final briefing. Of course, everyone was interested in making a good impression, and a number of people offered suggestions.

"One of them was a young Hauptmann—tall, blond, with all the correct decorations. His ideas were good, but what everyone remembered about him was how strongly he smelled of expensive eau de Cologne and how carefully tailored his uniform looked. After the meeting there was a luncheon with the senior command, and the young Hauptmann who smelled so pretty was seen at the same table with General Sperrle, who was in charge of all German forces in the theater. They seemed to be getting along quite well. Needless to say, after that luncheon no one ever saw the Hauptmann again.

"And, needless to say, the offensive was a disaster. The Republicans seemed to know all our dispositions and all our plans. Is it necessary to say anything more, or do you grasp my point?"

"Do you mean to say that . . . ?"

"Yes. That's precisely what I mean to say."

Weinschenk nodded, quite unnecessarily, and allowed himself the satisfaction of a tight, mirthless smile. There was another story he could have told, but he didn't think that Aarenhold would have appreciated the full significance of the parallel.

"The eau de Cologne was a stroke of genius," he went on. "His very conspicuousness protected him—one doesn't normally expect an infiltrator to present himself as a dandy. My point is that you mustn't allow yourself to put too much faith in machine guns and escorts of muscle-bound hoodlums. This man isn't the type to be impressed by brute force. He's likely to steal the cartridges out of your revolver if you approach him in that manner, merely as an object lesson. By the way, what arrangements have you made for Protze's security aboard ship?"

"Aboard ship?" Aarenhold seemed genuinely surprised by the question. "There's very little we can do aboard ship, but your American will be under the same limitation. Naturally a few of our men will stay with Protze until the ship leaves port, and after that he has his orders and a loaded pistol. He will remain in his cabin with the door locked, admitting only the steward, whom we know and have already cleared. Naturally from one point of view it would have been preferable if the satchel could be kept in the captain's safe, but . . ."

Weinschenk could feel a tightening in his chest. It had suddenly come to him with all the abrupt, catastrophic force of some massive physical breakdown, the answer he had been groping for since the early hours of the morning.

But Aarenhold hadn't noticed. What was he saying? Could any of it possibly matter now?

"Send someone down for the briefcase," Weinschenk interrupted, waving Aarenhold into silence with a peremptory gesture. "Send someone now, Leutnant."

For a moment Aarenhold didn't respond. He merely peered into the Hauptmann's face as if trying to unriddle some mystery there.

"Are you quite well, Herr Hauptmann?"

"Quite well, Herr Leutnant." Weinschenk smiled—it had occurred to him that since yesterday morning, when Protze had returned to announce that there would be a delay in sailing, security had been entirely the embassy's, and therefore Aarenhold's, responsibility. "Please fetch the briefcase."

"Yes, certainly."

Aarenhold pushed a button on the console on his desk and whispered a few words into the grid. He then sat down heavily in his chair, an inquiring look on his broad, smooth face. He didn't have the remotest notion what might have happened.

But Weinschenk did. What he had seen, with all the simplicity of truth, was that his American had not been seeking time, but opportunity. It was suddenly so obvious. The *Kungsholm* hadn't been delayed for any reason except so that Protze's briefcase could go—where else? Where anyone troubling to think about the question would have known it would have to go, into the embassy vault. The American would have realized that, and he would have understood that there was the last place he would be expected to come steal it.

So naturally that was where he had come.

Weinschenk experienced a giddy sense of relief, because it was now Aarenhold rather than he who would have to explain to Berlin how the most important diplomatic consignment of the war had been stolen practically from underneath his hand. And Aarenhold was Nebe's darling boy, so it was all in the Gruppenführer's lap now. Weinschenk, whose every movement took place under a cloud, was now the only one with clean hands—they would need him now if they wished to save themselves. The whole situation was delicious.

They waited in unbroken silence. Max remained with his back to the door, his hands clasped behind him as he carefully looked at nothing. Aarenhold remained at his desk, still perplexed, and Weinschenk sat unmoved and unmoving, his eyes never leaving Aarenhold's face. They might have passed five minutes together that way before Aarenhold all at once popped up straight in his chair and glanced around with the expression of a man who has been startled awake.

"You couldn't possibly be suggesting . . ." His voice trailed off, as if the thought was too improbable even to mention. "I assure you that the security here is . . ."

Weinschenk made no answer. The faintest suggestion of a smile played around his lips, but he said nothing.

After what seemed an eternity, a secretary came in, a model of German efficiency with her dark hair pulled back in a tight, uncompromising bun. She set the briefcase down on Aarenhold's desk, stood there for a moment at what almost amounted to attention, and, when Aarenhold waved her away, turned her back and marched out of the room. She was possibly all of twenty.

Aarenhold reached into the right-hand pocket of his tunic and produced a leather key case. The key to the satchel was so small it seemed to get lost in his thick fingers, or perhaps he was merely nervous. He tried it in the lock. There was the scraping sound of metal against metal. He tried again, and then again.

"Ach, Herr Leutnant! How very disagreeable for you!"

At a sign, Max stepped up to the desk, took the case from between Aarenhold's hands, and with a single brutal motion broke in the lid. The lock tore away, springing open like a child's toy.

"Yesterday's date," Weinschenk noted casually, looking over the folded newspaper his orderly had handed him. "The *Svenska Dagbladet*, as if there were any doubt. It would seem you've had a visitor in the last twenty-four hours."

He watched, his face expressionless, as Aarenhold sank slowly back down into his chair. They both knew what the consequences were likely to be; in the New Germany it was easy to slide across the spectrum of indictments from stupidity through criminal incompetence to treason. Doubtless at that moment Aarenhold was feeling the executioner's rope around his neck. Yes. The American, without knowing it, had done very well. The trap was closed not on its intended victim but on the men who had set it. The initiative had passed from Nebe to Weinschenk, who could now insist on a free hand to settle all the business that had been left unfinished since Spain. He would get the American, and the letter too, if he could. It was like the answer to a prayer.

"Of course, I'm sure we could come up with another of these," Weinschenk went on, recrossing his legs in the most casual way imaginable. His eyes rested thoughtfully on the smashed briefcase that sat like an accusation atop Aarenhold's desk. "I shall have to wire to Berlin for directions, of course—Gruppenführer Nebe will insist upon remaining fully informed, and I couldn't think of taking any action without his approval, but perhaps Herr Protze can still make his trip to the United States. To a courier, probably, one attaché case looks much like another, and there isn't any reason why it has to be *your* head which ends on a plate."

"Do you think not, Herr Hauptmann?"

Aarenhold leaned forward, his hands clasped together in what amounted to the most abject supplication. He was a pathetic enough sight.

"That depends, Herr Leutnant. That will be up to Gruppenführer Nebe."

XIII

By the middle of the morning David Steadman had established to his own satisfaction that Karen's apartment was being watched.

He bought himself a pair of field glasses, picked a building about a block away that gave him a good view of both sides of the street, and settled down on the roof to see what turned up. Sure enough, he spotted the same dark gray sedan, with the same dent in the right front fender and the same two guys inside, passing in front of her entrance and turning right into the next side street three times in the space of seventeen minutes. It would slow as it approached the apartment building, and some goon on the other sidewalk, who probably thought he was the cagiest thing since the introduction of the mail-order bride, would make a great production of taking off his hat and wiping the inside of the brim with a handkerchief so they would know that the quarry hadn't shown up yet.

They were British, of course—why should they be anyone else? The Germans would hardly have known to keep a watch on Karen Windermere's front door, and they would hardly have dared to do it so openly if they had. It was a little early yet to worry about one's enemies. One's friends were menacing enough.

For a moment, just a moment, he was worried that they might have done something to Karen, but then, it occurred to him, why should they?

Karen didn't know anything that could threaten them—at least, if she did she hadn't learned it from him. Karen was either an innocent bystander, someone they would just move out of the way so they could have a clear shot at him, or she was on their side. Why shouldn't she be on their side? After all, she was British too.

He wondered if Karen was up there waiting for him, or if they had already started her on her way back to England and the reception committee consisted of a couple of fellows with silencers screwed onto the muzzles of their pistols. He wondered if she had known all along it would end like this, or if that could have been something they had sprung on her at the last minute. Finally he decided to stop thinking about it.

But, really, this was the only logical conclusion for them. They didn't trust him—rightly so, as it turned out; after all, he really had peeked into their little surprise package—so they couldn't take the chance of leaving him alive. They weren't down there waiting to accept delivery. They didn't need an army for that. They weren't going to feel safe until Mr. David Steadman, late of Pittsburgh, Pennsylvania, and the recent unpleasantness in Spain, was washing out to sea with twenty or thirty pounds of scrap iron tied to his neck. He supposed he would have played it the same way in their shoes, so there was no point in taking the matter as a personal affront.

The British were no longer his friends and allies. It was just something he was going to have to learn to live with. He was back to his original starting point, where the only person on his side was himself.

Steadman took the stairway down from the roof—it was a large apartment building and he passed a few people in the hallways, but nobody seemed to think there was anything peculiar about his being there. He turned up the collar of his coat when he reached the outside, partly because it would be harder to see his face that way but mainly because there was a perfectly freezing wind at his back, and started looking around for a bus stop.

Walking around in the open didn't strike him just then as too terrific an idea. He wanted to make his getaway with a nice tight crowd packed around him. And he wanted to sit down and give some thought to what he was going to do with Uncle Adolf's little love note.

As much as he disliked the idea of being Hitler's mailman, the letter to Roosevelt had to get there. It wasn't a question of whether having the Pacific fleet blown up was a reasonable price for getting America into the war. It didn't matter, for present purposes, which side was right. The point was that nobody had designated David Steadman to make those decisions. He had enough on his conscience without that, so Roosevelt had to get his letter of warning; whether or not he chose to do anything about it—whether or not he even chose to believe it—was his problem.

It was a relief in a way. It was so disarmingly simple. A soldier fights and kills people, but that's all right because those people are trying to kill him. The ratio of blood guilt is one to one. The politicians could decide about balancing those hundred thousand lives against the demands of history and the honor of nations. It could all remain conveniently abstract for them. An ordinary man had no business with those decisions, not if he wanted to stay human. There were certain advantages to remaining a moral coward.

Which was fine as far as it went, but still left him with the problem of getting the letter delivered. And he supposed he might be allowed to regard staying alive as a reasonable secondary objective.

There probably wasn't a city west of Seuz where one didn't have to wait forever for the Sunday buses. Steadman hung back in the shadow of a doorway, watching the traffic go by and wondering with every passing car if it wasn't going to stop suddenly and he wasn't going to have to run like a rabbit from half a dozen guys with bulges under their coats. He wasn't very good at running. He still got shooting pains up his crotch if he just trotted along for a hundred yards or so, but he supposed he might be able to do a little better if he felt confident of catching a bullet in the ear the second he started slacking off. It was a great relief to him when, at about twelve minutes after eleven, a double-decker pulled up with a great puff of its hydraulic brakes and opened its door.

The only other passengers seemed to be middle-aged ladies, still in their Sunday best and with mesh shopping bags balanced on their knees. Steadman took a seat in the back, directly over the right wheel, and discovered that he had to fight to stay awake. He hadn't realized until that moment how tired he was.

Perhaps he really wasn't in the best shape to be deciding anything right then. Perhaps he ought to hole up somewhere for a few hours, get a little sleep, and then, with a clear head, start thinking about the problems of the world. God, he could hardly keep his eyes open.

The bus jolted along, and the winter sunshine came through the window and heated his face. The two women in front of him were chattering together pleasantly; Steadman listened without understanding a word. His hands lay in his lap, curled up together like a pair of small animals, and he breathed in the warm, stale air like perfume.

When he glanced up, he discovered they had already reached the center of town. The sidewalks were more crowded and people seemed to move with more purpose. He got off the bus and walked across the street to a movie house, where he paid the equivalent of twenty-five cents for a ticket to a comedy—at least, the characters on the posters were grinning like idiots, so a comedy seemed likeliest—and went inside and found himself a seat near a wall in the back. He was asleep before the house lights had dimmed.

The American embassy was unapproachable. Steadman might as well have tried to get inside the Kaaba. One gathered it hadn't taken very long for Major Horton's troops to figure out that nobody was coming back to the apartment on the Holländergaten and to draw all the obvious deductions, so they were out in force.

The embassy had the disadvantage of occupying a fairly open site. There was the sidewalk and then a fence of iron palings—you could have thrown a cat through them—and then forty or fifty feet of lawn and then the front entrance. The trees had lost all their leaves months ago, so there was no cover at all. If a man with a rifle wanted to kill you, all he needed was an open window on the other side of the street—at that distance he wouldn't even have to use a scope. There were even lookout cars parked at both ends of the block. It was like a goddamned shooting gallery.

And, yes, the British would be perfectly prepared to blow Mr. David Steadman away right on his ambassador's doorstep. They would feel that the stakes justified even this.

Steadman drove through in the back of a cab, keeping to the corner so there would be less chance of anyone spotting him, and he then told the driver to take him back downtown. It didn't look good. It just didn't look at all like a smart place to stick his head out. He would have to think of something else.

He considered phoning and arranging a meet somewhere away from the embassy, but that had two overwhelming disadvantages. First of all, the British probably had some of their own people on the inside, so how could he be sure he wouldn't be turning the letter over to a British agent? The only person he could possibly trust under these circumstances would be the ambassador himself, and how was he going to make himself believed? He could hear his pitch now: *I have a piece of correspondence here from Adolf Hitler to President Roosevelt. Be a darling and see that it gets delivered, would you? I'll wait for you at Harry's Bar until six this evening. Come alone.* Sure.

And the other problem was that, if there really were some of Horton's people inside, Steadman might never make it to Harry's Bar. It just wasn't going to work out.

He had walked for about twenty minutes after the cab dropped him off, and he was beginning to feel cold again. When he started looking for someplace to come inside, he looked across the avenue, across six lanes of traffic divided down the middle by a strip of concrete and what, under the snow, was probably grass, and saw a building that took up the whole block. It was called the Konsert Huset. Inside he followed the snaking current of people to a small auditorium, where he gathered he was about to hear a recital of violin music. A very young lady wearing a black sweater, with the wide, white collar of her blouse covering her shoulders, handed him a program and invited him to sit down.

The program, naturally, was unintelligible except for the actual listing of the selections, which for some reason was in French. Bach, Schubert, and somebody named Wieniawski, who came first. Steadman braced himself for the ordeal.

It wasn't so bad. Or, at least, you could ignore it. The violinist was a sad-looking fellow in his middle twenties, thin as a stick and already beginning to go bald. He wore wire-frame glasses and played with a passionate commitment not quite matched by his grasp of technique. Or perhaps the instrument was just a trifle squeaky. Steadman was a snob about violins. Had he kept up with Maestro Suvini, he probably would have inherited his stepfather's Guarneri, but he had heard it often enough to know such things could make a difference.

Of course he already knew what the next step would have to be. It was simply a question of nerving himself up for it. Major Horton might be able to keep him from passing the letter along to the Americans, but he wouldn't be able to work the same charm with the Germans. At least the Germans would know he wasn't pulling their leg.

He waited until after the Bach, which was very pretty, and then went out into the corridor during the intermission to see if he couldn't find a telephone. It was a long time before the embassy answered, and the operator didn't sound very glad to hear from him.

"Let me speak to your head of security," Steadman said in German. He waited, scowling out through the glass wall of the telephone booth, listening to the sound of pages being turned—apparently it wasn't so easy to find out where everyone was on a Sunday, even in the Third Reich.

"There is an officer on duty, if you . . ."

"I said the *head* of security, *Liebchen*, not some corporal. I'm not phoning to complain about the ambassador's cat. Just connect me—he won't be disappointed."

"I'm sorry, but Leutnant Aarenhold isn't available just at present. Could you possibly leave a message?"

Steadman told himself not to be angry, and then he realized that he wasn't angry at all. He was scared. It was like the two or three times he had been sent out into no-man's-land to wave a white flag and parley with the Nationalists for a truce in which to remove the wounded—he had never known whether they would be prepared to talk or would simply shoot him. He didn't like this eyeball-to-eyeball stuff.

But he would leave a message anyway.

"You tell him I'll call back in one hour. Tell him I know why the *Kungsholm* didn't sail on time, and that he's got a problem with his mailman. Don't worry about disturbing his day of rest—he'll be very interested. Remember, one hour."

He hung up the receiver and pressed his hand flat against the telephone-booth door. Instantly the glass around his fingers hazed over. He felt as if he had a fever or something. He could feel the veins in his neck throbbing like a tom-tom. One hour. He could almost hear that white flag fluttering in the cold Spanish wind.

The odds were about even. The initiative lay with Steadman but the Germans had manpower and organization. It went without saying that they would go back on any deal they made. They would want him as well as the letter, just so they could squeeze from him whatever the British might inadvertently have let drop. Besides, he had already killed two of their men, and they weren't very forgiving about that sort of thing. The problem was to set up a meeting he would be able to walk away from.

They didn't have a clue who he was. He might as well have been invisible.

There was a restaurant on the Bryggergatan, about half a block away from the central post office, where the front window was composed of diamond-shaped panes of pale yellow glass. There were a few little tables there; and anyone who walked by outside could get a good clear look at you. The only phone was behind the bar.

Aarenhold had his instructions; he was to wait there for a call. If he was a good boy and had come alone, he would be told where to go for the actual meeting. Steadman didn't have any illusions that there wouldn't be a battalion of security heavies all over the area, but at least this way the man wouldn't feel he had a license to be obvious about it.

"How do I know this isn't some sort of hoax?" the Leutnant had asked. It really wasn't such a stupid question.

"The combination of your vault is 61-15-23-70. If you look you'll find that the alarm switch under your basement staircase has been fixed.

Perhaps you'd like to hear what was in the attaché case that Herr Protze didn't take with him to the New World."

"No, not really, Mr . . ." Aarenhold had laughed uneasily, as if it were all just an undergraduate prank. "I suppose I have to call you something, haven't I?"

Steadman reached into his overcoat pocket and took out the diplomatic passport he had taken off that dead kid the night he landed. He turned back the cover with one hand and held it open against the wall of the phone booth.

"Grundmann—does that ring a bell?"

"Really, *mein Herr*, you have a grotesque sense of humor."

"Just show up, Leutnant. And if I see a lot of guys standing around with their hands in their pockets, we won't be having this conversation again."

Steadman took a long time making his approach. The Bryggergatan wasn't more than a few blocks, but there was plenty of foot traffic and he had lots of protective coloration. He carried a grocery bag—they wouldn't be looking for a man with a grocery bag—and he was reasonably certain that no one had spotted him. But perhaps that was only because he hadn't spotted them.

As he passed the restaurant, he tried to keep from slowing down. He would allow himself one quick look, just one. It was three-thirty in the afternoon; the place would be nearly empty. There shouldn't be that many choices. One look would have to be enough.

There was a single man leaning against the bar, holding a glass in his hand, his hat on a stool beside him. He was obviously waiting, but he wasn't Aarenhold. Steadman kept right on walking.

It was curious how he knew that. He had never seen Aarenhold, had never done anything more than talk to him for two or three minutes on the telephone, but he knew, with an eerie certainty, that this man leaning against the bar was not Aarenhold.

And the reason he was so sure, he suddenly realized, was that the man in the restaurant was known to him. This was someone he had seen before.

He got to the end of the block and waited for the signal light to change. It didn't matter who it was. The plan was still the same—he would go to the post office and make his call. If the Germans wanted to play bait-and-switch that was their business. What the hell did he care?

He was halfway across the street before he remembered.

In Spain a man made a point of knowing his enemies. This one, the last time he had seen him, had been wearing the uniform of a captain in the SS. Steadman had been sitting with a contact of his, a black-eyed, rather spectacular whore named Dolores, in a tavern in Madrid much favored by the Germans—as, indeed, was Dolores—and she had pointed him out.

"That one is Weinschenk," she had said, indicating with a raised eyebrow the man just coming in through the curtained doorway. For an instant his face had been flooded with the white autumn sunlight. "As a man he is not such a bad sort, but he is a bastard if he catches you."

Of course, by then Steadman knew all about Weinschenk.

It was the same man—perhaps not a bad sort, but a good servant of his masters. The same deep-set eyes in the same bony, exhausted face. Perhaps the hair had thinned a little, but everyone aged in three years. It was him. All the way from Spain, but it was him. Steadman would have been just as happy if it could have been someone else. Weinschenk had had a reputation, not just as a bastard—they were all bastards—but as a clever bastard. It really was just like old times.

"And watch out for the creature behind him. He is Max, Weinschenk's trained dog, always at his heels ready to do the Hauptmann's bidding. They say he can tear a man in half, from end to end, like a strip of paper."

Thank you for the warning, sweetheart, but the last time Steadman had seen Max he had left him bleeding through his fingers in a hotel corridor that very evening. He might even have killed him—perhaps that wouldn't be too much to ask. Anyway, it seemed probable that by now Weinschenk had picked himself up another grunting monster to watch his back. The Germans never seemed to run short.

There was a stack of empty shipping crates by the side entrance to the post office. Steadman dropped his groceries into one and pushed through the revolving doors and into the huge, empty cavern lined on three sides by mailboxes and clerk's windows. The floor was marble, and his footfalls sounded like cannon fire.

The bartender at the restaurant with the yellow windows connected him with "Herr Aarenhold" right away.

"Yes? Is this Mr. 'Grundmann'?" It was even the same voice.

"Tell me, Weinschenk, have you made colonel yet? We're both a long way from Madrid."

There was a short pause—shorter than Steadman had expected—and then a low, rather sinister laugh.

"So you know me, do you?" He was speaking in English now, as if they had dropped all pretense. "I am flattered, after all these years. But I assume we can still do business?"

"I called, didn't I? I don't know whether you've been in town long enough to do any sight-seeing—do you know where the railroad station is?"

"No, I have not that honor."

"Good. I'll meet you there in five minutes. And don't worry about finding me. I'll find you. If I like the setup I may even give you back what you've come for, but that's up to you."

"Oh, there will be no tricks, my friend. I've . . ."

Steadman didn't wait to hear the rest. He hung up the phone, waited about ten seconds, and dialed the same number again. Sure enough, what he got was a busy signal. Weinschenk was calling in reinforcements.

No tricks. Sure.

They didn't know him by sight. That was the one advantage left to him: He at least could recognize Weinschenk, but they wouldn't know who they were looking for. It was little enough upon which to hang your life.

Ordinarily, he would have just forgotten the whole thing and gone home. When they started playing it cute like this, then to hell with them. Your life had to be worth something. But there was the letter. How much was it worth to get that back on its merry way?

Of course, it wasn't any different for them.

Why *were* they playing it so cute? They knew now that Steadman was on to them, so why risk it? They would be getting the letter back, and that, you would think, should be enough for them. Why take the chance?

He waited in one of the lines in front of the ticket windows. It was a long line, and people in long lines get bored and look around them. No one would notice him there or think there was anything suspicious about his behavior. He had a good view of the stairway that led down from the street level—Weinschenk would come that way. He was taking his time.

It was hardly more than two blocks from the main post office building to the train station, and Steadman had run it. He couldn't believe they had gotten there ahead of him, even if they had a car somewhere. He hadn't seen anyone who looked the type. He would just have to wait.

Couldn't he just call it off, even now? Let them stand around with their guns bulging under their armpits—he could just take off, and live to play another day. What could be easier than to phone again tomorrow morning and say, "Your letter is in a package I've given to the luggage check at the railway station; you'll get the claim ticket in the mail"?

Except, of course, that then he would never know if the thing had gotten into the right hands. At least he didn't have to worry about Wein-

schenk being a British plant. There wasn't any second way. He would
have to take his chances with him, here and now.

Then he saw Weinschenk coming down the stairway. Alone.

Maybe it would be all right after all. Weinschenk walked slowly, his
hands dangling at his sides, not seeming to look for anyone. His face was
puckered and tense; he gave the impression of being seriously annoyed.
At least he hadn't come with a crowd.

The lower floor of the railroad station was like a long trench, with a
balcony, about five yards wide, running around all four sides at street
level. There wasn't much you could do at street level except buy a
newspaper, and there weren't any conspicuously unoccupied figures up
there scanning the floor. So maybe Weinschenk really had thought better
of it and had ordered his playmates out of the area. That would seem to
be the intelligent thing to do, and Weinschenk was not a stupid man.

He was pushed out of shape because he knew now he wasn't going to
get both the message and the messenger. He was the type who always
wanted it all. But not this time.

There were probably three hundred people down there on the main
floor, and the usual dull, muffled noise, like the rush of water underground, carried each of their separate sounds into oblivion. One couldn't
hear one's own footsteps. The air was thick and used up. It wasn't a place
where anyone lingered.

Weinschenk stationed himself at the mouth of the corridor at right
angles to the entrances to the various platforms. He looked at his watch
and frowned. He was making himself obvious.

It was one minute before four, and then the huge hand of the clock
over the information window slid up to the hour and it was four. There
wasn't anything to be gained by putting it off. Steadman broke away from
the line in front of the ticket counter, to the evident relief of the woman
behind him, and started making his slow, circular way toward the departure platforms and Weinschenk.

There were two ways of doing the thing. One was to walk past him as
if you didn't know he was there and then, at the last possible second,
before he realized you were upon him, thrust the letter into his hand,
smile, and keep going. You could be lost in the crowd before he had a
chance to summon aid.

That was fine except if Weinschenk wasn't interested in summoning
aid, if he had a gun under his coat and was willing to do the job himself.
Then he would have both the letter and you, and it wasn't as if no one
had ever committed a murder in a train station, in front of a few hundred
witnesses, and gotten away with it. On the whole, Steadman preferred

the second alternative: to come within, say, forty feet, give Weinschenk a waggle, and see how the man reacts. That way there was still room to get away.

Weinschenk had his hands in his pockets—not a particularly encouraging symptom—and his hat was pushed back on his head to reveal a considerable expanse of thinly covered scalp. He looked like a man waiting for his wife. It was just possible to imagine he might be ready to play straight. There was a pushcart out on that area of the floor; a woman was selling bunches of grapes wrapped in green tissue paper. Steadman stopped beside the cart, reached into his jacket for a few coins, and bought some of the grapes. Then, with one hand still hidden inside his overcoat so that Weinschenk could imagine that he might not be the only one carrying a concealed weapon, he turned around and faced him. Their eyes met, and Steadman grinned.

Everything would have been fine then if only Weinschenk had taken his hands out of his pockets and started to walk across that granite floor toward him. He could have had his precious letter and everyone could have left satisfied, but that wasn't what he did. He took his hand out of his pocket all right—one hand, his left one—but what he did with it was to flex the last two fingers downward, as if he wanted to see how far they would spread, and to glance at a spot someplace beyond Steadman's right shoulder. The son of a bitch was signaling for reinforcements.

Steadman didn't hesitate. He simply dropped the grapes and ran. He headed toward the platform entrances—there didn't seem to be a hole anywhere else—running just as fast as he could. These clowns weren't going to march him out of here with a gun in his back. Not this boy.

Weinschenk started moving too, and he was faster. He had maybe two or three steps farther to go, but by the time Steadman was almost to the first platform entrance he was very nearly on him.

Steadman kicked out to the side and caught Weinschenk a glancing blow to the knee. It was enough. Weinschenk went down, hard. Just as he reached the entrance, Steadman risked a quick look behind him to see if anyone else was gaining.

Good Christ, it was that gorilla Max! Big as life, with his coattails flapping behind him and a Luger in his fist, he looked like a tackle for Notre Dame.

Steadman dodged inside, onto the boardwalk in front of the platforms where he was covered by shadow.

Behind him he heard the crack of a pistol shot—Jesus, what were these people thinking about?—and he cut down a platform, which he happened to notice, for no particular reason, was marked with a large white "5," and kept going. All he could hope was that there was a train there, and that it was ready to leave in the next two or three seconds.

No such luck. The train was there, but as he ran past the third-class carriages it was obvious that no one was in any hurry. Children had their heads and arms stuck out through the open windows, and people were standing in the aisles. Plenty of time.

He turned to look again, hoping against hope that the great ape had given up or lost him in the darkness or had fallen down and broken his neck, but he was still back there, King Kong in his city tweeds. The platform was crowded; they both had to dodge and weave to keep from running people over, not that that would have much bothered Max.

Steadman suddenly realized that he was nearing the end of the train, and therefore the end of anywhere more to run to. He glanced up at the first-class carriages, each compartment with its own little outside door—thank God for the European class system, where that sort of thing was still possible—and grabbed the first handle he could reach, pulled it down, and swung himself up and inside.

Just as he cleared the platform, he heard another shot and felt something tug at his sleeve. Right beside him a woman screamed; he looked at her, a well-appointed lady in her mid-fifties, and saw her standing there with a large, ragged hole in her left cheekbone. For an instant there wasn't any blood, and then it poured out, red and shining, and still she didn't move. She just screamed. Steadman kept right on going.

What was that animal up to? It didn't make any sense!

Probably he would remember the four people in that compartment until his dying day. There was a young couple, both in new clothes—perhaps they were just setting out on their honeymoon. The man had his arm over the girl's shoulders and was holding her fingers in his other hand. A man in a black suit, with a gigantic mustache and his hands balanced on his knees. Near the window on the same side, with an empty seat between them, a woman in her thirties in a lilac dress; she had been reading a book, which she held in her trembling hands. They were all staring at him as if he were a visitation of the Eternally Damned.

But there was no time to stop. Steadman threw himself through the still open door to the corridor, ran to the end of the carriage, hit the connecting door to the next, and was out on the narrow little steel gangway without ever breaking stride. When he got down to the tracks he kept right on running. There was only one direction—away from that maniac with the Luger.

There was an empty set of tracks, and then a train at rest. Steadman rolled under the wheels and hid there, trying to catch his breath, trying to listen for footsteps on the gravel roadbed. Max wouldn't dare hang around very much longer. After all, Sweden had laws against shooting people, even if you were in the SS—especially if you were in the SS—and there were always a few policemen around a train station.

It wasn't until he had been under there for perhaps as long as a full minute that he noticed the blood trickling down over the back of his hand and realized he had been shot. The bullet that had made such a mess of that woman's face must have grazed him as well. The thought had barely had time to form in his mind before he was aware of a burning pain in his upper arm. But there would be time to worry about that later.

Between the steel rail and the edge of the platform was a narrow band of sunlight. He was almost at the end of the station, beyond where the metal awnings enclosed the platform like the vault of a church, so he could hear the wind stirring and see the sunlight. That band was suddenly broken by a flicker of shadow, and Steadman could hear the sound of footsteps. He knew, by an instinct he couldn't have explained, that Max had finally run out of time.

By the time he managed to crawl back out onto the roadbed, his shoulder was really beginning to stiffen up. There was steam coming from the brake cylinders of the engine ahead, so he decided this was as good a time as any to make his escape. He didn't know what was waiting for him back inside—he didn't want to know. He pulled himself along to a gangway between cars and climbed aboard. Almost at once the train jolted forward and they were on their way.

He was tired, he was dirty, he had a notch chopped out of his left triceps, and he didn't have a clue where the hell he was heading, but he had a compartment to himself and he was alive. One mustn't complain.

There was a bathroom of sorts at the end of the carriage, where Steadman peeled off his overcoat and found that his jacket and shirt were stiff with blood. The wound itself wasn't so terrible; it seemed to be reasonably clean, and the bullet hadn't touched the bone. He ripped off his shirtsleeve and used it for a bandage. It would do until he got to where he was going.

The compartment was still empty when he got back. He threw himself into the seat nearest the window and closed his eyes. All he wanted was a little sleep.

He heard the door slam and saw a man in a blue uniform standing over him, frowning. It was only the conductor.

"I don't have a ticket," Steadman said evenly, in English. What the hell. What could they do to him? "Could you sell me one?"

The conductor's eyes narrowed, which caused his tan face to break into a series of roughly parallel creases. He looked as if he were probably close to sixty and could tear a telephone book in half any time he liked. He also looked as if he thought Steadman was trying to fiddle him, or perhaps he just didn't understand English.

"Are you hurt, sir?" He made a languid gesture at the bloodstained hole in Steadman's overcoat—so much for the language barrier. "Do you need a doctor?"

"No, I just need a ticket. Where are we going?"

"This train goes to Norrköping, and then on to Helsingborg. The fare to Helsingborg is fifty kronor—do you want to go there?"

"Fine."

Steadman reached into his inside jacket pocket and extracted his wallet, where he had what little was left of the money Karen had gotten for him from the British embassy. He would have enough to buy this ticket, and maybe to get him out of the country, but after that things were going to tighten up. The only checkbook he had brought with him was to a bank in London, and probably Horton and his pals would be looking for something like that. It would be a new experience, being flat broke.

"There was trouble back at the station," the conductor murmured, all of his attention apparently absorbed by the operation of punching Steadman's ticket. "Somebody said a woman was shot."

He looked at Steadman with not so much suspicion as wariness. He wanted an explanation.

"So was I. Did they catch the man?"

The conductor shook his head. And then, all at once, something seemed to occur to him.

"Does it have to do with the war, sir?" he asked, with a kind of reverence. He seemed almost ashamed of the question.

"Yes, it has to do with the war."

"And are you English, sir?"

There was nothing Steadman could do except to nod.

"Then no one will disturb you here, sir. I have a first-aid kit. If you will give me your coat I will see if it can be cleaned off a little." He handed Steadman his ticket with great solemnity, as if it sealed some sort of understanding between them.

Steadman could have wept with gratitude. Perhaps, even now, there was some hope for the human race.

XIV

NOVEMBER 3, 1941

The Mosquito was much less crowded flying home. Karen was all by herself.

It had started the moment David had passed out through the door of her cousin's flat; from that moment, even while the place was crowded with tense, unpleasant men from the embassy, who had expected her to make them coffee and to answer their telephone calls for them, she had been by herself.

It was odd how the worst things always arrived carrying the sense that they had been expected all along. Nothing could have predicted for her that David would turn into a traitor, but the feeling of betrayal had hardly come as much of a shock. It seemed to be her lot in life that no man would ever live up to what she hoped for him, so perhaps she simply hoped too much. First Bertie with his nervous breakdown and his cold, unyielding rejection, and then David, who had disappeared like a thief. She didn't believe in coincidence. It must be something within herself.

And now, it seemed, she would have the solitude to sort it all out.

In Scotland they gave her a voucher for a troop train that was leaving that morning and told her she would be expected to report as soon as she arrived in London, but someone must have crossed a wire because Brian Horton was at the Aberdeen station waiting for her.

"How was your flight?" he asked, hunching his shoulders and pushing his hands deep into the pockets of his trench coat—it was bitterly cold. His eyes wandered nervously over her in a way that suggested he really didn't care one whit about her flight. "Things didn't work out, but that couldn't have been your fault. No one is blaming you."

He smiled tensely. He didn't even believe it himself.

The platform was jammed with soldiers, standing around in little groups, with their packs resting against their legs, smoking cigarettes and talking in low voices and staring at the handful of women who had come to see some few of them off. Since Karen was accompanied by an officer, they hardly glanced at her. Some of them hardly seemed to be out of their teens.

"Have you had anything to eat?"

Brian jerked his head toward a wooden sign that read Commissary. It was so bright against the faded shingle wall that it must certainly have been put up since the spring. Karen looked away in distaste.

"No—no, thank you. I'm not hungry."

They hardly spoke again until it was time to board. It was a heavy, embarrassed silence—they seemed unable even to look at each other— but to stand around exchanging small talk would have been worse, and to mention what was on both their minds impossible. There would be time enough for that when they were sitting down and the train had left. Certainly Brian could have come for no other reason.

There was only one first-class carriage, reserved for the officers. Brian, who was carrying a suitcase, hoisted it into the overhead rack in one of the front compartments and slid the door closed. During the rest of the trip, which lasted until after midnight, no one else attempted to enter, even though the train must have been crowded. Certainly someone had issued orders.

"We don't have any idea where he is," Brian said suddenly, adjusting himself on the seat cushions and smoothing down the end of his mustache with his middle fingertip. "We know he's left Stockholm—there was a bit of a ruckus at the railroad station there; our information is that he shot a woman—but after that he seems to have just disappeared. I suppose the Gestapo's got him by now."

He smiled faintly, as if the idea gave him some sort of satisfaction, and crossed his arms over his chest. In that moment, all Karen could think about was the pistol she had given David at almost their last moment before parting.

If someone should catch you, I thought that with a silencer you might have at least a fighting chance of getting away.

"If anybody catches me, then that'll mean I'm blown and it won't matter whether I get away or not.

It'll matter to me.

But why should David have shot a woman in the Stockholm railway station? And what did Brian mean by "the Gestapo's got him by now"? Did he mean they had caught him or that he had turned himself over to them? Where could he possibly go if he left Sweden? He wouldn't be able to get out of Europe, and there was nowhere to go that the Nazis hadn't occupied. It didn't make very much sense.

She had a feeling that Brian was waiting for her to ask him to explain himself, but on small things like the truth she found she no longer trusted him. Hadn't she trusted David?

"Aren't you going to ask me if I knew what he had planned?" She let her eyes grow large, intending to show her contempt. She wanted to insult him, but there was just that much sweetness in her face that she couldn't ever have succeeded in insulting any man.

"No, I'm not going to ask," he said, the smile becoming frozen on his lips—he didn't seem at all happy. "As I've said, it couldn't have been your fault."

"How—how could you know that?"

"If you insist I say it, we had your cousin's flat wired."

"Oh, God."

Brian's face took on a waxen immobility. Nothing seemed alive except his eyes, but they said a great deal about the struggle that was taking place inside Karen's old admirer. He seemed ashamed, and not so much because of what he had caused to be done—there was little enough to suggest he felt any scruples about a trifling matter like that—but because he knew now that David Steadman was her lover. He had had to listen to their little endearments, and the groaning of the bedsprings. And she hoped he had suffered for it.

"It's the sort of thing one has to learn to live with," he said finally.

No, it wasn't—it was disgusting. It was like being violated, and he could sit there and smile kindly and announce that one had to learn to live with it. God, she wished she could pay him back somehow for this. She could just imagine some technician somewhere, with earphones clamped over his head, snickering as he monitored the recording.

"Where did you put the microphone, under the bed?"

"Oh, come now, Karen. It isn't as bad as all that." He shrugged his shoulders, making a face as if he were shocked himself. "In a war we give up things, and in our war we give up our privacy. It's all part of the necessary horror, but the point is that *you* were cleared."

"Does that make a difference?"

She turned her head to look out at the gray winter landscape, miles and miles of pale, snow-dappled fields, and in the far distance the sea. She felt as if she hadn't moved in hours.

"Yes, it makes a difference. We may need you again, you know—provided Steadman puts his nose up somewhere. Somebody is bound to catch him, and even if it's the Gestapo we might still be able to pry him loose—these things are done, you know. And if and when we get him back, we're going to need all the leverage we can manage."

What was he talking about? Karen pressed her forehead against the cold window glass and wondered why her eyes were burning. Outside, for just an instant, she caught a glimpse of a great shaggy ox, the color of wheat, who picked up his head to stare at the train rolling past. Her throat ached, as if someone had a hand around her larynx and was squeezing hard. What could this man possibly want from her now?

"Is that what you came all this way to tell me?" she asked, swallowing a little gulp of air and trying not to look as if she cared about anything, least of all what Brian Horton and the War Ministry might want with her now. "But perhaps you just happened to be there. A short vacation? The salmon were running?"

"No, I came up here to tell you that Bertie has died. It happened the morning after you left."

For the rest of her life Karen would wonder what she had felt in that first moment. Surprise? Yes. Perhaps relief? Sorrow? Guilt? Anger? Was this the final desertion? Then whose? Perhaps she didn't feel anything. Perhaps there was only a kind of numbness.

There was a question she wanted to ask. She shaped her mouth to pronounce the first syllable, but nothing seemed to come out. And then that but no other. A little panting sound. That wouldn't do. She decided she didn't want to know after all.

"I don't know quite how to say this . . . I'm afraid he did away with himself." Brian paused for a moment, looking just as if he were frightened someone was about to strike him. And then he began smoothing down the end of his mustache again, with the same slow deliberation that somehow reminded one of a cat. "They fished his body out of the Medway, but he seems to have shot himself. The funeral was yesterday—I came up here as soon as . . . Well, that afternoon. I'm sorry."

They had even buried him without her? Her own husband, and she had missed his funeral? With a kind of inward cringing, she caught herself wondering what Bertie's mother must have thought.

When they arrived in Paddington Station, she got away from Brian and caught a bus to her flat. Whatever they wanted with her at the ministry, it could wait until after she had had a hot bath and a few hours to herself. It was the first time she had been on a bus after blackout, and the feeling was eerie. One sensed rather than saw the street below; it was rather like being at the bottom of a well.

It was only then, in the dark bus, surrounded by strangers as unreal as ghosts, that she allowed herself to think about Bertie. Was this what it had been like for him all these months, engulfed in darkness and shadow? Had the world perished for him like this? She could feel the tears coursing down her face. She had been his widow for a long time already, so the sense of loss had long since become a thing to which she had grown accustomed; but somehow, and for the first time, now she could imagine what that separation, not only from her but from everyone and everything, must have been like for him. It was a peculiar kind of grief, like a discovery. Like the unearthing of some terrible crime.

They made her wait for a long time. It was one of those subterranean office complexes where the seepage from the Thames had left strange stains on the walls and there was a constant humming from the ventilation fans. She had a wooden chair and an ashtray stand and had to share a room about the size of a coal hole with a WRENS typist who spent every minute of the two hours they were together working over her fingernails. It was like the solitude of the confessional after the priest has left.

Perhaps they had done it purposely. Perhaps they wanted her to spend some time under that faint official displeasure that is always implied by a government waiting room. Perhaps they wanted her to feel that now she had lost everything: husband, lover, the respect and confidence of the War Ministry. But it wasn't working.

All she could feel was an overpowering resentment. Their war, with its efficiency and its inhuman logic, had taken Bertie, and now they had robbed her of David as well. For a day or two she had had a sense that life was beginning again for her, and now David was a fugitive inside occupied Europe and she would probably never see him again. But if they expected her to believe that he had suddenly become a villain, they had wasted their effort.

She kept remembering how those two men from the embassy had shown up at Griselde's flat within an hour of David's leaving. They had

been listening to every word they had said—Brian had admitted that—
and they had come as soon as they were sure David was on his way.

There had been something about those two. They weren't just ordinary
embassy couriers or something; they were too wary, too alert. They had
been like predatory animals. What would they have done if David had
returned? Killed him? Killed her as well? That no longer seemed to her
so terribly unlikely.

And if they were prepared to kill him already then, what possible claim
could they have made on his loyalty?

Why hadn't he come back? Had he known somehow? How could he
have known? It seemed a circle from which there was no way out.

A door opened from the corridor, and the WRENS smoothed back
her hay-colored hair, put away her nail file, and left without a glance.
At almost the same time Karen heard a soft cough from the inner office,
followed by footsteps on a linoleum floor, followed by the opening of a
second door. It was like a piece of stage business they had planned for
her benefit alone.

"Karen, could you come in now?"

But it wasn't "they." It was merely Brian Horton.

He had undergone a transformation of sorts, even in the few hours
since they had parted on the platform at Paddington Station. The waxen
mask was firmly in place now—he was no longer the family friend or
the old suitor; he was the official spokesman of the ministry now. He
extended his hand, not so much in greeting as to draw her into the room
like a prisoner at the end of a noose. By the merest glance he indicated
the chair on which she was to take her seat.

And, of course, there was no explanation of the change in office.
Perhaps he was important enough now to have more than one. Perhaps
he merely wanted her to think so. What difference did it make?

"Our business in Stockholm wasn't much of a success, was it," he
said. It wasn't a question, but a working postulate. It was as if they were
meeting again for the first time, as if the train ride together had never
happened.

Brian sat down behind a desk cluttered with telephones and manila
file folders with secrecy classifications stamped in red letters on the covers;
he laced his fingers together and seemed to squeeze something between
his hands.

"I wonder where your friend Mr. Steadman hopes to sell what he has
so cleverly stolen. In certain circles it would doubtless be worth a great
deal of money."

Karen hardly knew what to say. She tried to feel angry, but under the

pressure of this sudden change in their relationship she was frankly in-
timidated. It was difficult to guess what was true and what wasn't.

"David Steadman is independently a very wealthy man," she said
finally, glancing up from the point of her left shoe, which had seemed
to occupy her attention for so long. "I don't think it's very probable that
money could have been a motive."

"Then perhaps he's undergone a conversion. At any rate, he seems to
have changed sides rather dramatically."

Brian unlaced his fingers, looked at them for a moment as if inspecting
for damage, and dropped his hands out of sight behind the desk. The
action suggested a certain impatience—one might almost have said anger—
which seemed to include both David and herself. Or perhaps he was
merely annoyed with the necessity of explanation.

"The details are still a bit vague, but he shot a woman while trying to
make good his escape—that should tell you something. She died yesterday
morning. Perhaps he attempted to make a deal with the Germans and it
came unstuck." Brian smiled a cheerless smile. "At any rate, he's on the
run. Eventually we'll get what's been happening sorted out."

"Why are you explaining all this to me, Brian?"

"I told you, my dear." He looked at her through eyes suddenly wide
with astonishment at her simplicity. "We intend to get him back, one
way or the other, and when we do we're going to have to involve you
again. You know, you got us into this ridiculous dilemma, and you're
going to have to help us get out."

"I don't see how I could help you. I also don't see why I should."

"Women so rarely do."

It was a tense moment. The man seemed almost to be daring her to
respond, but Karen saw quickly enough the uselessness of it. Nothing
she could say would be very likely to impress him, not in his present
mood.

When the silence began to grow awkward, he brought one hand out
from under the desk and touched the knot of his tie with the thumb and
first finger, indicating that he was ready to continue.

"Nevertheless, you will help us," he said. "This matter goes quite
beyond any personal considerations either one of us might care to bring
to it. Catching Mr. Steadman may not be enough; we may still need
something to use against him, and you're one of the few weapons we
have. Everyone has to remain loyal to something—in his case, it would
appear to be you."

He took one of the manila file folders off the stack on the right-hand
side of his desk and stood up, holding it out to her.

"Here—take a look at it. Perhaps something here might stir your memory. You seem to need reminding which side you're on."

It was a typed transcript of a conversation. The speakers were designated as W and S. She didn't have to read more than a line or two to understand.

"Yes, that's correct." Brian's face was as blank as marble. Even his irritation seemed to have disappeared. "Your last night with him, word for word. Keep it. I have another copy and I'm sure I can count on your discretion with classified material."

"What do you want with me? Just what do you want?"

Wasn't there anything to be left for her? Karen could feel her eyes filling up with tears—she simply couldn't help it. She didn't trust herself to speak. It wasn't anything as trivial as embarrassment. It was a bitterness so deep there wasn't room even for anger. Now, finally, she had lost the last shred.

"I want you to take that home with you and read it." The fingers laced themselves back together, and the dead face came back to life. "I want you to realize the power you have over this man. And, when the time comes, I want you to use it to help us turn him inside out."

After he had ordered a car to take Karen back to her flat, Brian Horton started out on the short walk from the ministry to his own digs in Chandos Place. It was hardly past the middle of the morning, but he simply had to get away for a while. He needed a stiff drink and a few hours of quiet before lunch.

At the start of the war, after he had been assigned to the Sector, he had leased a little three-room affair as close to his office as he could manage. He had ended up on the second floor of a poky little building where, if he looked out his kitchen window, he could just see the top of Nelson's Column. Aside from summer visits to his mother in Lancashire, which hardly counted, it was the first time since his passing out of Sandhurst that he had had his own place, away from barracks.

He didn't like it. He didn't like the wallpaper or the rented furniture or the way his bedroom faced out onto a street lined with tobacconists' shops and Italian restaurants. It was all too depressingly civilian, and he couldn't wait until the war was over and he could rejoin his old regiment.

However, at that moment it was the only spot on earth where he could be sure of being alone until he had digested his appalling interview with Karen Windermere. As soon as he was inside the door, he set his briefcase on one of the overstuffed and uncomfortable chairs in the sitting room and went into the kitchen to make himself a large brandy and soda. He needed it. He needed to get just a little stiff if he was to regain his composure.

There was hardly anything left in the bottle, and decent brandy was becoming indecently expensive as supplies ran out—it might be years before an invasion of France was possible—but Horton felt that in the present emergency he was justified in the extravagance. He poured himself about three fingers, hunted around under the sink until he found the siphon bottle, and sat down at the kitchen table, where the slanting sunlight crossed over the lower part of his face. Within three or four minutes he was beginning to feel pleasantly numb, and the scene with Karen had stopped playing over and over again in his mind.

He had hated every minute of it. Reading that transcript alone in his office had been bad enough, but then to have to show it to her . . . Nothing he had ever had to do in his life had left him feeling so humiliated, so dreadfully mean. He was sure now, quite sure, that Karen would never forgive him. He could hardly blame her.

And that bounder Steadman was to blame, playing around with his friend's wife like that. The two of them had sounded like a couple of moonstruck adolescents.

Now Steadman was running around somewhere in occupied Europe, he shouldn't wonder—there seemed little enough reason for him to stay in Sweden, where, between the Germans and the British, both of whom would be watching every ship that left port, right down to the ferries, he was bottled up as tight as a man could be.

Steadman would head for Portugal. He was an old hand there; doubtless he had friends who would still help him. And one could travel to anywhere from Portugal—in Portugal, except for all that hothouse intrigue in the sidewalk cafés, the war hardly existed.

Horton would send out some discreet alarms, just to see that someone would have orders about what to do if Steadman turned up there, but it didn't seem very probable that he could get so far. Certainly the Germans could catch him before then. After all, the man wasn't invisible.

It would serve the bastard right. Horton took another long pull on his brandy and soda and noticed that his face was beginning to heat up and that his breathing had become slow and deep, almost as if he had fallen into a catnap. It was very agreeable.

Steadman was a clever and resourceful man—the Foreign Ministry had sent along abstracts from the Spanish intelligence reports on him, and they made very gaudy reading—but the odds were heavily in favor of the Germans. After all, it was their territory he was traveling over, and they weren't precisely inexperienced in this sort of thing. He would lead them a merry chase, but they would nab him in the end.

It was to be hoped he *would* lead them a merry chase. It would be a disaster if they caught him too quickly. It wouldn't do at all.

Because Steadman had to make it at least as far as France. There was almost no resistance movement worth mentioning inside Germany, but if he could just haul himself across the border there might be some hope of getting him safely out.

In France there was an underground dependent upon the British for weapons and logistical support—an underground which, thank God, had no truck with de Gaulle and his crowd; the last thing anyone needed was to put that Don Quixote in touch with a secret of such magnitude. Churchill would have a fit. He hardly even trusted de Gaulle with his telephone number.

Steadman had to make it at least that far, otherwise he would simply disappear into some Gestapo dungeon and no one would ever hear from him again.

So, let all men of goodwill hope that David Steadman lived up to his reputation for cunning and courage, damn his soul.

XV

NOVEMBER 4, 1941

Getting into the Third Reich was almost as hard as getting out. At one point, the waters separating Sweden and Germany were only about sixty miles wide—a night's journey there and back for some fisherman who wanted to make a fast few thousand kronor—but try finding a boat.

"Denmark is easy," Steadman was told. "We do a brisk business with Denmark. We can drop you off any night you like, and the Germans will never know the difference."

Steadman shook his head. "No, it has to be Germany."

He had worked it out: There was no land route out of Denmark except through Germany anyway, so Denmark would just mean one more border crossing. He had no papers, and after he bribed his way across he would have very little money—none, really; what good would Swedish kronor be to him? And the only other currency he had was a few British pound notes. He didn't know a word of Danish. It was just too many risks. It had to be Germany, provided he could get anyone to take him.

Gjesling scratched at the bare scalp under his woolen seaman's cap, and a worried expression came into his pale blue eyes. He didn't much like it.

"The Germans patrol those waters," he said, his thin, strong face puckered with worry. "And the winds through there at night can be pretty bad—of course, we could always go out in broad daylight and do some fishing. You know, let the patrols get used to us. Then maybe we could slip through and I could be home in my bed by three or four in the morning. But a risk like that, it'll cost you plenty."

Steadman took out his wallet, extracted the entire contents, and spread them out on the table in Gjesling's galley.

"That's it. That's all I have. You can have that, and this." He took off the gold-mounted wristwatch his stepfather had given him for his fifteenth birthday and set it on top of the notes. "That cleans me out. Will you do it for that, yes or no?"

Gjesling considered for a moment and then nodded. He wasn't a bad man. His family was Norwegian, so he was no lover of the Nazis, but most people have to have a motive to take chances. Steadman couldn't really blame him.

They started out the next morning at dawn.

Gjesling had been one of the fortuitous discoveries, one of those rare pieces of luck that you learned to push for everything they were worth. Steadman had taken the train all the way to the end of the line, to a city called Helsingborg, and then caught a bus south. There wasn't very much south of Helsingborg, and when he had run out of the conviction that he was doing himself any good by touring, he had gotten out at a fishing town called Skanör. He bought himself lunch and then took a stroll down by the dock.

He didn't have anything clearly in mind; he was just window-shopping. He was no sailor. He didn't imagine he could manage to get across the Baltic Straits by himself, even if he did manage to steal a boat and evade the Swedish shore patrol. And he didn't have a clue about how he could find someone he could trust not to sell him out to the Germans as soon as they cleared land. It was a bad situation.

And then he saw a man sitting on a wooden box in the stern of a fishing smack, repairing a net that was spread out over his legs like an invalid's blanket. The boat was tied up, but it rose and fell with the swell of the tide, and traces of gasoline smeared the water in the berth. There was a paper sign on the side of the cabin, like a public notice. Since it was in Swedish, Steadman didn't have any idea what it could mean. He decided to take a chance anyway.

"You interested in renting this boat?" he asked in English, pointing to the sign.

"That sign says I must sell it. I owe money to the bank for it."

The man's hands never stopped working on the net that covered his lap in folds, and as he looked at Steadman he wasn't so much smiling as squinting into the sun. He didn't have anything more to add, but the tilt of his head suggested that he was still listening.

"How much?"

"Two thousand three hundred kronor."

"I have nearly that in my pocket. I'll ask you again—are you interested in a charter?"

So they cut their deal.

"You can sleep here tonight," Gjesling told him, pointing to a roll of blankets at the foot of a plank bed in the narrow little ship's cabin. "It will be safer and will cost you nothing."

Which was a nice way of saying that he didn't want Steadman wasting money he already looked upon as his own.

"In the morning I'll bring some clothes. If the Germans stop us, it's better just to pretend you work on the boat than to try hiding you. You look like a Viking anyway." He grinned, and with a deft movement threw the net into a corner of the stern.

After he left, Steadman began opening drawers and looking into boxes, trying to find the first-aid kit. As soon as he had turned up a small piece of oilcloth as well, he took out the letter—that ghastly document for which his life was now little more than a vehicle—wrapped it in two thicknesses of the oilcloth, sealed it shut, and attached it along the side of his rib cage with four strips of surgical tape. If he was going for a sea voyage, he wanted to keep the goods safe and dry.

When he tried to stretch out on the plank bed, he discovered that it was about six inches too short.

He had a heavy black sweater and a knitted cap, and a pair of cotton work gloves to hide his hands. "Nobody who looks at your hands will believe you are a sailor," Gjesling told him, and he was probably right. When they started out the harbor was blanketed in fog.

"Why does anybody want to escape *into* Germany these days?"

It was a good question, and Steadman told him the story he had made up the night before, lying there in the dark galley, listening to the waves against the wharf pilings. It was a good story, full of telling little details, about how his girlfriend, who was half Jewish, had been arrested and he was desperate to get her out. The girlfriend lived in Magdeburg, and a cousin had written to him to America. The Germans had denied him a visa, so he had to get in illegally. He had worked out all the angles.

"If she's really been arrested, I don't know what you'll be able to do," Gjesling commented. He was a practical man and saw the problem from that point of view, but apparently it hadn't occurred to him that it might all be just a story. "They've probably taken her to a concentration camp, and you'll never be able to get her out of there. We hear stories about what's happening. It's a shame."

"I have to try anyway," Steadman answered, feeling just a little ashamed of his sham nobility. He was thinking of Karen, wondering what she made of her knight errant these days, wondering if she was back in England and if she . . .

Gjesling only shrugged his shoulders.

"I'm glad I'm no longer a young man," he said.

It was a little short of two in the afternoon, and they were lying in quiet water, when they saw the first German patrol boat.

There was a wind that was slowly driving them farther and farther out into the gulf, but they were nowhere near the zone within which the Germans felt themselves free to stop and search. The boat was larger than Steadman had imagined, low in the water and sleek. He saw it as gray, but really at that distance, and in the light fog that still hung over the water, it could have been any color. He could feel someone's field glasses on them for a moment as the Germans slowed to have a look, and then they were gone.

"They'll be back in a few hours to see if we've moved," Gjesling said, the flat of his hand shading his eyes as he watched the patrol boat disappear. "We'll just drift with the current. They'll decide we're harmless and forget all about us. They aren't such bad ones in the navy."

It was a bitterly cold day. The fog seeped right through your clothes and you felt as if you were standing there naked. Steadman couldn't remember ever having been so uncomfortable in his life, not even in Spain. To kill the time he let Gjesling teach him how to patch nets.

And, sure enough, three hours later the German patrol boat was back.

"See? What did I tell you." Gjesling grinned, showing a gold-capped tooth in his upper jaw. He stopped grinning when the Germans made it obvious that this time they were coming in for a closer look.

"HALT!"

The German captain was standing on his bridge with a megaphone. You would have imagined that even he could have seen the command was unnecessary—they hadn't been under power for several hours. Steadman continued fiddling with the net. It wasn't the first time he had been looked over by an enemy sentry.

There was a sailor standing amidships, cradling a machine gun, which he was very careful not to point at anyone, in the crook of his arm. He was only about seventeen and looked scared to death. The only other crewman visible was small and thirtyish, with rimless spectacles that suggested a village schoolmaster. He stood beside the captain and acted as interpreter, and since the captain was one of those officers who couldn't seem to speak below a bark Steadman had no trouble following at least the German end of the transmission.

"The *Kapitän* would like to inquire if you are disabled and request assistance," the schoolmaster shouted, although the two boats were now no more than twenty to twenty-five feet apart. Gjesling smiled and shook his head, explaining that they were just getting ready to lay out their nets. The two men seemed to be on excellent terms, so probably this wasn't their first encounter. Steadman kept his head bent sullenly over his work, trying to give the impression of complete indifference. He had taken his gloves off to manage the nets. His face wasn't tanned enough. They were sure to spot something wrong. That kid with the machine gun gave him the fantods.

"The *Kapitän* says it must be taking you a long time. We were by three hours ago and still you have your nets aboard."

The schoolmaster pointed to Steadman, whose legs were covered with them. It was a good point. He was curious to see how Gjesling would answer.

Gjesling merely smiled again—or, rather, since it was the same smile, made it a little broader—and followed the Germans' gaze to where Steadman was sitting on the well cover. He said something, and the schoolmaster nodded and laughed. There was a translation and then the captain laughed. Steadman forced himself to assume a slow, bashful grin—it seemed as if he had fouled the nets putting them away the night before, but what could you expect from a landlubber? He was Gjesling's cousin, fresh off the farm.

Over the prow of the German boat, the sun was already glowing like an ember on the waterline. In an hour it would be dark as the inside of a rock. The captain looked at the lurid pink horizon and then turned back to Gjesling and smiled.

"It's getting late," he shouted in German. "Home for supper." And then he laughed. They all laughed, one after the other, in rotation, even if they were presumed not to have understood a word.

In five minutes the Germans were gone. You couldn't even hear their engines.

"Their base is in Denmark," Gjesling said tensely. The episode seemed to have sobered him considerably, so that now he was like a man under fire. "We'll wait half an hour, and then head south. I don't mind telling you, I'll be glad when this is over."

It was after nine-thirty when they first spotted the lights of the German coast. There weren't many; this didn't seem to be a very densely populated area. They looked to be about two miles distant.

They were running without any lights of their own, and Steadman wondered about rocks. He wondered about whether anyone on shore would be able to hear the sound of their engine. He wondered what the hell he was going to do when he got on shore, a hundred and fifty miles from Hamburg and without a brass farthing.

Gjesling was on his bridge, managing the wheel with a set, grim expression on his face.

Gradually the lights began to drift away. They were running parallel to the coast now, leaving the inhabited part behind them. The moon was about three quarters full and cast a sheen on the tops of the black waves. Finally Gjesling cut the engine and disappeared into his cabin. When he returned there was a huge, old-fashioned army revolver in his hand.

"We're close enough," he said. "I want you over the side."

In those first few seconds, Steadman had the brassy taste of fear in his mouth. He couldn't move, he couldn't think. He could only see the muzzle of Gjesling's revolver and wonder what the bullet would feel like when it went tearing through his right lung. He could feel where the letter was taped to his rib cage; it was like the bull's eye of a target.

And then he wondered why he was so goddamned surprised, and when he was finally going to grow up and learn that this was the way the world was organized. What other sort of send-off had he expected, a bouquet of flowers and a kiss? Gjesling was thinking about Gjesling. He didn't give a damn whether his passenger landed safely, just so long as he could turn around and go home to his nice safe bed in Skanör. Such was life.

For a moment Steadman considered rushing him—he was calm now, scared but calm, and his mind was operating again, which was what mattered. The idea had a lot to recommend it: They weren't more than a few feet apart, and most people weren't ready to shoot from one second to the next. He thought perhaps he could make it without catching a bullet, but what then?

Probably Gjesling had been thinking about rocks too, and it wasn't going to make Steadman's escape any easier if there was a smashed-up boat on the beach tomorrow morning. The police would start wondering what it had been doing there, and where the crew was. And it was possible Gjesling might get a shot off. Even if he missed, the report might be enough to bring somebody out for a look. It wasn't worth the risks.

"That water is ice cold. How far will I have to swim?"

"About two hundred meters."

"If I make it I'll be half dead, with nowhere to crawl in out of the cold. All you'd have to do would be to turn on your running lights for a few seconds and maybe we could find a pier or something."

"I can't risk it." Gjesling's voice was tight, and his hand seemed to be shaking as it held the revolver. It was possible he was nerving himself up to shoot. "I've done all I can for you. From here on you'll have to take your chances."

"How do I know it isn't four hundred meters? Or five? Turn on your lights for a moment so I can at least get a look at the shore."

"Would you rather I just shot you now?"

Put that way, it wasn't much of a choice. With the hopelessness of a condemned criminal, Steadman glanced down at his shoes, wondering if he should take them off, if they would drag him down in the water. What the hell, he decided: he was probably going to drown anyway, and he couldn't fancy wandering around in the dark and cold in his bare feet. He would keep them.

"So long, pal," he said, stepping up onto the rail. "Thanks for nothing."

In the first second after he hit the water, he thought perhaps it had already killed him. It was so cold that when he broke back to the surface he could hardly force himself to breathe, and every muscle in his body felt as if it were cramping up. He hurt everywhere. How the hell was he going to swim any two hundred meters in this stuff?

One stroke at a time, it would seem. One stroke at a time.

It was several seconds before he even remembered about the boat, and by then it was already pulling away.

Which direction was the shore? Everything was uniformly black around him; there wasn't a thing to stop him from swimming straight back out into the gulf. He could just swim and swim, until he sank with exhaustion. The bullet wound in his arm felt like it was burning, and some salt water had gone down the wrong way. He didn't think he had ever been so frightened in his life.

Come on, Davey, pull yourself together. Start thinking or you really will peg out.

A wave came up and slapped him in the face. As he tried to wipe the water out of his eyes it occurred to him that the waves would be going toward the shore. He twisted himself around in that direction and tried to focus. Sure enough, he could make out slight variations in the dark gray that was almost black—there was a landfall in front of him. He forced himself to take a deep breath and kicked off.

Everything hurt. His arms and legs weighed him down like lead. He would swim a few strokes and then coast, letting the waves break over him, and then push himself on a little farther. Every once in a while he would let his legs drop down and feel for the bottom with his toes. It was never there. Then he would try to find the shore again, with its broken lines of gray against gray, and swim on. All the while he couldn't get over the idea that for all he could do perhaps the tide was pulling him farther and farther out to sea, that he might as well just give up and let it happen.

It wasn't very long before he discovered that his fingers were getting numb. He could feel the cold, but that was about all. His hands were like flippers, stiff and useless, and there was a line of burning pain that kept creeping higher and higher up his arms—he felt as if they were being cut away from him a slice at a time.

I'll die pretty soon like this, he thought. I'll freeze up and drown and not even know that it's happening to me.

Finally he was sure he couldn't make another yard. He would just lie there, he decided, and if he drowned then he drowned. He found it hard to give a damn.

Slowly his legs drifted down in the water. He could hardly feel them anymore; they were just weights at the other end of his body. It wouldn't be much longer before he was sucked under completely. The idea no longer appalled him very much.

What was that? His foot seemed to catch on something—he felt it the way you feel something you touch with the end of a stick. He wondered what the hell it could be.

And then he realized that the edge of his shoe was scraping back and forth against the sand. He was touching bottom. He couldn't be more than a few dozen yards from shore.

It seemed stupid and pointless and—yes—a little cowardly to let himself die when he could probably save himself with a few kicks. He still had that much left in him. He really ought to try. He really ought.

One hand over the other, he started to drag himself forward through the water. It was slow going—his arms felt as if they were made out of bread dough and weighed a hundred pounds apiece—and at first it didn't seem to make any difference. He wasn't going anywhere. But then his legs started to float up again. Some salt water went up his nose, and he tried to spit it out. He tried to kick his legs. At least he wasn't sinking anymore.

Whether it was his own efforts or merely the tide he would never know, but pretty soon he found the water was only chest deep. He could walk then, just allow himself to be pushed forward by the waves. When he staggered onto the beach he forced himself to keep going until he was above the waterline, and then he fell to his knees and then over on his face. It just wasn't in him to move any farther. He would have to wait until he could catch his breath.

Everything was clear enough in the moonlight. He didn't even have to turn his head; he could see the shingle beach stretching up to where it met the foot of a sandy bluff. He could even make out the grass growing on the edge of the bluff, waving faintly in the sea breeze like the fringed border of a shawl. He was alive. What the hell, he was alive.

But he wasn't likely to stay that way if he didn't get moving. He was freezing cold, colder even than he had been in the water, but at least he could feel it. He wasn't numb anymore. But if he allowed himself to lie there much longer he wouldn't be able to move and the numbness would come back. He had to get the blood pumping through his arms and legs. He had to move.

By the time he had scrambled up to the foot of the bluff, which mercifully was only about four feet high, he was convinced he was going to be all right. Everything ached with cold, but the very pain was a kind of guarantee against dying of exposure. Now all he had to do was to get in out of the wind somewhere.

The ground was waste, as far as he could make out. Nobody had even bothered to put a fence up anywhere. He couldn't see a light. He couldn't see anything that told him that there were human beings anywhere around. But there had to be lights—he had seen them from Gjesling's boat. He had seen them from the right-hand side, so now, with his back to the sea, if he headed right he should find them. Anyway, it was a direction.

His clothes, naturally, were wet through and hung clammily against his body. But he couldn't go naked; at least this way there was something between him and the wind. He wondered what he would do if he caught pneumonia. He could hardly check into a hospital in the middle of Hitler's Thousand Year Reich, not without papers or money. He couldn't even rent a hotel room. He ran both hands backward over his head to squeeze the water out.

He had no idea how far he had walked before he saw the first light.

It was the window of a farmhouse. The people inside were probably just getting ready for bed. Without thinking, Steadman glanced down to check the time and then remembered that bastard Gjesling had his wristwatch. But probably it wasn't much later than eleven—the last hour had only seemed like an eternity. Still, farming people were normally long since asleep by this hour.

No, it wasn't a farmhouse. It was a barn. Finally, there was a split-rail fence, and Steadman could see clearly where he was. There was a plowed field and then a little cluster of buildings, and the one with the light in it was much too large to be anything except a barn.

He crouched down next to the clapboard wall and listened, but there wasn't a sound from inside. The window was too high up for him to reach. Now, resting still beside the wall, he felt the cold worse than ever. He had to get inside, even if it meant killing somebody to do it. He reached down inside his trouser leg, which was stiff with cold and salt, and closed his fingers around the haft of his knife. Those people in the barn had never done him any harm, but if it was going to be him or them it was going to be them. He was beginning to shiver uncontrollably.

He started working his way around to the front entrance, trying not to stumble. He might have the knife, but just then he didn't feel he would be much of a match for anybody. There just wasn't any choice.

When he got to the corner of the building he threw himself down on the ground, burying his head in his arms. The doors were squeaking on their hinges and three or four men were coming out, talking softly among themselves as if they were great respecters of the night's quiet. They hadn't seen him—why should they? Their minds were elsewhere. One of them closed the doors behind them, not bothering to swing the crossbar into place. There had been a death in the family.

He couldn't pick up more than a few snatches, but sometimes the tone of voice is more eloquent than any words. And then there were the silences. The bereavement was almost palpable.

He watched them trudging across the empty yard to the farmhouse, one of them, a little broader across the back than the others, swinging a gasoline lantern down by his knee, and his eyes filled with tears. He didn't even know why. He was tired and cold and the world was a scene of suffering, that was probably why. He didn't know why anyone troubled to go on living.

When they were gone, and he could no longer even see the glimmer of a light through the farmhouse windows, Steadman got up and slipped in through the barn doors.

It was impossibly dark inside, except for a single broad beam of moonlight that streamed in through a window. It fell on an open stall, where a black colt, its spindly legs hardly thicker than a broom handle, was lying on a bed of hay. Its eye was glassy and half closed; it was quite dead. That was what had kept those men up past bedtime and thus possibly saved Steadman's life.

There was a horse blanket draped over the side of the stall. It was half an inch thick and rough as a board, but who the hell cared? He took it down and started feeling around for the ladder into the hayloft. City boy that he was, he knew about haylofts.

It was warm inside. There was a pleasant smell of something like ammonia in the air. He found a place between two bales of something wrapped in burlap, stripped off his clothes, and wrung them out. He could hear the water dripping on the loft floor. Then he wrapped himself in the horse blanket and lay down, pressing his back against the burlap. He was asleep almost at once.

XVI

He was drowning. He could feel the water closing over his head. It was pouring down his nostrils, hot as burning gasoline, and there wasn't anything he could do except wake up.

The barn was quiet. He didn't have any idea what time it was. He was shivering, and his face felt hot. He was in big trouble.

Gradually, after he had sat up and was pulling the blanket around his shoulders to fight the chill, he could hear a few disconnected sounds that managed to dispel the lingering suspicion that he was still dreaming, or had gone off his head with fever. A horse's hoof clicked against a stall floor, the wind whispered through the chinks in the hayloft wall. He put his hands over his face and was surprised at how cold they were.

His shirt and trousers were still damp, and his shoes were sodden and clammy. That would be priority number one: He had to get a dry change of clothes. Then he had to get some food. Then he had to get the hell out of there.

There was a loft door through which, presumably, they brought in the hay; it was fastened shut from the inside with a metal latch. You opened it a crack and you had a pretty good view of the farmhouse and the whole yard. There was a second building that looked like a kind of dormitory—at least there were curtains on the windows and the front door was newly painted; nobody would go to that kind of trouble with a tack room. The shadows on the ground suggested it might already be the middle of the morning, so Steadman figured he'd been asleep a full twelve hours. He must have needed it.

People worked on farms. They didn't lie around in the bunkhouse reading back issues of the *National Geographic*. So maybe, if he could sneak over there without being seen, Steadman figured he might be able to raid the place for something to wear. Of course, the problem was to find out whether anyone was at home in the farmhouse.

There was no cover. Nowhere. He would have to walk straight across the yard, big as life. There were windows around all four sides of the farmhouse, so all someone would have to do was to be in the wrong room at the wrong time and happen to turn his head . . .

And then Steadman noticed a length of stovepipe peeking over the edge of the roofline on the other side of the building. There was a thin trickle of smoke beginning to sneak out from beneath the little cone-shaped cap that kept out the rainwater. Someone was starting to cook lunch.

And if you're cooking lunch on one side of a house, you can't see who's walking around the other.

Steadman climbed down from the loft, holding on to the ladder for dear life. He was still feeling shaky and feverish, and he didn't seem to have much strength left. His shoulder wound, he noticed, had opened up again and the blood was oozing thickly into his shirt.

During the course of the morning, someone must have come in and taken away the dead colt, because the stall was empty.

The yard was hard-packed earth, so no one heard him. No dogs came out and barked at him. There weren't any screams from the second-story windows. The bunkhouse door wasn't even locked. Well, it wouldn't be.

There were four beds inside, and a couple of wardrobes about the size of packing cases. A number of elliptical rag rugs punctuated the floor. It was all very homey. Steadman began going through the wardrobes, hoping somebody was his size.

He had to pick in odd lots: one fellow's shirts were about right, but his legs were too short. Finally he managed everything, even a jacket and a hat, but the shoes were hopeless. His feet were simply too damn large; he had had the same problem over and over again in Spain. He would have to keep the pair he had.

As he was buttoning up the heavy woolen jacket he had found draped over the back of a chair, he experienced a moment of terrible misgiving and reached inside his shirt to pull the letter free from his chest. With trembling fingers he unwrapped the oilcloth, unfolded the single sheet of paper, and turned it this way and that, checking both the back and front. It was all right, the oilcloth had kept out the Baltic. He folded it back up and put it in the jacket pocket.

When he was finished, he rolled his old clothes up in a bundle and stuck them away at the bottom of a drawer. There wasn't any money or anything like that he could use, but at the back of one of the wardrobes he found a small bottle of something that was probably the local version of white lightning. Steadman decided he would take that too.

It wouldn't be more than a couple of hours after they got back from their work, certainly no later than tomorrow morning, before these people discovered that they had been robbed. That meant Steadman didn't dare spend another night in the barn. His little dip the previous evening had chilled him right through, and if he wasn't very careful he would end up dead in a ditch somewhere—he was feeling pretty peaked as it was— but he had to get out of there or he would find himself in the hands of the Gestapo. There just wasn't any third choice.

It would have been nice to have gotten something to eat, though.

He was starting from scratch. It was like being born naked into the world all over again, only this time there was no mother and no millionaire father to cushion him against the shock.

He had nothing to think about now but the letter—that was the single imperative. He had considered simply dropping it in the mail while he was in Sweden, but the document itself meant almost nothing unless he was there himself to see it reached the proper hands and to explain how he had got it. By itself, it was too easily dismissed—such things were probably forged every day, and this wasn't anything anyone wanted to believe—but if he could deliver it in person he could serve as a kind of hostage to its authenticity. After all, there was probably some law against crying wolf about enemy attacks; they could throw him in the jug if it turned out he was lying. And with a living witness, they might not have the nerve to just sit back and do nothing.

He would get his brother Carl to fix it for him. Carl was now board chairman and principal stockholder of Steadman Tool and Die, and a very important man in Republican politics. Carl was a carbon copy of their father—he was an isolationist and hated Roosevelt with the pure passion a godly man should reserve for sin, but Carl was his best bet. Nobody, not even a president of the United States, had ever succeeded in ignoring Carl.

So all he, David Steadman, that feckless adventurer, had to concern himself with was getting away from Europe with his skin.

And he had plans toward that end, if he could just contrive to live so long. If he made it as far as Lisbon, all he had to do was to send a cable and help would be on its way.

Arsène Vidocq owed him, and Arsène Vidocq was the kind of man who didn't say no when you called in that sort of a debt. Arsène would come to Lisbon if he had to swim.

The man was a wonder with counterfeit papers and that sort of nonsense. He would bring money—he would bring an army if he had to. It would be all right if Steadman could just make it as far as Lisbon.

He got up from where he had been sitting on one of the beds and checked front and back through the windows to make sure no one was in evidence and that smoke was still rising from the kitchen chimney before he retraced his steps back to the barn. There was nothing there he particularly wanted, but the barn itself would screen his departure. There had been a road out there last night, running along the split-rail fence, and a road had to lead somewhere. He didn't even have any very definite idea about where along the German coast he was, so one direction was as good as another. From here on it was strictly potluck.

By the middle of the afternoon he had walked far enough to have escaped any indication that he was near the sea. The salt tang on the wind had been submerged in the smells of turned earth and meadow grass, and he couldn't even feel the damp. He had met no one on the road, and there didn't seem to be any signs. His fever wasn't any better, and he was near the end of his strength. He had come about ten miles.

It was going to rain in an hour or so. The sky was precisely the color of lead, and at the horizon black clouds were boiling up, ready to sweep over the smooth landscape like spilled paint. It was a matter of urgency now to find somewhere in out of the weather.

There was a building up ahead, the first one Steadman had seen since before noon. It was simply a dark speck in the distance—it could have been anything from a palace to a tool shed: he didn't even know how far away it was—but it was something to fix on. He started counting his steps.

It was the only thing he remembered from high school Latin. Caesar's legions had measured everything in *milia passuum*, which was supposed to be a hundred or so yards short of a mile. Every time the right foot struck the ground . . . It was something to occupy him, a little vacation from thinking about how much his bones ached or how his face felt like it was on fire. He could be sick anytime. The opportunity would still be there when he had finished.

He stopped counting after twelve hundred paces.

What he had seen as one building was actually two, the second a little behind the first but painted the same blinding white. There was a house and a garage—or what looked like a garage, since the doors were the right size. The house was remarkably small and even from the outside gave the impression of having been designed for maximum efficient use of space. You wondered what the builder could have been worried about, since there seemed to be all the room in the world.

Steadman decided there was nothing to be gained by being cagey. He went straight up to the front door, rehearsing in his mind the story he had prepared. He had been fired from his farming job—he hadn't been much good as a farmhand, but he was afraid of being drafted into the army—and now he was on his way home. The night before he had slept out in the open, where he had both caught cold and gotten robbed. It was a story calculated to be believed. People were always ready to believe you when you put yourself in an unflattering light. He was from the south, around Munich, which would account for the difference in his accent.

Except that there was nobody home to listen to it. He knocked at the door, waited, knocked again, waited . . . As he stood on the porch the first large, widely spaced drops of rain came down; he could hear them hitting the roof, clicking like fingerpops. Steadman gave the door a kick directly under the knob, and it sprang open as if it had been waiting for him.

The first thing he found was a snug little kitchen—a tiled floor, pretty yellow wallpaper, a small round table covered with oilcloth—and the first thing he did was to start looking for something to eat. What he found was a couple of tins of canned meat, half a dozen hardtack biscuits in a paper sack, and—rarity of rarities—a carton of loose tea with about four spoonfuls left inside. Now, if he could just swing some hot water . . .

There was an old-fashioned handpump water sluice by the sink. He tried it a few times and finally managed to produce a trickle. He wondered if he dared start a fire going.

It was a coal stove, and he was some time getting it to light. He just couldn't resist it. He wanted to be warm, inside and out, and there wasn't another house around for as far as he could see. He needed some time to recover himself. He needed that stove going.

After he had eaten the canned meat and the biscuits and drunk the tea, he took the heavy crockery mug he had been using and filled it halfway with the liquor he had stolen that morning, topping it up with hot water from an iron kettle. It tasted like nailpolish remover, but in

Spain the conventional wisdom had been that hot water and Moroccan rum could bake out any fever short of mortal. When he had it about a quarter down, he gathered up the kettle and his booze and went upstairs—the other side of the cure was a warm bed.

This seemed to be his lucky day. In the larger of the two upstairs rooms he found the genuine article, the sort of bed that was always featured prominently in dirty jokes. A massive oak double, a regular four-poster. In a closet he found pillows and a thick down-filled comforter. He was set.

He lay down, propping himself up with some pillows, listening to the springs creak, wondering how many men and women had had it out together on this ancient plain of battle. The varnish on the footboard was darkened with age and covered with a fine spiderweb of cracks like an unrestored Rembrandt. In a bed like this marriage must be a solid, tangible comfort, like roast beef or the *Times* crossword puzzle.

Steadman poured himself another mug of hot water and hooch, and by the time he was finished with it he was beginning to sweat pleasantly. He was relaxed and suddenly rather melancholy, so he assumed he was probably getting just a little tight.

His mind returned by a kind of natural inertia to Karen Windermere.

There wasn't going to be any big oak four-poster in their future. They had had a couple of nights together in borrowed rooms, but that was going to be the end of it.

For a while he had persuaded himself that Bertie might have been brought to allowing her a nice quiet divorce—he was giving the pretty definite impression that he had lost interest, so he might not have minded. But Steadman didn't have to look very far to know that was all garbage, because neither he nor Karen could have brought themselves to go up there to that haunted hall in Kent and ask him. It would have been like stealing the casters off somebody's wheelchair.

So the whole thing, the whole charming, longed-for interlude had been a blind alley from the start, even before he had gotten curious in that Swedish coffee shop and had had his peek into Hitler's mailbag. Falling in love just didn't pay anymore.

But he couldn't help himself. All he could think about was how pretty Karen Windermere had been that first afternoon when she had poured him a cup of tea and handed him a little plate of cookies.

"So you've taken the Wildfell cottage?" she had asked, smiling that kind, soft smile that said, *We must say something, mustn't we? We don't always have to stay strangers.* She had been wearing an ivory blouse with long sleeves and ruffles around the neckline, and she had seemed an angel to him. He could hardly speak.

And then, when Bertie had gone into the drink, Steadman had driven her up to the hospital and sat outside with her while they waited for the doctor to come out and report on the damage.

"He'll be all right, won't he, David?" She had pressed up beside him on that narrow wooden bench and held his hands in both of hers as if she were afraid that to let go was to lose everything. "He's lasted all this time, so it can't be too awful, can it?"

"No—I'm sure he'll be good as new."

And all the while, David Steadman, friend of the family, was eaten up inside with love and guilt in about equal proportions because, of course, he knew that the net had closed around him a long time ago.

He was getting very drunk; he knew that too. In a minute, if he wasn't careful, he would start to sniffle like a baby. The only dignified thing left to do was to fall into a stupor before he had a chance to disgrace himself utterly, so he poured what was left of the white lightning into his mug, diluted it down with a splash from the kettle, and drank it off like so much lemonade. After about fifteen seconds, he began to feel it, the immediate answer to all his little psychological discomforts, coursing through him like novocaine. He closed his eyes and dropped off to sleep.

When he woke up, the first thing he saw was the fierce sliver of sunlight that ran across the carpeted floor like some sort of flaw in the design. The second thing he saw was the guy standing in the bedroom doorway. He was much more interesting because he had a shotgun threaded through his arm. He didn't look very pleased.

"Who are you?" Steadman asked, gratified with himself for having had the presence of mind to put the question into German.

"I think that is for you to answer," the man said. He was a big, dark brute in a blue seaman's coat and a pair of badly wrinkled corduroy trousers. He was wearing a billed cap that somehow made his forehead look prehistorically low over a face that seemed hewn out of hardwood with an axe, and he hadn't shaved that morning. His eyes glittered like cheap glass.

Steadman began to make a few tentative moves toward getting out of bed—more to see how they were received by his visitor than because he wanted to go anywhere. He liked it in bed. It was warm there, and he knew that when he got up he was going to have to kill this joker, or get killed himself, and neither alternative was very attractive. Somehow the fellow didn't look as if he would take the attempt in a spirit of disinterested sportsmanship.

"You just stay there," he said, raising the muzzle of his shotgun a few degrees to punctuate the sentence. Steadman sank almost gratefully back against the feather pillows. "You broke the back door. You come here to rob the place?"

"No, I came to get in out of the rain, and because I was sick and needed to lie down."

"You don't look sick."

"I got better."

The man nodded, but there was nothing in the gesture that suggested any willingness to believe. He had heard, that was all.

"I look after the property here," he volunteered, quite unnecessarily, since he was the one with the shotgun. "The people live in Bremen—they come for the summers. They pay me to check that everything is all right."

"Everything is fine. I just took a little food, that was all. A man has a right to save his life."

"You broke the door too." He nodded again. He was like someone going over a checklist. Each item seemed to tally for him.

Certain things were obvious, even then. The first was that this guy had decided he wasn't going to shoot anybody, at least not that very minute. He wasn't going to plaster the bedroom walls with hair and brains; he was probably going to take Steadman outside, and there he would see about finishing him off. The corollary was obvious: Steadman had between the bed and the staircase to jump him, or he was going to end up cold meat.

The second thing was that the son of a bitch was lying.

Who ever heard of a watchman checking in at the crack of dawn? Hell, it probably wasn't much after five-thirty in the morning. And why should he bring a gun with him? If you want to stop burglars you don't come in the morning, you come at night. And if you don't want to stop burglars you don't bring a gun.

Besides, Steadman figured, if I had property to watch, would I hire this mug? It would be like engaging Alistair Crowley as the village parson.

"I worked on a farm around here," he said, falling in with his cover story. "I got fired."

"Oh, yes—I think maybe I seen you around somewhere." The shotgun muzzle lowered maybe an inch, and the hacked-out, glittering eyes narrowed in what was probably supposed to be a smile of sudden recognition.

Steadman again began to lift himself from the pillows, crooking his leg so that he could get at his knife under cover of the down comforter. He slid the haft up his sleeve until he could grasp the thick edge of the blade between thumb and first finger. This place probably had a basement, and he didn't want to be invited down there.

"You saw the smoke, didn't you." Steadman forced himself to grin.

"Last night, you saw the smoke from the kitchen chimney and you decided you'd come for a look. Why didn't you come then?"

"My wife, she . . ." He didn't continue. This wasn't a clever man, and you could tell he knew he had said more than he should have.

"She wouldn't have approved? Probably not."

It was like an understanding between them. They both knew why he had waited, and why he had brought the gun with him. Somebody new was in the empty house, probably someone from the city who could be counted on to sleep late in the morning, probably someone with money, since everyone from the city had money. So this one, who was not clever but who owned a shotgun, had crept out of bed a little earlier than usual, taking with him the shotgun he probably kept wrapped in an oily bedsheet in a closet. He thought no one would notice if it was gone for a few hours—he would put the gun back when he returned home for his lunch. No one would remember when a stranger or two were found murdered in the basement of a house that was only occupied in the summers, and he would have the money from their wallets and their jewelry and watches. He could hide them somewhere and sell them off when everyone had forgotten. It was the kind of crime that would attract a certain sort of man.

The trick was to get beyond the muzzle of the gun, so that even if it went off all the pellets would go harmlessly into the wall. Steadman had been zinged once already in the past few days, and he had an unpleasant impression that he might not get away this time with just a messy surface scratch. He didn't want to be chewed to pieces with number-nine birdshot.

"You come downstairs with me," the man said, frowning suddenly. He made a short sweeping motion with the shotgun barrel. "You don't give me any trouble. You shouldn't be here."

You neither, pal. But Steadman got up, swinging his legs over the edge of the bed, taking his time about it like a man who wakes up in the morning with a thousand little sore places in his muscles and joints, a man who couldn't execute a sudden movement without snapping in two. His friend with the shotgun stepped a little out of the doorway to make room for him, lowering the muzzle—it was the sort of little courtesy that was simply a matter of reflex—so it wouldn't be in the way. In that instant he gave Steadman his one and only chance.

They were about seven feet apart, which Steadman reduced down to five by the simple expediency of standing up. He took a step toward the door and then allowed his left leg to collapse underneath him; it was just ambiguous enough a movement that the other man didn't know quite how to react, and it brought Steadman that extra few feet.

He reached out and grabbed at the barrel of the shotgun with his left hand. He didn't have a good hold, and the thing almost jerked itself free as it went off. The sound was deafening in that enclosed space—it could even have been both barrels at once. Steadman let the knife drop into his hand and struck out for whatever he could get, which turned out to be the man's leg, just an inch or so above the knee.

It was astonishing how quickly people can react when they find themselves with a knife blade sticking into their thigh. This one stiffened up straight, almost snapping to attention. It was easy to take him down then. Steadman just pushed forward from where he was crouched and hit him in the legs like a football tackle. After that it was nothing but a wrestling match.

The shotgun was forgotten. Everything was forgotten as the man struggled in a blind panic to defend himself. He just wanted Steadman off him. He clawed like an animal. He pushed with the heels of his hands. He did everything but bite and spit. Steadman went for the face, bringing his palm straight down on the nose so that it split open like a grape. With the other hand, which his opponent was too busy to remember even existed, he carried the knife up to the jawline and jammed it in just at the crease above the larynx. He didn't stop pushing until the man went suddenly stiff, and then relaxed and was limply quiet. It was all over.

When you killed a man with a knife you were close enough to smell his last breath as his rib cage collapsed. There was a ghastly kind of intimacy about it. But there was no pleasure when your target was pouring his blood out over your hands and you could feel his dead fingers loosening their grip on your arm. It was something to which you might grow hardened, but which never entirely lost its capacity to unnerve and humiliate you, and to remind you that life's seeming suppleness was nothing but a cruel illusion.

Maybe the British were right. Maybe the smart thing was to let the Japanese launch their surprise attack. You kill a few thousand sailors and sink a few ships, and suddenly America is in the war and it's that much closer to being finished. Maybe in the long run they would pile up fewer corpses that way. He didn't know.

If by some miracle he ever got to New York alive, maybe he didn't know what he would finally do. Maybe, in the end, he would just take Herr Hitler's brotherly warning and use it for kindling. For the first time that occurred to him as a serious possibility, and it was a frightening idea. He didn't want to have that kind of power conferred on him. He preferred to be responsible only for those murders he had committed in his own person.

XVII

NOVEMBER 5, 1941

The night after he returned from Sweden, Weinschenk's wife asked him if he had heard anything recently of Ion Lupescu.

"I was planning on a small dinner this Friday, and I phoned several times. It's as if he's dropped off the face of the earth."

Weinschenk turned around from the door of their bedroom closet, where he was hanging up the spare suit he had taken with him on his trip, and looked at her. She was sitting on a low chair covered with dark pink velvet, in a cream negligee that suited her and was probably intended as part of his welcome home—Magda had a marvelous sense of the obvious—and it was clear that there was nothing of suspicion in her question.

The beauty of many southern women was of a type that faded early. Magda was now thirty, and she was beginning to collect a few faint lines around her mouth and eyes. In another five years she would be hard-featured, and then perhaps lovers like Ion Lupescu would be more difficult to acquire. Weinschenk tried to imagine that day, tried to imagine how he would feel when other men no longer wanted his wife, and decided that he would be glad. Because he would still love her, because then perhaps she would be grateful. Perhaps by then she would have learned to put some value on a constant heart.

But he wouldn't have to wait that long to be able to forget about Ion Lupescu. At that moment, Ion Lupescu was in Switzerland under the protection of the British. He had fled almost as soon as he had heard about von Abeken's suicide.

And who could blame him? In recent years, "suicide" had become a very flexible term. Some people received help.

Ion, not knowing whether his contact inside the Foreign Office had really blown his brains out or had died at the hands of some Gestapo interrogation team, had decided that it was a moment for discretion and had announced that he was taking a skiing vacation. Weinschenk was pleased on a number of accounts—for reasons personal and professional, the last thing he wanted was for the Rumanian third secretary to begin answering questions in a police dungeon.

But there was no thought of that now. Magda had cooked dinner tonight, which was unusual since lately she had grown to dislike domestic routine. She was making everything very agreeable. Perhaps she felt deserted by her lover and was trying to ingratiate herself back into the safety of marriage. Whatever the reason, Weinschenk was little disposed to complain. She had poured the wine with her very own white hand and had allowed him the special dispensation of a cigarette with his coffee. Probably not even Ion Lupescu, with all his oily Balkan charm, had been permitted to smoke in her presence.

And now, while he finished his unpacking and listened to the tinkle of a piano recital coming from the radio in another room, she had made it remarkably plain to him that she was prepared to see to it that he enjoyed himself tonight, if only he would. He watched the outline of her strong, elegant legs under the cream-colored silk and began the process of hypnotizing himself into believing that she might really still care for him after all, that perhaps there had never been any lovers, or that perhaps they had never really touched her heart.

It was only later, as he lay in bed, staring up at the dark ceiling and trying to hold fast to the illusion of a passionate happiness, that it occurred to him to wonder why suddenly Magda should have become so very solicitous of his inner comfort. It couldn't be something as simple as the disappearance of Lupescu—it couldn't be that.

She seemed to know somehow that the Stockholm venture had changed his prospects. She was trying to attach herself to that success, just as, all these years, she had tried to find other protectors. She was all compliance and easy sweetness. This was probably how she had treated her lovers.

But if she knew that he was now in the ascendancy, who had told her? Who else knew? Nebe?

Yes, Nebe?

In all respects, his return to Berlin had taken on something of the character of a triumphal procession. He seemed at one stroke to have regained everything: his sense of the significance of life, the attention of his wife, and the esteem of his superior. His victory over Nebe had been so total that the Obergruppenführer had actually sued for peace and offered himself as an ally. And all of this in spite of the fact that the Führer's letter to President Roosevelt was still lost and the American who had stolen it was still at dangerous liberty.

But the blame for all that had fallen on Aarenhold, who, it seemed, had proved simply too tempting a scapegoat for Nebe to resist.

"We shall have to have him shot," he had confided. He had even moved away from behind his desk, relinquishing the nimbus of the late-afternoon sunlight, to sit across from Weinschenk in a pair of chairs separated only by a small table. They had suddenly become colleagues. "The security arrangements in Stockholm were entirely in his charge, and he botched things disastrously. Besides, by now he knows too much. Sooner or later we shall have to shoot him. I've already issued orders for his recall, to be followed immediately by a telegram congratulating him on his promotion to Hauptmann—it wouldn't do if he decided to turn his coat."

"No, it wouldn't."

Nebe frowned, simultaneously raising his eyebrows in a curious admission of weakness. Obviously it hurt his vanity to have to sacrifice a protégé like this, but the Gruppenführer had very little choice; the lines that creased his high, white forehead conceded as much.

This was actually, Weinschenk realized all at once, the very first time he had ever had an opportunity to examine his immediate superior at such disarmingly close range. They didn't meet socially—at least, they hadn't thus far, although that seemed likely to change—and Nebe had never before withdrawn himself from the protection of his picture window. Besides, it wasn't considered good manners to look directly at a senior officer while one received one's orders. However, everything of that kind had changed.

It wasn't a very elevating study. The upholstery salesman was still quite visible in the SS colonel's uniform. Nebe had a domed skull bracketed on either side by long black hair swept back over slightly protruding ears, the effect of which was to emphasize his baldness. A short mustache, grown like everyone else's in imitation of the Führer and therefore without visible effect on his face, separated a long nose from a discontented mouth that looked like a fold in the skin. His eyes were light brown and restless. He seemed determined to be cordial, and the attitude didn't suit him.

Had Magda really taken up with this lout? It seemed past imagining.

"I suppose he's lost to us now," Nebe continued, with a faint shrug of his shoulders. "By now the British must surely have spirited this curious American of yours well out of our reach."

He seemed resigned to conceding that the venture had been a total loss. Weinschenk could only smile.

"I don't think so. He's playing some game of his own, I think. He wouldn't have tried to sell the letter back to us if he weren't. Why should he?"

And, in fact, Weinschenk expected the American to turn up at almost any moment—not in Berlin, of course, but somewhere. He would enter the territories under German control, and then it would simply be a matter of catching him.

Where else did he have to go? Weinschenk had checked, and the British had agents on every ship leaving Sweden. All they had to do was to receive a signal from one of them and, considering what was at stake, the Royal Navy wouldn't hesitate for a moment to stop a neutral vessel on the high seas to remove so significant a person.

Still, Weinschenk had been less than candid when he had said that his American had wanted to sell the letter. One develops a sense of a man, and this one was not mercenary. A mercenary would not take such appalling risks, and this man's history was an unbroken series of hazards.

So what did he want? And, more important, who was he? The first was a problem for deduction, the second for research.

The SS was very good at research. It had been easy enough to find out the American's name—even a photograph, although it was some nine years out of date.

"He speaks excellent German, but with a slight overlay of Swiss, I think." Weinschenk was from the south himself and therefore sensitive to that particular set of dialectical differences. He smiled, wishing to be believed but not wishing to claim anything for himself beyond the obvious. "He is tall and blond. Look through the school records. He must have learned early, and one couldn't pick up an accent like that in a week. There must be some trace of him somewhere. I'd put his age at thirty-one or -two."

The file clerk understood and nodded. They were all women, gray little things like field mice but susceptible to a certain amount of cultivation. Weinschenk had learned the value of having friends on all levels—dependents, people willing to do him favors in exchange for nylon stockings and cigarettes. This was how the Reich was actually governed.

And in an hour he had several choices, close to fifty. There had been no shortage of tall, blond Americans seeking the polish of an European education, and they liked to have themselves appear in official portraits. Perhaps this was a demand their relatives made of them. Weinschenk shuffled through a stack of glossy, curling photographs until he found one with a familiar face.

A young man, standing in the second row of a group of young men, looking slightly self-conscious with the arms of a tennis sweater tied loosely around his neck. Yes, it was him.

"Find out all you can about this one," Weinschenk said, drawing a circle in heavy ink around the familiar face. "See if there are other photographs."

There were none, but other information was by no means lacking. It seemed that on the basis of his Aryan appearance and his hereditary position in the international business community the SS had tried to recruit Mr. David Steadman as early as 1932. The Swiss Party organizations had invited him to meetings and courted him with persistence until it became clear that he wasn't interested in standing as the Gauleiter of Pittsburgh, Pennsylvania. Still, as a result they knew a great deal about him.

But the most important thing, as far as Weinschenk was concerned, was that now he had a name. He was David Steadman. Weinschenk had spoken to him on the telephone and seen him in the flesh, and now he knew what to call him. A man under those circumstances ceases to be a specter. If he can appear in a photograph he is a man like other men.

Yes. He was David Steadman, a student of philosophy at the University of Geneva until his return to America in 1936, when he ceased to be an object of SS surveillance—they assumed he was still there. He was wealthy in his own right, having inherited money from his mother, and his father was one of the most powerful men of business in the Western Hemisphere. His scornful rejection of the Cause had been greatly lamented.

And what connection could there be between this shining playboy and the tricky, ruthless, apparently fearless individual who had almost killed Max in Spain and then, three years later, stolen perhaps the greatest secret of the war from the very strongroom of the German embassy in Stockholm? None, except that they happened to be the same person. None at all.

And he was now somewhere within the territories of the Reich, that was almost certain. The thought was so intoxicating that Weinschenk found himself utterly unable to keep still. His office could not contain him; he found it absolutely necessary to put the dossier away in his desk and take a walk around the gardens behind Security Department headquarters to settle his nerves.

It was a bitterly cold morning, and the lawns were spangled with yellow leaves. In another month it would be emphatically winter. Weinschenk hardly noticed. He was too excited. David Steadman, hitherto nameless, was virtually in his grasp. The humiliation of Spain would finally be redressed. Anything, anything at all seemed possible.

He glanced up at the row upon row of windows, most of them half obscured by droplets of condensation so that they looked like blocks of bearded faces, and the thought of the busy hum inside made him smile with childish delight. Yes, he still loved the SS, in spite of everything. He knew he had been right to join at the university. It was still possible to do great deeds in the SS. The SS was the golden road.

And then he thought of the letter—that damned letter, which the Führer had been persuaded to sign no doubt against his real instincts—and his heart quailed within him. He would have to see Nebe again. They would have to decide upon a policy or they might both be lost.

"No, there is nothing we can do about the letter now—we can't even admit we know it's missing. Can you imagine any of us explaining this to the Führer, perhaps asking him to write another? It would put the SS in a very peculiar light. And the Führer wouldn't blame Aarenhold—he's very probably never even heard of Aarenhold and, besides, that isn't the way his mind works. No, he'll blame Himmler, and Himmler will blame us. It's a good thing you persuaded Aarenhold to send off that dummy attaché case. That way we'll at least have some breathing time."

Nebe was frightened too. One could see that in the peculiar, strained expression of his face, as if the skin had been stretched tight. The fingers of his right hand were tapping unrhythmically against the arm of his chair. Of course he was aware of the risks.

"The best thing would be if you could get it back from this fellow Steadman when you catch him."

"To have Steadman is not necessarily to have the letter," Weinschenk said quietly, in the tone of someone breaking bad news. "He is not a fool. God alone knows what arrangements he may have made. If he senses we are closing in, he may hide it."

"Then you'll have to sweat him for it, won't you. And when you've found out what he's done with it, you'll have to kill him. He knows far too much and, besides, he's just as valuable a trophy dead as alive—you have my permission to carry his head back to Madrid on the point of a stake if you like.

"You can catch him, can't you?" Nebe's ferocity disappeared almost at once, making plain that it had been nothing more than a reflection of his fear. The upholstery salesman was worried about his position.

"Oh, yes—I can catch him." Weinschenk smiled understandingly. He was the repository for all the Gruppenführer's trust.

"You didn't do so brilliantly against him in Spain."

"In Spain one had to contend with the Spaniards," he answered, nodding, having decided to overlook the implied malice. "The Falangist police were stupid, or uncooperative, or worse. Chiefly, I think, they wanted to catch Steadman for themselves and preferred that he go free rather than that we have the glory. Everything in that country is a matter of personal prestige. But such difficulties won't present themselves here."

"No. Of course not."

The two men sat quietly for a moment, avoiding each other's eyes. The only sound was a faint ticking from the heating coil; one couldn't even hear the traffic. Everything seemed muffled.

"If I can obtain the letter, can you procure its delivery?" Weinschenk shifted uneasily in his chair. It had occurred to him that such a thing might be just possible—unlikely, but possible. It frightened him even to ask the question.

"The question is what I will have to do if you *don't* obtain the letter," Nebe answered, smiling in a way little calculated to set one's mind at ease. "Washington will of course immediately notify Berlin when the courier arrives and his attaché case is discovered to be full of old magazines, but we can let him take the blame for that. He will have had the papers switched on him while visiting a prostitute in New York—that has a nice believable ring to it. I think we can manage, provided the ambassador agrees to go along. And I have a thing or two on Thomsen in my files that should guarantee his cooperation. It would, however, put us in a much better position if we had the letter."

Weinschenk could see that. After all, nothing remains a secret forever, no matter how many like Aarenhold are stood up against a wall. It was all bound to come out, sooner or later, and the resulting purge would sweep them all away.

The Gruppenführer nodded approvingly, quite as if all the strings were already in his hands.

"The courier's presumed failure will put the Foreign Ministry in disgrace, and then if we could come up with the letter . . . We would have saved the Führer from the possibility of considerable embarrassment in front of his allies—after all, what would the Japanese think if the letter were ever made public? If we get it back, however, the Führer will be too pleased to ask any awkward questions, and you and I will be safe. More than safe."

Nebe frowned suddenly, as if displeased in some perfectly trivial way.

"I do not think the letter should ever be delivered. The Reichsführer doesn't think so either. What should we have to fear from the Americans that we should sue for peace like this? Our armies are within striking distance of Moscow—the war in Russia will be over within two months. I'm sure that von Ribbentrop tricked our Führer into signing, and if we are very careful we can use this little mischance to bring the champagne salesman down for once and all. Foreign affairs should be an SS concern, don't you agree?"

Not knowing what to answer, Weinschenk merely smiled. It seemed to be enough.

"But we must get the letter, Herr Hauptmann. Once we have it, and von Ribbentrop is safely in Dachau, then I'm sure the decision to deliver it will be rescinded. Can you get the letter, Herr Hauptmann?"

"I can try. I shall have to get Steadman first."

"Oh, you must get them both. You must, or all our heads may yet be on the block."

"As I have said, Herr Gruppenführer, I can try."

XVIII

NOVEMBER 8, 1941

Steadman spent his first night in Hamburg at the bottom of a sewer main with about seven hundred other people, waiting out an air raid. There was no light and they all sat in stinking, ankle-deep water, doubled up like embryos and with their hands clapped over their ears whenever the crash of bombs overhead got close enough to shake down clouds of rusty scale and excrement. It was like being inside a tom-tom. It was impossible to believe that the concrete and pavement overhead weren't about to collapse and bury them forever under a thousand tons of clammy, airless rubble. In the intervals, when the bombing tapered off, you could hear whispering in the darkness as here and there people recited the Lord's Prayer. *Vater unser, der im Himmel ist . . .* Perhaps they had been praying all along, even through the worst of it, but somehow Steadman didn't think so. Steadman had been through all this before, during the London Blitz, but it still scared the hell out of him.

He had hitched a ride in aboard a produce truck, telling the driver a story about being a fisherman on his way to try and join the navy. The driver was very patriotic and had approved. He had even bought Steadman a drink in Ahrensburg as a kind of send-off.

The plan was to try to equip himself with papers somehow and then to head south by train into occupied France. Then, if he could just cross into Vichy—the border was supposed to be a bitch, but there was probably a way—the rest of the trip to Lisbon wouldn't be too bad. He had about fourteen hundred miles to go, provided he wasn't arrested on the spot because he couldn't produce a satisfactory identity. Provided he wasn't blown to pieces.

The old man crouched next to him in the sewer main kept asking how the British—even the British—could do anything as terrible as bomb civilian targets. His outrage was nearly comical. And then, after the hours of noise and terror and discomfort had worn him down, he began to weep softly, as if he hardly had the strength left even for that.

In the morning, when they started crawling out through a manhole cover into the pale, misty sunshine, Steadman was surprised to find how many soldiers there were about. Home-front troops, fresh from a decent night's sleep in barracks that were outside the target area, their eyes fierce as they paced around with submachine guns. Once in a while they would stop someone, spin him around to face a wall, and conduct a search. They were looking for something.

Steadman kept away from the main streets, so he didn't have much trouble avoiding them. It wasn't going to be possible to do that for very long, however.

He needed an identity, something that would render him invisible. Something that would allow him to travel without worrying about being asked to present a permit. He would have to give the question some thought, but right at the moment what he needed was some breakfast and maybe a couple of hours' sleep. The sewer hadn't been terribly restful.

The man with the shotgun had had twenty-eight marks on him, and after two days twenty-eight marks begin to stretch a little thin. But there was still enough left for a decent breakfast, if he could find a place that would sell it to him. Bombed cities tended to be a trifle disorganized.

But by nine o'clock he had found a lunchroom that was just opening up in the basement of a half-ruined building. A heavy blond woman of about sixty was sweeping the concrete dust and broken glass from her stairs; she glanced up at Steadman and smiled.

"No coffee. No, only *Ersatz*. No tea either. I can't remember the last time we had tea."

But there were scrambled eggs and toast, and the *Ersatz* wasn't any worse than the British version. The proprietress was also good company, which made up for a lot. It seemed years since Steadman had held an ordinary conversation, in any language.

"Were you here last night?" she asked. "Was it bad?"

Steadman nodded—guilty on both counts. "Were you?"

"No. I stay with my sister in the suburbs. Five miles each way, but it's better than getting killed or spending the night in a hole. At six o'clock I lock the door and start walking. If it's here when I come back in the morning, fine. If not, at least I'm not a corpse inside. Five nights now, and still they haven't put me out of business."

"Will they be back tonight, do you think?"

"Sure." She nodded slowly, closing her eyes as she did it. The impression was that the British had taken her into their confidence. "Two more nights. They give you a week of it, and then they let you catch your breath. Nice of them, eh? They go someplace else and bomb them to hell, but they'll be back. Funny way to fight a war, eh?"

She poured him another cup of *Ersatz* with that careless air that lets you know it's on the house. She was a nice old broad.

She wore a scratchy-looking gray sweater that probably could have used a trip to the cleaners, and the gold bangles at her wrists tinkled like Ceylonese temple bells. She was looking Steadman over very carefully.

"You know, I'm in good with the police," she said finally. "You know why? They come here and drink my *Ersatz*—all they want, free. How much can anybody stand, eh?"

It was a joke. It was very funny, so Steadman did his best to laugh. All that came out was a soundless *huh!*

She smiled at him. She understood all about him, the smile seemed to imply. It wasn't a comforting thought.

"I used to do a little business in the black market, so I learned to be nice to the police. I learned all about the police, eh? I think maybe you know all about the police too."

It was one of those awkward moments when you knew you were expected to say something—some password, maybe; a signal that it was all right to stop talking in code—but you were goddamned if you knew what it was. Steadman wondered if he wasn't being invited into a trap.

"I don't work for anyone except myself, mother. So stop worrying."

He took another sip from the thick-sided crockery mug and set it down again, sliding his hand over the top, his fingers gripping the sides like talons. She was standing within a foot or so; there wouldn't have been any problem about catching her a blow on the side of the head that would put her down forever. She might be a nice old broad, but there wasn't any occasion for playing games.

"In these times you get to know who you can trust." She glanced down at the back of his hand as if she could read his mind. "I think maybe you have a problem with the police. Maybe you run away from the army or something? I could use a smart boy who knows what's what. You look tired. I got a shower back there, if the pipes aren't broken. You could get some sleep with nobody bothering you."

There was a coaxing look in her eyes. For a grotesque moment Steadman wondered whether she might not be casting her net for him, but then he decided not.

. . . *some sleep with nobody bothering you.* No, the lady was lusting after something else.

What the hell, he might as well take the chance. The odds were so heavily against him it hardly made any difference.

"I have no papers," he said, leaning forward on the narrow wooden counter. "I have no money. And you're right, I have a problem with the police. It wouldn't pay you to sell me, though. You wouldn't want to get involved."

"Did you run away from the army?"

"No."

"No?" She looked genuinely surprised. "Then it *must* be bad for you."

"It's bad enough."

She seemed to consider all the possibilities. Her head tilted to one side and then the other, and the great mass of her brittle, dyed hair sagged and rustled against her shoulders.

"You aren't one of those British, are you? I heard they shot down some of the bombers last night—you couldn't be one of them."

"No." Steadman was actually able to smile. "No, I promise that much. I didn't drop from the sky. Nobody loves me over there."

"Well, I'm glad to hear that! If it isn't political it's all right." She grinned ferociously at him, showing the gold caps on some of her teeth. Perhaps now she felt herself licensed to believe anything she liked.

"Could you go to Frankfurt for me?" she asked. It was important to her. She could tell.

"One direction is as good as another. What's in Frankfurt?"

"My ex-husband. I want to send him something."

She went into her back room for a moment, and when she came out again she slid a small green-covered booklet across the counter to him. It was only a few pages thick and not much larger than a library card. It documented that someone named Josef Matzky had been a member in good standing of the National Socialist Party since 1932; there was even a photograph. Josef Matzky, if that was really his name, didn't look like a Nazi. Josef Matzky looked like the man behind the ribbon counter at Woolworth's.

"We were divorced a long time ago," she said, an anxious, guilty quaver in her voice. "It wasn't nice, but it was a long time ago. He has to get out of the country now and he can't get a passport."

She didn't have to spell it out for him—if you didn't have the right sort of grandparents these days you were in all kinds of trouble.

"How much did this thing cost you?"

"Six hundred marks. If they catch up with him it'll mean the work camps in Poland, or worse. I can't go myself—I can't get the permits to travel, not after paying for this. It's hard to get all the way to Frankfurt."

"I might not make it either."

"I got a hunch this trouble of yours didn't start yesterday—you been running a long time?" She smiled at him quizzically, showing her gold dental work again. "You made it this far."

It was an unanswerable argument. The whole thing was unanswerable. And pathetic, and kind of grand. A poor faded old hag had laid out her savings to buy passage to safety for her cast-off husband, and she was ready to trust a complete stranger with it because she didn't have any choice. The world was rotten straight through that it did such things to people.

"I can give you seventy marks—maybe eighty. Is Frankfurt on your way?"

"How do you know I won't take your money and drop this in the next trash barrel?" He pushed it back over the counter to her, feeling like Judas Iscariot. "You don't know me."

"You get to know, in these times."

He stayed all that day in Frau Maurer's back room. He was asleep most of the time, but every so often she would come in to wake him up and give him something to eat. He seemed to need food even worse than he needed sleep. He couldn't seem to get enough. And while he ate he would listen to Frau Maurer telling him what he would need to know to get to Frankfurt and deliver Josef Matzky's identity card.

"What's his real name?"

"Josef Gottschalk. He's a Jew—does that make a difference to you?"

"No."

"He's a chemist, so they've left him alone up until the last few months. Perhaps they didn't even know he was a Jew. That happens sometimes." She shrugged her shoulders, as if the failure of the present government to hunt Josef Gottschalk to his doom were something that needed to be apologized for. "I got a letter from him in August. He says they even read his mail. He's been evicted from his apartment and is staying with a friend."

"He might think I'm trying to trap him—the police do things like that, you know."

"I know. Tell him you have something for 'Beppo.' " She smiled. "I don't suppose anyone's called him that in thirty years."

And at six o'clock Frau Maurer locked up her little lunchroom, which had hardly had a customer all day, and started on her walk to her sister's place in the suburbs. Steadman went with her for the first block, and they separated at the corner, precisely as if they had never seen each other before in their lives. Frau Maurer worried about her friends the police.

"You had better wait until dark," she had told him. "There are soldiers around, and they'll shoot anyone they think may be looting. It isn't safe to be on the streets in daylight unless you look like you know your own business, but after dark most of them are too frightened of the bombing to wait around. That's the best time."

Steadman's plan of last resort was to get to the railroad yards and stow away aboard a freight car headed south. If he absolutely had to he could crawl into the undercarriage and ride between the wheels.

What he really needed was a set of papers, and that meant he was going to have to kill someone.

The streets were dark and almost empty—it was even spookier here than it had been in London at the height of the Blitz. If you met anyone on the sidewalk, he treated you to a scared look and scurried away. Probably all this had been a tremendous shock to their feelings of invincibility. Steadman walked quickly, his hands thrust deep into his jacket pockets, as if he had somewhere very definite to go and people were waiting for him. Already he could see the beams from the searchlights nervously feeling around in the sky for enemy bombers.

Maybe this would be the last killing.

He would pick someone where the physical resemblance was strong enough to satisfy the casual scrutiny of border guards. In northern Germany, where tall blond men were ten to the yard, that shouldn't be terribly difficult.

It was close to nine o'clock before Steadman heard the drumbeat of flak guns announcing the beginnings of that night's bombing raid. In a few minutes he would be able to hear the plane engines, and then the bombs would start falling. It was all perfectly familiar, a routine he had learned in London. He was already in the southern part of the city and the planes would have come in from the North Sea to avoid crossing Axis territory in daylight; it would be fifteen or twenty minutes before he had to start worrying about where to hide his head.

There was a good moon out. You wondered if that made things easier for the British bombardiers all those thousands of feet up, if Hamburg wasn't all laid out beneath them like a relief map. It wasn't a thought you wanted to dwell on.

The first bombs fell very far away. He could hear the concussion, a dim sound, like someone punching a pillow, and as he turned around he could just make out a flicker of yellow light on the northern skyline.

There were still people on the streets, but most of them were running now, trying to find someplace underground. The soldiers had been all gone for hours. There was no law now. If anyone was in charge, it was the British, and they were too high up to make any use of it. The police, if they hadn't run for cover with everybody else, were no longer the agents of the all-powerful state—they were only individual men with guns. And it would stay that way until morning. Steadman felt an exhilarating sense of personal freedom.

Except that someone was following him.

It hadn't been very hard to spot him. Everyone was interested in the progress of the bombers; it was natural to glance back over your shoulder at the fires raging in the northern districts—you could see the lurid orange and yellow flames dimly reflected in the upper windows of buildings, and the smoke was visible even in the dark—and that was where he was, about half a block back and on the other side of the street, a man in a black leather overcoat and a wide-brim hat of indeterminate color. After Steadman had seen him twice he slowed his own pace just to make sure. Everyone was passing him now; he was almost in the way. But when he looked around a third time, the man in the leather coat was still there, keeping pace with him step for step.

Well—what to do? If the whole question didn't become academic within the next two or three minutes—the bombers overhead were dropping flares; you could almost read a newspaper it was so light outside; five blocks away buildings were lurching over on their sides like drunks dancing on a slippery floor, and the sounds of the detonations hit you with an unnervingly physical shock—if the pair of them, along with a lot of other people, weren't blown to pieces almost at once, then Steadman was going to have to put the gentleman's lights out.

He was Gestapo, of course. They all loved those leather overcoats, wearing them like uniforms, even in the Spanish summer. If the Nazis were ever defeated, their passion for display, for self-dramatization, would have had a big hand in it. This one was Gestapo right down to his shoelaces.

When the building across the street exploded like a paper bag, Steadman dove headfirst down the closest basement stairway, rolling as he hit the first step and tucking himself up into a ball so that he bounced down into the darkness and fetched up with a crash into a row of garbage cans. Over his head the world was coming to an end—chunks of burning white phosphorus, big enough to cook dinner over, ricocheted off the walls and skittered out into the street like beads of water on a hot stove. From the noise you might have imagined somebody was out there punching six-foot holes in the asphalt with the blunt end of a tire iron. It was terrific, like nothing he could have believed, sheer chaos. He kept himself curled up, his eyes opening and shutting in time to the explosions, thrilled and terrified. He hardly thought a thing about it—there simply wasn't attention left for such considerations—when, a few seconds later, he discovered that he had company down in his hole.

It was him, of course. Steadman could see him quite clearly in the light from the flares. He was squatting in a corner; he looked as if he was trying to regain his balance, so maybe he had jumped over the railing. He had lost his hat and there was a large gash, as straight as if it had been made with a ruler, over his left eyebrow. He was holding a pistol in his hand and grinning.

"Herr Steadman?"

"Are you out of your fucking *mind?*" Steadman screamed in English. They were in the middle of a bombing raid, with the whole street falling down around their ears, and this stupid bastard wanted to make a pinch. It was simply past believing.

The grin wavered for an instant, but the pistol stayed steady as a rock. He probably would have been tall if he had been foolish enough to stand up, and his dishwater-blond hair was cut so short it could hardly take a part. He was probably about twenty-eight, and you could have supposed he was making his first arrest, he was so pleased with himself.

"You will come with me, Herr Steadman? I have been following you for nearly three quarters of an hour, just to be sure."

They both ducked as a tremendous explosion rocked them in their cellar landing like dice in a cup. A fine spray of gritty, glittering dust began to filter down on them from the street. The young policeman waited for a second or two and then rose to his feet—yes, he was that foolish.

"Come, up!"

He motioned to Steadman with the muzzle of his pistol, but Steadman still couldn't believe he was serious.

The stairway was the sort of logistical problem that perhaps they hadn't covered at Gestapo school. It was on the policeman's side of the landing, and his glance kept flickering between it and Steadman because naturally he realized that if he let his prisoner pass up first he would be letting him in close enough to run the chance of getting jumped. He didn't want that; he didn't seem to know quite what he should do. Finally he started to back up the stairway himself, feeling his way up the steps with the heels of his shoes.

"Come, come!" he said, as if the sound of the English word made him feel uncomfortable. He was holding the pistol as if he planned to use it; Steadman picked himself up and ventured a step forward. That seemed to make his captor very happy. He actually smiled.

"Come. There's nothing to fear now. They've gone a—"

He never got to finish the sentence. Behind him there was a blinding white light, silent as death, and then the roar and the impact reached them in the same instant. Steadman had the impression that the policeman was coming toward him, but then everything seemed to be coming toward him. He had just time enough to realize what had happened, and to begin raising his arm to fend it off, when suddenly the white glare turned to red, and then to black, and he felt himself falling backward into an emptiness that closed over him like oblivion.

When he first woke up he couldn't seem to place where he was and, since he hurt through every inch, it didn't really seem all that worthwhile to try remembering. He was lying there—at least, he assumed he was lying somewhere, since he could feel the pressure strongest against his back and behind the crook of his knees—and his eyes were shut, but he was awake. Somehow that all by itself struck him as a remarkable accomplishment. He tried the experiment of opening and closing his left hand, and when that worked he tried opening his eyes. It didn't help. He couldn't see a goddamned thing.

But that, he finally decided, was because there was something in the way. And, besides, it was the middle of the night. Jesus, he felt awful, as if someone had taken a hammer and broken each and every tiny little bone in turn.

And then he remembered the explosion.

The British had been tricky. There had been a little lull, just enough to make you think they had passed on overhead and were busy blowing up people farther south. And then, *KA-BAM!*

The object lying on top of him and obstructing his view was, he discovered, a dead body.

He tried clearing a little room for himself and made some progress. The cellar landing was half full of chunks of plaster and cement, pieces of board, unidentifiable objects of various shapes and sizes, and the corpse of a tall, blond Gestapo agent in a leather overcoat. Steadman, after much effort and several halts to catch his breath and reassure himself that none of his appendages had been broken off, managed to climb out from underneath for a look. The bombers were gone and, reflected against the wall behind him, he could see the shadows of smoky flames. It was quiet except for the sound of the building burning across the street, which must have taken a whole stick of bombs in a direct hit; there was no sign of anyone around.

A little careful examination with the tips of his fingers revealed to him why the side of his face hurt so much. There was a lump about the size of a walnut over his right cheekbone, and the slightest touch set it throbbing like an electric engine. Probably a piece of flying cement had caught him. There didn't seem to be any functional damage. Everything seemed to work. In a day or so he would probably have a lovely collection of purplish-black bruises, but he was alive and ambulatory and didn't seem to be bleeding anywhere.

The policeman hadn't fared so well. He was already slightly cold to the touch. Probably he had been dead at least an hour. Aside from the cut on his forehead, there wasn't a mark on him. He must have died from the concussion. And the fact that he had played it so cautious and had gone up that stairway first was probably what had saved Steadman's life.

He looked at the man's dead face, which showed no sign of the violence of his end, and an idea occurred to him.

Why not? This one was tall and fair-haired—they were probably both of a height and fairly close in general build—and God knows he hadn't any need for anything anymore except a few cubic yards of cool earth. Steadman was probably three or four years older, but people aged fast in wartime. If he got himself a haircut and put something over the goose egg on his face, he might just be able to pass. People didn't ask for a perfect likeness when you carried all the signs of having been in an accident. He slipped the watch, which miraculously was still ticking, off the man's wrist and, with perhaps unseemly haste, began going through his pockets.

There was a leather cardholder, containing everything necessary to establish Dieter Kroll as a corporal in the *Geheime Staatspolizei*—the picture, blessedly, was terrible, shadowy and slightly blurred, as if the photographer had been in a hurry. There was a billfold containing something in excess of two hundred marks. There was a pocket handkerchief, some change, a religious medal attached to a short bit of ribbon—did people in the Gestapo go in for that sort of thing?

There was also a photograph, about four inches square. Steadman peered at it for several seconds in the uncertain light from the conflagration across the street. The face—and that was all there was, just a face—was unsettlingly familiar.

And then, of course, he realized. It was a photograph of himself.

Well, naturally. The little creep had called him by his name, hadn't he? They had his face and his name already, only six days after the dustup in Stockholm. You had to hand it to these people—they did their homework.

And apparently they had launched a manhunt. They might be looking for him all over Europe. Or maybe they just knew where to look.

Steadman felt himself go cold all over, like a presentiment of death.

Where was the son of a bitch's gun? He had been waving it in Steadman's face the very second the bomb blast had killed him, so it had to be around somewhere. Finally he found it, lodged between the wall and part of a board. It looked as if it would still work, and now he was going to need all the help he could get.

The next part he didn't like one little bit, but he needed more than just money and a card that said he worked for Hitler. He had to dress the part as well.

Ten minutes later, he stepped off the top of the stairway onto the sidewalk. The whole street had changed—most of it wasn't there anymore. No one was around, and the fires were simply burning themselves out. Pressed up against the side of a building, miraculously undamaged, was the hat that went with the leather overcoat and the seven-millimeter Luger. Steadman tried it on and discovered that it was a reasonable fit. He wondered how far he still had to walk to the train station.

XIX

The only train out that morning was carrying soldiers to garrison duty in the Netherlands. Steadman went along only as far as Göttingen. No one seemed surprised or suspicious when he requested to be taken aboard; he wasn't even required to purchase a ticket. He found himself in a first-class compartment full of junior officers, and they tended to give him a wide berth, but otherwise all he had to do was to show his card and the world belonged to him.

In Göttingen he decided to have his hair cut and get his clothes cleaned. People under nightly visitation from the Royal Air Force probably don't even notice one another's appearance, but in Göttingen, where the war hadn't left any visible marks, he suspected his godlike authority as a member of the Secret Police might suffer a little if he went around looking like a bum.

The barbershop was an agreeable sort of joint, with a cast-iron stove in the back corner and chairs covered with faded, cigarette-burned green cloth. The barber was extremely careful about shaving around the lump on Steadman's cheekbone. Apparently he too knew all about black leather overcoats, because all the time he was scalping his customer he was testifying to his enthusiasm for the war and the current regime.

"I bet they bring Stalin back to Berlin in a cage," he said, making a pass through the air with the point of his scissors—it was a movement wonderfully expressive of his contempt for the Russian army. "Those people all stand under a meter and a half and have pointed heads; how long can they hold out against the Wehrmacht? I bet we have peace by Christmas."

He grinned. He was a fat man who looked like he grinned a lot; his face seemed to pucker and fold as if the expression were habitual. But he was frightened. In Spain, Steadman had heard the same line from shoemakers and bus drivers and the old women who sold wine by the glass at corner stalls—they saw his militia jacket and the rifle slung over his shoulder, and they smiled and talked about the glories of the workers' state. Three quarters of them had probably sympathized with Franco.

It was the same everywhere in Europe. For ten years now it had been just the same—everybody was afraid.

So the fat barber, whose hands were covered with huge, bronze-colored freckles and who knew all about the Gestapo, cut Steadman's hair and told him how much he admired Heinrich Himmler.

Steadman hardly recognized himself when he was finished. For two marks the barber's wife had taken his trousers and jacket and loaned him her husband's bathrobe while she sponged and pressed them until they looked like new. Even the black leather overcoat had benefited from a little warm water and saddle soap. He walked back out onto the street the complete policeman, ready to inspire terror in anyone. He decided he needed to get some aspirin. He really was covered with bruises, and the pain was making him feel sick to his stomach.

"What did you do to yourself?" the barber had asked in amazement, looking at the purple knob over his cheekbone. "Or perhaps I shouldn't be nosy."

Steadman had let him wrap a hot towel around that side of his face and took refuge in silence. That was one nice thing about pretending to be a Gestapo agent—people expected you to be close-mouthed and secretive.

The old city of Göttingen looked as if history had left it behind. There were the timbered buildings and baroque church steeples that gave the impression that nobody here had ever heard of inflation, defeat, social collapse, Hitler, the Third Reich, war. The whole cycle of the last thirty years seemed somehow to have been ignored. It was an impression you could maintain right up until the moment you crossed over the main square, in front of the town hall with its faintly Gothic brownstone façade and its red roof, and saw the sign pointing down the Horst Wessel Strasse.

Steadman bought four lengths of dried sausage at the butcher shop and started eating them on his way back to the railway station. He decided that if he could find a bottle of schnapps he would buy that too. The aspirin wasn't doing him much good—he could hardly chew, his face hurt so much. He thought he would try getting drunk.

The soreness from his wounded shoulder had spread to his chest, his face throbbed, and he could barely move for the little stabs of pain that seemed to be his punishment for having survived the bomb that killed Korporal Kroll. And on top of everything else, his fever seemed to have come back. He had come approximately seven hundred miles since Stockholm; if things kept up at their present pace he would die of his injuries long before he got as far as the French border.

Of course, the big problem was making up his mind what to do next. He could either go on to Cologne and make his way into France through Belgium, or he could go down to Frankfurt and then Strasbourg, where all he would have to do was to walk from one side of town to the other. He had promised Frau Maurer—well, perhaps not promised; that might be laying it on a bit thick—but he had certainly implied to her that he would go to Frankfurt and take care of the little matter of Beppo's identity card. He had accepted seventy marks. He had let her believe he . . .

What the hell, he could let the train schedules decide. He would go whichever way would get him out of Germany the faster, since the risks were probably about the same. And if his way led him through Frankfurt, it wouldn't kill him to stop off for an hour and run such a simple errand for Frau Maurer. But if the next train leaving was for Cologne, then that would be tough on everybody.

"No—you have to transfer at Lahn if you want to go to Cologne. That's a bad line; they bomb the track all the time. You still want to go there?"

The ticket seller looked at him speculatively, blinking behind his eyeglasses as if he couldn't believe that anyone would want to change trains at Lahn. He seemed genuinely pleased when Steadman shook his head and asked for a one-way passage to Frankfurt.

"Is there a tavern around here anywhere? I need a drink."

Steadman took a window seat in a second-class compartment on the four-fifteen train, which was only three quarters of an hour late, a small bottle of French brandy, for which he had paid only about seventy-five pfennig—somebody was making a good thing out of the occupation—in the pocket of his overcoat. Aside from the inevitable soldiers, there were very few passengers and they all regarded Steadman with evident distaste. You had the sense that even here in Germany the Gestapo was not universally loved.

He took the bottle out of his pocket, broke the seal, and took a long, burning swallow. Doubtless his fellow travelers thought he was just no end of a vulgarian for drinking right out of the bottle like that—and in a public place, too. Well, to hell with them. He felt a rush of heat as the cognac hit his stomach. He wondered how much it would take to make him feel numb; they wouldn't reach Frankfurt before morning and he wanted to sleep. He took another swig, and the man across the aisle gave him a black look—the son of a bitch looked like an undertaker. Fuck 'em. If the moldy little bastard made a fuss, Steadman decided that maybe he might just arrest him. He almost laughed out loud at his own joke, but instead he had another drink. Yes, he was definitely beginning to feel better.

He had finished his sausages a long time ago, but all the cognac in the world couldn't seem to wash the taste out of his mouth. He found himself thinking about lamb chops and canned artichoke hearts. He thought about warm apartments in Stockholm, and warm beds. He thought about Karen.

Jesus, it had been better half an hour ago when the only pain he felt had been in his body. He shouldn't drink, he decided. He got too depressed when he drank.

That night with Karen, that had been the last time, the last moment, when he had put any value on his own life. Probably he would never be that happy again, ever. Probably he would never see her again. In fact, it would be better if he never did. What could they possibly say to each other? No, all of that was finished.

But he couldn't resist the tug of recollection. He closed his eyes and tried to remember what she had looked like, every line. A couple of days, that was all they would ever have had.

"Maybe we could come back here when the war is over. Do you think so, David? Do you think we could?"

And she had turned her head toward him and touched his face with the tips of her fingers, her little head nestled on the edge of the pillow. She had been smiling, but there was just that uncertainty that could have turned her smile into anything.

"I don't know—when the war is over, maybe. Could we make it in the summer, though?"

That had been enough. Her laughter sounded like the tinkling of glass. But there had been no more questions about the future.

He decided he didn't want to think about Karen anymore, so he took another drink. When he held the bottle up to the light, he discovered that it was already about two thirds gone. Good. Then maybe so was he.

* * *

There was a cold fog all around the railroad station when Steadman arrived. He had slept soundly—or, as soundly as one can sleep sitting up in a moving train—and the only trace left on him by his pint of cognac was a kind of emotional anesthesia. He couldn't seem to move his attention either forward or back, so fear and sorrow didn't exist for him. There was only the moment, what he would do over the next hour or so, where he would get some breakfast, whether he should buy his ticket to Strasbourg now or wait.

He had exactly three hours between trains if you could believe the schedule, and that was certainly enough time to take care of his errand for Frau Maurer. Besides, he didn't know how many of those photographs were floating around, and it didn't strike him as a particularly good idea to hang about on the platform giving the police and the stationmaster plenty of time to figure out where they had seen that face before. Perhaps he was just being vain; perhaps the search for him was still confined to the north. But he didn't care to take the risk.

Josef Gottschalk's friend lived on the other side of the River Main, which was probably something like three hundred yards wide at the point where the bridge crossed it. Steadman looked down at the water, which was gray and wrinkled like the skin of an elephant, and felt the cold wind and began to wake up again. That only meant that he began to feel fear again, but fear had become enough of a constant in his life that he hardly noticed it. Its revival was almost a physical pleasure, like the return of sensation after your foot's gone to sleep.

He had decided that the great thing was to avoid being taken alive. It was the SS that was after him, and the SS seemed to be playing some game of their own. In any case, no cause he was interested in was going to be advanced by turning the letter over to the likes of Captain Egon Weinschenk.

So if it came to that, he decided, he would try to ditch the letter. Beyond that, he had a pistol; he could kill himself if he absolutely had to. He thought, however, he would simply raise the price of arresting him to something higher than the Germans would be prepared to pay. The clip in Dieter Kroll's Luger contained seven rounds. That should be enough.

Away from the main boulevards, all the apartment buildings looked the same. They were all the same sandstone exterior, with the flight of stairs to the upper stories on the left side and everything trimmed with the same dark stained wood. It seemed to be a fairly prosperous district where Herr Peter Döhlmann lived; you heard the sounds of children's laughter coming from the back gardens, and the people on the sidewalks were well-dressed and carried with them that preoccupied air that was characteristic of the European middle classes. The streets had been cleaned recently, which, in the third year into a war, said a great deal. It didn't seem the sort of place where a Josef Gottschalk would be able to hide out for very long—someone would be sure to turn him in. After all, having hounded, penniless Jews around was bad for the neighborhood.

Steadman found the correct street—at the railroad station he had purchased a small city map from an elderly woman at the newspaper kiosk who, from her habitual expression, seemed to suspect all her customers of being spies—and the mailbox at the correct number directed him to the third-floor apartment. *P. Döhlmann, Baumeister*, said the card that had been attached to the wood with shiny-headed tacks. He climbed the stairs with a certain unfocused apprehension, feeling in his pocket to make sure the phony identity papers were still there.

There wasn't any answer.

It was a quarter after eight, by which time most people in that part of the world were already in their offices, sorting the pencils. But an architect might work at home. Herr P. Döhlmann might even be retired. Steadman rang the bell again, leaving his finger on the button for about fifteen seconds—the sound he heard from behind the rough oak door was hollow, almost plaintive. There was nobody there.

In two hours and forty-two minutes the train for Strasbourg would be on its way, and there could be no shadow of an excuse for not being on it. But perhaps, if there was somebody at home in the apartment below, it might be possible to find out where Herr P. Döhlmann spent his mornings away from number 91, Harsewinklestrasse. Maybe there was a park around the corner where he went to feed the pigeons.

The man who answered the door at the second-floor apartment was about forty-five and wearing a pair of carpet slippers. His blue trousers looked like, a million years ago, they had been the lesser half of a pretty decent suit, but it had been a while since they had had their creases pressed and they were covered with small shiny patches that suggested ancient food stains. Their owner blinked at Steadman out of a meaty, unhealthy-looking face that could have stood shaving.

"The man upstairs, he's not at home," Steadman announced. "I wonder if you could tell me where I might find him."

"Who wants to know?" The meaty face hardened. Heavy, iron-colored eyebrows lowered accusingly.

Steadman took out Dieter Kroll's identity card and held it up at eye level just long enough for the words *Geheime Staatspolizei* to register and then quickly put it back in his pocket.

"Where does Herr Döhlmann work?"

"At Dachau, I should think, by this time." Herr Döhlmann's neighbor grinned unpleasantly. "You fellows came and took him off last week—him and that Jew friend of his. I should think you would have known."

Steadman couldn't have said why he was so shocked—after all, it wasn't as if the possibility had never occurred to him. And it wasn't as if Peter Döhlmann and Josef Gottschalk were his intimate friends. There was no reason why he should have taken the news of their arrest as a personal grief, and yet he did. He could feel something cold trickling down the inside of his chest, as if his heart were melting ice.

Döhlmann might survive. The Nazis might content themselves with sentencing him to five or ten years of slave labor somewhere, and if they lost the war there might be something left of him when it was over. But Gottschalk was as good as dead. Nobody really believed the official German government line about "deporting" Jews to work in the East; the rumors had it that they were being shipped to Poland in cattle cars to be shot.

The man from the second floor was looking at him through narrow, suspicious eyes.

"Is everything all right?" he asked finally.

"Yes—yes, everything is fine. It seems I've come for nothing." Steadman forced himself to smile.

The man peered at him for a few more seconds, frowning disapprovingly, and then closed his door. Steadman took the stairs back down to the wide, uncluttered sidewalk and began making his way back to the railroad station.

Should he write to Frau Maurer? No, it wouldn't do her any good to know what had happened, and he might only get her into trouble. Possibly, if she ever found out the truth, she would think that Steadman had done a bunk with her money, never even trying to get to Frankfurt; but that didn't seem an adequate reason for putting her life in danger. The Nazis did read people's mail.

Poor Beppo. These days you didn't even have to put on a uniform to get swept into the meat grinder. If you were a Jew or a Communist or a Social Democrat or a Slav, that seemed to be enough. In Spain, one half of the country had made up its mind to annihilate the other, and now that mentality seemed to embrace the whole world.

XX

Weinschenk had read the report a dozen times. He had studied the photographs and he could still hardly believe it. It was all actually happening, precisely the way he had predicted. Steadman was in Germany.

A fisherman is found dead in a deserted house along the Pomeranian coast, a local scoundrel named Geelmaack who had no legitimate reason for being there. There were signs of a struggle—a shotgun is discovered lying beside the body, both barrels having been discharged into the floor, and Geelmaack is stabbed in the leg. There is also a small incision under the jaw, and that is what killed him. The body is not much more than forty-eight hours when discovered. That was the day before yesterday.

Weinschenk particularly liked the photographs of the body. A considerable quantity of blood was visible, most of it having trickled out of the wound under the jaw. One could see that the knife blade must have been about three centimeters wide. Knifings were not so common within the Reich that this could have been the handiwork of anyone except the durable Mr. David Steadman, who had somehow managed to make his way past the shore patrols to kill Geelmaack and was probably at that moment halfway through Germany. One wondered where he could be heading.

"You recognize the style, Max?" Weinschenk showed the top photograph to his aide as they sat together having breakfast in a roadside *Gasthaus* outside of Hünfeld—they had driven all night to be in Stuttgart and have a chance of being in on the kill. "That is what you probably would have looked like if our friend had been in less of a hurry that night in Madrid."

Max's eyes reflected a yellowish light and he growled, baring his teeth slightly. Weinschenk reached over and turned the photograph face down as the waitress approached with a tray of covered dishes. It wasn't very pretty, and she was frightened enough of Max as things were.

"I wonder which direction he'll take," Weinchenk said, as much to himself as to Max, who didn't concern himself with the speculative side of their work and, in any case, was at that moment entirely devoted to a huge plate of scrambled eggs. "He'll have to make for some neutral country—Switzerland, do you think? No, the border is too well guarded and, besides, how would he get out? No—I think he'll head back toward Spain and then on to Portugal. He knows that part of the world. Doubtless he still has friends there who would help him."

Max glared at him for a moment, allowing his fork to hang suspended in the air in front of his mouth. Just catch him, he seemed to be saying. Just put him within my reach, and you'll never have to think about him again. There won't be anything to think about.

"Yes, I know. I've told you, when we've got him—and after we've squeezed everything out of him—you can finish him off. Any way you like."

However, this was a game with limited options. Steadman had gone to the considerable trouble of having himself smuggled out of Sweden, and he had to go somewhere. England was, of course, out of the question. If he had wanted to get back to England, all he would have had to do was to turn himself in at the British embassy in Stockholm. Doubtless the British were as much interested in peeling his skin off as anyone.

Unless he intended to spend the rest of his life as a hunted man within German-occupied Europe, he had to go to either Switzerland or Portugal. And since Switzerland was entirely surrounded by Axis territory, that left Portugal.

He would go through Germany to France, from France to Spain, from Spain to Portugal. From there he could probably arrange passage to the United States—that seemed the logical goal. A man who could cross a hostile continent could probably arrange anything. But where would he enter France? That was the really interesting question.

Weinschenk's best guess was that he would cross the border somewhere in the south, where he would have the shortest distance through occupied territory. Vichy was only some two hundred or so kilometers from, for instance, Freiburg, and if he crossed at Strasbourg he wouldn't even have to worry about the Rhine.

The Rhine. Of course—Steadman would have to think about the Rhine. Steadman, after all, had gone to school in Zürich, so, along with all the other little schoolboys, he would have learned all about the Rhine. The damned river was thirteen hundred kilometers long. One couldn't very well just ignore it.

Considered simply as an obstacle, it was formidable enough. In places it was seven or eight hundred meters wide and, this time of year, cold as the grave. Furthermore, it was carefully watched. Out of force of habit the Germans had annexed Alsace again, but the obsession with keeping that border scrupulously defended had proved difficult to overcome. There were watchtowers; soldiers with binoculars studied every leaf that floated by. All they would have to do if they saw Steadman in a boat would be to pick up the telephone and a squad of frontier guards would be there to meet him on the other side. Because that was now German territory as well.

Steadman would think long and hard about the problem of the Rhine.

How would he be traveling? By rail? Yes. It was the quickest and safest, and he would be clever enough to find a way around the travel restrictions. He would take his seat, pulling his hat down over his eyes, and allow the most efficient transportation system in Europe to carry him along. Yes. Probably he would even have hit upon a way to have the Reich pay his fare.

There was a railroad bridge at Strasbourg. All he would have to do was ride across.

"Max, I think we will go on to Strasbourg."

But they stopped off in Frankfurt to check in with the local SS office. It was on the way, and Weinschenk wanted to see if there had been any developments.

"Something has turned up," said a tall, cadaverous Hauptmann who introduced himself as Kleefeld. The man's head seemed too large for his body, and his hand, when he offered it after the required salute, was as lifeless as a piece of chilled fish. He had an odd way of smiling, with the left side of his mouth only; it seemed to be something of which he was perfectly unconscious. "An informer has identified this person Steadman. He seems to have been in the city within the past four hours. We have a dragnet out for him, of course."

He smiled his odd smile, which somehow took on a defensive character, as if he expected one to strike him.

"Is it certain? Is it absolutely certain?" Only by the greatest exercise of self-control could Weinschenk refrain from grasping the Hauptmann by the lapel and shaking him.

"Oh, yes, quite certain." Kleefeld blinked slowly—while his eyes were closed he looked quite dead. "We have the informer. Would you like to talk to him yourself?"

"Yes—yes, by all means. And please provide me with a local railroad schedule."

"Just as you wish."

The informer's name was Stöhr, and he was unsavory in the extreme. He looked like a butcher, although Kleefeld had described him as the owner of a small hardware business, and his trousers were unclean. That such a filthy jackal should have a hand in bringing down a lion like Steadman was almost too much to be borne.

"He asked about Döhlmann," Stöhr announced—one had the impression he was already well on the way to having his part memorized. "He had a card from the Gestapo, but why shouldn't a Gestapo agent know that Döhlmann had already been arrested? Besides, he seemed so shaken when I told him—it wasn't what one would expect. So I decided to report the incident."

He seemed very proud of himself. His deductive powers were obviously of a very high order, and his loyalty to the state a matter beyond any dispute. He was obviously a very fine fellow. Weinschenk disliked him intensely.

"What was the name on the card?"

"I don't know. He really didn't give me time to read it."

"It would have been helpful to know." Weinschenk smiled. It gave him a certain perverse satisfaction to realize that Steadman had been wandering through Germany passing himself off as a member of the police. "What time precisely did he pay this call on you?"

"I can tell you that exactly, Herr Hauptmann," Stöhr answered quickly, as if relieved at this opportunity to redeem himself after the fiasco about the card. "I had just finished my second cup of coffee, and on weekdays . . ."

"The time, Herr Stöhr."

"Eight-seventeen, Herr Hauptmann. I looked at the kitchen clock when I heard the doorbell."

"Thank you, Herr Stöhr."

Weinschenk took off his hat and set it down on the corner of the desk against which he was leaning. Then he glanced at his watch and consulted the railway schedule which had just been handed to him by one of Kleefeld's aides. It was almost half past twelve, and a train for Strasbourg had left at twelve minutes to eleven. Once again the clever bastard had slipped through their fingers. Weinschenk wasn't quite sure how he felt, so he assumed a haughty tranquillity.

"At what time did Herr Stöhr make his report?" he asked calmly. He raised his eyebrows in friendly inquisitiveness, but Hauptmann Kleefeld's mouth still twitched into his peculiar half smile.

"At around ten-thirty. Naturally Steadman was the first thing I thought of, and he made the identification from your photograph at once. My men were on the street immediately."

"Ten-thirty?" Weinschenk's gaze settled on Herr Stöhr, who was sitting on a small wooden chair that seemed hardly strong enough to bear his weight. Herr Stöhr, naturally, was embarrassed.

"I hadn't even shaved yet, Herr Hauptmann." He smiled apologetically. "How was I to know it would be important. And your office is quite on the other side of town, and I had one or two things . . ."

"Ten-*THIRTY?*"

Weinschenk took a step forward and struck Stöhr squarely in the middle of the face with his gloved fist. Stöhr and his chair both went straight over backward, landing on the floor with a loud smack.

"Herr Hauptmann," Weinschenk asked, looking at Kleefeld as if he might be ready to repeat the performance—he was perfectly beside himself. "I assume you have the usual facilities in your basement."

Kleefeld nodded stiffly. They were both looking down at Stöhr, whose nose was streaming blood but who hadn't as yet found the courage to move.

"Max, take this one downstairs and shoot him."

For several seconds they could hear the hardware merchant screaming as he was dragged down the corridor. It was a terrible sound, which ended abruptly for no immediately obvious reason. Weinschenk turned to his colleague and smiled.

"I expect Max is bouncing him down the stairs. He always does that when they make too much noise—you have no idea how quiet a man becomes when he's had three or four ribs broken."

Kleefeld said nothing—even the twitch on the left side of his mouth had stopped. His eyes, buried deep in their sockets, seemed to glow. It was an odd way for a man to behave who had reached the rank of Hauptmann in the SS.

"This Döhlmann who was arrested, is he still alive?"

"I really don't know," Kleefeld murmured, as if to himself. Then he glanced up at Weinschenk and once more assumed his cringing smile. "I suppose that could be checked."

"Then I suggest you do that. We might as well take care of all the loose ends at once."

"Stöhr was a valuable informant."

"He was an idiot. If he'd come with his story even an hour sooner . . ." Weinschenk paused and looked around him as if surprised to find himself in that particular room. The whole time the muscles in his jaw were working with fierce, mechanical regularity. "In any case, in an operation of this importance . . . But, of course, you don't have any idea of its importance, do you, Kleefeld. Lucky for you."

Weinschenk placed a call to the SS detachment in Strasbourg. Beyond that, there didn't seem anything else to do here. He was impatient to be on his way.

"Did Stöhr add anything to the description?" he asked, taking up his hat from the corner of Kleefeld's desk. "Steadman must have changed himself a little that no one has spotted him before this."

"Only that there was a large bruise on his cheek, along with a few scratches. Stöhr said he looked as if he'd been in a fight."

"I doubt very much if that was what happened. Steadman isn't the sort of man one can simply beat up." He drew his mouth into a mirthless smile. "How was he dressed?"

"A black leather overcoat and a dark gray hat—quite the standard outfit."

"Yes. I wonder how he got it."

And after that there seemed to be nothing more to say. Max had returned from his business below stairs and was standing at parade rest in the doorway, looking rather as if he actually were the door. The two officers exchanged a brief, formal salute and Weinschenk and his aide went back down to the interior courtyard and their car.

It was close to two hundred kilometers to Strasbourg. The train would probably take something like three hours, and Steadman had a head start of nearly two. There was no possibility of getting there ahead of him. Weinschenk didn't dare risk contacting the train directly—what could he do, tell the engineer to slow down? Order an unscheduled stop? Steadman would realize at once what was going on and they would never find him. In this instance it was particularly important not to underestimate one's antagonist.

So it would be necessary to depend on the Strasbourg office.

The road was clear of traffic and Max wasn't wasting any time. The countryside was green and pleasant, even this late into the year, and here and there the road skirted close enough to the Rhine that one could catch a glimpse of it in the distance. At one point they passed a neat little farmhouse, and Weinschenk glanced out his window to see that the fence facing the road was merely a blur of white pickets.

He was glad to be back in the south, where he had grown up and still felt at home. The south was the real Germany—in Berlin they put raspberry syrup in their beer and sat around in cafés, just like the French. One only had to compare Berlin with, say, Munich to see everything that was wrong with the country, and if the Movement had become corrupted it was because the center of authority had been transplanted to the arid, godless soil of Prussia. It was said that the Führer hated Berlin, that after the war he planned to move the capital back to Bavaria, where it had all begun.

When the war was over, Weinschenk decided, he would seek a transfer to Munich—yes, to Munich. He and Magda could go hiking on weekends, just as they had when he was a student. Perhaps he would even take up collecting wild flowers again. It had been quite a mania with him when he was in his early twenties; he wondered what had ever become of his albums of dried specimens. Somewhere along the way they had probably gotten lost. So many things had gotten lost since then.

He glanced over Max's shoulder and noticed that they were going at better than a hundred and ten kilometers an hour. Max was impatient—he wanted to see the American carried away from the train station in chains.

But was Steadman the type to surrender quietly to a mob of Gestapo thugs? What would he do if they ran him to ground in some corner of a railroad yard—surrender like a sensible chap and come out quietly with his hands knitted together over the top of his head? It seemed an unlikely enough possibility. Under those circumstances, all Weinschenk would have for his trouble would be a corpse.

It wasn't enough. It wouldn't do by half. He didn't want Steadman carried back to SS headquarters in a body bag—that wouldn't be much of a triumph. He needed him alive, so he could be made to talk. Steadman had stolen the Führer's letter, practically from beneath Weinschenk's hand, and he had to be forced to give it back. He had to believe he was wriggling through the net, right up to the last second; he had to be led along until the web pulled tight around him.

Which meant that the Strasbourg Gestapo had to be restrained.

"Max, pull in at the next town. I need to make a telephone call."

XXI

Steadman had always rather enjoyed train rides. They were associated in his mind with summer holidays, when Herr Käselau would pack wife and stepson off to Viareggio a week early and then go to visit his mother in Basel before coming down to join them. There would always be a great bustle at the station, a promise of important things ahead, with the luggage being handed in through the open window of their compartment, with a wicker picnic basket packed according to Herr Käselau's rather lavish ideas of what such an expedition required—two bottles of white wine, a roast chicken wrapped in oilpaper, a pot of goose liver, hard crusty rolls the size of tea saucers, and, generally, in a white box tied up with string, a whole chocolate cake—with presents of money and repeated warnings against the local water, with Herr Käselau standing beside the tracks as they pulled away, waving his handkerchief to them like an offer of truce.

He would have to proceed on foot after he reached Strasbourg. The border with France would have roadblocks. It would have to be through the fields, and at night.

There had been a time when he had traveled halfway across Spain like that, sleeping in hayricks during the day and keeping off the roads. It was fine as long as they weren't actively trailing you, and the cold at night wasn't bad as long as you kept moving.

It was nearly two o'clock in the afternoon. They would be coming into the station in another ten or twelve minutes; for some reason this particular train had stayed remarkably close to schedule.

And then, unaccountably, they began to slow down. Outside there were still fields. He could see the Rhine—no, it was too narrow to be the Rhine; it had to be one of its tributaries—and beyond that the low hills of the Black Forest. They hadn't even reached the suburbs of Strasbourg yet, and already the fucking train was slowing down.

Steadman checked the schedule he had picked up in Frankfurt, and there was no mention of any stops between Roppenheim and Strasbourg. He checked down the list of local stations—Drusenheim, Weyersheim, Wantzenau—and decided they must be coming into Wantzenau. What was in Wantzenau?

What was in Wantzenau was a pair of Gestapo plainclothesmen, as alike as two pumpkins, standing at either end of the platform. They didn't have any luggage, not even so much as a briefcase, but they were obviously waiting for the train. They were coming on board to search it.

There were about a dozen carriages on the train, and Steadman was sitting in the third one from the engine. He saw the first of these sentinels of the Reich through his window and immediately moved to a seat on the other side. Then he moved to the platform between cars—if they wanted to search the train they could do it without him. He was getting off. He removed his overcoat and rolled it up like a parcel, because if they were looking for him he must have been spotted somewhere in Frankfurt and they would have his description. Taking off your coat wasn't much of a disguise, but it was a start.

He didn't see Tweedledum until he got off, mixed in with a family group so that he might have seemed like one of them; after all, the police were looking for a man on his own. Number Two, just a figure in a leather overcoat with his hat pulled down low over his eyes as if he were the one trying to make a getaway, never even turned around to check on departing passengers but just stepped aboard the front of the first carriage. When Steadman could risk a quick glance at the other end of the platform, he wasn't particularly surprised to discover that Number One was already gone. As soon as he got clear of the train he stuffed his oh-so-distinctive overcoat in a trash barrel.

Well, this was all he needed. He was stuck in a little dorf with the goons in hot pursuit. It would only take them four or five minutes to search the train and satisfy themselves that he wasn't there—they might even manage before it left the station; they might even hold the train until they were finished. And as soon as they knew their quarry had flown they would put in a call and the immediate area would start swarming with police. They might even have a couple of backup men waiting out on the street. They might have spotted him already. It was a hell of a fix.

There wasn't anything to do except to brazen it out.

Dieter Kroll's pistol was stuck in his belt. He slid his hand in under his jacket and closed his fingers around the long grip. He would make it very expensive for them if it came to that.

The street outside the train station had that forlorn, transient quality one associates with such places. It was simply somewhere people passed through on their way to somewhere else; even the lot on the other side was vacant. There were two or three cars still waiting to pick people up, none of them taxis. Steadman looked them over and settled on a black Mercedes, the driver of which made a phlegmatic impression and had black and silver hair crinkled profusely over both his head and the backs of his hands, which were holding the steering wheel in a loose, untroubled manner, as if they had to go somewhere and that was as good a place as any. Fine—what was needed was a calm type.

Steadman walked up from behind, opened the rear left-hand door, and got in. The Luger was out and pointed in the right direction. The driver turned around, doubtless to say something, but his eyes never got any farther than the muzzle of Steadman's pistol.

"I hope you're the reasonable sort," Steadman said tensely. "Otherwise I'm afraid your brains are going to be decorating the windscreen."

It was a bad monent. You never knew how someone was going to react to having a gun pointed at him—more than a few people got uncontrollably hysterical. Fortunately, this guy didn't seem to be one of them.

"This isn't very smart," he said finally, in the rich, heavy accent of southern Germany. He looked like the sort of man who took life easy— he probably weighed better than a hundred kilos—and somehow you had the impression he had been through this sort of thing before. Steadman noticed that he kept his hands out in plain sight.

"Probably not—is that a professional judgment?" He grinned, wondering why it hadn't dawned on him before that this might be the driver for the boys who that very minute were so busy running up and down the length of his train. A big black Mercedes, that would be just their style. "Either way, I suggest you get this thing out of here. I'm not anxious to meet up with your friends. Move it."

The driver took his hint, and within a few seconds they were already out of sight of the train station. Three quarters of a mile carried them right out of town, and when he saw a roadsign pointing to Strasbourg Steadman decided they had gone far enough.

"Pull over," he said. "This is fine."

There was a stand of pine next to the road, the impenetrable bluish-black stuff that doesn't seem to grow anywhere else in the world. You could walk forty feet into it and never even know the road was there.

"Out. You first."

For perhaps the first time the driver seemed to realize that he was in a fair way of being dead. His heavy-lidded eyes widened, and he started to open his mouth to say something but thought better of it. After all, what good would it do? He had probably taken a few men into the woods to blow their heads off himself, and probably they had had something to say about it too. Wasn't the whole world just like the Gestapo?

The driver kept his hands over his head, and for that reason, or perhaps simply because fear had that effect on him, his progress across the uneven ground was accompanied by a certain unsteadiness. Finally, when they had gone perhaps a hundred feet, Steadman told him to lean against a tree. It was time to find out if he was armed.

"That's right, let your arms take the weight. And don't get ambitious—you wouldn't be the first man to die trying."

Sure enough, there was a gun. A pistol, the exact duplicate of the one Steadman had been carrying ever since Hamburg. The Gestapo must pass them out like party favors.

"Take off your necktie—slowly."

The man did as he was told. He undid the knot with thick, clumsy fingers, and when he was finished he held the tie out to Steadman.

"Just drop it on the ground. You're probably tired. Why don't you go sit down with your back against that tree."

He grinned. He was having a certain amount of fun with this boy. Somebody else could be scared for a change. He waited until the driver was sitting on the ground, with both feet straight out in front of him, and then he picked up the tie.

It was a big tree, probably as much as a meter all the way round. Steadman crouched down behind it and grabbed one of the man's hands, pulling it backward sharply and tying a quick loop around the wrist. In a few seconds he had both hands tied, close enough together so that the fingers could almost touch.

"How much do you like your life, friend?" Steadman rested the muzzle of his Luger against the soft spot underneath the German's right ear. "Because if it's your ambition to die for the Fatherland, we can manage that right here and now."

"I think you plan to shoot me anyway. I think I can say anything I like and still you will kill me."

It was spoken, one had to admit, with a certain dignity. Steadman was still crouched behind the tree and therefore couldn't see the man's face, but there was less fear in his voice than one would have expected.

"Silly boy—what would I gain by killing you? The fact that you're missing will tell your colleagues everything you could. I'm sure they're already looking for the car, so I'll have to get rid of it as soon as I'm away from here."

It seemed a perfectly reasonable argument. The man twisted his head around, scraping it against the trunk of the tree, so that he could see Steadman's face. Yes, he was afraid.

"They say you've killed many men," he said, blinking painfully. "They warned us that you . . ."

His voice trailed off, as if he wasn't sure he cared risking the truth. Steadman felt a certain coldness in his chest.

"I'm not in the SS, friend. I don't kill just for the fun of it."

"What do you want to know?"

What he wanted to know was how hard the Gestapo was down on him, but Georg—that was his name, Georg—wasn't able to be much help. He was just a driver; all he heard was the gossip.

"You've been the big item for a couple of days now," he said, smiling tentatively, as if he expected Steadman to be flattered. "They want you bad. Somebody named Weinschenk is giving orders that you're not even to be interrogated, just held in cold storage until the Berlin office can take possession. We got the nod a little after lunch to come and scoop you up at the railroad station."

"How many teams did they send, Georg? Who is 'we'?"

"Just the one car. I drive for two fellows, always the same. Just us. No one else."

He wanted to be believed. You could see it in his eyes. He wasn't interested in martyrdom.

"Okay."

Georg didn't have to be told not to start yelling his head off until he heard the car drive away—he didn't want Steadman coming back and putting a pill in his ear. There was an etiquette to these matters which they both understood. The necktie was probably good for about twenty minutes' lead, but by then he didn't expect to be anywhere around.

The Mercedes was surprisingly powerful, so possibly the Gestapo had them souped up. Steadman kept his foot on the accelerator until he was doing about eighty kilometers an hour. He didn't want to attract a lot of attention, and he felt as if everybody in Germany could see him for a hundred miles. He would be glad to get rid of the thing.

They would be watching the trains now. They would be watching for this car. He didn't dare go near Strasbourg, although that would have been the easiest place to get lost for a while, because that was what they would be expecting him to do. The next couple of hours were going to be a problem.

Why the hell had they only sent the one car? It wasn't a question of feeling slighted—Steadman thought he could live without the honor of being the most hunted man in Europe—but if they were that hot after him it just didn't make a great deal of sense. They had known he was on that train and they had sent out exactly two goons to make the pinch. Something was wrong.

Well, it wasn't going to do him any good to torture himself about it. If they caught him they could amuse themselves by explaining how clever they had been, and if they didn't he couldn't give a damn.

After about forty-five minutes he decided he had pushed his luck with the car just about far enough and started looking around for a good place to get rid of it. That wasn't really very difficult—there were all kinds of little turnoffs into the forest, gravel-covered roads hardly wider than footpaths that were probably used twenty times in the year. He settled on one, drove in a hundred yards or so, and parked. He left Georg's Luger on the front seat, just keeping the clip. The clip was all he was going to need, and he was in for a long walk.

It was after four o'clock in the afternoon and none too warm. He wished he had been able to keep Dieter Kroll's leather overcoat, but you couldn't have everything. And he couldn't remember the last time he'd had had a hot meal.

The direction he wanted was southwest. If he stayed on that course—and stayed out of sight—he would be across into Vichy inside of a week. He was a good walker and could do thirty-five or forty miles a day, although he didn't know how that was going to work out at night. Maybe he would have a bit of luck and find another car to steal.

As the sky began changing from dove gray to slate, Steadman decided he needed something to eat. He was near the top of a low hill, and as he reached the summit he could see the twinkle of lights from a village the map in the glove compartment of the Mercedes designated as Schirmeck. The bottoms of his trousers were wet from the long grass, and his nose never seemed to stop running. It was going to have to be this place and no other.

The Germans liked to eat—even Hitler hadn't been able to change that. They liked overheated rooms and long tables and the cat rubbing its back against their ankles. They favored dumplings and meat covered with gravy and sweet, heavy desserts. It was a moral certainty with them that a virtuous man always rose from dinner feeling slightly sick. So naturally this village, like all the others, had a *Gasthaus*.

It wasn't much larger than the living room of a good-sized private home, and the claustrophobic feeling was increased by the heavy wood paneling. There were deer heads mounted on the walls. The air was heavy with the mingled smell of cooked meat and burning pine logs. Somewhere a gramophone was playing a sentimental tune with violins like syrup. The Germans liked that too.

Steadman took a table near the fireplace. Nobody seemed to pay the slightest attention to him but there wasn't any reason why they should. There had been a rack of newspapers near the door and he had taken one. As he waited to give his order he scanned the lead items in the *Strassburger Illustrierte Zeitung* to discover if Winston Churchill had been dragged to Berlin in chains yet. Apparently not. The war in Russia was as good as over, he discovered. And America, notwithstanding Roosevelt and the Jews, was beginning to see how clearly her interests lay with the Reich. It all went with the sentimental music and the *Pfannkuchen*.

The waitress came, a nice elderly lady with white hair and a white lace apron over her peasant dress, and Steadman looked at the blackboard she brought with her and decided on the venison and the potato pancakes. He would drink the house wine, which was white and spiced—in Alsace they spoke German and drank wine, and in Lorraine they spoke French and drank beer; it was one of Europe's great cultural mysteries—and he didn't want any dessert, just coffee. It wouldn't be real coffee, of course, but it was the thought that mattered. She brought him a little plate of sausage pieces wrapped in pastry, just so he wouldn't starve to death while he waited.

As gradually the fire thawed him out, Steadman discovered that he was getting the shakes again. He decided that when the war was over he would go back and settle with that goddamn Norwegian. He felt awful.

Why hadn't they nabbed him at the train station? They had had their chance—why hadn't they sealed off the whole area? It was almost as if they had wanted him to get through. Perhaps Weinschenk was simply getting arrogant, or perhaps he had something else entirely in mind.

Weinschenk. He was the clever type. He prided himself on it. He would take the devious way for choice. Well, maybe this one time he had outsmarted himself.

You didn't get just a glass of wine—the Germans couldn't understand anyone drinking just one glass of anything. You got a carafe. The stuff was a wonderful fruity flavor and Steadman had the impression it cleared his head.

It was very pleasant here. The fire was just far enough away to be comfortable, and he was beginning to get sleepy. Maybe he could find somewhere to hole up for a few hours and get some rest before he started his trek. That might be the best idea.

He had once asked Herr Käselau why he had moved to Switzerland, and had been told, "This is what Germany was like before the Great War." Maybe so. Herr Käselau hadn't approved of the Weimar Republic, and still less of Hitler, but they had all gone to Stuttgart for the ballet a few times every year and that had always been Steadman's view of the country. Once, in '28, they had seen a street demonstration by the brownshirts, but for the most part his stepfather had shielded them from German politics the way parents of a certain class in England won't let their children play in the neighborhood for fear of their picking up "common" accents. The Nazis weren't particularly dangerous; they simply weren't refined.

Well, even Herr Käselau had lived to outgrow that idea.

When he had finished his coffee, which tasted like boiled wood shavings, Steadman paid his tab and left. There was a row of overcoats hanging from hooks near the door; he snagged off the one that looked biggest and walked out with it. Nobody seemed to notice.

Outside, the street was dark. Perhaps even in a little dorf like this they were afraid of British bombers. Hardly anyone was out; Steadman could hear the sound of his own footprints quite distinctly.

The cold woke him up again, and he remembered that he was in a hostile country where the police were anxious to start work on his fingernails. In Stockholm they had been content with trying to kill him, but here it would be different. Here they would be all prepared to settle down to a nice, long, uncomfortable interrogation.

Somehow the atmosphere had changed—it was as if he had stepped out into a different world. The shadow that gathered around the feet of buildings looked darker, and there was an indefinable menace in the air. Suddenly Steadman felt himself in immediate danger, although he couldn't have said precisely why. Something was threatening him, something just beyond his line of vision. He slipped his pistol into the pocket of his overcoat, which was cut for a man with shorter arms than his, and kept his fingers closed over it.

There was a clock tower somewhere, and when it struck the quarter hour Steadman nearly fainted. This was ridiculous; he was just letting his nerves get the better of him. It was the occupational hazard of fugitives.

A man passed him on the sidewalk, glancing at him with frightened eyes, and he knew he was kidding himself. Something was up—everybody seemed to know about it except him.

What was he listening for? In Spain he had discovered that you heard all sorts of things if you took the trouble. The trick was to hear with something more than the conscious mind, to become simply a receiver for all the little sounds that floated around you, to stop trying to interpret. That was how you survived.

They had dogged him to this place. It wasn't so much a discovery as something he suddenly just admitted to himself. He had been spotted and now they were out there, circling around for the kill.

He kept on walking in the same direction, and as he passed into the shadow of a building he fished the letter out of the pocket of his trousers, folded it into a small square with his right hand, and started looking for somewhere he could get rid of it. If he turned out to be wrong, and nobody jumped him, he could always circle back and retrieve it, but he couldn't take a chance on being wrong. For the rest, he wasn't making any particular effort to appear inconspicuous. If they had seen him, they had seen him. There wasn't anything he could do about it.

There was a church ahead, with its porch, which was flush with the sidewalk, shrouded in darkness. In European churches there was almost always a poor box right next to the door. It was Monday night; probably the priest emptied the box after services on Sunday, so that would be a safe hiding place for nearly a week. If he never came back, and the priest found the letter, he might turn it over to the police, but he would be more likely to burn it—ordinary people didn't want to become involved in state secrets, not in Nazi Germany. The poor father would probably have wit enough to know such knowledge could lead to his sudden and permanent disappearance. Under the circumstances, the poor box was Steadman's best bet.

He slipped inside the shadowy porch, found the box, and dropped his tiny square of paper inside. No one could have seen him do it, but if anyone was watching they might wonder why he had made the slight detour. He started undoing the buttons of his fly so he could leave something behind to account for his wanting a few seconds of privacy. Let them think the worst.

Half a minute later, he was on his way again. The street was quiet. Perhaps he really was just getting paranoid.

And then, all at once, he could hear the sound of running feet behind him. He didn't stop to look; he just bolted. The first alleyway, he ducked inside and kept right on running. There was a board fence at the end—

for a moment he thought he had boxed himself in, and then he saw that the alley took a right-hand turn. As he threw himself that way, nearly stumbling over a pile of empty paint cans, he heard a sound like someone coughing and, almost simultaneously and directly behind his head, the crack of a bullet splintering wood. They weren't kidding.

And then the pursuit stopped. Steadman found himself out on a side street, and suddenly there was no one following him. He ran a bit farther, zig-zagging between rows of houses, and then slowed down. Maybe he had lost them. In any case, it seemed that they had given up. He tried remembering how to breathe.

A car began turning the corner ahead, its headlights out, and he stepped into the narrow space between two buildings, hardly wide enough for two men to walk abreast, and waited.

They were getting out—he heard the car door slam and the sound of footsteps. At the end of the passageway there was a wooden gate. That would have to do. Just as they were about to reach the opening he closed the gate behind him soundlessly. For the moment, he was safe again.

Apparently not. As he turned around, a yellow light flashed in his eyes. For an instant he could see nothing. And then, the shape of someone behind the light. His hand went to his pocket.

"Don't try, Mr. Steadman."

He recognized the voice of Weinschenk. The flashlight beam dropped a few feet, and he could make out the narrow silhouette in the darkness.

"It would be a thousand pities to kill you now."

But you couldn't stop what had to be. He almost felt sorry for Weinschenk as he drew the pistol from his overcoat pocket, but it was time now to die.

He couldn't have described the sensation that shot down his arm—it felt as if it were being twisted off, and suddenly he could no longer move his hand. It opened seemingly of its own accord, and the Luger dropped to the pavement with a clatter. He heard a growling in his ear, like an animal, or the low hum of a machine, and, as he tried to turn, something struck him on the side of the head. He felt the impact, that was all. After that, there was nothing.

XXII

NOVEMBER 11, 1941

Until the night they called her in, Karen had imagined they might have forgotten all about her.

The weather had turned suddenly cold, with sharp winds that blew pieces of newspaper down the streets and made them snap against the walls of buildings like pieces of flying shrapnel, but she hardly noticed. She hardly left her flat anymore. She had stopped going to work, but no one called to complain. It was as if she had died.

"He's gone into business for himself," Brian had warned her. "I don't know what sort of a game he thinks he's playing, but it'll end badly. Either we'll get him or the Jerries will, and the results won't be much different. If we need you, we'll let you know."

Her first day back, after the unavoidable preliminaries were over, she took a train out to Kent to see where they had buried Bertie. The family had a certain local standing, so anyone would have imagined they could have done better than the poky little back corner of the churchyard where one could look through the iron palings at the bus stop and the turf accountant's office. Even the warden was ashamed.

"We couldn't help it, my lady," he said, leaning uneasily on a garden rake. "The vault was filled in his lordship's grandfather's time, and we're hard pressed to find room for anybody these last few years. Just the old families, you understand."

No, she didn't understand, but it hardly mattered. She looked down at the fresh-turned earth and tried to grasp that that was her husband beneath her feet, Bertie the Brave, whom somehow, somewhere along the line, she had ceased to love. It didn't seem quite fair.

So many hearts seemed buried in one grave. David and Bertie both— it seemed this horrible war had murdered them both.

Brian was right, of course. The responsibility was hers. One's relationship to the causes of things mattered very little. Nothing she had done or not done would have changed the outcome for Bertie, but that didn't alter the way she felt. Events could move in parallel—she had turned her back on him and he had died. Perhaps the case wasn't so different for David.

She had brought a little bouquet of violets with her because Bertie had always loved violets and she found herself unable to resist the gesture. She laid them on the spot where in another year the headstone would rest, if there was anyone left to see to it, and turned away. She would never come back, she knew that. Somehow it would be impossible.

There were things to see to at the house—she had regained possession with Bertie's death, but the idea of living there again never entered her head. Perhaps, after the war, she would sell it. The keys to his desk were where he had always kept them, as probably every servant in the house knew, at the bottom of his handkerchief box, and when she went through his papers she found everything was in order. She had half expected to find a note, but there was nothing like that. There was nothing to suggest any idea of her had crossed his mind in the last few days of his life. The cook asked if she would be wanting dinner, but Karen shook her head and said no. She would take the evening train back to town.

When she got back to her flat, the transcript Brian had given her was still waiting there on her nightstand. She didn't want to look at it, so she went into her kitchen to make herself a cup of tea.

David had shot a woman trying to escape from the train station in Stockholm. She had died the next morning. In all probability he had used the gun Karen had given him. Did that make her an accessory before the fact? Had he really done such a thing, or were they lying to her?

The War Ministry had wired her bedroom and listened while she and David made love. An hour after he left, two silent, ferocious men had rung the doorbell and occupied the flat like an invading army. The orders Brian had given David were, on the face of it, confused, so their real motives might have been anything. And yet they expected her to accept with blind faith that the man she loved was a murderer and a traitor. They expected her, if and when the time came, to help them interrogate him, to persuade him to return whatever it was he had stolen from the Germans. They expected a great deal.

They had expected a great deal of Bertie, and it seemed to have broken him. Honor, King, and country—they were the magic words that were supposed to settle everything. Perhaps for men like Brian Horton they actually did, but Bertie still had some small claim to her loyalty, and because of that she was no longer sure.

She decided that she would disobey her instructions. She wouldn't read the transcript. She wanted her memories of that night left as they were.

Thus began the term of her widowhood. She just withdrew, and stayed in her flat, and read back numbers of *Country Life*.

The following morning her mother arrived from Surrey. She had phoned and couldn't be dissuaded; it was simply inconceivable to her that a woman who had just lost her husband, regardless of the context, didn't need the company and consolation of her mother. Besides, Karen suspected, winter in the country was beginning to bore her.

"You weren't here for the funeral, dear," she said, as soon as she had taken her suitcase into the bedroom and come back to sit in Bertie's chair. "It made a very odd impression. Didn't you know?"

She had taken off her jacket, and the pale cream of her long-sleeved blouse looked very starched and fresh. From the way she was sitting, with her hands crossed in her lap and her ankles pulled together, Karen could tell that in another few minutes she would be asking for her midafternoon coffee and would be very put out that there wasn't any date bread. She was only a few years over fifty, had lost her figure in her thirties, and, as anyone could have guessed from the peculiar lightless quality of her pale blue eyes, had learned next to nothing from life. Between mother and daughter there subsisted the dumb affection of natures that have no sympathy with one another.

"No. I didn't hear until night before last." Karen smiled uncertainly. "I went down yesterday to see how everything was."

"Yes—well, as you can imagine, all old Lady Windermere could talk about was the fact that nobody seemed to be able to find you."

It was obvious she was waiting for Karen to explain herself—and just as obvious she had her own suspicions where the explanation might lie. One could see it in the crinkling around her eyes. The war didn't have any reality for her; nothing had really changed since the summer of 1939. If a young woman who is estranged from her husband should happen to disappear for a few days, well then . . . It wasn't her fault. It was simply the way her mind worked.

"I can't discuss that with you," Karen said, scanning the wall behind her mother's chair, resigned to not being believed. "I don't mean that I won't discuss it with you, but that I can't. You know where I've been working."

"Yes, well . . ."

Not another word would be spoken on the subject. Lady Ridley was a gentlewoman who had discharged her motherly duty, so the matter was closed. This, of course, indicated nothing whatever about her private opinions.

"Would you like some coffee, mother?"

"Now that Bertie's gone, I hope you won't be taking up with that hideous, social-climbing American." Lady Ridley smiled in a way that suggested she was merely tightening the muscles of her face. "I never could abide him—they all have way too much money and no breeding."

"Mother . . ."

"Well, are you? I noticed he wasn't at the funeral either, but of course I didn't say anything."

The two women sat staring at each other for several seconds, during which the situation could have gone absolutely anywhere. When Lady Ridley realized this she smiled again.

"Yes, dear, I will have some coffee. Thank you. I suppose it's only chicory, but you can't help that."

After the first day, her mother's presence seemed to make very little difference. Lady Ridley had many friends in London and, of course, the shops were a standing temptation to anyone from a village the size of Thursley. Sir Arnold Ridley had been dead for eleven years; no one could criticize his widow for wishing to enjoy the pleasures of the metropolis. Karen would see her again in the evening—her mother was terrified of being bombed, and nothing could convince her that the raids were for the most part a thing of the past—and, besides, in her present state of mind it hardly mattered to her whether she was alone or not.

Except to go down to the Cromwell Road to fetch in provisions, Karen was getting out of the habit of dressing during the day. She would sit around in her bathrobe, wondering why she didn't have the energy to do anything more. Perhaps it was just as well that her mother had come; otherwise she might really have gone into a slide. It wasn't grief precisely.

One had to remember in order to grieve, and she was refusing to remember. She was refusing everything.

And then the phone rang.

"No, I can't come over," Karen said. "I have my mother here with me and, besides, I don't see that we have very much left to talk about."

"Then I'll have to come there. It's very simple, Karen—either you come to me or I shan't have any choice about coming to you, mother or no mother."

"All right. Tomorrow morning."

"I'm afraid not. I'm afraid it has to be at once."

It was a cold night, and there didn't seem to be any taxis running. Karen gathered her coat as tightly around her shoulders as she could and started walking. She had told her mother not to wait up for her.

She still didn't understand why she was going. She had come to dislike Brian Horton, so what did he represent to her that she would drop everything and walk all the way over to the War Ministry simply because he had told her she must? Bertie had severed that tie, and in the end had parted from life too. Perhaps that was it. Perhaps she wasn't prepared to surrender so much, to accept the responsibility. She didn't really know.

In any case, she hadn't committed herself to anything. She could go and listen and still walk away. There wasn't any law . . .

It was astonishing the way Belgravia emptied after dark. Once one crossed Sloane Street it was like being in a city abandoned. The blackout was observed so scrupulously that there wasn't even a sliver of light from behind a curtain. Karen managed to walk three blocks before she saw signs of life—a couple getting out of a taxi. Perhaps she wouldn't have to walk after all. She raised her hand, and the driver must have seen her because he pulled up at the corner and waited for her.

There was nobody else in the waiting room this time, and the door to Brian's office had been left ajar. Brian appeared at the threshold to wave her inside—he wasn't wearing a tie, and the bags under his eyes had taken on a faintly purplish tinge. His whole attitude suggested a resigned exhaustion.

"Did you read the transcript?" he asked, the way her teachers used to ask, *Did you read the chapter on the early Tudors?*

"No. It's in a locked drawer in my flat. I haven't gotten around to burning it yet."

Without waiting to be asked, she sat down. Brian took his place behind the cluttered desk and smoothed down the left end of his mustache with the tip of his little finger.

"You know, Karen, I'm beginning to wonder if you're everything we could hope for in a security risk." He paused for a moment, evidently expecting a response. When there wasn't one, he sighed faintly and knitted his fingers together over his chest. Very gradually the knuckles began going white. "However, it seems that we have remarkably little choice but to assume that we can continue to rely on you."

Karen smiled. The smile said, *Do you expect me to be grateful? Pleased? I'm not.*

"Do you have any idea how precariously the war is balanced right now?" Brian asked, relaxing the tension in his fingers and bringing the tips together so that he seemed to be confirming they were still a match. "Hitler is within a few miles of Moscow, and we don't know what the political situation is there—it's perfectly possible those people might go for some kind of separate arrangement. They're exhausted. And if the Germans manage to take the Russians out, we'll be right back where we were a year ago. Alone. Do you imagine the Americans will continue to help us then?"

For a moment it was possible to believe that he was seriously asking the question. He leaned forward, resting his elbows on the desk, his tired eyes watching her in a nervous, questioning way. And then suddenly he dropped back against his chair.

He made a weary movement with his hand, as if waving away a fly.

"Winston can make all the heroic speeches in Parliament he wants," Horton went on, his voice a hopeless monotone. "But there are certain economic realities to the situation that cannot be glossed over. If America doesn't enter the war within the next few months, then I'm afraid we might just be for it. The Russians aren't the only ones who are nearing the end of their tether. Hitler may win by spring, but if he doesn't he's finished. We know that, and so does he. And right now I'd rather be in his position than ours."

He stopped for a moment. The gloomy idea seemed to possess him, and his eyes took on a cloudy, lifeless quality—he might have been seeing the Wehrmacht parade march up the Mall in front of Buckingham Palace. It was an eloquent silence.

"Which brings us back to your friend Mr. David Steadman."

Karen felt her face suddenly going hot. It was the surprise as much as anything. What did David have to do with the Russians? What was the man talking about?

"I don't follow you," she said finally, a little astonished at the sound of her own voice.

"Don't you?" Brian smiled unpleasantly and his eyebrows shot up. "No, perhaps you don't. You don't know what it was that Mr. Steadman was sent along to lift for us, do you."

"Am I about to find out?"

As if on cue, a secretary came in through the door, waited a moment until she was able to catch Brian's eye, and then laid a file folder on the desk in front of him. She smelled very strongly of gardenia toilet water, which for some reason struck Karen as rather out of place in the War Ministry. Brian's gaze followed the secretary back to the door, but only, one sensed, to confirm that she was closing it behind her. He set his left hand down over the folder as if about to take his oath on it.

"Would it be enough if I told you that if you believe that Mr. Steadman has the outcome of the war in his pocket you wouldn't be wrong by very much?"

He sat quite still. One had the impression that he was studying Karen to read her reaction.

"No—perhaps you're right not to be satisfied with that." He smiled again, this time without actual malice. "I suppose I wouldn't believe it either if I were in your shoes."

"I don't see why, I . . . ."

She really didn't know what she was trying to say. She only knew that she didn't want to hear anything more and that, at the same time, she was powerless to avoid it. It was obvious even to Brian that she was a captive now—one could see it in her eyes.

"Hitler has made certain diplomatic overtures," he went on, quite as if she hadn't spoken at all. "Or, perhaps more accurately, someone within his circle has made them, and he hasn't entirely withheld his blessing—there seems to have been some sort of power struggle within the Nazi hierarchy over this matter and we can't be certain who is on which side. In either case, certain proposals have been put to the United States about the continuation of the war, proposals which President Roosevelt may find himself powerless to reject. If that turns out to be the case, then I'm afraid we've lost. If the United States remains neutral for, say, another six months, I think it's likely that by next summer we may be suing the Germans for peace."

"But David . . ."

"David? Yes, David. David is the issue." Brian lifted his hand and drew it slowly back to his breast. His eyebrows came closer together, and the impression of concentrated attention was almost painful. "That was what David stole in Stockholm—the letter containing Hitler's proposals to guarantee the continued neutrality of the United States. That's what we're expecting you to talk him into handing over to us."

Tears began forming in Karen's eyes. She knew it was cowardly of her, but she simply couldn't help herself. There was a pain in her throat that felt as if it might actually split her open. For several seconds she was quite incapable of making a sound, and then, finally . . .

"How can he?" she said, in a voice that was hardly more than a choked whisper. "Why are you telling me all this? What difference can it make? He's in Europe—the Germans may have him already, so how can I make him do anything? He's run away."

"Yes—he's run away. But the Germans don't have the Continent quite all to themselves. We have a few friends who might be able to assist us." Brian's face began to relax. He was actually grinning. "I think we might have him back in our hands before long."

XXIII

They had taken his wristwatch, so he didn't have any clear idea how long he had been out. It must have been awhile, though. He had cloudy recollections of being moved—hands gripping him under the armpits, voices, the lid of a car trunk closing over him. They must have given him something to keep him quiet. He had an unnatural, throbbing headache, and there was a terrible taste in his mouth.

He was lying on his back when he woke up. There was a bright yellow ceiling light behind heavy wire mesh. Perhaps they were afraid of people cutting their throats with pieces of the bulb, or perhaps they just didn't want you to be able to put it out. He couldn't have reached it anyway; the ceiling was a good twelve feet high.

He closed his eyes again. He had seen enough. A wave of nausea passed over him as he thought about what an idiot he had been. Nothing could be worse than this, not even death. He had let himself fall into the hands of the Gestapo, and now they would smash the bones in his fingers and attach electrodes to his genitals and try to break him down. The best thing he could hope for was that they would make a mistake and kill him before he lost the will to hold out.

They would kill him anyway, sooner or later—nobody ever got away alive from a place like this. They might find the letter by themselves, or it might not make any difference whether they found it or not. All he knew was he had no right to make his exit from this world a little easier by giving them what they wanted. There was too much at stake for that, so he would have to accept the fact of dying in uncertainty. As long as he was alive and the secret was safe, there was hope. If by some miracle he did get out . . .

But he couldn't count on that. He couldn't even think about it. He would die here—all he could do was try to make the right choice between available alternatives. Better to have his heart give out under torture than to wait for a bullet in the brain, longing for it because he had spilled his guts to these animals and could no longer bear the shame of breathing. Anything was better than that.

His attention was attracted by a sound, a metallic click, and he saw that someone was watching him through the narrow eyeslit in the upper part of the cell door. He could detect a trace of movement, that was all; he wasn't even curious enough to wonder who it was.

This was all such a grotesque joke that he nearly laughed. The Germans are the enemy. The Germans want the letter back so it can be delivered to President Roosevelt. The British are on the side of the angels. The British want to kill him and burn the letter. He tries to return the letter to the Germans, and they're not interested. They try to kill him. Nobody seems to know what anybody wants, except that everybody wants David Steadman's heart cut up in quarters.

Well, maybe there was an easy way out after all. Maybe, if Weinschenk would listen to reason, Steadman could just give the fucking letter back and be done with it. Weinschenk would kill him anyway—Weinschenk seemed to have a score to settle—but maybe everybody could just forget about the broken knuckles and the fried testicles.

Of course, that would be what they would want him to think. That would make everything easier for them. He would have to keep reminding himself that the decision was not his to make—he didn't know what the hell game the Germans were playing.

From this moment on, he thought, everything is strategy. They have pain and fear, but I have the letter. The real question is not whether a man's nerve endings can hold out longer than his heart, but whether he can be tricked into believing what isn't true.

That was why the Germans had taken away his wristwatch. They didn't even want him to be sure what time it was.

The cell was tiny, perhaps six feet by twelve—when he got up he would measure it exactly. The walls were white ceramic brick, like bathroom tile. He would count them and, when he was sure no one was looking, mark a few of them so he would know if they were moving him from one cell to another.

His bed was simply a tick filled with straw, resting on a metal frame. There were no blankets. The tick, when he concentrated enough to notice, smelled like vomit.

He was cold. Why hadn't he noticed before that the cell was like a meat locker? He was so cold that he began to shiver, and then, abruptly, he forced himself to stop. That would be just another of their tactics, to try wearing him down with small physical discomforts. So what if he was cold? He had been cold before.

Nothing that could happen would be so very terrible, he told himself. What made torture so frightening? Pain? He had been in pain before. When he was shot at Artesa de Segre. In the dentist's chair. He had known a man once who had sawn through his own thumb trying to get disentangled from a parachute halter; the son of a bitch had cut himself down and run a hundred yards before he even noticed what had happened. Torture was bad because you expected it to be bad, because you allowed your mind to rest on how bad it was going to be. You scared yourself into it.

And you believed in the future. Rousseau said that existence was nothing but disconnected instants of experience, that our sense of continuity with ourselves was an illusion. Okay. He would play it that way. He would take it one experience at a time. He would work from the assumption that his life was only the one thought in his mind, the one moment of sensation. There was no future, no past. Only now.

He was hungry. Maybe that should give him some idea how long they had had him—he had just eaten when he was captured. Or maybe they had pumped his stomach, or he had thrown up. Maybe the stink from the mattress ticking was his own. There wasn't any way of knowing.

And, besides, he was supposed to stop thinking about having had a past. There was only now.

And then he remembered Karen, and tears flooded his eyes, and he decided that Rousseau must have been full of shit.

So it would be just a question of holding out, after all.

Oh, God, was it really going to end like this? Had he lived through all those years in Spain and all that had happened in the past several days to die in a stinking cell, beaten to death by some sadist the SS had probably pulled out of a lunatic asylum? And that was the very best he could hope for.

Karen would never know what had happened to him. They would burn his body and flush the ashes into a sewer, and he would just disappear. And even if she did know, she wouldn't think there was anything terrific about it even if he did hold out. He wouldn't be dying for her side. It would be better if he just forgot all about Karen.

It was still him against them, and they didn't have quite all the weapons. He would hang on to that thought.

They were still out there, on the other side of the cell door, still watching him. The bastards.

The eyeslit closed with the same sharp click, like a glass rod snapped in two, and Steadman lay waiting in suspense. But when the door opened it was only a man in a long white coat, like a doctor's smock, carrying a black medical bag—he might even have been a doctor, if the Gestapo wanted to go to the trouble. Apparently they just thought to see what kind of shape he was in before they began the main entertainment.

He was a small man, with a round unsmiling face and hands of almost feminine delicacy. He never spoke and never looked directly at his patient, not the way a man would who didn't wish to avoid even the slightest human contact. It was only a cursory examination: He pulled down the lower lid of Steadman's left eye, he counted the pulse, he held the back of his hand on Steadman's forehead. Then he was done. The medical bag was never opened. He waited for someone outside to open the door for him and then was gone. He didn't seem to enjoy his work.

It wasn't until he was alone again that Steadman realized how weak he felt—perhaps it was the experience of being regarded as a patient that made him think about it, but suddenly he wasn't sure he would be able to rise to his feet even if he wanted to. He decided to attempt the experiment—a foot slid over the edge of the bedstead and hit the floor heel first with a smack. It took him a good five minutes before he could gain a sitting position, and when he had made it he leaned forward, resting his elbows against his knees, absolutely exhausted. No, he was not in the greatest shape. What the hell had they given him?

He was still sitting up when the door opened again and Weinschenk came in. He was carrying a wooden chair.

"Feeling any better?" he said pleasantly as he positioned the chair in the center of the floor and sat down. "Did you realize you had pneumonia? The doctors have given you something for it they say should clear everything up in a day or two. In a way, you're lucky we caught you."

He spoke in English. He smiled. His legs were crossed and his hat was resting upside down on a corner of the bed. Apparently that was the way he was going to play it, at least for openers.

"Thanks a lot."

Weinschenk's smile became knowing, almost intimate. He appreciated the irony. He might wear the uniform of the SS, he seemed to be suggesting, but that didn't stop him from being a good fellow. After all this time, the two of them were almost boon companions.

"You can't imagine how I've been looking forward to this," he said, stretching slightly in the chair, as if from pure excess of good feeling. He was a few years younger than Steadman had expected—of course, he had never seen Weinschenk except from a distance, and a man always looks younger with his hat off. He was going a little bald as well, which had a humanizing effect. It was only when you watched the muscles working around the jawline, where the skin seemed thin as paper, that you could identify this as the Hauptmann Weinschenk who used to interrogate prisoners in batches of three, shooting the first two at the outset and then putting the pistol against the third man's head and asking him if he had anything he wished to say. No, he wasn't the least bit human.

Steadman decided he was tired. He wanted to lie down again, but his feet seemed to weigh about forty pounds apiece. So instead he sat looking at Weinschenk through eyes that felt too large for their sockets, wishing he would be a nice boy and go away.

"It's been a good hunt," Weinschenk continued. "How did you happen to catch pneumonia?"

"Swimming across the Baltic from Sweden."

Weinschenk looked doubtful for a moment and then laughed. He seemed prepared to accept anything.

"And what did you do with the Führer's letter?"

Suddenly everything changed. The smile on Weinschenk's face was no longer friendly and encouraging—he had reverted to type. Well, it had to start sometime.

"What do you care?" Steadman asked—he didn't give the impression of being much interested in the answer. "You could have had it back in Stockholm, but you got cute. Now I'm not so sure you can be trusted with it."

To hell with this—he was tired of games. By putting his hands together under his knees, he managed, one at a time, to get his legs back on the bed so he could lie down again. He was tired of the exertion of trying to look properly defiant. Weinschenk bored him.

Weinschenk too seemed bored. He shrugged his shoulders, and the heavy black material of his uniform stirred slightly.

"You have been searched, of course," he said finally. "While you were unconscious we even X-rayed your stomach. Obviously you have disposed of the letter somehow, but I'll tell you in advance that the letter is a secondary consideration, even for me. We mean to have it back, but the principal thing is to guarantee your silence—and I'm sure you know how they plan to achieve that. But I can see to it you have a relatively painless and dignified death if you will simply tell me what you have done with the letter."

Weinschenk peered into his face for a moment, as if he expected an answer that instant. Finally he seemed to lose interest, and he resumed his attitude of bored melancholy.

"It will never be delivered in any case." Weinschenk's eyes closed and then opened again with trancelike slowness as he spoke. "No matter what arrangements you have made you must realize the situation is hopeless, so why put yourself through the ordeal of an interrogation that can only end one way? You know the kinds of things that happen to people in places like this—why put yourself through that?"

"Maybe I'll be the exception. Maybe I'll hold out until the British are marching on Berlin and you'll have to shoot me as a safety precaution. You never know about that sort of thing."

He tried to grin, but he didn't have the impression he had made much of a success of it. Weinschenk merely shook his head.

"There are no exceptions. Everyone breaks in the end—you know that." He leaned forward, resting his elbows on the thigh of his left leg, and his eyes were almost mournful.

"I bear you no ill will," he went on. "You made me look rather bad in Spain; it wasn't the best thing for my career. But I've always respected you as a man, Steadman. I don't like to think of you ending your life as you will be when the brutes they have here are quite finished with you. I am being honest—I hope you appreciate that. They will get the letter out of you one way or the other, and there won't be a thing you will be able to do about it. No disgrace can attach to you. A man's honor lies in the recognition of facts."

Steadman glanced toward the door and noticed that the eyeslit was still open. The light beyond it flickered off and on, as if someone were out in the corridor, walking back and forth. Yes, he could hear the sound of boot heels on the floor.

He felt a terrible despair. It was an almost physical affliction, a draining of what little strength was remaining to him. Because it was obvious now that he had fallen into the hands of a lunatic.

Somewhere in this building there were guys waiting to pull him to pieces, one raw nerve fiber at a time, and Weinschenk could talk about personal honor, and his career, and how he bore no ill will. People were dying all over Europe. History was being served back and forth like a tennis ball, but what mattered to Egon Weinschenk was whether or not he made his next promotion and if his hands remained clean. How could you talk to someone who seemed to think the war was some sort of personal contest between just the two of them—as if they mattered?

Weinschenk was mad—that was what it all meant, the whole ludicrous scene. Weinschenk was announcing that he was out of his head, that they were no longer playing tragedy but farce.

"Maybe I burned it, *mein Herr*—did you ever think of that?"

"You would never have burned it, Steadman." The Hauptmann's face hardened and there was a certain hint of accusation in his voice, as if he felt himself betrayed. "You have hidden it somewhere. You could walk out of here tonight and have it back in your hands before morning— I know you much too well not to know that. But you *are* going to tell, and we *are* going to get the letter back."

"Explain to me why you want it, Weinschenk. Maybe you can have it without any fuss."

Steadman closed his eyes, covering them with his arm. He was very close to caving in and he knew it. He wasn't even sure he didn't want to. What the hell, he was going to be dead anyway. How was it any of his business?

"We want to keep it away from the British," Weinschenk answered, his voice registering a certain disappointed surprise, as if he had expected Steadman to have figured it all out for himself. "Think of how embarrassing it would be for us with the Japanese, if, for instance, Churchill decided to publish the thing in the newspapers."

"But you don't plan to deliver it, do you."

"We will see to it that something is delivered to your President Roosevelt, but it is by no means certain that it will be the Führer's letter. We have no interest in promoting Herr von Ribbentrop's diplomatic maneuvering. Why should we concern ourselves with that?"

We? That would be the SS, of course. Of course, thought Steadman, wondering why he pestered himself with silly questions. The SS would be just as happy if their sacred Führer's letter ended up in the paper shredder and all those American sailors ended up in the Deep Six. What difference did it make to them whether the United States entered the war, since, it would seem, *their* war was with the Reich Foreign Office?

"No, it doesn't make any difference." Weinschenk shook his head, almost as if he could read your mind. "You Americans think you hold the balance, but you don't. The Führer has been persuaded by unscrupulous men that he must stay on terms of peace with your nation of mongrels, but why should Germany have to plead with anyone? If you entered the war tomorrow, it would be a year at least before you could land a soldier, and we will have finished our business with both Russia and Britain long before that."

"Terrific. I'm frightfully pleased for you."

Steadman managed to turn his head toward Weinschenk and show his teeth in a ratty, mocking grin. Somehow having that last option closed on him made everything easier. He wouldn't have fancied doing a deal with the Germans anyway.

But was there anything else he could even imagine as a way out? Could he get them to kill him somehow? Could he goad them to do that? You had to play it very carefully when you were torturing a man for information. You couldn't be tricked into losing your temper. You didn't dare get carried away.

"In an hour you will be turned over to the professionals," Weinschenk said, standing up from his chair. He allowed the fingertips of his left hand to touch lightly against the backrest as he reached down and picked up his hat from the bed. The interview seemed to be drawing to a close. "Don't imagine they will be betrayed into any mistakes—these men are very experienced. I give you an hour to consider the future, Herr Stead-man. One hour."

XXIV

Doubtless so that he could be on hand to take the credit, Gruppen-führer Nebe had come to Strasbourg by special military plane the instant he received word of Steadman's capture. He had been around all that afternoon and evening, making his authority felt and annoying everyone. He was waiting in the prison commandant's office when Weinschenk returned.

"How is our patient?" he asked, smiling ferociously. "Is he ready to be put to the question?"

"Yes, he's quite ready. I rather suspect he's somewhat more ready than we are."

Weinschenk threw his cap onto the commandant's desk and sat down heavily in his chair. He wished Nebe had stayed in Berlin—the man grated on his nerves at any time, but now . . . He was weary and depressed, and he couldn't shake the nagging suspicion that he was about to make some ghastly mistake, something for which he might never be able to forgive himself, no matter how well everything worked out. It was almost like having a bad conscience.

"Are you going to witness the interrogation?" Nebe leaned against a corner of the desk, his arms crossed, his cap pushed back on his nearly naked scalp. Weinschenk looked at him and wondered, quite irrelevantly, if that was what he was going to look like himself in another ten years' time.

"No." He shook his head, frowning. "No, not actually present. I'll just come in from time to time to see if he's ready to break, but for tactical reasons it's better if he doesn't associate me too directly with the . . . What about yourself? You might find it instructive."

Nebe was much too shocked at the suggestion to notice his subordinate's irony. A perfectly visible shudder passed over him, and his eyes narrowed with disgust.

"No, thank you," he answered, a shade too loud. "That sort of thing turns my stomach. I'm not a criminal, you know." It was several seconds before he was once again entirely placid.

"Fortunately this business shouldn't take very long. I've advised the Reichsführer of the situation, and he's awaiting my report. Besides, one doesn't relish . . ."

The smile returned, but there was nothing of ferocity in it now. Weinschenk could barely contain his annoyance at the man.

"I'm sorry you saw fit to mention any of this to the Reichsführer," he said blandly. He could just imagine what Himmler's reaction must have been—he only hoped Nebe had laid it on thick enough about how they had arranged for the Foreign Ministry to take the blame. "Personally, I think 'this business,' as you call it, may take quite some time. And I wouldn't, if I were you, have quite so much faith that pair of 'technicians' who accompanied you here are going to be able to manage. He isn't exactly a debutante, you know. I think it entirely possible that he may die under torture without giving us any useful information whatsoever."

He smiled tightly at Nebe's bewildered expression. The idea gave him a certain satisfaction. It would serve the little mediocrity right, him and Himmler both. It would be delicious if Steadman ended by cheating them all—or, at least, the idea was delicious. The fact might be another matter.

"The Reichsführer will not be pleased if you are unable to produce the letter," Nebe said, as if the statement by itself removed every difficulty. He pushed himself away from the desk and let his arms drift down to his sides, coming to a kind of shuffling attention. "If he is to discredit von Ribbentrop, he needs the letter. He needs it to show that the SS has been looking to the security of the Reich while the Foreign Minister has risked losing the Japanese alliance with his irresponsible diplomatic adventures. But we need the proof, Hauptmann—we need to retrieve the Foreign Ministry's blunder or people might begin to ask if the blunder might not have been ours in the first place. I can't risk shooting everyone who might know or suspect something about that disgraceful affair in Stockholm."

"If *I* am unable to produce it?" Weinschenk raised his eyebrows in contemptuous reproach. "Are those degenerates you brought with you from Berlin *my* concern?"

Weinschenk would never know what he might have said next, what indiscretion might have escaped him, if the door had not swung silently open at that moment to reveal Max's gigantic shape filling up the frame with the black outline of his uniform. His aide didn't step inside, but his eyes glowed with a peculiar yellowish light and his mouth opened soundlessly to reveal his clenched teeth. In any case, his meaning was clear enough. Steadman was about to be removed to his place of trial.

Weinschenk rose slowly from his chair, picked up his hat, and fixed it squarely on his head, as if he intended it to stay there forever.

"Allow me to remind you of something, Herr Gruppenführer," he said as he turned to his superior officer with a faint, indecipherable smile. "We have limited time, so our approach to the problem of Mr. Steadman's reluctance to confide in us will be necessarily unsubtle. Not every man can be broken by the use of physical pain alone, not unless you are quite at leisure to strip away his defenses one layer after another. This is no frightened schoolteacher we have to deal with here. It will be a close race to see which goes first, his will or his nervous system. He might die on us, you know. Or he might go mad without telling us a thing. It wouldn't surprise me at all, knowing him as I do, if he's still laughing in our faces as he slips into some dark nightmare of his own where we'll never be able to reach him. Come along, Max."

There was almost something of triumph in his manner as the Hauptmann looked back at Gruppenführer Nebe from the dimly lit hallway. If anyone had been watching—anyone except Max, for whom, presumably, the conversations of his superiors were as unintelligible as bird cries—they might even have assumed that Weinschenk was enjoying a moment of cold, passionless revenge.

When they came to fetch him, they decided he should be able to walk to what they called the Interrogation Chamber, and when he had trouble complying they had a good time bouncing him off the corridor walls. It wasn't much worse than a lot of college initiations, but it set the tone.

Actually, Steadman was feeling somewhat better. After fifty or sixty feet he was beginning to get the hang of using his legs again, but there were certain advantages to seeming weaker and more helpless than in fact he was. He wasn't going to waste them on a couple of goons who looked as if they hadn't been out of school three months.

The corridor was so cold that the walls were sweating, and he was naked. They took him to a room that was empty except for a wooden chair. Steadman tried to sit down on it and was immediately caught along the side of the head with a truncheon.

He lay there on the dirty floor, watching his two guards, waiting to see what they expected him to do next. They were both about nineteen—big farm lads with clear complexions. One of them was blond and one had hair of that light brown which, from an ideological point of view, was almost as good. It was the blond who had hit him; he was still weighing the stick in his hand, hoping he would have another chance. The sight of a naked man lying on the floor with a welt above his ear was making them laugh.

There was a mirror bolted to the opposite wall. Of course, no one in a torture chamber has much use for a mirror—Steadman would have given very favorable odds that somebody, probably Weinschenk, was in the next room, enjoying the view. They were all so fucking obvious it was almost embarrassing.

And then the door opened and his two guards snapped to attention like mechanical toys as two more men, both of them in white hospital smocks, like consulting physicians, came in and closed it behind them. Lately the bad guys only seemed to arrive in pairs.

One of them carried another wooden chair, a duplicate of the one already in the room, and the other carried nothing except an extremely shiny pair of handcuffs. The man with the chair could have sold ice cream for a living—he was small and short, rather soft-looking, with brown glassy eyes and dark brown hair; he had a thin little mustache that might have been intended for a joke—but the other one, the fellow with the handcuffs, was genuinely scary.

Steadman had seen the type before—war attracted them like flies. He probably weighed two hundred and seventy pounds, and he was a good six four or five. An almost invisible bristle of whitish blond hair covered the sides of his head, but for the rest he looked as if someone had gone over him with a pair of tweezers. Tiny blue eyes glittered in his pig's face and the smile on his lips looked permanent, like the smile of an idiot. His arms were as thick as fireplace logs. You could hear him breathe in little squeaking pants; he was really looking forward to this. He was the type that sane societies keep locked away where they can't hurt anyone.

He held out the handcuffs to the guard with the blond hair, who, along with his buddy, grabbed Steadman by the arms and hoisted him into the same chair they had clubbed him for trying to sit in not four minutes before. The blond one stepped in back of him and cuffed his wrists together, threading the chair behind one of the leg supports. Now he couldn't get up without bringing the chair with him. In fact, he had to slide down to keep the handcuffs from digging into the flesh. It was very uncomfortable.

The guards left.

Without a word, the big creep started to work him over, very systematically, with his huge fists. He concentrated on Steadman's face, first one side and then the other, squeaking and whimpering with pleasure. At first Steadman tried to taunt him to make him angry enough that he would forget himself and hit too hard, but it didn't work. He was being careful—apparently he didn't want the party to end for a long time— and, besides, after a while Steadman discovered that he couldn't talk very well.

Smack! He would feel the impact and hear the sound and then, a second or two later, there would be a great welling up of pain on that side of his face. Smack! And we would start all over again. His head felt the size of a basketball and seemed to burn. His right eye was closing fast, and he could taste blood. Smack! The disgusting bastard was working on the bruises now—there probably wasn't anything else left to aim at.

Every once in a while there would be a pause, and the great ape would lift Steadman's head by the chin and survey his handiwork. It was revolting to listen to his squeaky breathing and to feel his damp, hot hands on you.

And then it was back to work, and he had other things to think about.

It felt like hours and then, suddenly, it stopped. After a few minutes, when he could catch his breath a little, Steadman looked up and saw that Weinschenk had sometime or other entered the room, as silent as a shade.

"Max, escort these two outside and see that they wait there. Get them out of my sight."

The Hauptmann stood regarding him for a moment, his head cocked a little to one side, one gloved hand holding the other, and then he reached into the side pocket of his tunic and produced a key. After he had unlocked the handcuffs, Steadman made a stab at clouting him on the head, but Weinschenk didn't have any trouble dodging out of the way. Steadman was so weak and groggy that even if the blow had managed to connect he couldn't have expected it to do much damage. After nearly falling off the chair, he decided to give up trying to be a tough guy and slumped back, letting his arms dangle lifelessly.

It seemed a long time before he could catch his breath. His lips, even his tongue, felt swollen and shapeless. When he opened his mouth he had to be careful to keep from biting himself, and the blood running down his throat made him cough. Finally he spat up a massive black clot of something, and then his lungs seemed to work a little better.

Weinschenk had pulled up the other chair and sat down. They were facing one another. With the tip of his finger he described an arc through the air, tracing the ragged line of scars down Steadman's abdomen and left thigh.

"Spain?" he asked. Steadman nodded wearily. "Artesa de Segre?"

"What of it?"

"You have no idea how much time we spent searching for you among the dead and wounded," Weinschenk said evenly, carefully twitching up his trouser legs. "We had heard from a prisoner that the American they called *El Cortador* had been a casualty; it would have meant a great deal to me to have had the fact confirmed. How did you get away?"

"It's a long story."

Weinschenk seemed to consider this answer, his hands neatly folded in his lap, and then he smiled.

"I hope you appreciate that I didn't allow them to break your nose," he said—he really was crazy. "But not even my superiors imagine that you can be made to talk by anything so obvious. You know, of course, that there is more to come, and it will be much worse."

"I know."

"Then save yourself, my friend." Weinschenk actually reached out and rested his hand on Steadman's forearm. It was an extraordinary thing for him to do under the circumstances. "The end will be the same, in any case. Why allow these revolting degenerates to reduce you to jelly? You make me wish I had shot you when I had the chance—this degrades us both."

In the long silence that followed, Steadman merely glowered at him. He hated Weinschenk. He hated his compassion—he didn't care whether it was real or just another pantomime—and he hated his ridiculous, perversely genteel notions of honor.

"Tell me about Artesa de Segre," Weinschenk said finally. He smiled kindly. He was your dearest friend.

"You tell me," Steadman answered. The words were soft and indistinct, like pieces of dough. "You tell me. Was it you who ordered the wounded shot at Solsona. Was it you?"

"Yes, it was me. We all have our duty."

"Then you are a piece of shit." Steadman looked up at him through swollen, half-closed eyes, experiencing an agony of grief and hatred. "I'll never tell you anything. Not even my favorite color."

A light seemed to go off in Weinschenk's face. He was angry—he was actually shocked. He wasn't used to hearing people talk to him like that. Finally, after what seemed a remarkably long time but probably wasn't more than five or six seconds, he managed to master his features and stood up.

"Max, if he were allowed his way, would tear you to pieces," the Hauptmann said, his voice quivering with rage. "He feels cheated that he hasn't been allowed to take personal revenge for Madrid, but perhaps what lies ahead for you will satisfy even him. I never wanted this, Steadman—you can believe that. Now it must all be on your own head."

As if on cue, the door opened and the two white-suited interrogators entered, the smaller of whom was carrying a black box, about the size and shape of a sewing machine case. The other one had a portable table under his arm, with the legs folded flat against the bottom. They were followed by Max, who, when he looked at Steadman, drew back his lips in a cruel grin.

"I would direct your attention to a peculiarity of our back wall," Weinschenk went on, nodding in that direction. "Take a close look, Mr. Steadman—touch it with your hand."

Max quickly paced off the few feet that separated them and picked Steadman up by the shoulder like a length of garden hose. A quick, deft motion sent Steadman clattering to the floor at the back of the room.

He could hardly avoid a "close look" now. What he noticed first as he struggled up into a sitting position was that the wall seemed to glitter slightly, almost as if it were wet. He touched it and felt the cold—it really was wet. And when he took his hand away he discovered that his fingers had left a slight impression.

"Clay." Weinschenk sounded as if he were announcing the solution to a riddle. "A special composition—an excellent conductor of electricity."

Steadman looked down at the corner to his right and saw that the fat boy was attaching a pair of heavy black wires to a small grid. His pink, hairless hands were screwing down the bolts with almost comical delicacy.

"I will leave you now, Mr. Steadman. Remember that if you wish to end this sorry business all you have to do is to say so. It will last no longer than you wish it to."

The door closed behind him.

"Steh' auf!"

When he had gained his feet, he felt the fat boy's hand in the center of his back, pushing him flat against the wall. He pressed his face to it, otherwise he would have fallen down. He was so frightened he could hardly bring himself to breathe.

With the first surge of current he tried to scream, but nothing would come out. He found he couldn't pull himself away—his fingernails seemed to dig into the clay of their own accord. He felt everything in his body tightening unbearably, twisting like a dishrag being wrung out. The muscles in his arms and chest seemed ready to splinter. His back would break any minute. Without willing it, he jerked back and forth, up and down. Pain wasn't just something that was happening to him. Pain was all there was. He was like a fly caught in amber, except that the amber was his own pain.

Then, finally, he found his voice and screamed, filling his ears with the sound of his own shrieking.

A curtain of black came down over his mind, and everything stopped.

XXV

They woke him up with cold water and then propped him against the clay wall again. They did that three or four times—toward the end he was a little vague about the count—and then Weinschenk decided that was enough for that day and the two guards came in and dragged Steadman back to his cell. He didn't remember the trip, but when he came around again and noticed how the tops of his feet were skinned he guessed that was how they must have done it. The cell was freezing but he couldn't seem to muster the precision of movement to dress himself. All that voltage seemed to have done something to his muscles, so he dragged his clothes up on the bed with him, spread them out over his body as best he could, and lost consciousness.

He woke up feeling a lot better—maybe this sort of thing was good for you. Maybe if he ever got out he would set up a health spa in the Swiss Alps, where he would stand people against electrified walls and see if they would light up. He might make his fortune that way.

Except, of course, that he wasn't ever getting out.

He tried to sit up, and when he discovered he could do that he got out of bed and walked around a little. The first time he could walk the length of the cell, back and forth, four times before he had to sit down again. He was almost as good as new.

The sour-looking doctor came back and listened to his heart with a stethoscope. He didn't say anything—Steadman imagined he would in all probability never hear the man's voice—but the expression on his face suggested that he didn't like what he heard.

After that they brought him something to eat. He got a piece of bread and a metal bowl filled with a kind of soup that smelled like sewage and was a mysterious purplish brown—when you passed a spoon through it you turned up things of indeterminate color and unimaginable origin. Steadman ate it tentatively; it tasted as bad as he could have expected, but he was hungry. Then he ate the bread, which he had been saving to clean the taste of the soup out of his mouth. It was surprisingly good bread. When he was finished he lay down again and had a rest. He felt reasonably confident about the next couple of hours—you retched your guts out after they turned off the current, and they weren't likely to feed him just so he could spill the stuff all over their floor.

It was impossible to be accurate about the passage of time, but Steadman slept again and woke up again and was hungry again, and still no one came for him. Apparently they had decided to give him a rest. Perhaps they wanted him to have plenty of opportunity to think, so that the clay wall could grow in his imagination, so he would be in a proper frame of mind to collapse when they dragged him back.

They hadn't actually asked him anything. They had just put him against the wall and turned on the current. Would he have told them anything if they had asked? He didn't know.

He looked down at his hands and discovered that the fingernails were black. The beds were bruised and tender—he had done that to himself, digging into the clay. A few more times and the nails would probably start peeling off like old wallpaper.

He tried not to think about it. He tried not to think about anything. He tried to sleep, and for the rest to keep his mind a blank.

His face felt raw. He didn't have a mirror, of course, but he could tell it was swollen. He couldn't even smile without it starting to throb, so he didn't smile. He waited, as impassive as a mandarin, for the next round.

Once he woke up and found Weinschenk sitting at the foot of the bed. The Hauptmann was resting his elbows against his knees, and his face seemed worn. He looked like a man with a lot on his mind.

"How did you get out of Artesa de Segre?" he asked. This once Steadman did smile—he didn't care how much his face hurt.

"I have a pair of magic combat boots," he said. "I put them on and I can walk through walls. Why is it so important to you to know?"

Weinschenk drew himself up straight, turning his eyes away to face the wall.

"I never even found out your name." His right hand, lying in his lap, was clenching and unclenching rhythmically. "You just disappeared. I never even knew where to look for you."

"Then you were pretty stupid. Franco's police had a make on me four weeks after the collapse. I had one of them come and visit me in Paris. They've been dunning the British government ever since, trying to have me extradited."

"They couldn't possibly do that."

"That's what the British told them. I'm surprised you didn't know all about it."

The clenched hand finally stayed open, and Hauptmann Weinschenk sat staring at it as if he couldn't remember ever having seen it before.

"I was in Berlin," he said finally. "In something like disgrace, thanks to you. And, in any case, we have lost all official interest in Spanish internal affairs. Or perhaps they simply didn't choose to tell me."

He closed his eyes for a long moment. He seemed to be reliving some buried humiliation.

"But now we can fill in all the blank periods, can't we." The smile on his face wasn't very comforting—the Spanish business, for some reason, seemed to stand even ahead of his Führer's letter in importance. Now even a friendly chat about old times had the character of a compromising admission. "How did you get out of Artesa de Segre?"

"I told you—magic combat boots."

"Max!"

The door opened with a clang, but you hardly noticed the difference, so completely did the corporal of the SS fill its space. He stepped inside, glanced down at Steadman, and bared his teeth.

"You know, if you're not careful that ape will kill me one of these dark nights and mess up everything for you. Wouldn't that be a pity?"

Max made a grab for him, but Steadman didn't wait. He rolled off the bed and scrambled for the corner of the room, leaving his shoes behind him—the bastards had confiscated the laces, damn them. In his stocking feet he made ready to defend himself, but Max didn't follow.

"Don't be an idiot, Steadman." The Hauptmann made a gesture with his left hand and his orderly stepped back toward the open doorway. "He could pull you apart. What could you do about it?"

"Tell him to stay away from me, Weinschenk. Tell him to remember Madrid, or I'll . . ."

"Oh, I assure you, he never forgets Madrid." Weinschenk was relaxed again, his thumbs hooked over the top of his wide black uniform belt.

"But what can you do, *Cortador?*" he went on, just as if he really wanted to know. "Your knife is in a drawer in my office. I plan to keep it as a remembrance. What can you possibly do?"

"Keep him off me, or you'll both find out."

The two men exchanged a wordless glance—they both knew perfectly well what he was talking about, that he was prepared to force the issue, that it would be to the death if Max tried to touch him again.

They came again for him that night. He had nothing against which to measure time except his daily meal, which he settled upon as midafternoon, and the few hours when the light in his cell went out and he was allowed to sleep. It could have been anytime, but by that reckoning it was night when they came and woke him out of a deep, dreamless sleep.

This time they didn't have to drag him, and when one of them tried to push him along he stepped back and drove the point of his elbow into the nasty little brat's guts, using everything he had. It cost him a beating, right there in the corridor, but not a very bad one, and, in any case, it had been worth it. They just kicked him around a little—doubtless they had their orders—and they stopped when they saw he was prepared to fight back. It was different, one gathered, when they realized they had to be ready to kill him if they wanted to play rough.

He made it to Weinschenk's little visiting room without much more than a couple of sore ribs.

"I heard noises outside. You shouldn't be so hard on them, Mr. Steadman. After all, they're only boys, and that sort of thing is bad for prison morale."

Weinschenk sat in a chair, smoking a cigarette and smiling contemptuously at the two guards. Max was absent, but the huge bastard with the piglike, hairless face was standing behind the Hauptmann's chair, wheezing in anticipation. The ice cream salesman was sitting behind his little control box. Everything was ready. Weinschenk seemed not to notice; he leaned back in his chair, looking at Steadman as if they were the only two adults in a room full of small children. One of the guards, the blond one, started to say something—he seemed to fancy himself insulted—but Weinschenk raised his hand in a peremptory demand for silence. He didn't even look at the man.

Finally he got up and left, as if the scene depressed him.

As soon as the door closed, the fat boy grabbed Steadman by the shoulders and threw him against the wall, hard enough to knock the wind out of him. Almost at once the current went on, and Steadman found himself screaming without any voice. They turned it off and on, off and on; he was twitching like the flicker at the end of a whip. At the finish he sank down to the floor, drenched in sweat and trembling uncontrollably, as if he had been dipped in ice water. There were great red welts over his hands and arms and across his body, everywhere he had been in contact with the wall. He couldn't seem to make one thought follow another; he couldn't even remember how he had gotten there. All he could do was whimper softly, covering his face with his arms and wishing he were dead.

After a while he became aware that Weinschenk was kneeling down beside him, talking to him in a low voice—he might just as easily have been shouting, because it all seemed to fade in and out, crackling in his ears like a bad radio signal.

"You've made a mess, did you . . . all over the floor. I should . . . so that you . . ."

Weinschenk was holding him up by the hair, looking down into his face, not letting him turn away. It hardly mattered—it was only half real. Steadman could hardly place who he was.

But gradually things began coming back into focus. The waves stopped crashing in Steadman's ears, and he remembered that he was there to be tortured for information. He also remembered that he wasn't going to give it.

"What happened at Artesa de Segre?" Weinschenk's voice was almost pleading. "You're a brave man, Steadman—braver than I am. You've proved that. I would have spoken long before this. But you must tell me what happened. How did you get away?"

Steadman tried to think—get away from where? He coughed; it seemed to come from deep inside him, and to bring everything up with it. He smiled through his bruised lips. He was suddenly very happy.

"Boots," he whispered. "I tol' you—fuckin' boots . . ."

"What did you do with the Führer's letter? Tell me, Steadman. You *will* tell me."

Steadman trembled and cried—the tears coursed down his face; he couldn't seem to help himself—but he said nothing. He shook his head and said nothing.

"Damn you, Steadman. Damn you and damn your wretched bravery. I may learn to hate you all over again for the things you force me to do to you."

When he could no longer stand on his own, ropes went around his wrists and he was hoisted up from a couple of hooks in the ceiling. He could try pushing himself away, but when the current went up and the muscles in his arms started jerking wildly he would fall back against the wall, hitting it with the whole length of his body, and that was terrible. That was like being scorched through, all at once. When he was able to breathe, all he could do was scream, but most of the time he couldn't even breathe. When he blacked out, someone would bring him around again with a rag smelling of ammonia. He didn't have any idea how many times that happened.

The questions were always the same. What happened at Artesa de Segre? Where was the letter? They seemed to have equal importance in Weinschenk's mind—or perhaps he didn't care what the questions were. It would be so easy to lead from one to the next. All secrets were the same—to have one was to have them all. But so far . . . So far . . .

Steadman was near the end of his tether. He couldn't remember why he wasn't answering the questions. He didn't even understand them anymore. He didn't understand anything. His mind was just a spinning blackness.

"He's had enough for now," Weinschenk said, holding Steadman's head up by the hair and pulling back an eyelid. "Any more of this for a while and he'll simply die. He'll die laughing at us."

The ice cream salesman opened the door, and the two guards came in and carried Steadman back to his cell.

As he lay there in the dark—the overhead light was on, but Steadman couldn't see it as more than a dim, hazy glow, something immeasurably distant—he wondered if he hadn't gone mad. The thought kept skipping back into his mind, like the half-dozen notes that repeat over and over on a flawed gramophone record. Am I mad? Nothing is real anymore. I can't make sense of anything. Am I mad?

Eventually his mind began to clear, and he was seized with a blind, unbearable terror. Weinschenk wouldn't care what he told him. He could confess to any crime, give him anything he asked for, and it wouldn't matter. All of that was just the excuse. Weinschenk was killing him by degrees, would make his death as long and painful as he could. Weinschenk was like a little boy twisting the legs off a spider.

Nothing was worth that kind of death.

If he could have believed that telling what he had done with the letter would save him, if Weinschenk had come to him at that moment and offered him an easy death, at that moment he would have told. He knew that, and he was too crushed even to feel shame.

But it wasn't Weinschenk who came. It was the doctor. The little round-faced man sat down on the edge of the bed. He put his small, effeminate hand on Steadman's forehead and pushed back the sodden hair. His eyes were dark and anxious.

"They haven't given you the full dose yet," he said, in peculiarly accented German—clearly it wasn't his mother tongue. "I've told them that your heart wouldn't take it, that your pneumonia is still hanging on. It might even be true, but the point is that they believe it. Can you hold out for another day?"

"What time is it?"

"What difference does that make?" The doctor looked surprised, and then he looked at his wristwatch. "It's twenty minutes after nine."

"In the morning or the evening?"

"The evening."

Steadman smiled to himself. Then he hadn't been so very far wrong after all. Somehow to know the time was to regain something of himself. He would be all right now.

"I can hold out."

"Good. I'll be back tomorrow evening. Wait until then."

He didn't say anything more, and Steadman didn't ask. The doctor rose to his feet and passed out of sight into the corridor. The door slammed shut as if of its own accord, and Steadman was left once more alone.

I'll be back tomorrow evening. What did that mean? Death? An injection of cyanide? Was it all some sort of trap, one of Weinschenk's little refinements? He would wait and see. He would fool them by expecting nothing. He knew the time. He had his strength back.

The next day there was no food. It didn't make any difference— Steadman's hands had developed an uncontrollable palsy and, besides, he couldn't have kept anything down. If they were trying to starve him into submission they were making a mistake. Pain, when it reaches a certain level of intensity, allows for no competing miseries.

Instead of bringing his food, they came early to make him strip off his clothes and march him to the interrogation room.

Weinschenk was there already. He smiled politely and invited Steadman to sit down.

"You've held out for two days," he said, leaning back against the door with his hands clasped in front of him. He was like a trainer issuing a progress report on his star athlete. "No one here has ever seen that before, but of course they haven't begun getting the hardened resistance types here in Strasbourg yet."

"Is that where we are?"

Weinschenk nodded.

"What time is it?"

Weinschenk glanced at his wristwatch.

"Nine-fifteen. Why?"

"In the morning or afternoon?"

"Morning. Why?"

"Nothing."

The Hauptmann shrugged. He gave the impression that he wished to be considered amiable. It was an old technique.

"The question is," he went on, after a short pause during which he stood staring at the tips of his fingers. "The question is, why persist? Everyone breaks eventually. And if you're hoping we'll kill you by accident . . ."

He smiled again. It was a pitying smile. The smile we reserve for children and fools. That wasn't, it said, a mistake into which a man of Steadman's experience should allow himself to fall.

"Maybe I won't break." Steadman had trouble with the words. He had to speak slowly or the syllables jumbled up together. "Maybe I enjoy making you look stupid. Maybe that's enough."

He tried to smile at Weinschenk, but the muscles in his face weren't cooperating; he didn't know what he looked like.

"I'm not the one sitting naked in a prison torture chamber," Weinschenk said coldly. His thin face appeared seamed and unyielding, as if the skin had dried to vellum. "In any case, I've decided we've wasted enough time with you. Perhaps we might just let the electricity kill you this time. Perhaps your little secrets aren't so terribly important as you imagine."

Can you hold out for another day? Yes, of course. They had just wanted to give him a ray of hope so the darkness would be all the blacker when it disappeared. Steadman congratulated himself on having foreseen it and wondered why he still felt so stricken.

Max had somehow positioned himself just a few feet from the chair where Steadman was pondering his own sagacity, and his eyes were resting on the groove in Steadman's shoulder where he had been shot in the Stockholm railroad station. The edges were still red and angry, and the scab looked like cracked leather. All at once, there he was, his huge hands crushing Steadman's arms, and then he pressed the point of his thumb against the wound until he drew blood. He was peeling it open as if he wanted to rub it away. Steadman could feel it all the way down his arm.

"Max—stop it, Max. Stop it at once, do you hear me?"

A few minutes later they had him up on the hooks again, only this time they were using handcuffs instead of ropes. The handcuffs cut into his wrists and he couldn't touch the floor with both feet at once. As they turned up the current, the handcuffs felt as if they would burn through his hands.

"Tell me about the letter," Weinschenk said—maybe it was Wein-schenk. Maybe that was what he was saying. "The letter. The letter. The letter . . ."

Steadman didn't know where he was. He was somewhere in the room—he could see them, all of them. Weinschenk, Max, the interrogators in their white hospital gowns, himself. He was somebody else, watching himself. And it was so sad. He felt so sorry. There wasn't anything he could do to stop it. He was there, but they couldn't hear him shouting to them to stop.

When they threw water on him to bring him around, he saw that his hands had turned a peculiar glassy blue. He couldn't feel them—the cuffs must have cut off the circulation. He was glad, because now they had stopped hurting.

Can you hold out for another day?

In any case, I've decided we've wasted enough time with you.

He wished whoever was screaming would stop. If they stopped, maybe he could go to sleep. He just wanted to sleep.

"Bring him down. Get him out of here. It doesn't get us anywhere if he doesn't even know what is happening to him."

When he woke up he was back in his cell. "Woke up" was perhaps too strong—he hadn't been so much unconscious as . . . What? Cloudy. Very far away from himself. It was difficult to sort out.

His memories of the past few hours were disconnected—little splinters of time that didn't seem to mean much, or to have anything to do with David Steadman, who was lying in his cell, trying to figure out why he wasn't dead.

Weinschenk had been hopping mad. But not at him, at someone else. There had been a scene in the interrogation room—Steadman could still hear the shouting, like echoes in the dark. Weinschenk and another officer, someone he had never seen before, had been fighting over him like a couple of dogs over a scrap of stinking meat.

Steadman laughed quietly, and then stopped because it hurt to laugh. He didn't care. He was winning. If he could hold out just a little longer, Weinschenk would lose control of himself.

It was difficult to be afraid of death from the perspective of a Gestapo prison cell.

Was this one of Rousseau's disconnected instants? If it was, it was a pretty good one. It was possible, he was discovering, to languish in pain as if it were a feather bed—all you needed was the consciousness that the worst was, for the moment, distant, and, in any case, not more than you could bear. Perhaps to have lost the fear of death was the final happiness.

He must have drifted off to sleep, because it was only gradually that he realized there was someone there with him, holding him down. He opened his eyes. It was the doctor, and his hand was on Steadman's forehead.

"You're in a bad way," he said, smiling sadly out of his anxious brown eyes. "I'll have to give you something to bring you around."

He brought the black medical bag up onto his lap and took out a hypodermic syringe that looked as if it had been prepared in advance—the tip of the needle was wrapped in a loose wad of cotton. He pinched up a fold of Steadman's arm muscle and injected the full load. Steadman could feel it coursing through him even before the needle was pulled out.

Oh, the good doctor! How nice it was to be able to think well of somebody!

"There now," he said, snapping the bag closed. "Now you'll be in fit condition to get out of here."

What was the man talking about? Get out of where?

After a furtive glance back at the door, the doctor undid the middle button of his white smock and reached inside. There was the sound of something tearing, and in a few seconds the hand came back out holding a small, flat automatic pistol with three flaps of white gauze attached to it, which the doctor set about pulling off with quick, deft movements. He had carried the thing into a Nazi prison taped under his armpit—the risks that represented were staggering.

There was no pillow, but the doctor put his hand under Steadman's shoulders and with astonishing strength lifted him a few inches away from the mattress ticking and slipped the pistol underneath.

"You'll know what to do and when to do it," he whispered. "Just a few more hours."

He smiled again, as if he didn't even believe it himself.

XXVI

Steadman lay there for a long time without moving. The pistol was directly under his left shoulder blade, and its hammer shroud seemed to be resting on a nerve. That was all right; he liked the feel of it, reminding him that it really was there, that he hadn't dreamed the whole thing.

Suddenly his mind filled with suspicion; he reached back and pulled the pistol out where he could see it. Rolling over on his side, so his body would shield what he was doing from the eye slit, he prized out the clip. Yes, there really were bullets in the thing, six of them. Of course, they might have had the powder taken out of them, but there wasn't any obvious evidence of tampering. For the moment, he was prepared to operate on the assumption that the thing would actually go off if he pulled the trigger.

In that sense his basic problem was already solved. He now had the option, anytime he cared to exercise it, of stuffing the muzzle into his mouth and blowing his brains out. Wouldn't that annoy Weinschenk! Or he could wait upon events. The doctor had spoken of getting out. That didn't seem a very realistic possibility—one man with a pistol doesn't break out of a Gestapo jail all by himself.

You'll know what to do and when to do it, he had said. It was a touching display of faith, but what did it mean?

He pressed the clip home again and returned the pistol to its position under his left shoulder blade. Everything would make itself clear in time, and at least he wasn't going back for any more of Weinschenk's clay wall.

His heart, he noticed, was beating very fast. That was natural enough under the circumstances, but Steadman had an idea it had more to do with whatever had been in that hypodermic needle than with his suddenly enhanced prospects of survival. Also, the pain in his face and hands, where it was worst, was beginning to subside a little. He wished he knew how long the effects of whatever he had been given were likely to last; that by itself might tell him how long he had to wait for whatever was coming.

His clothes were still at the foot of the bed. He stood up and started putting them on. He felt little inclination to meet the future stark naked.

Everything seemed to work again, even his fingers. He could button his shirt, which had become something of a lost art, and his legs no longer threatened to give way under him. The pistol went into his back pocket; he stood so that no one looking in from outside could have seen the lump it made.

Just let somebody come in—that blond creep, for instance—and with what pleasure Steadman would scatter his brains all over the wall. He promised himself that no matter how things worked out he would kill at least a couple of these goons. He had killed often enough in the last five years, and never with anything except a kind of cold revulsion; this time he would enjoy the work.

Getting dressed made him tired. He sat down on the bed, wishing he had something to eat. His mouth felt dried out, as if someone had gone over it with sandpaper. Suddenly all confidence left him—he would probably be dead in two hours' time. Now that he could imagine some other possibility, the fear of death returned to him. He hadn't been afraid when the alternative was nothing but pain and self-betrayal.

For no particular reason, he started thinking about Karen, wondering where she was and what she was doing. He didn't want to think of Stockholm, even though she had been his there; she was tied up in his mind with the ordinary details of life. He remembered her playing with her Labrador retriever—what had that dog's name been? She would kneel down and gather her skirt in around her legs and put her arms around its neck, laughing for pure happiness at the sun and the pleasure of a dumb animal's affection.

Then along had come the war to make everything go smash. How was he ever going to make all that up to her?

The floor was like a slab of ice. He started to put his feet into his shoes but then remembered that they didn't have any laces. Better to do without them—in an emergency he would probably fall all over himself if he tried to keep them on. Besides, a man in his bare feet is quieter.

He was going to get out of this place, or he was going to leave his corpse in a gutter trying. The day would come when he would find that son of a bitch Weinschenk again, and he would cut his throat for him. Slowly. An inch at a time.

The ceiling light in his cell began to dim. They expected him to go to sleep now. He lay down like a good boy and even closed his eyes. There wasn't anything to see anyway. He would listen. That was how he would know the moment had come, by listening for it.

Every ten or fifteen minutes he would hear footsteps approaching, then a shadow would pass over the eyeslit of Steadman's cell door, and then the footsteps would fade away and die. The guards were doing their rounds—perhaps they looked in, perhaps not. The cell was dark; there wouldn't be anything to see, but perhaps they had their orders. It would be very German of them to look into the empty blackness of the prisoners' cells; a man could have an ostrich in with him and they would never know. Everything was drill for the Germans, drill and routine. They imagined that to be their great strength, but it was where they showed themselves the weakest. It wasn't wise to put one's faith in a system.

The ceiling light had been out for perhaps an hour when gradually Steadman became aware of some change in the atmosphere. It was like a slight rise in the temperature, except it wasn't that. It was a sound— so silent, so pale as to be almost invisible.

Suddenly he sat up. In an instant he had the pistol, working the slide to put a cartridge in the chamber. *You'll know what to do and when to do it.* The sound he had almost not heard was now quite distinct in his mind. It was an alarm bell.

There were other sounds now—men running, and voices.

The light in his cell popped back on. They would be coming around to check again any second now, only this time they would be more thorough. They wouldn't know, of course, whether somebody was breaking in or breaking out, but prisons weren't such nice places that people ever breached the alarm except to steal someone. They would want to reassure themselves that everyone was still tucked in bed.

Steadman got up and placed his back against the wall, to the left of the cell door, away from the hinges. When they checked they wouldn't see anything except a dent in the mattress. That would make them nervous, so they . . .

If they had any brains, they wouldn't be timid about opening the door with a push. It was a massive iron mother—it probably weighed a good hundred and fifty pounds—and anyone standing on the wrong side when it swung in would find himself with one hell of a flat nose. Only idiots hid behind doors.

He could hear them at the other cells now. There were something like eight or ten of them in a row, and Steadman's was almost in the center. He would be number five, probably—he couldn't be sure.

They were opening the doors, all of them. Number one, slam. Number two, slam. It was like waiting for the dentist.

Number four, slam.

No, he would be number six. He waited, with the pistol held beside his ear, pointing toward the ceiling. In a few seconds, whether he liked it or not, he would be on the loose again. He decided that he liked it.

Number five, slam.

The door lurched open with a sudden movement and the first guard came in right behind it. It was Blondie—oh, good. He looked around him, startled for an instant not to find anyone lying on the bed. For an instant he stood perfectly still, and in that instant he died.

Steadman put the gun straight up to his head, just behind the ear, and pulled the trigger.

A person tends to go rigid when all at once he gets a hole punched through his brain. At that range the shot seems to go off with a little twanging sound, and there's a smell of gunpowder and burnt hair in the air, and there's a slight lurch away from the impact before he goes over like a roll of carpet slipping off the back of a truck.

But Steadman wasn't standing around to admire. Blondie had a friend, right behind him. The poor slob was just raising his gun when Steadman swung around and shot him, twice, both rounds going just an inch or so to the side of his nose. It was a very messy way to die.

Fine—that was one score settled. Steadman chanced a quick look up and down the corridor, but there didn't seem to be anyone else around. They wouldn't be long, not now that guns had started going off. He scooped up one of the two Lugers that were now lying on the floor, picked a direction—one was as good as another, since he didn't have a clue which way was out—and started up at a loping run.

He could hear people shouting from behind the locked cell doors, but he didn't have any keys. The general confusion might have been helpful, but probably all he would have bought these people was a quick trip to the incinerator—what were they supposed to do when the guards broke out the machine guns? It wasn't a time to be philanthropic.

He threw himself past a corner, a pistol in each hand now, expecting to be burned down, but again there was nobody. Either it was an understaffed prison—did the Germans have understaffed prisons? Was such a thing imaginable?—or the real party was somewhere else.

Somebody was providing a distraction for him, it suddenly dawned on him. There wasn't a soul in this section except the two boys regularly assigned to it, and they were both dead. Somebody was going to a lot of trouble.

It wasn't a very long time before he had trouble of his own. You go any distance in a prison, pretty soon you run into a locked door. Steadman put his hand on the knob, just to be sure, and shook it. Nothing doing.

He looked around—there was a stairway just behind him, but it didn't lead to anything except another door, doubtless also locked. No. He would stay on the one floor. People might be looking for him—people other than the Germans—and he wanted them to be able to find him. He pointed the Luger, which was the heavier of the two pistols, square at the lock of the door in front of him, turned his face away, and started firing.

Once, twice, three times. A splinter of wood the size of a tenpenny nail buried itself in his right leg, just above the knee; he pulled it out with an impatient movement and threw it away. The door was standing open about three quarters of an inch. So far, so good.

There were people on the other side. They were both carrying what looked like machine pistols, and both were aimed straight at Steadman's chest, but fortunately neither man was wearing a uniform. One of them, a short, dark little creature in a black sweater with a black knitted cap pulled down over his ears, looked at him with something that could perfectly well have been hatred, and then lowered the muzzle of his weapon about an inch.

"*Etes-vous Steadman?*" he asked in a tense, hoarse voice. He really wanted to know.

It occurred to Steadman in that instant that it was just as possible that these two, for reasons best known to themselves, had been sent here not to rescue but to kill him. Just at that moment, the way this guy was looking at him, that seemed a distinct possibility.

But then the doctor could have done that job a lot easier with his needle. No—these weren't the enemy. He nodded slowly.

"Steadman. Right. David Steadman."

"*Bien!*"

The hard little mouth broke into a grin. It was a pretty sight, something you wanted to remember forever.

The other man, who was taller and younger and dressed in a shabby double-breasted suit of some indistinct shade of gray over his open blue workshirt, motioned him forward with a wave of his thin hand. Introductions were over. It was time to get out of there.

They all ran together, Steadman taking up the rear. They went through another door, this one intact and ajar—there was a dead German guard lying beside it, with a large, gory hole where his right eye had been—and then down a staircase and along a corridor that seemed to run parallel to the one they had just taken a floor above. There were no more Germans, alive or dead.

At that moment they began to hear fast, heavy footsteps, a single man but coming down on them quickly.

"We have a car," the tall one said, pointing to a door—it was glass halfway down, and there was a number painted on it at eye level; it was probably somebody's office during the day. "Through here, please."

The footsteps behind them were becoming louder. In a few seconds whoever it was would turn the corner and see them. It wasn't necessary to ask twice.

The room was dark and much colder than the corridor. Papers on the desk were stirring in the breeze from an open window, through which came a few traces of pale, reflected light, just enough to render visible the outlines of a few pieces of stark furniture. The three of them stood still, waiting in silence. It wasn't safe to risk making a sound while pursuit was so close.

The footsteps had slowed to a walk. He was still alone, whoever he was, but there weren't any guarantees that others weren't closing in. Steadman turned around, glancing back at the door, and a cold hand closed over his heart when he saw that there was a narrow bar of light across the floor—someone had left the damn door slightly open.

It could only be a second or two now before the man outside passed by and saw. It was too late in the game to risk a gunshot—that would bring the whole building down on them. Steadman moved over to the desk and began sliding the middle drawer open. The other two watched him with worried, uncomprehending expressions. What was he going to do if there wasn't . . . ?

But there was. A pair of scissors. Not ideal, not the barber's shears with pointed tips like a stiletto, but you couldn't ask for miracles. He put his two middle fingers through the wider loop of the handle and wrapped the rest of his hand around the other. It was a clumsy grip, but the best he could manage.

He wouldn't wait for their friend outside to find them. Everybody in the building would be armed, and not with scissors—he couldn't risk him getting a shot off. He watched the shadow passing across the glass top of the door. He put his hand on the knob and pulled it suddenly open. There were no strangers outside.

"*Wie geht's Ihnen, Max?*"

There was a moment of stunned surprise. That was what he had counted on. Max's head turned a few inches toward him, and the yellow eyes widened in recognition—he wasn't glad to see him was old Max. Steadman picked his spot, just on the inside seam of the shirt pocket, and struck home with everything that was in him.

The scissors went in with the dull sound of a teaspoon falling to the carpeted floor. There was no resistance; the points must have gone between Max's ribs without even touching the bone. Steadman took his hand away, but for some reason he couldn't find it in himself to step back and out of reach. They stood there like that for what seemed like a long time, hardly more than two feet apart.

At first Max didn't look anything except surprised. Perhaps he hadn't noticed yet that he was stabbed; his eyes searched Steadman's face with astonishment. So it's come to this, he seemed to be saying. After all these years, this is how it ends.

Then he tried to raise his right arm—he wanted to get a shot off; he was still thinking all that mattered—but the arm wouldn't work. Instead, the fingers uncurled and the Luger dropped to the floor and skittered away. He was already dead. The scissors were sticking a good couple of inches into his heart, but he didn't know that yet. He was still thinking about how he wanted to kill David Steadman for what he had done to him all those years ago in a hotel corridor in Madrid.

Suddenly his face grew pinched with pain, or hatred, or both. He grabbed the front of Steadman's shirt with his left hand, his fingers pulling tightly. He looked as if he wanted to say something, but what could Max have said, then or any other time, to anybody? Then, from one second to the next, something seemed to go out behind his eyes and he was dead. He went down on his knees and then straight over onto his face.

Steadman grabbed him by the coat collar and dragged him inside. He left a thick smear of blood over the doorsill, but there wasn't time to worry about that.

"Let's get out of here," he whispered thickly.

As they approached the window, Steadman could see that that side of the prison faced onto another building and that there another window, just opposite, was standing open. The distance between them couldn't have been more than seven or eight feet.

A face appeared across the abyss; it grinned at them. Another second and there was a wooden ladder sliding across the distance—they had their bridge out.

"You go first," the tall man said, touching him on the arm.

Steadman turned around for an instant and looked at the corpse on the floor. Max seemed to be grinning at him through half-closed eyes, as if he had finally caught on to the great joke. The scissors were buried under his massive body, but blood was welling out onto the linoleum. This time at least, Steadman thought to himself, he had finished the job.

When they were all across, one of them closed the window and they started running over the empty floor of what looked like a warehouse. Their footfalls sounded unnaturally loud. They took a stairway down a couple of floors, opened a door, and there it was. Their car was parked in a silent alleyway, where you could have imagined the whole world was quietly sleeping. The man who had opened the window stayed behind. He grinned again, raising his arm to them as they drove away.

It was almost too easy. Steadman stretched out on the back seat, both to keep out of sight and because he was so used up he could hardly breathe, and listened to the two men up front as they talked to each other in the peculiarly accented French of that region. He had learned the language in school, but it had been years since he had spoken more than a few words at a time, so he couldn't manage much more than to follow the drift. Still, just the sound of it was strangely comforting.

They didn't speed. Nobody seemed to be after them. Two blocks from the prison there wasn't a sign that everything wasn't just as it should be. They never even came across a traffic cop. Within twenty minutes they were out of the city and bumping along a narrow road lined with stone fences. It seemed they had gotten away clear.

"You had a bad time," the tall one said to him, resting his arm on the back of his seat and smiling. His English was heavily accented but clear. "We heard they were giving you a bad time."

"It wasn't a holiday, but it's over."

"*Boches!*" The man made a face in disgust. "What can you expect of them, eh? We kill them all before we finish. Alsace will be French again."

Steadman contented himself with a smile—it wasn't a statement that looked for any response, and he was too tired to talk much. He watched the darkness slip by outside and wondered where they were heading. He was just curious. He didn't really care.

"Here—have some coffee. It doesn't taste like much, but it is hot."

A thermos jug made its way over the seatback, and Steadman unscrewed the top. The stuff almost scalded his throat, but even that was welcome. He felt it going down through him, and for the first time in days he experienced a sense of physical comfort. It was almost luxurious there on the back seat. He took another swallow.

It was only after the second mouthful was down that he noticed the aftertaste, the faint chemical odor that seemed to rise up to his nostrils, and he found himself asking the questions for which there hadn't been any time before. Who were these people? How had they known that the Germans had nabbed him, and why should they have cared? You don't risk something like this for a stranger, but they had called him by name, so he wasn't that. What the hell was going on?

The thin one was watching him speculatively. Suddenly these people weren't his friends anymore. Steadman began to reach for the pistol that was in his waistband, but that was when it hit him. It was like some enormous weight pressing down on him; everything slowed almost to nothing. His fingers closed around the pistol grip, but he couldn't pull it loose. It seemed to be rooted there under his belt.

Someone—he couldn't see who; it was just a shape, a vague shadow—reached over and took the gun from him, and then a huge hand settled over his face and everything went black.

XXVII

A few hours after he had been notified of Steadman's escape, Egon Weinschenk was sitting behind his desk at the office loaned to him at the Kippenheim prison in Strasbourg, his pistol resting on the blotter pad in front of him as he contemplated the ruin of his life. Everything was quiet now. The cellblocks were locked down tight, the corpses had been cleared away and removed to the basement morgue—there were no prisoners, since none of the attackers had allowed themselves to be captured alive, but something might be done toward identifying them through their dead—and heavily armed columns were fanned out through the immediate area, trying to find some trace of the Reich's most important fugitive. Weinschenk didn't delude himself that there was any chance of that at all.

He had arrived just as they were loading Max onto a stretcher; the expression on his dead face had been like a rebuke. *Why didn't you let me kill him when we had the chance?* he seemed to be asking. *Now he's killed me. What I feared all along would happen has happened, and he's killed me. Why isn't Steadman dead instead of me?*

And, of course, it had been Steadman who had killed him. Who else would have used a pair of scissors like that? So the American's triumph was as complete as he could have wished.

Poor Max. He was really nothing more than a brute, but, funnily enough, Weinschenk had experienced something like real grief when he had discovered him dead. They had been through a great deal together, had come to share something like the dumb intimacy of couples who have been married for decades—in fact, wouldn't it be truthful to say that he had trusted Max more than, perhaps, he had ever trusted his faithless, well-loved wife? He would miss his Caliban, for whose death he could not help but blame himself bitterly. Would he ever feel safe again?

But since, it seemed, now his own life was to be measured out in minutes, perhaps it hardly mattered.

Poor Max had hated Steadman. It had all been so simple for Max.

Because, for all that he recognized his own existence as shipwrecked and blasted by this new twisting of the coil, for all that there was really nothing left for him to do except to put a bullet through his head before Nebe had him arrested, he couldn't quite suppress a certain perverse sense of triumph. Because they had tried to degrade Steadman to their own level. They had assumed that every man was just the same as themselves, mere lumps of muscle and nerve tissue with no higher ambition than to avoid pain and death. They had been wrong. They had misunderstood David Steadman and, by extension, Egon Weinschenk as well. His escape, his victory over them, was a kind of vindication.

There was only one man in Europe who had the slightest chance of stopping David Steadman from doing everything he had set out to do, and that man was about to shoot himself.

It was all so childishly clear. These brigands who had stolen his prisoner, could it possibly matter who they were? They worked for the British— that was the important point. Who else in the wide world would put such a high price on the possession of this one man? And the British, like the Germans before them, would learn that it was one thing to capture David Steadman and quite another to keep him.

So. They would spirit him away—to England, one imagined—and there the fun would begin all over again.

The great thing, the only important thing, was to know where Steadman would go when he inevitably succeeded in escaping from the British.

Weinschenk was reasonably sure he knew—there simply weren't that many alternatives. And he was the only person left whose ambitions with regard to Mr. Steadman were modest enough to have some chance of success. He didn't care anything about the letter. He didn't want to take him prisoner and rack his body in hopes of breaking his will—not anymore. He merely wanted to kill him.

But that was not to be. By now someone would have told the Gruppenführer what had happened, and Weinschenk knew what to expect from that direction. Nebe was the ranking officer on the scene; Steadman's escape would be laid at his door unless he could find some means of distracting attention from his own incompetence. His response would be instinctive—his immediate subordinates, Weinschenk among them, would be taken to one of the basement execution chambers, and Nebe would write a lurid report hinting at treachery. In the present atmosphere, it might even work.

There was a possibility, just a possibility, that if Weinschenk took his own life—and thus appeared to assume responsibility—his disgrace might not extend to his widow. For all that Nebe had probably enjoyed the pleasures of her bed, Magda's position as the wife of a condemned traitor would be extremely precarious—assuming, of course, that Weinschenk somehow survived even long enough for that. Death sentences had a way of extending themselves through families, like the taint of some contagious disease, and Magda would not enjoy Dachau.

Over the last few years he had almost convinced himself that he hated his wife, but this moment of extremity proved that, quite the contrary, her hold over him was as strong as ever.

And his mother would be all right—there was an insurance policy. The shock, of course, would be bad for her, but there was a decent chance that the circumstances of his death would be kept a secret from her. The SS was very sensitive about its public popularity and would go to ridiculous lengths to preserve the fiction that anyone wearing its uniform was a German hero. His mother would grieve, but she would not starve. And she would not be ashamed.

The gun was lying there in front of him. He had heard that the safest way was to fire up through the roof of the mouth, and he had no inclination to end up maimed but alive. Death, of course, would be instantaneous. There would be no pain. It seemed unlikely that he would even hear the shot that killed him. It was simply a question of nerving oneself up to do the thing.

And then he heard footsteps in the hallway and, without thinking, slipped his pistol back into his holster and stood up. He was perfectly relaxed, there was no hint of his intention in his face, when the door pushed open and Gruppenführer Nebe burst in like a man searching for a place of refuge.

"This is a fine mess," he said, hardly looking at Weinschenk—he might even have fancied himself alone in the room. "That's just all that I can say. This is certainly a fine mess."

"Yes." Weinschenk's lips were drawn tight in a cruel, ironical smile—seeing his superior officer like that was just what he needed to bring him back to life. "I can imagine that it must have come as something of a surprise."

Nebe actually started at the sound, and his head snapped around on the end of his neck as if it were operated by a spring. At first his expression indicated nothing except blank surprise, but gradually, as he recovered himself, it hardened into its usual hauteur.

"I shouldn't like to be in *your* shoes . . ." The sentence died off in a shrug. Nebe seemed to forget all about it, and about Weinschenk as well, as he slumped into the chair his subordinate had so recently occupied, propping his elbows against the desktop and burying his face in his hands.

For several seconds the two men seemed to ignore each other's existence. It was clear that Nebe was still merely responding to the fact of Steadman's escape; for the moment, he was too overwhelmed to have given any thought to what he should do next. That would come with time, but for a few hours at least Weinschenk could feel himself safe.

Weinschenk found it rather humiliating to reflect how relieved he felt at the prospect of a brief extension of life. Nothing had really changed, of course, but there were still those few hours in which to breathe and move his limbs and allow the procession of ideas to float across his mind. He would enjoy them with the shamefaced pleasure of a child in possession of stolen sweets. After all, it was something simply to be alive.

"But I'm sure they'll find him." Nebe drew his long fingers across his eyelids and sat up. "How far can he have gotten? We'll search every house if we have to—we'll comb him out. Someone will know something, and then we'll throw him right back into that cell."

"This is France, Herr Gruppenführer. The local people . . ."

"This is GERMANY, Herr Hauptmann!" he shouted, almost bouncing up and down in his chair. "This is part of the Reich now!"

Weinschenk glanced down at the toe of his left boot. For all that he regarded himself as a fervent patriot, these outbursts of chauvinism embarrassed him. They were so beside the point.

"Nonetheless," he began finally, when he was certain of not being interrupted again. "Nonetheless, the Resistance is very well organized in Alsace, and supported by a significant share of the population. They will find many willing to hide them. Doubtless they have made their plans in advance—they have the advantage of having taken the initiative. And now they have Steadman. We must anticipate events and move accordingly. But I am of the opinion that we will not see Steadman again inside the continent of Europe. If the patrols recapture him it will only be through some fluke."

"Perhaps you imagine you can read his mind?"

Nebe was regarding him with scarcely concealed contempt from above his clenched hands. His breezy, mocking tone was belied by the muscular tension that showed in his whitened knuckles. Weinschenk merely smiled.

"Well enough. At present his purposes are well served. He will probably be in England within a few days, but he will not stay there. I believe we can count on seeing him take ship from Ireland within, say, a week."

"Ireland?" The Gruppenführer leaned back in his chair, pulling his hands apart and coughing out a single, voiceless syllable of laughter. "You must be mad. What would he be doing in Ireland?"

"Escaping. It is a neutral country and close enough to be almost inevitable. That is where I think he will go."

"Don't be ridiculous. If what you conjecture about this escape is true, he will probably be dead. He is a British prisoner."

And now it was Weinschenk's turn to laugh.

"He was a German prisoner, if you will remember. I don't imagine the British will fare any better with him." The Hauptmann shifted his weight from one leg to the other and clasped his hands together behind his back. "He will go to Ireland—to Dublin, I would guess. It would be easy enough to check. We could be there to meet him."

In the silence that followed, Weinschenk tried to shake off the feeling of unreality that seemed to hang chillingly around his shoulders like an overcoat wet through by the rain. Could this conversation really be taking place? The Gruppenführer seemed to have no more solid existence than a shadow.

But it was happening. They were probably both marked for death by now—surely someone had telephoned Berlin—but, like ghosts condemned to repeat forever the patterns of their long-extinguished lives, they continued pretending that they still had some small measure of control over the events that were resistlessly carrying them into oblivion. They were both dead men, without the dignity to lie down and be still.

Or, perhaps not. Nebe was squirming in his chair, and the hair above his ears was hanging down in limp strands. There was something he was holding back, something he couldn't bear keeping to himself. It would almost have been possible to feel sorry for him.

"Well, we shall have to have him back long before then," he said at last, his voice sounding hoarse and exhausted. He looked up at his subordinate with eyes that were almost pleading. "The Reichsführer had me on the line not twenty minutes ago—he couldn't sleep, he told me; he wanted to know how things were proceeding with our prisoner. I told him that everything was in order, that we expected a breakthrough within the next several hours. I told him he could rely on us."

"You fool. You panicked."

Weinschenk was so astonished that it almost amounted to a kind of awe. He started to say something more and then discovered that his voice had deserted him.

He wondered if Himmler could have known the truth already. He could imagine that cold, calm face listening while Nebe made reassuring sounds through six hundred kilometers of telephone wire—had he noticed the faint undertone of despairing fear, or had he grown used to that from the men who lived under the shadow of his hand? But whether he had known then or not, he would know soon enough. And he would never forgive. The Reichsführer was really, in his way, a man of very narrow principles, and he would never forgive a lie.

"You poor fool," Weinschenk managed finally—the words seemed to choke him, so that he cleared his throat before going on. "You've killed yourself. You're as good as dead already."

Gruppenführer Nebe appeared not to have heard him. His weary, bloodshot eyes flickered aimlessly around the room, and his lips had drawn back from his teeth as if of their own accord. In all, the effect was sufficiently grotesque for anyone. And then, all at once, he looked at Weinschenk and scowled.

"And what of you, Herr Hauptmann? Or don't you imagine his arm can reach that far down?"

But Weinschenk didn't answer. He had already discounted the Gruppenführer and he couldn't be bothered. The nature of the problem had changed out of all recognition. The Gruppenführer had become quite irrelevant.

Now there was no one who could profit from using Weinschenk as a scapegoat. Weinschenk hadn't been responsible for the escape—Himmler wouldn't blame him for that, not if there were no one around to fan his suspicions. Himmler would blame Nebe now.

All Weinschenk had to do was to keep outside of the Reichsführer's grasp for a while—and, of course, catch and kill David Steadman. If he turned up again with that business settled, everything would be forgiven. Himmler had a known weakness for swashbuckling. Weinschenk would be received back like the hero in a boys' adventure novel.

The only condition was that Nebe would have to be already dead by the time the Reichsführer began making up his mind about whom to punish. A suicide has tacitly accepted all the blame, only now the suicide would have to be Nebe instead of Weinschenk.

The Hauptmann stepped over to the door, which was still standing partially open. He glanced out into the corridor. There was no one around, thank God.

"Where do you think you're going, Weinschenk?"

Nebe was still sitting behind the desk, and he seemed disposed to be quarrelsome. Weinschenk smiled at him benignly and, with his right side partially hidden by the edge of the door, unsnapped the flap of his holster. The Gruppenführer was left-handed; it would be important to remember that.

"Are you thinking of sneaking back to Berlin?" Nebe went on, watching through narrowed, fretful eyes as his subordinate quietly closed the door and came slowly around toward his left side. He was merely irritable because he was frightened. He suspected nothing.

"Perhaps you have some idea of getting your pretty wife to intercede for you. Perhaps you can play the pimp to Reichsführer Himmler as well—God knows, you must be sufficiently skilled at it by now."

And he laughed. Weinschenk was standing directly beside him, and still he laughed like a maniac. In a way, Weinschenk was grateful, since it made everything so much easier.

"No, I'm not going to Berlin. I'm going to Ireland." He slipped the pistol out of its holster. "And you are going even farther."

Before Nebe had a chance to react, Weinschenk leveled the pistol at a point just above his left ear and pulled the trigger. The shot made more noise than Weinschenk had imagined possible, and Nebe's head bounced away from the impact, precisely as if it had been struck with a hammer. The bullet went straight through, tearing a large hole. There was so much blood that Weinschenk had to step back quickly to keep it from spattering on his tunic.

After a few seconds, Nebe slumped quietly forward until his shattered head was lying on the surface of the desktop. His eyes were still open, and he looked as if he had died in the act of trying to say something. Weinschenk put his pistol in the dead hand, closing the fingers around the grip. Then he took Nebe's pistol out of its holster and put it into his own. No one was likely to check the serial numbers. No one was likely to doubt that Nebe had simply blown his brains out. No one would expect him to have done anything else.

As he closed the office door behind him, he decided that he probably had about twelve hours before anyone would think to wonder where he was. By then, if he drove fast enough, he could be most of the way to Portugal.

Yes—he would find Steadman and save himself and his Führer. It was for this that he had been preserved.

XXVIII

NOVEMBER 14, 1941

Steadman woke up in an attic room, on an iron bedstead—there was no mattress—directly under the peak of the roof. Had he tried to sit up his head would just barely have cleared the ceiling ridge, but he was very far from wanting to sit up.

It must have been broad day outside because a few bars of dusty sunlight were coming through the slats of the ventilating grille. There were a couple of ancient steamer trunks and a chest of drawers against one wall. Everything suggested he was in a private house, but that was the absolute limit of his information.

He tried listening for outside noises, just to try and discover if he was still in the city or if they had him squirreled away in some farmhouse, but after a few minutes he gave up. As his mind cleared he discovered that the sound he had been endeavoring with such attention to make out was nothing more than the throbbing of his own head.

It wasn't one of his better days. When he had attempted to turn over onto his side, the racket from the naked bedsprings actually made him sick to his stomach. It was then he noticed that they had chained his legs to the footboard.

He didn't have to be told that these people, whoever they might be, were working for Major Brian Horton and Company. It went by process of elimination: once you discounted the SS—and after the way things had gone during the escape, it seemed a pretty safe thing to discount the SS—Horton was all there was left. Who else cared? Who else knew? Probably not even this crowd who had nabbed him.

But he really wasn't up to detailed speculation about much of anything. That stuff in the coffee had given him a terrible headache—it seemed to extend straight down to about his knees. They could have spared the leg braces. Nobody was going anywhere for a while.

After an hour or so, someone brought him some breakfast. It looked like it probably would have been a pretty good breakfast, but he couldn't eat it. It lay on the floor beside his bed until the grease on the omelet had congealed into an opaque, whitish sheen. There was also some red wine, however, in a carafe that must have held close to a quart, and he managed about three swallows of that. He had the impression it made him feel better.

The attic had been deathly cold when he came to, but the temperature built steadily so that by what he concluded must have been noon, when the bars of sunlight from the ventilating grille dug into the floor directly beneath their source, he was tolerably comfortable. His headache and the carafe of wine were both just about gone, and he was beginning in a melancholy way to consider his situation.

As soon as the British had him, the fun would start all over again. Perhaps they wouldn't be quite so scientific as the SS—new technological wrinkles like Weinschenk's electrified wall might not be the fashion yet in Major Horton's circles—but the general drift would be the same. Steadman decided to give over thinking about what new horrors awaited him until the time. He had to make up his mind as to what he should do about the letter, and he had to figure some way of arranging another escape.

Both problems seemed insoluble—hell, he couldn't even get off this fucking bed.

He would have to wait upon events. He didn't know where he was, or even who had him. There was no one he could trust. How should there be? He would see what presented itself.

But at least, for the moment, he didn't have some goon pounding on him. He would have a chance to recover.

There was a staircase leading down from the center of the room, as if someone had cut a pie-shaped wedge out of the floor. The door at the bottom was slightly ajar. Every so often Steadman would hear murmured voices or see a band of shadow come peeking through the open doorway, so there was probably a guard posted outside. It was a reasonable precaution. Once in a while he would even get a visitor—the door would swing open wide enough for one of his captors to slip inside for a quick look. They never said anything, but he gathered he was an object of some curiosity.

Around one o'clock the door opened again, and this time a man with old blue cotton coveralls over a collarless shirt carried a tray noisily up the stairs. His sleeves were rolled up over arms matted with black hair and he hadn't shaved in two or three days, which gave his flat, snub-nosed face a ferocious appearance. He was probably around forty, but the bags under his watery brown eyes were heavy enough to make him look even older. He set the tray on the floor, as if there were no reason why either one of them should care what he did with it, and sat down on the foot of the bed.

"So it is really you, eh?" he said in heavily accented French. "When I heard the name I decided to come up and have a look for myself."

Steadman pulled himself into a sitting posture—it was a trifle disconcerting to have someone stare at him so openly—and then, quite suddenly, the man smiled. His teeth were stained almost black with tobacco, but he clearly intended to be friendly.

"You don't remember me, do you, eh?"

"No, I . . ."

"But I remember you." The smile broadened, and the man nodded his head furiously. "I was in Spain, and I remember *le Coupeur*. A friend of mine introduced us, although I don't think he had met you before either. I shook your hand. That was in Manresa, just before the end. They said afterward that you had been killed."

"I was—almost. I got out by accident." Steadman grinned, just as wide as he could manage. He couldn't have placed this guy in a million years, and he couldn't even remember Manresa—there had been lots to think about at the time—but he wasn't going to let an opportunity like this get away from him. If people wanted to reminisce about the honored past, he was game.

"And now it seems we are on different sides. Strange."

"I don't know. As you see, the Germans still don't like me very much."

It seemed to be the right answer—this man was predisposed to think well of him and, under the circumstances, Steadman was prepared to trade a little on his gaudy reputation. He had always been slightly ashamed of the nickname, which in Spanish meant either "cutter" or "butcher," but he knew that it had been intended as a great compliment and that, in any case, this was not the moment to be fastidious. *El Cortador, le*

Coupeur, Jack the Ripper—what did he care? If it got the job done, his good friend from Manresa, his brother in arms, could call him anything he liked.

This time the meal tray carried a whole bottle of red wine. It seemed they didn't mind how stewed he kept himself. Steadman picked the bottle up by the neck, took a long swallow, and held it out to his sympathetic jailer.

"Have some," he said, perhaps a little solemnly. "A drink in honor of our fallen brothers."

"God rest their souls."

It didn't take many minutes or much wine before they were both feeling damply sentimental. Étienne—that was his name, Étienne—confided to Steadman that he had been a Communist since the age of sixteen. He was a man who believed in causes, a patriot of the world. It was probably even true—not everyone with a great soul looked like Cary Grant.

And he liked Steadman—*le Coupeur*. That was the important thing. They were old comrades in the struggle for a better world.

"Tell me," Steadman asked, pouring out the last of the wine into a cracked tea mug they had taken to using as a glass. They were both just a little drunk by then, but Étienne, who had had most of the wine, was just a little drunker. "Tell me, why do a bunch of French Marxists go to all this trouble just to rescue *le Coupeur?* For old times' sake?"

They both laughed. It was a joke. Étienne put his thick arm across Steadman's shoulders and waggled a finger unsteadily. He smelled rather strongly of garlic. Their two heads were very close together because Étienne was about to confide a secret.

"No, my friend. No, it's . . ." And then he had to pause, and giggle quietly to himself because he remembered Steadman's little witticism. "No, it's that you are worth a lot of money. You must have done something very bad because we are going to sell you to the British and they are paying a vast sum in gold for you. Arms, too. My head reels just to think of it."

"I stole something from the Germans for them and then kept it. I stole a secret. They tried to trick me into betraying my own country, but I got wise and ran away. The British are without honor in this."

There was a moment of silence, during which Étienne scratched his neck with the heavy, dark talons of his left hand—he was considering the matter.

"Yes," he said finally. "That is like the British. They did not help us in Spain. If they had helped us, perhaps we might have won."

After a few more minutes of leaden silence, he got up and started down the stairway with the untouched breakfast tray between his hands—heavily, like a man with a burden. There was simply nothing more to be said. Steadman waited until he was gone and then started work on the lunch Étienne had brought. He was astonishingly hungry.

He figured they were waiting until nightfall before they tried moving him to some more secure location—certainly they wouldn't ask Horton to come to a private house. They would probably drug him again so they wouldn't have to watch out for both him and the Germans, and then it would be off to some defensible spot, probably in the mountains, where they could stop worrying about getting arrested. Horton could be in France tomorrow.

The attic was getting hot. As he sat up on the bed, Steadman could feel the sweat trickling down his back under his shirt. He felt stuffed; he probably hadn't eaten that much the whole time the Germans had him. It was a pleasantly uncomfortable sensation.

He also ached just about everywhere, and the tips of his fingers felt as if they had been burned off. This had been a bad trip in terms of general wear and tear. He wondered how long it would take him to heal up again, and if he would live to find out.

The sunlight from the ventilation grille had almost crossed to the other side of the floor when the attic door opened once more and Étienne came trudging up the stairway again, carrying another bottle of wine. This time, when he sat down on the edge of the bed, there were no smiles.

"We've been having a long talk downstairs," he said. He was perfectly sober now and had even shaved—he was there in his official capacity. "A few of us were in Spain, so we have the decency to feel ashamed that we cannot just let you go. We have no love for the British, and you are *le Coupeur*, but we cannot do it. We need their gold to finance the resistance. You understand, it was a military decision."

During the time he spoke, the believer in causes kept his wine bottle close to his side, as if he were a trifle embarrassed by its presence. The cork had been pulled, of course. Perhaps it was drugged. Or perhaps Étienne, the patriot of the world, no longer felt himself to stand on drinking terms with his illustrious and valuable prisoner.

Steadman waited, saying nothing. When the Frenchman had done, he turned his eyes away. Yes, the wine bottle was drugged.

"Did I ever ask you to let me go?"

Steadman allowed his voice to go heavy with ice. It wasn't very good manners, even for a prisoner, but he felt bound to push his advantage just as far as it would stand.

"No—you did not. You have been very understanding."

The situation had its ludicrous side, to be sure. But Étienne the proletarian roughneck, with his ridiculous delicacy of feeling, was all that Steadman had to work with for the moment, so he was very little inclined to laughter.

"But I suppose you would be willing to perform a small service for me, provided it did not jeopardize your arrangement with the British—and involved no risk to yourself?"

Steadman assumed he would wonder for the remainder of his short life if ever he had had so much riding on a single question.

For a long moment the Frenchman looked as if he hadn't understood, or couldn't believe that anyone would have the effrontery to insult him so. Steadman began to entertain a suspicion that perhaps he had laid the malicious irony on just a trifle thick.

But that wasn't it at all. What he had seen in Étienne's broad, troubled face was not anger but relief. Heaven be praised, the Communist romantic was beginning to see a way out of his difficulty.

His difficulty—his, not Steadman's. The French were marvelous.

"My first loyalty must be to *la Patrie*," he said cautiously, wiping his eye with the back of a hairy knuckle. Yes, he was actually going to carry it through. "But, that aside, I am prepared to do whatever you ask of me."

While Steadman was still digesting his good luck, the Frenchman passed his wine bottle from one hand to the other and set it on the floor, as if now they had reached an understanding about it.

All at once his face brightened.

"This thing you would have of me," he asked suddenly, "would it be to help you escape from the British once we have received their gold?" The idea seemed to have a certain attraction for him.

But Steadman shook his head.

"No. I want you to rob a poor box."

"The village is called Schirmeck. It's about forty kilometers south and west of Strasbourg. Do you know it?"

"Yes, of course." Étienne made an expansive gesture with his left hand. "My mother's sister used to live nearby—I could be there and return in two hours. What do you wish me to do with this letter when I have it, give it back to you?"

"No. I don't know what I want you to do with it. Maybe nothing."

Steadman could feel the cold gathering in his stomach, a kind of physical desperation, as if his fear had begun leaking through him like ice water. He couldn't see anything in front of him, nothing beyond the end of this probably rather pointless conspiracy.

"Just hang on to it," he went on finally. "You could ask again sometime before they hand me over to the British—I might have thought of an answer for you by then. Will you be staying around that long?"

"I hadn't considered the matter, but I suppose so. No one would tell me I could not."

"Do you know any German?"

The Frenchman shrugged in a Gallic, noncommittal way.

"A few words—enough to get by in this part of the country. Why?"

"For your own peace of mind, don't read the letter. Just put it in your pocket and leave it there."

"Monsieur, I can barely read French."

"Lucky for you."

When he was alone again, Steadman stared down at the bottle of wine Étienne had left so ostentatiously on the floor, wondering if it would taste as bad as the coffee they had drugged last time and where, after he drank it, he would wake up. In twenty-four hours, probably, he would be on a plane back to England and the French resistance would have their money. It seemed that everyone except him was making his way in the world.

There was nothing waiting for him in England except pain, failure, and death. There weren't going to be any reunions; he was a chump even to think about it. Karen was probably down in Kent, reading the sporting pages to her husband and wondering how she had ever been demented enough to become involved with as unreliable an item as David Steadman.

Well, so what? What should he care? He was probably going to be a corpse before he was five days older. He didn't have any business loving anybody.

At this precise moment he was hated by the Germans, the British, the head of the Spanish government, his father's ghost, and the woman he loved. There was no particular reason to add the French, so he decided he might as well be cooperative. After all, a deal was a deal. He picked up the bottle, pulled the cork, and took a long swallow. When the level in the neck had dropped about four inches, he replaced the cork and set the bottle back down on the floor. Then he lay flat on the bed, folding his hands over his belly, and waited. Within less than a minute, he could feel the numbness creeping stealthily into his brain.

XXIX

NOVEMBER 15, 1941

It makes one feel funny having to do with chaps like these, but there's the war for you. I dare say this isn't the only queer trick Winston has pulled in his time."

Brian Horton touched the tip of his mustache with the nail of his little finger, looking around him with what amounted to embarrassment. He didn't like the pine forest. He didn't like the squalid little tents and the cooking utensils scattered around the stones of improvised fires. And he didn't like the Communists; he watched them with the worried disdain of someone afraid he might catch a disease among such people. He was regular army—he might have felt he had a standard to maintain.

Karen had hardly been able to believe her ears when Brian finally let her in on the secret: "The Gestapo caught up with him in Strasbourg—not a bad run for a man on his own, but I don't suppose even he thought it could last forever. Our best information is that he's still alive and holding out. We've arranged to have the Maquis lift him."

"The *Maquis?*"

"It means 'bush,' or something like that. They're guerrilla bands, mostly Communists, I'm afraid. They've been underground since before the war, so they don't much like de Gaulle and the Free French—lucky break for us as it happens. Anyway, they'll get Steadman out of that prison."

So they had left that very night, as soon as they received the shortwave signal confirming that David was out of German hands. By prearrangement, Brian picked her up in front of the Victoria and Albert Museum, and they drove to an airfield near Windsor. There were two other men in the car, big, sullen men who didn't look like officers and who sat together on the front seat without even glancing back.

"Interrogation specialists," Brian murmured finally. "They'll be coming along too."

By the time they set down in that deserted wheatfield in Alsace, it was so close to dawn that the poor pilot had to fly on to Switzerland rather than risk recrossing occupied France in daylight. The man who picked them up drove them straight up into the Vosges Mountains; when they ran out of road, they had to hike, up through switchback trails that hardly seemed more than a scratch in the dirt. It was midafternoon before they arrived. The Germans would have required a division to take this place—provided, of course, that they could ever have found it.

The snow on the ground was still patchy. There was no wind to speak of, and the sun was so strong one was almost uncomfortable. Everywhere there was the smell of pine and, when they stopped for water beside one of the dozens of little streams that crossed their trail, the water was delicious and so cold it made one's throat ache. It was odd to be in so beautiful a place and to know that men with hunting rifles were watching one's every move. Karen never saw any of them; but she heard the whistled signals being passed up the mountain ahead of them.

Except for the stacks of weapons that seemed to be everywhere, the Maquis stronghold might have been taken for a holiday camp. There were women about—not many, but enough to give the impression of normal life—and even a few children. Here and there one saw somebody wearing the Cross of Lorraine on an armband, but not very often. The British arrivals were regarded with undisguised suspicion.

Without quite acknowledging it to herself, Karen had somehow expected that David would be there to welcome them. She had imagined that his might be the first face she would see. It wasn't. He was nowhere in evidence. She hadn't realized until that moment, when she could measure it against her disappointment, how badly she had wanted this reunion.

Perhaps he was dead. Perhaps the escape had been a failure, or they had arrived too late and found the Germans had already killed him.

Brian's worry, she knew, was that he might talk before the Maquis could reach him, but for her the concern was much more personal. She just wanted him back; she didn't care about the terms.

But he wasn't dead. As she listened to the conversation in halting French between Brian Horton and a small man in a black sweater who seemed to be in authority, it became clear that David was alive, that the Maquis had him, and that he had not broken. He was a prisoner, a valuable property, and the Maquis wanted full value for him.

"No. Of course not—how could I have brought the arms with me? I have the gold. You'll have to be satisfied with that for the moment. Have we ever broken our word to you?"

The man in the black sweater looked less than convinced. He dug the heel of his boot into the ground as if testing its resilience. He frowned with concentration. He wanted something more than the bare word of an Englishman from the class of the oppressors.

"You have the gold?" he asked finally.

"I have it. I said I have it." Brian started undoing the buttons around the waistline of his shirt, and in a moment he had extracted a wide canvas belt, snaking it out like a tapeworm. The belt looked heavy and thick—it couldn't have been much fun dragging it over all those miles of mountain trail.

"You'll find a hundred and twenty ounces pure in there," he said, dropping the belt contemptuously to the ground. "Given what gold buys on the black market these days, that should come close to five thousand pounds sterling. And that's only the down payment."

"Then you can have him."

The Frenchman didn't look particularly satisfied with his bargain, but it was made. He gave a sign with his left hand, bringing it out to shoulder level and snapping his fingers, and a boy of about fifteen, with hair the color of butter, came out of nowhere and gathered up the belt that was still lying in the dirt. It seemed to be an embarrassment to everybody.

At that moment a tall man in a threadbare gray suit—an odd costume for such a place, Karen had to think—stepped out of one of the nearer tents, walked up to Brian, and smiled. He had three or four days' growth of beard on his chin, but nothing about him suggested that he had ever worked with his hands. In the lapel of his jacket was a small pin enameled red and shaped like a five-pointed star.

"You wish to see him?" he asked in a tone that hardly guaranteed the wish would be gratified. "He is asleep now. We have been keeping him asleep—that is no timid maiden you have there. I saw him kill a German with a pair of scissors the night before last. It was a pleasure to witness."

The expression on his face suggested he was measuring the new arrivals against the man they had come to claim as their prisoner, and he seemed amused by the contrast.

"What do you want with this one, eh?" The tall Frenchman shifted from one foot to the other, somehow giving the impression that he had taken a proprietary interest in David Steadman, as if the prestige of his prisoner were intimately involved with his own. "What did he do that he is worth so much money?"

."That's rather our business."

The French Communist and the British career soldier regarded each other from either side of a chasm of natural antipathy. Anyone might have imagined they were about to come to blows, and then the Frenchman smiled once more.

"We lost three men getting him out of that Gestapo prison, monsieur. I have an idea that makes it our business as well."

"Nevertheless, you aren't going to find out. Just reconcile yourself to that as best you can."

A graceful Gallic shrug seemed to be all the reply Major Horton was perceived to deserve.

"Well, he's in there." The arm of the threadbare gray suit pointed back to the tent from which its owner had issued a few moments before. "He'll wake up in another quarter of an hour, and then you can decide what to do with him. If it occurs to you that you need any assistance, just ask anyone to fetch you Raymond—it is a *nom de guerre.*"

Raymond glanced at Karen, and his eyebrows went up in comic resignation. A second later he seemed to be nowhere in sight.

Karen peered at the narrow tent flap beyond the shadow of which David was sleeping his drugged sleep. It occurred to her that now she would probably find out something like the truth of what had happened back in Stockholm, of why he had run away and what he had stolen to make himself such a threat to everything that was represented by the War Ministry, and she discovered that she wasn't at all eager for it. What should she care? Her husband was dead and the man she loved was asleep forty feet away in a canvas tent. Wasn't that enough for her to know?

Brian Horton seemed to measure the ground with his eyes and then paced over and lifted up the tent flap with a sweeping motion of his left arm. He craned his neck peering into the gloomy interior and then came back, from all appearances very well satisfied.

"It's him," he said, his voice fairly booming. "Out like a light. He looks awful."

That thought seemed to allow him a certain pleasure, as if it solved no end of difficulties. He smiled, so that the broad ends of his heavy, salt-and-pepper mustache reached nearly to the edges of his face.

"I think we ought to have a doctor check him. The Gestapo had three days in which to put their questions, so we ought to be sure he'll stand up to it before we begin ourselves."

Karen glanced away. Brian was beginning to frighten her, and she didn't particularly want him to see that.

"Surely we'll take him back to England before any of that," she said, trying to keep her voice level. "Surely it can wait that long."

"Naseby, have a word with that Raymond fellow. See if he can't come up with somebody." As the man drifted off, Brian frowned at the tent. Probably he hadn't even noticed that anyone had spoken. Then his eyes turned toward Karen, and their expression became at once cunning and cruel.

"Perhaps you'd better come with me," he said.

The atmosphere inside the tent was humid and stale, as if the air had been breathed to exhaustion. Brian raised the flaps at both ends, more to let in some light than to provide for ventilation, but it had that effect as well. David was lying on his back, and when a bar of sun crossed his face he grimaced in his sleep and turned his head away. From the way his arms moved at his sides, one could see that his dreams were far from restful.

"Oh, my God, what have they done to him?" Karen murmured. She picked up one of his hands. The fingernails were rimmed with dried blood and half torn away, and the tips were so bruised they actually looked black. His face was swollen and mottled with purplish bruises. He looked like some of the pilots in the hospital where Bertie had stayed immediately after he was rescued, only they had been burned. The practical results didn't seem to be very different.

"They've been asking him questions for three days—from the look of things, I'd say we were lucky they didn't have a chance to make it four."

Using his thumb and first finger, Brian prized open David's left eye and then let it snap shut again. With the flat of his hand he began slapping him gently on the cheek. Finally, after perhaps three quarters of a minute, David started to react, but it was a long time before he gave any indication that he was returning to consciousness. At last he lay blinking at the sunlight. He hardly seemed to know where he was.

The interrogation specialist now identified as Naseby came in at that moment and knelt down beside Brian, glancing uneasily at their prisoner. He was a dark man, with massive eyebrows, and there was something peevish in his expression.

"I'm afraid it's negative about the doctor, sir," he said, in what amounted to a sickroom whisper. "He says it's too dangerous."

David looked up at them and grinned.

"Now at least I know who paid the tab," he said, sliding a hand in behind his neck. "How've you been, major?"

His eyes shifted nervously to Karen, as if he were ashamed that she should see him like this. It was something that only lasted for an instant—probably no one else had even noticed it—but she felt her heart contract painfully, telling her she shouldn't have come.

"I'm afraid I couldn't get your package for you. I couldn't talk the safe open." He was looking at Brian, just as if they were the only two people there, and he was mocking him. It was terrible to watch—he was almost inviting them to take up where the Germans had left off. He didn't seem to care.

All at once he sat up. Half a minute before one wouldn't have suspected that he was capable of such rapid movement. He looked at Brian and his face went stony.

"That's quite right, Mr. Steadman. We mean to have it." Brian stood up, dusting off his knees with a flapping motion of his hand that suggested a certain fastidious intolerance. "The corporal and I will leave you now. Perhaps Lady Windermere would be good enough to explain our position—perhaps you'll find it more agreeable coming from her."

His face crinkled in a strained smile. Even that was a warning. As he left, he dropped the tent flap behind him with a delicacy the irony of which it would have been difficult to overlook.

As soon as they were alone, David put his hand out and grasped her arm just below the elbow. At first she thought it was intended as an embrace, but he pulled her toward him with a suddenness that had nothing to do with love.

"Listen," he whispered, holding her close to him with a grip that threatened to break her arm. "Listen to me, Karen. We won't have more than a few minutes. They'll be taking me back to England—I don't plan to give them any choice. And when they do you've got to find out where they intend to stash me and tell Vidocq. Arsène Vidocq. You remember him—I brought him to dinner one night. He's got a gas station, in Winchester, I think. Tell him where they've got me. He'll know what to do. You understand? Tell him, Karen."

But she was shaking her head, and her eyes were brimming with tears. She couldn't help him. How could he think she could help him?

"Give them what they want," she sobbed quietly. Her free arm was around his neck now—his poor face was so battered; she didn't want to hurt him—and she pressed her cheek against his temple and whispered into his ear, the way one might comfort a child. "Whatever it is, give it to them. It can't be worth all this. Give it to them."

He released her arm, almost threw it away, and she could feel him pulling himself free from her embrace.

"You don't understand. You don't even know what it is, do you." He held her by the shoulders and she looked away. She couldn't face him when he was like this. "Don't you see? They'll kill me. The minute they have it I'm as good as dead. They can't leave me running around loose with a secret like this."

He was so fierce about it. His eyes, in their swollen, blackened sockets, almost glowed, and his fingers . . .

"You're hurting me, David. Please . . ."

"I'm sorry."

He released her at once, his hands dropping down into his lap—he seemed not to know what to do with them now.

"They could put you in protective custody, David. They do that, until the end of the war. It's called . . ."

"There won't be any time limit on this one, sweetheart." With the tips of his bruised fingers, he brushed a wisp of hair away from her face. Where before there had been an almost desperate harshness, now there was only tenderness—he was once more what he had always been. "You have to help me. It's not just my life, it's . . ."

Once more he drew her to him. His hands cradled her face, and his lips almost brushed against hers.

"What's the date?" he asked.

What was he saying? There was a pleading in his eyes that almost broke her heart.

"What?"

"What's today's date?"

"It's the fifteenth. November the fifteenth. It's a Saturday. Why?" For some reason she felt a surge of disappointment.

"In three weeks, maybe less, the Japanese will attack the American Pacific fleet anchored at Hawaii. Do you understand me, Karen? In three weeks. The Germans know it. The British know it. Everybody knows it but those poor slobs waiting in Pearl Harbor. That's the secret your friend is ready to kill me for. Do you understand? He *wants* it to happen."

It seemed like forever before she could bring herself to do anything except stare. The words, the individual sentences, were clear enough, but they didn't seem to have any relationship to what she had always taken to be real life. She wasn't so much shocked as stunned. She couldn't seem to get past a panicky confusion that wouldn't allow her to feel anything else—to feel anything as it should be felt.

He was lying. He had to be lying. Such a thing simply wasn't possible.

"David, did you kill a woman in Stockholm?"

"No—what are you talking about?" He shook his head. He really didn't seem to know anything about it.

"In the train station. They said you shot a woman."

"That was the Germans. They were shooting at me and missed. Did she die?"

"Yes."

He seemed to cloud over for a moment, as if lost in some ugly memory, and then his mind snapped back. Suddenly nothing mattered but the two of them, and this terrible secret.

"Whatever you do, don't let Horton guess that I've told you." The ball of his thumb glided over her cheek, and his eyes pleaded with her. No, he wasn't lying. "These guys aren't kidding. They'll kill you too if they think you're a threat. Tell Vidocq."

She couldn't. He must know that—it would be treason. She couldn't go against her own country, not just because he told her to. Not just because she loved him. Not even for that. How could she tell him? How could she make him understand that it wasn't possible?

"Bertie died."

The tears were running down her face. She was helpless to stop them— she didn't even want to. What had made her tell him that? Of all things, why that?

"I'm sorry. Oh, God, baby, I'm sorry."

And to his everlasting credit, he really was. All one had to do was to look at him. Bertie had been his friend. In a day, or even an hour, he might see something more than that, but for now . . .

"Get out of here," he said finally. "Tell them I'm not buying, that I won't even talk to you. For God's sake, stay alive."

Outside, after the tent, the bright sunlight was like an affliction. She had to shade her eyes, and that was just as well because she wasn't any longer sure enough of herself not to welcome an excuse to hide her face for a moment.

Brian and the two interrogation specialists were standing together beside a clump of trees that marked the southeast corner of the camp. The man called Naseby had his head bent and his arms crossed over his chest; he seemed to be listening to his superior officer with utter concentration, but Brian was turned aside and his lips were sealed in a straight thin line under his mustache. By the time she reached him, she was composed enough that they wouldn't imagine she had been listening to the War Ministry's most closely guarded secrets.

"I can't help you," she said. They were free to interpret that any way they liked.

Brian frowned, his eyes searching her face. He seemed to have expected something of the kind. And, yes, he would kill her if he thought she knew—he would do it with hardly a qualm.

"I expect it was very upsetting for you to see him under such circumstances," he said, shifting his weight from one leg to the other. He seemed even more than usually guarded and wary. "I expect you found you had a lot to talk about."

Suddenly, in one of those flashes of insight that come to people whose feelings have been worked to a morbid sensitivity, Karen realized that he was jealous, that he hated her at that moment, that she had never stood in more danger in her life. He would have welcomed an excuse to order her death. She smiled—it was a crooked, painful smile, the only kind of which she was capable. It seemed to send the right message.

"I told him that my husband had died. They were good friends, as you know. I think he was sorry to hear it."

Yes. Put like that, it sounded like an episode from a film. The husband and the lover, and all such good friends. But if one could stand to seem so contemptible, one could always count upon being believed.

Yes. Brian believed her. A woman who could reduce everything to the level of her private life wasn't anyone to whom such a secret would be confided.

"Yes, I'm sure of that," he said. Even as he stood there looking at her, he seemed to have dismissed her from his mind. "Then I suppose we'll have to find other means of bringing Mr. Steadman around."

But still he kept insisting. He kept at her all the rest of the day, as if he couldn't bring himself to part with the idea that she would be the instrument of David Steadman's destruction.

"I really do think you could have another go," he said to her. They were sitting together on a log, eating a thick, perfectly delicious stew from metal dishes. It was a quarter to six in the evening, and the foreigners were being served dinner first. "I'd still be willing to bet that you could get him to come clean with us if you tried. For his sake you ought to, you know. It's going to get messy if he holds out much longer."

His mustache made him seem to frown absurdly, but the threat in his words was apparent enough. He was ready to do anything to get David to talk.

"Listen, old girl, there's a good deal at stake here . . ."

"Don't call me 'old girl,' Brian."

"Sorry."

They went on eating in silence, and as soon as his plate was light enough to allow him to without seeming rude, Brian got up and shoveled his uneaten stew into the fire. She didn't see him again for a couple of hours.

She thought they would all leave the next morning, but about ten o'clock she was surprised to find herself the only one prepared to go. When she ventured near David's tent she could understand why.

Even from outside she could hear the distinct smack of wood on human flesh. At first there was no other sound, and then, finally, a pale, hollow groaning. She lifted up the flap to look inside and dropped it again almost at once. She found it hard to believe her eyes.

All at once Brian's hand was on her shoulder. He spun her around almost before she had a chance to realize he was there.

"You stay away from this," he said tensely. "This isn't any of your business." He looked as if he might do anything. He was almost frantic.

"You're breaking his hands! Damn you, you can't do that!"

And then Karen Windermere did something she had never in her life thought she would ever do—she went for Brian's face with her fingernails. It was purely a matter of instinct. She was beside herself; she hardly knew what she was about. Brian swept her aside as easily as he might have brushed a speck of dirt from his lapels. She fell to the ground, skinning her hands. He seemed to be daring her to get up.

It seemed to go on forever. The dull sound of a thin wooden cane striking over and over again, the moan that finally became a strangled sob, a moment of silence, a muffled question, silence, and the cane again. All the while Brian stood there watching her, glaring at her as if he hated her more than anyone in the world, and there seemed to be nothing she could do to stop that terrible sound, as regular as the ticking of a clock.

She had known Brian Horton for years, and she hadn't imagined he could be capable of this. She would kill him. If she ever had the chance she would kill him.

"Stop this," she shouted. "Stop this, stop this . . ." Until her voice trailed off because she was choking in her own tears.

Finally, the tall Frenchman in the shabby double-breasted coat strolled up. He seemed to have come out of nowhere. He smiled. And then his hand went inside his lapel, and when he brought it back out it was holding a pistol, an ugly, sleek mechanism such as she had never seen before. He was pointing it directly at Brian's heart.

"You will call a halt to this, major. Now."

The pleasant smile on his face never wavered. All at once the sound of the interrogation ended, and the man whose name Karen had never heard stepped outside. Behind him was another from the Maquis, also holding a pistol. In his other hand was the cane.

"You will not do this, major. Not here." Raymond shook his head slowly. He seemed to think the two Englishmen were somehow comical. "If you will be so good, major. We are Communists here. There are men in this camp who have been fighting the Fascists since 1936, when your country's government would not raise a finger to help us. They remember Monsieur Steadman from those days."

He put away his pistol and took the cane, sliding its edge down the palm of his hand. And then suddenly he broke it, just snapped it in two.

"We don't know what he is supposed to have done," he went on, his eyes narrowing slightly. "We have sold him to you because we need money and guns, and what you do with him when you have him home among your own we leave to you. But, as I said, some of us have long memories, and some of us have promised to kill you pigs of Englishmen if you touch him again."

Karen got up slowly. No one seemed to notice her, and she was just as happy. She felt a change taking place within her, a shifting of her center of gravity, and suddenly she knew that she didn't care about anything except the fact that now she was on David's side. Somehow the Frenchman had settled that for her when he broke the cane.

"Very well." Brian's smile was breezy, almost contemptuous, as if such considerations of ancient loyalty were unintelligible to him. "As you wish. I suppose we shall have to take him back with us now."

XXX

They brought David down the mountain on a stretcher. He was kept drugged the whole time and then loaded onto the back of a hay truck, with the bales stacked around him like the blocks of a tomb. The French wouldn't allow any of the British soldiers anywhere near him; they were even driven to the airstrip in a separate car, accompanied the whole time by armed men so that it amounted to a kind of tacit arrest. Karen rode with them. Probably no one would have stopped her if she had tried to stay with David, but she decided that would probably have been a tactical error.

They kept to narrow little country roads the Germans probably didn't even know existed. They were in Lorraine now, where French was spoken and people resented their annexation to the Reich. Provided one was careful, there was little enough danger of being betrayed to the Gestapo.

Karen had made a great point of apologizing to Brian for her behavior—she could understand that these things were necessary; it was just that she had never seen . . .

He seemed to understand, or perhaps he simply didn't care one way or the other, but she achieved her object. She was back in his good graces.

"I understand," he said, patting her on the wrist. "It's not the sort of thing anyone likes. It's a savage war, and we have to fight it that way. The Nazis aren't giving us any choice."

He smiled sadly. He seemed to feel rather sorry for himself, but at least he had accepted Karen back into the club. She was entirely sympathetic to the necessity of beating the backs of a man's hands until they were so swollen he couldn't even bend his fingers. Of course it was a dreadful thing for someone of Brian's sensitive nature to have to order done.

They didn't talk for most of the journey. After dark they drove with only their side lights on, and they hardly encountered a soul.

Their airstrip was nothing except a muddy field next to an apple orchard. Karen looked at her wristwatch. It was only a few minutes after nine P.M.; the plane wouldn't arrive for hours. There was a cold wind, so everyone stayed in the car. The truck that had brought David was parked about a dozen yards away.

"What are they going to do with him?" she asked, allowing her eyes to fill up with tears—it wasn't a very difficult performance; all she had to do was to remember the way David had looked while they had carried him down to the road, the way his face had twitched in his sleep. "It isn't going to be anymore . . . ?"

Brian smoothed down the tips of his mustache and cleared his throat. He was embarrassed. He had forgotten about the savagery of war—he was basically a rather pedestrian little man, and all this had taken him out of his depth.

"No—I shouldn't think so. Once we get him home, it'll be all narcotics and sleeplessness. Not much fun but a great deal less wearing on the nervous system."

He smiled, making one wonder to whose nervous system he could have been referring.

"They keep a place in Buckinghamshire for just such cases. I expect it'll be something of a rest cure for him after what he's been through."

"And when they've found out what they want to know?"

It wasn't a question Karen much wanted answered—she suspected she already knew the answer and, besides, she could hardly afford to believe anything Brian would tell her. But it was time to change the subject. He was beginning to look restless, as if he realized he had been talking out of turn.

She smiled at him bravely. She was only a woman, after all, and naturally she would allow herself to be guided.

"Oh—nothing very drastic, I should think." He was lying. Anyone could have seen from the way his eyes wavered that he was lying. David was as good as dead if these people had their way. "Prison—protective custody—for the duration. Perhaps not even that long."

He seemed anxious to end the conversation. He recrossed his legs and started fidgeting apprehensively with the last button of his overcoat, and all the time his eyes were trained on the back of the truck where David Steadman was lying, probably wondering how long it would be before they could begin cracking him open like a walnut.

But the joke was on them because they were already too late. The letter for which they were preparing to destroy the man she loved was nearer than they could have any idea but already far out of reach. At that moment she was carrying it, neatly folded, inside her brassiere.

There were good people everywhere—these French guerrillas, of whom Brian was so contemptuous, had already seen that David was in the right. Yesterday evening, while Brian was huddled with their leader Raymond, one of them, a great bearlike man in blue coveralls, had sat down beside her at the fire and, with a gesture she had at first interpreted as a clumsy pass, had slipped a square of paper, no larger than a library card, inside the palm of her hand. There were people all around, all talking to one another and studiously avoiding any notice of who might or might not be having a quiet word with the British lady of uncertain loyalties. One had the sense that perhaps this little scene had been arranged in advance.

"You now have what they seek with so much treasure and blood, madame," he murmured. "And, more than that, you have David Steadman's life in your keeping. If you decide to give that piece of paper to your major, he will surely kill *le Coupeur* as soon as he has the chance."

"What did you call him?"

"He has many names, but only one life, madame. He asked me to do this thing, and I have done it. I hope his trust in both of us has not been misplaced."

And then the man got up, casually dusted off the seat of his trousers, and strolled away. And now Karen carried David's life close to her heart.

Her betrayal of her own side troubled her less than she would have imagined. Brian and the men like him, these really weren't very nice people, Karen thought to herself. It was a bad war, but there was an unseemly haste in the way they welcomed their opportunity.

The plane landed a few minutes after one o'clock in the morning, and the stretcher was put aboard first. As they took off, they could still see the Frenchmen standing around in the flickering light from their kerosene lanterns.

It was a long flight, and no one was very interested in talking. They were all given leather flying suits except David, who was merely covered with a couple of blankets. It was probably a mercy that he was asleep during the entire trip. The cabin was brutally cold.

They landed at the airfield near Southend. There was an ambulance waiting—there was even a red cross painted across the rear doors—and David was whisked away as if his very existence were a state secret. Karen caught a ride to the railroad station, where the train to London was ready to leave within twenty minutes. Brian didn't seem to think there was anything unusual about her wanting to get away. He was probably glad to have her off his hands.

She had lots of time to think on the train. She didn't really believe that Vidocq would have much success in getting David out of a secret military installation, in Buckinghamshire or anywhere else— David was probably just grasping at straws. The army was, after all, the army.

But that wasn't her decision. They were going to kill David—or, just as likely, turn his brain into raspberry treacle—and if there was anything anyone could do to prevent that . . .

David had told her to find out where they were taking him and to contact Arsène Vidocq, and these were things she simply had to do. The war had taken Bertie away from her, but it wasn't going to take David. Not if there was any way she could prevent it.

So it was necessary to come up with something a little more specific by way of an address than "Buckinghamshire."

It was almost six in the morning when she reached London. She took a taxi from Liverpool Street Station and reached her flat by twenty after. It was perhaps unfortunate that the sound of her running a bath woke up her mother.

"Good heavens, child, where have you *been?*" Lady Ridley stood in the bathroom doorway, clutching her black satin eyeshade in her left hand while she steadied herself dramatically against the sink. "You can't imagine *what* went through my mind when you disappeared like that. You *might* at least have left me a *note.*"

"I've been in France, mother. How are you for petrol coupons?"

Karen was in a great hurry. Her clothes were lying in a little heap in the middle of the floor, and she wasn't finding it easy to wash herself in some seven inches of bathwater.

"You might have been killed in a *bomb*ing raid. You might . . ."

"There hasn't been a bombing raid over London in weeks. Petrol coupons, mother—try to think. Have you got any?"

"Well, yes, I suppose. If you put it like *that.*" For a moment she was sulky—Karen wasn't properly sympathetic to a mother's feelings. The business of the petrol coupons, however, provided its own interesting possibilities. "Why *should*n't I have coupons? When one lives alone in the country one never *goes* anywhere. What were you doing in France, dear?"

Lady Ridley was looking at her daughter through narrow, speculative eyes. It was obvious that the fact of France's being under German occupation had temporarily slipped her mind.

"Mother, if you have any please go get them. I'm in a hurry this morning."

By seven-thirty Karen was climbing the steps of the War Ministry, just in time for the shift change.

As usual, the vast corridors were crowded with people, none of whom seemed to find anything remarkable in her presence. She crept along, staying close to the wall, fighting against the idiotic idea that everyone was staring at her, that she was about to be arrested by a massive military policeman with a bristling mustache. She had reached the point of absolute decision. If she proceeded any farther she would be committing treason. But the thought merely crossed her mind as a settled fact. If that was what it was, then fine. Treason was merely a word, and somehow she knew, without having to work it all out, that David's was the right side to be on.

There was just that level of informality on Operational Sector Three that the director's door was usually left unlocked and there was no great difficulty about getting at the record books. Everyone had clearance and nothing was kept there that had more than a Grade Four security rating, so why make a great issue of access? That sort of thing merely got in the way of general efficiency.

Brian wouldn't be in this morning. Probably he wouldn't show up at all—he had a proprietary interest in David Steadman, and he wasn't about to relinquish it. Karen slipped into his office and let the door close behind her. Everyone was already too busy to have noticed.

She could feel her heart pounding as she went through the drawers of his desk. If a clerk should happen to walk in just then . . .

The *Directory of Permanent Installations* was under a box of carbon paper. There was only one listing for Buckinghamshire under "Interrogation": The Willows, Long Crendon. She put the directory back, closed the drawer, and left the office. Her mother's Rolls was parked just a block and a half away from Trafalgar Square, and Winchester would be a good two-hour drive. The specialists at Long Crendon had their orders. They were probably working on David that very moment.

By ten that morning she was within sight of the cathedral spire, and by a quarter after she had found that there was an automobile repair business on Ranlagh Road that listed an "A. Vidocq" as proprietor. She asked directions from a schoolboy on a bicycle.

The "business" wasn't much larger than a private garage. There were three rather expensive-looking cars in various stages of dismantling and a tiny room with a metal sign reading Office on the door. Vidocq was sitting behind his desk, blowing on a cup of tea. He looked up at Karen and frowned.

"You want something, madame?" he asked. The sleeves of his shirt were rolled up over his heavy arms, and he seemed oblivious to the fact that the temperature inside was probably hovering around fifty degrees.

"My name is Karen Windermere. I don't suppose you remember . . .

Vidocq's face brightened, and he ran the palm of his hand over his nearly naked scalp.

"Of course!" he bellowed. "Dinner that time with David—you are the pretty one with the big house. How is your husband?"

"I'm afraid he died."

"Ah, well—then you can marry my friend David."

He grinned. Naturally he had guessed, on the basis of a single evening, everything that it had taken Karen months to sort out for herself. It had all been so obvious that now it could stand as the subject of a joke.

"David is the reason I've come," she said slowly, all at once no longer sure of anything. "He sent me—he's in trouble. He's being held at a military interrogation center in Buckinghamshire, and he wants you to get him out."

She told him the whole story, everything she knew. It was a relief in a way, and he sat there listening silently, nodding every so often but not offering any comment, occasionally making a note on the back of an envelope.

"Yes. It is just the sort of thing he would do." A worried look came into Vidocq's eyes. "This place, this Willows, have you ever seen it?"

"No—I've never seen it."

She hardly dared breathe. She didn't have any idea whether he would do the thing or not. She could think of a hundred reasons why he might refuse—it was like watching the black wig being placed on the judge's head.

"If you don't help him, he'll die," she said finally, not even trying to keep her voice steady. She would use any weapon to make this man say yes. She didn't care what she did. It was David's life. "He would have come for you. You know him—you know he wouldn't refuse."

"My dear madame, there is no question of refusing." He smiled as he reached across the desk and touched her on the back of the hand with the tip of a blunt finger. And then the smile faded.

"But you know nothing of this place where he is being held?"

"Nothing."

"It doesn't matter," he said, shrugging his shoulders. "We will get him out. The British are fine people, but they are like children in these matters. For some reason, as long as they are in their own country they feel perfectly safe."

XXXI

Vidocq had the devil of a time with pretty Lady Windermere—she simply would not be persuaded to go back to London.

"You will only be in the way, madame," he told her. It was always difficult to convince a woman that she would only be in the way; Vidocq hardly even knew whether he believed it himself.

"I've been trained. You'll see—I won't be in the way. This is something I have to do. Please."

And the expression on her face as the tears welled in her beautiful eyes seemed to say that she was determined not to be put off. When they were like that, women were tougher than any man.

"David would not want your life to be put at risk. Think of him."

"My life is useless to me unless we can get him back."

Well, and she was a bewitching little creature. It was easy enough to see why David was in love with this one, although he had always been sentimental about women.

"As you wish, madame."

David had gotten himself into trouble over some great secret. This story about the Japanese might or might not be true—it was evident that the little madame would tell any story if she thought it would help to save her lover—but David had sent her, and David would not ask his friends to risk everything merely to save his life. That would be the one reason to bring them, but he would never have asked if that were all. So there would have to be something more.

But what did Arsène Vidocq care about the British and their secrets? He had buried all that sort of idealism in Spain. He would never again hazard his neck for an abstraction.

David Steadman, on the other hand, was his friend, who had twice saved him from joining the honored, nameless dead in that terrible little war, and such debts it was a privilege to repay.

And Arsène Vidocq knew he would not be alone in thinking so.

Thus he excused himself from Lady Windermere, went across the street to a public house to purchase two box lunches, placed a couple of long-distance telephone calls from a booth around the corner from his flat and, having gone back to the garage to close it up and collect the lady and his car, drove off to find the Willows, Long Crendon, Buckinghamshire. In his trunk were a few souvenirs from *la guerre* he suspected might turn out to be useful.

It was after two when they arrived in Long Crendon, but the house he was looking for wouldn't be right in the heart of things—the British liked to preserve a decent privacy when they did something of which they were ashamed. They would pick a place where they didn't have to worry about the neighbors. So Vidocq drove straight through, taking the road to the northeast that led away from the main highway. The map he had purchased from a bookseller in Stokenchurch indicated that the road formed a loop heading back into town, so it seemed reasonable to assume that any large houses listing Long Crendon as an address would have their entrances along there.

Sure enough, after about twenty minutes he came across the metal gate with the word Willows written in elaborate scrollwork across the archway. Vidocq, you are such a clever fellow, he thought to himself. Now all you have to do is to find some way of getting close enough to have a good look.

"Madame, we will drive on perhaps another quarter of a mile and then stop. You will be so good as to wait for me in the car? And if anyone should pass and inquire, you will perhaps tell them you are having engine trouble? A maiden in distress—who could be so wooden as not to believe you?"

Two hours later they were in Oxford, in the lobby of the Hotel Prince Regent, where a dapper little Spaniard with close-cropped hair and a mustache that looked as though it might have been painted on was waiting for them by the entrance to the bar.

"Come upstairs," he said to Vidocq, throwing a suspicious glance at Lady Windermere. "I have taken a room so we can have a place to talk. The others have already arrived." He took Lady Windermere by the elbow and guided her toward the elevator, just as if he were in the parlor of his own home.

The room was on the third story. There was a window that faced out onto the street, and in front of it was a small round table where two men were playing chess on a miniature board. Both of them wore uncomfortable-looking blue suits and starched collars that seemed to go three quarters of the way up their necks; they were in the cement business together and, so it was rumored, doing pretty well out of the war. They were Mario Grinaldi and Luca Poggio, and good Communists in spite of everything. Luca Poggio, who at twenty-eight was the senior partner, glanced around for an instant, smiled at the woman from behind thick glasses that made him look like a character out of a Dickens novel, and was about to get up when his attention was drawn back to the game by the fact that Grinaldi had just decided to move his knight. On top of the dresser against the opposing wall were lined up three bottles of red wine. None of them had been opened yet.

"Put the game away," said the little Spaniard, dropping down onto a corner of the bed. "Arsène has been out to look at the house, and the impression is that it won't be easy."

Vidocq was standing by the dresser, his hand clamped around the neck of one of the wine bottles. It was just about the right temperature— probably they had been chilled first and then allowed to stand. Probably, in a place like this, they had cost two or three pounds a bottle, but men on the eve of a battle didn't care how they spent their money. Vidocq looked at the label, frowned, and took his jackknife, which included a corkscrew, out of his pocket.

"Have you any glasses?" he asked. One sniff at the cork told him the stuff was rubbish. It could be left to breathe all afternoon without improving any, so they might as well drink it right away.

When they had all had a little wine and could feel comfortable, Vidocq took up a position with the window to his back and crossed his arms over his chest. There were certain necessary formalities.

"It is more than possible some of us may be dead by tomorrow morning," he began, uncomfortably aware of the cold windowpane behind him. "Besides, this is England—the end of the line for all of us. If we are found out, there will be no other place of exile. We will be killing Englishmen this time. If anyone has any second thoughts, now is the moment to back out. David would understand."

Of course, such a thing was inconceivable, and they all knew it. After a moment of silence, the Spaniard, whose name was Marañosa and who four weeks earlier had been part of a convict gang building roads in Segovia, made an impatient gesture with his right hand to indicate that the subject was closed.

"Proceed," he said, in the shaky English of a man who had learned the language out of a book. As his hand returned to his lap, he reached across with the other to pull the long, brilliantly white shirtcuff back into place. It was already an automatic piece of business; there were manacle scars on his wrists which he wished to hide.

Lady Windermere, who had been listening in silence but with visible anguish, threw him a look of gratitude which he was too much of a gentleman to acknowledge.

"Proceed," repeated Luca Poggio, nodding. Grinaldi said nothing, but nodded as well.

"All right, then." Vidocq smiled and then leaned forward, pulling the chessboard to the center of the table and gently sweeping the pieces to one side with the edge of his hand.

"The house is here," he went on, tracing around the edge of the chessboard with the tip of his finger. "It is old, Victorian. Many odd corners and places to conceal ourselves on the outside, which is good. Probably many small rooms and staircases on the inside, which is bad. A crazy house, where they will know their way and we won't. Also, all the windows above the first floor are barred—perhaps the British have taken themselves over a lunatic asylum."

"Where is David in all this?" asked Luca Poggio. The cement contractor was a practical man, and the expression on his face betrayed a certain impatience with the historical side of the question.

"I don't know. That is something we are going to have to find out."

"It is a thousand pities we don't have David with us," Marañosa said in Spanish. He shrugged his shoulders, as if in relief. It was probably a strain for him to follow the conversation in English, but for the Italians the problems were reversed—it had been common enough to fight for Spain on the Republican side and never to have learned to manage the language.

"Yes." Vidocq nodded and smiled at the irony. "He was always good at finding out things like that, wasn't he."

"We will have to take a prisoner," said Grinaldi. It was the first time he had spoken and they all looked at him with a certain surprise. He was quite right, of course, but somehow it was indelicate to speak of such things so early.

"Tell us about the security," said Luca Poggio.

"Again, good and bad." There was a slight film of dust on the table. At the edge closest to him, he wiped the wood clean with a long, heavy sweep of his fingers. "Here, in the north, there are trees, plenty of cover, but only up to within sixty to sixty-five meters of the house. Otherwise the ground is clear. There are floodlights, but only around the house itself. When I was there, only two men were on patrol. No dogs, but they were carrying rifles. I suppose we shall have to kill them."

Vidocq glanced quickly at Lady Windermere, whose face mirrored a kind of hopeless wretchedness. But still she said nothing—she was a good woman. At last she nodded.

In that uncomfortable silence the same thought was in all their minds—that this wouldn't be like the old days, that it was one thing to kill German Fascists, or even the Nationalists of General Franco, but that it was something else again to kill British soldiers while Britain was at war with Hitler.

"Well, let us not feel it too deeply," said Grinaldi at last, pouring himself another glass of wine and sliding the bottle across the table toward Vidocq. As far as he was concerned, the woman might not even have been there. "Where were the British in 1938, eh? And where was David?"

The question of the prisoner was perhaps the most urgent. They all knew they were working against time.

"We must assume they plan to kill him as soon as he breaks—that seems to be what he believes himself." Vidocq looked down at the chessboard and frowned.

"David is tough," answered Luca Poggio, grinning and looking around at the others as if the fact constituted some sort of personal triumph. "They will find they cannot break him just overnight."

"Yes, David is tough. But the Germans have had him for three days before the British, and there are limits to what anyone can stand."

"Then it must be tonight."

It was Marañosa who had spoken. He made a gesture with his hand and shoulder, a beautiful, eloquent, profoundly Spanish gesture reminding them that David Steadman had not thought of the risks when, all alone, he had ventured into a country where there was a price on his head and had plucked a friend from the slow death of a twenty-year sentence at hard labor. They all owed similar debts, so the risks didn't matter. None of them could disagree.

"Yes, it must be tonight."

This was followed by the comforting reflection that soldiers stationed at home had nothing to do with their evenings, even in the middle of a war. Certainly many of them would have leave. The officers surely would be going into town for a friendly pint or two and a little relaxation—it shouldn't be such a difficult thing to find someone to answer their inquiries.

It was a technique they all knew from Spain, a little trick of David's. All that was necessary was to wait for the man alone on the open road.

They waited in two cars, parked about a hundred yards apart, along the road that led from the Willows into Long Crendon. All they had to do was to keep still until someone came out. It was eight in the evening, and the officer's mess would be over now; they wouldn't have to linger long.

Vidocq fidgeted in the driver's seat of the lead car, hoping that the Willows contingent weren't all family men, the type to stay in barracks and play cards. There was a public house in town called the White Horse—they always seemed to be called the White Horse, as if the British had no imagination—and the barmaid was pretty. It stood to reason that someone from inside David's new prison would be counting the money in his pocket and thinking about the barmaid's laughter.

Lady Windermere was on the front seat beside him. A man and a woman out together were less conspicuous and, besides, he discovered that she had a certain tranquilizing effect.

"It will be all right," he said finally, hardly knowing that he had spoken until she turned her head to look at him. She smiled, but there was something full of tragedy in that smile.

"I know. I believe you."

The first two cars that passed them were carrying two or three people each. They all wore uniforms, as far as Vidocq could tell—it had perhaps reached the point in wartime England that a uniform was less conspicuous than civilian clothes, even if one worked at a secret government installation for the torturing of prisoners. After them there was no one.

A long time passed, but there were no more cars. Vidocq looked at his wristwatch—it was twenty minutes past eight. At the half hour he rolled down his window about two inches, hoping perhaps to hear something before he could see it, but there was nothing. After a while the draft began to bother him and he rolled the window back up.

It wasn't until ten minutes before nine that he saw another pair of headlights coming through the metal gate. He turned on his sidelights and touched his brake pedal, signaling the car behind him to make ready.

It was a man, alone. Vidocq started his engine, allowing the car to gain a slight lead. In a moment the three of them, the car from the Willows, Vidocq, and the car driven by Luca Poggio, formed a little caravan. None of them was going faster than thirty miles an hour.

Vidocq waited until they were well away from the gate and then began picking up speed. He passed in the other lane and then fell back in front of the Willows car, slowing back down. Thirty-five, thirty—he could see the other car's lights coming up on him through the rearview mirror. It was time for Luca to make his move.

Sure enough, Luca also drew into the other lane as if to pass, but when he had come even with the other car he simply stayed there. They had it boxed in. Vidocq hit his brakes, hard.

Few things in life could ever be expected to happen so smoothly. There was a squeal of rubber on asphalt, the blast of a car horn, and suddenly all three of them had come to a halt. Of course, their subject might simply have thrown his car into reverse; he might have risked scraping his paintwork on the stone wall that ran along that section of the road. But he did none of these things. He was an Englishman. He didn't inhabit a world in which anyone had anything to fear from strangers on a dark stretch of road. He simply waited while Vidocq got out and started walking back toward him. Probably he was already rehearsing all the irate speeches he would make.

But Vidocq never gave him the chance.

"I say, you can't . . . ."

But before he could finish the sentence, Vidocq had jerked open the car door, grabbed him by the collar, and pulled. The element of surprise was everything; he never even tried to resist, he simply fell out onto the ground. Vidocq kicked him deftly in the pit of the stomach—after that he would have other things to think about than fighting back—and then he reached down and, with the thumb and first finger of his right hand, squeezed tightly on a pair of nerves that ran along either side of the man's neck. After a few seconds even the groaning stopped.

"All right, Luca, help me get him into the truck. Mario, you drive his car. This is not a safe place to stay."

The spot where they all gathered was only about three quarters of a mile from the Willows, but the man in the truck of Luca Poggio's car had no way of knowing that. He might have been anywhere for all he could have told. He was still unconscious when they opened the trunk.

By then they all had black ski masks over their faces, and Lady Windermere was still sitting in the car. Vidocq was the only one of them he had seen, and him only for an instant. There would be no problem of being identified later, so there would be no absolute necessity for killing this one. That would be up to him.

Vidocq took his wallet, which contained about fifteen pounds and a set of papers made out in the name of Lieutenant Edgar Rice Phillips. Lieutenant Phillips' hands and ankles had been bound with a thin grade of wire that was used for the coils of electromagnets—if one struggled against it, all it did was cut deeper—and his eyes were covered with white adhesive tape. In an exercise of this sort, the subject always tended to be more cooperative when he felt completely helpless.

They waited a few minutes as Lieutenant Phillips woke up, allowing him to recover from the first blush of panic, and then Vidocq took a large military revolver, the one he had carried in Spain, and pressed the muzzle into the soft flesh under the corner of the lieutenant's jaw.

"We wish to ask you a few questions," he said quietly. "If you give us the answers we are looking for, everything will be fine. If you lie to us, or if you decide to be a hero and say nothing, then I will pull the trigger of this very powerful pistol. That will produce a terrible racket, but of course you will not hear it. You will be dead, with your brains scattered around for yards and yards. Do you understand me?"

There was a slight nod—the lieutenant seemed afraid to move his head very much. Perhaps he thought the pistol against his throat might go off by accident. In any case, he was afraid and he was listening. That was all that mattered.

"Either last night or this morning, you received a new prisoner. Tall, thin, blond, badly bruised around the face and hands. His name is Steadman, yes?"

A surprisingly pink tongue came out and played across the dry lips. Phillips wanted to speak but didn't quite dare. Vidocq eased back a shade with the muzzle of his gun.

"A new prisoner, yes," the lieutenant whispered. He was very young, about twenty-two or -three, and heavy almost to the point of grossness. His lank brown hair was hanging down into his face. "We never know the names, but that's him. In for questioning."

He was working hard to catch his breath, moving his head around as if he could see through the tape over his eyes. Vidocq brought the pistol back up to his throat and all that stopped.

"I will now tell you something. We are going to take our friend Steadman out of there, tonight. Doubtless some people will die—some of you, perhaps some of us—but he is worth many lives. Perhaps fewer will die if we know where to look for our friend, if you tell us. In any case, if you tell us you will not be one of them. Remember, you can save no one except yourself."

He decided the young Mr. Phillips would need a moment to consider, so he waited in silence. The young always needed a moment before they could be brought to believe in the possibility of death.

"Now—will you tell us? Or do you prefer that we kill you now, this minute?"

"I'll tell you. Oh, God, I'll tell you! Please . . ."

So it was to be easy, after all. Vidocq glanced around at the masked figures who were standing on either side of him with their arms folded across their chests, noticed that the license plate of one of their cars was visible and made a sign to Grinaldi to cover it up—there was no light, but a frightened man sometimes notices things and there was nothing to be gained by taking an unnecessary risk. When it was done, he reached down, took the corner of the piece of tape over Phillips' eyes, and pulled it loose with a quick, rough motion. The lieutenant whimpered and clapped his hands over his smarting eyelids. Well, possibly it hadn't been a very pleasant experience; Vidocq thought he could see pieces of lash sticking to the tape.

"Now—listen to me." He took Phillips by the hair and pulled his head up. "I will give you pencil and paper, and you will draw for us a map. The whole house, floor by floor. Then I will lock you in the trunk of your car again, and I will tape your mouth so you cannot cry out—not that anyone could hear you if you did. If the map is accurate, and everything goes well, we will be back in a few hours to let you out. The trunk is airtight, but you will have enough air to last that long. If you have betrayed us, and all of us are captured or killed, then you will suffocate long before anyone finds you. If any of us escapes the trap you have set for us, you can be sure we will come back here—a man can be made to die very painfully from just a single bullet wound."

No, this one didn't wish to die, painfully or otherwise. They would have their map, for all the good it would do them. They would not have to go rushing in like blind cattle.

Vidocq turned to Grinaldi, who was leaning against the fender of Lieutenant Phillips' car.

"Fetch the lamp," he said, and the thing was done.

Within a quarter of an hour they were ready to leave. The lieutenant was back inside the car trunk and Lady Windermere had come out from the front seat to join them. She was holding a machine pistol, but in her hands it looked like simply a large piece of metal. It had been agreed that Lady Windermere would stay with the prisoner.

"We will be back soon," Vidocq told her, his voice low and confiding— he had developed a certain liking for this woman who was so willing to do evil for the sake of his friend David. She was no weakling. David had done well for himself.

"We will bring David back."

"Yes."

Vidocq glanced at her face for a moment, smiling uncertainly, and then went to join the others. He had lost his taste for making promises.

Once they got inside, it would all be reasonably straightforward. David was being kept in a small room in the back. He never left it; when they wished him to answer questions, they came to him. That part of the house was reached most conveniently through a stairway that ran into the old servants' quarters. There were only two doors in the way. It would be a walk.

Once they got inside.

But there were still all those yards of lawn to cover, and the two guards. The guards were armed with semiautomatic rifles and the floodlights were never turned off, not even during the day.

They decided to wait until just before four in the morning, when even the liveliest celebrants would be sleeping heavily.

The great problem was to keep the guards from raising an alarm. Unfortunately there was no solution except to kill them—the difficulty would be to do it quietly.

Which was the principal reason they had thought to include Marañosa. Marañosa was the best rifle shot Vidocq had ever seen, perhaps the best rifle shot fighting on the Republican side, and Vidocq happened to have a seven-millimeter bolt-action Mauser for which a gunsmith in Paris had built a special silencer. It was the perfect weapon for the present emergency: the bullets were hollow-point and would splinter on contact, which guaranteed one's kill provided the placement was right and also prevented them from passing straight through the target to flatten out on the wall behind. It was surprising how much noise that could make.

The only question was whether, after only four weeks, Marañosa's nerves had recovered sufficiently to allow him to do it.

"It will require considerable delicacy—he will have to die without making a sound. Are you up to that?"

"I shall have to be." Marañosa moved his shoulders in resignation. "One could wish he were not a moving target."

"Perhaps we can find a way to make him stand still."

They waited together in the dark apron of woods that came closest to the house, Vidocq, Marañosa, and Mario Grinaldi. Luca Poggio was waiting out by the gate; at a signal he would come straight in through the driveway, park his car beside the door through which they would carry out David, and hold his position against all comers until they could all make their escape. Provided it worked, it was a beautiful plan.

While they gave Luca Poggio time to get into position, they teased Grinaldi about his recent marriage.

"Perhaps that is what I should do," Vidocq said as he wiped his face with his ski mask. For some reason he was sweating heavily on this rather cool night. "Perhaps I should find myself a nice English girl and settle down."

"I advise against it," Grinaldi answered. "You would find it a great disappointment."

They all laughed quietly, not because Grinaldi was so droll but because they were all on edge.

At five minutes before four, Vidocq decided it was time.

"I can buy you perhaps two seconds," he said, putting his hand on Marañosa's shoulder. Marañosa was already crouched beside a tree stump which would serve him for a shooting stand. "Try not to waste them."

The guards went round and round, as guards did everywhere. They both were circling the house anti-clockwise, so one was always on one side with the other on the other. If Marañosa could take care of Number One, they could all cross over to the house and then deal with Number Two at their leisure as he came around. All Marañosa had to do was to remember how to shoot.

Vidocq took up his position about thirty feet from Marañosa's right, and they all waited for the guard to come round again.

It only took a few seconds. Vidocq had been timing them, and they each made the full circuit in about seven minutes. They wore the khaki fatigues of combat soldiers, but they were only boys. The poor little toads.

He stepped over a fallen log and out onto the grass. There was very little light; the guard wouldn't be able to see him unless he looked hard, but Vidocq was going to give him a reason. He cupped his hands over his mouth to produce a fluttering, birdlike whistle—there was a bird in Spain that had just that cry, and the sound would carry a long way.

At first the guard didn't notice, so Vidocq tried again, raising the pitch a bit. This time the guard hesitated for an instant.

Over here, blockhead. Vidocq whistled again and then began waving his left arm. That worked almost too well—the guard froze in his tracks, stared straight at him for a few seconds, and then began to slide the rifle from his shoulder.

He never made it. To his left, Vidocq heard a faint thump, as if someone had struck the soft earth with his fist, and the guard pitched over without even unlocking his knees.

Nobody wasted any time. They all started running toward the house, just as fast as their legs would carry them. Grinaldi got there first; he was standing over the body when Vidocq and Marañosa arrived.

It wasn't a very pretty sight. The bullet had entered the man's neck, apparently severing an artery before hitting the spine. There was a great deal of blood around—some of it seemed to have spurted out a distance of some five or six feet. One bleeds to death almost instantly.

But they had all seen dead bodies before. Vidocq took the rifle from Marañosa's shoulder and handed it to Grinaldi. It was well not to put too much on any one man.

"Go around and take care of the other one," he whispered. As soon as Grinaldi was out of sight, he and Marañosa began dragging the body into a clump of bushes beside the house. There was nothing they could do about the blood, but at least this way someone looking out through a window wouldn't have a corpse to gasp at.

When Grinaldi came back, no one asked him any questions. One could see from the expression on his face that now there was another body in the bushes. They all started around together to the old pantry door.

It was locked, of course, but what difference did that make? Vidocq took the wallet from his back pocket and extracted a thin piece of glittering steel, like a sewing needle except longer. They were inside in a few seconds.

Grinaldi would wait for them there, guarding their escape. The other two started making their silent way up the staircase that led to the old servants' quarters. Marañosa had a tiny electric torch that threw a beam of light perhaps six inches wide, but otherwise they had to make their way in the darkness. When they reached the second locked door, Marañosa held the torch while Vidocq worked with his needle. They both knew they were almost there.

What they found on the other side was a corridor, a hardwood floor carpeted with a Persian runner. At the end it seemed to open out into some sort of vestibule, where a dim light was visible. That was where they headed.

The guard—he looked for all the world like a hospital attendant, even down to the white trousers and shirt—was sitting behind a desk, reading a magazine. He looked up, saw Vidocq's revolver pointing at his head, and opened his mouth without uttering a sound.

"No heroics," Vidocq murmured. "Stay quiet, and you may live to see the sun rise. You have a prisoner—tall, blond, a bruised face?"

The guard nodded stiffly. One might have thought the joints in his neck had frozen shut.

"Well—take us to him. Be quick about it."

There was a ring of keys hanging from a hook on the wall behind the desk. The guard rose out of his chair and, without taking his eyes off Vidocq's gun, reached back to fetch it. Unlike the boys standing sentry outside, this one was almost middle-aged and had the look of a man who has spent long years working in prisons. Vidocq knew the type.

They walked back down the corridor together, the guard in front, until they reached a heavy door with a tiny window just at eye level—the glass was reinforced with wire, the kind behind which chickens are kept, and the door, although painted white like the corridor, was chipped here and there so one could see that it was made of metal.

"Open it."

The guard inserted his key and pulled the door toward him by its handle. It swung open like a bank vault. Inside, a man was lying on a narrow cot; he was bound up in one of those white canvas camisoles by means of which madmen are kept restrained, and his eyes, when he looked toward them, were wild with fright.

"My God," Vidocq whispered, "what have they done to him?"

They cut David out of the straitjacket and got him to his feet, but he didn't show any signs of recognizing them. He was quiet and peaceful, but badly frightened.

"What have you done to him?" Marañosa snarled, poking the guard in the chest with the muzzle of his pistol. "What kinds of dogs are you?"

The guard didn't know—he only worked there; the doctors gave the injections. He didn't know anything about it.

Probably all over Europe little men were telling themselves the same thing.

"Let's get him out of here," Vidocq said. He slung David's arm over his shoulder and they started out the door. "You stay where you are."

The guard took the hint and sat down on the mattress so recently occupied by his prisoner. He was content to have the cell door closed behind him—it meant that he would be allowed to live.

It was slow going down the corridor. David could hardly drag his feet; he seemed bewildered and talked in single words that made no obvious sense.

"Quiet . . . postman . . . home . . ."

And then, suddenly, a door at the opposite end of the corridor flew open, and there was a sound of running, and they had a couple of soldiers coming straight down on them. That shit of a guard must have pressed an alarm button somewhere.

Vidocq was running now, dragging David with him. If he could reach the door to the stairway he had a chance. He heard a shot behind him and realized that Marañosa was covering them from the rear.

There was a great deal of shooting now—a bullet buried itself in the wall next to his head. They were almost to the stairwell now.

He pushed David through and, glancing back over his shoulder, was just in time to see Marañosa stumble and fall, the bullets taking great chunks out of his chest. For just an instant their eyes met and Marañosa managed a feeble gesture with his left hand. *I'm finished and we both know it,* he seemed to say—*get out of here.* Vidocq dove through the open doorway, kicking it shut behind him. There was no more time to play nursemaid. He threw David over his shoulder, a little surprised at how light he was, and ran.

Grinaldi was waiting in the pantry and, astonishingly, Luca Poggio's car was already standing outside with its doors open.

"I gave a yell as soon as I heard the shots," Grinaldi said, almost shouting. "Where is Marañosa?"

"Marañosa isn't coming."

They didn't wait any longer. They were inside the car and moving when the first soldier burst out through the pantry door into the yard. Vidocq took his time, aiming carefully through his rolled-down window, and shot him straight through the heart. The more the merrier, he decided.

As they broke through the iron gateway to the road, Vidocq kept watching through the rear window, but no cars followed them. They wouldn't have had a chance yet to get them out, and by the time they did this one would be abandoned and they would have transferred to Grinaldi's rather gaudy dark-green Packard. No one would be looking for them in that, and it seemed unlikely, considering the circumstances, that David's captors would dare to call attention to themselves by calling up a manhunt.

By sunrise they were already beyond Oxford, on the road that led west to Cheltenham and, finally, to the sea and safety. As the light dawned, David seemed to begin to come back to himself. He was resting, his head against Vidocq's shoulder, and suddenly he turned and looked up into his face.

"Is it you, Arsène?" he whispered. "Is it really you?"

"Yes, my friend. It is I, and no one else. And you are safe."

It seemed to be more than he could bear. He buried his head in Vidocq's sleeve and wept like a child.

XXXII

NOVEMBER 20, 1941

By the Thursday after his rescue, Steadman was nearly his old self again. The British had pumped him full of stuff that induced some very disagreeable effects—paranoia, hallucinations, the inability to tell if he was dreaming or awake—but after he had slept through most of Tuesday and Wednesday all of that passed off.

Vidocq would bring him around when it was time for him to eat or climb into a boat or look bright-eyed and alert for the benefit of some policeman or railway conductor, but for the rest he was treated as just so much cargo and allowed to doze as much as he liked.

And when he would wake up, Karen was always there. She held his hand and smiled a little anxiously; she seemed never to leave his side. All the time he was fighting his way out of the nightmare, she kept him anchored to the love of the light.

Anyway, his memories of the trip to Ireland were fairly sketchy.

Grinaldi and Luca Poggio separated in Worchester and went back to their cement business, and Vidocq bought three tickets on the train to Holyhead, where a friend of his was waiting with a boat. Steadman was put into a cot made up in one of the storage compartments, and they went across at night and landed a dozen or so miles above Dublin. There wasn't anything illegal about the trip—it wasn't absolutely necessary that they carry on like gun runners—but Vidocq figured there was no point in taking chances. They stayed in a town called Balbriggan until Steadman had come all the way out of his trance.

On the morning they were to take the bus to Dublin, Steadman decided that he was steady enough on his feet to risk a little walk.

"Well, one supposes your lady will be able to nursemaid you, my friend." Vidocq smiled knowingly. "You still carry that little revolver in your handbag, yes, madame?"

Balbriggan wasn't much of a town. You turned a corner and you were back in the country, where green fields stood separated from the road by low stone fences. It was very pleasant, and Karen walked beside him with her arm threaded through his. She was to stay behind. Steadman had put his foot down—there was always the chance there would be a watch up in the big cities, and he didn't want Karen to be seen with him so she could end up in a prison cell back in England. In an hour they would part. It was possible they might never see each other again.

"I wonder if the memory of this business isn't going to stand between us for the rest of our lives," he said finally. There seemed to be so much he had wanted to say and then, suddenly, when the moment came, he hardly felt able to utter a word. "I never wanted you to be involved. You have to believe that, Karen."

"I know."

For a long while after that they walked along together in silence. It was as if they had become separated from time, from the sequence of events that had brought them to this place, as if for the moment, as long as they said nothing, they could hold on to the illusion of being free. To be together, to be silent and to feel the pressure of their arms touching, was a kind of ecstasy.

"Sometime it has to be over, doesn't it?" she asked. She didn't look at him. She really didn't expect him to have an answer. "The war—everything—it will be over someday."

"Will it? I can't imagine . . ."

"I love you, David." She turned to him, clutching the front of his coat fiercely. The tears were starting up in her eyes, and her face reflected a smothered agony that seemed ready to break her heart. "I love you. I'd do it all again. That's all that matters."

It wasn't, and they both knew it, but what difference did the truth make? For that one moment they belonged to each other, and for them that was enough.

*　　*　　*

Vidocq had always been a great one when it came to documents; he always seemed to know the best local forger, and he had a careful eye for detecting the kinds of mistakes that got you in the lockup. The passport he managed for Steadman was an absolute work of art, good and used-looking and with all the right visa and port-of-entry stamps. Even the picture was perfect—somehow the photographer had managed to get rid of all the bruises, so that Steadman looked about twenty-eight years old and as innocent as a cherub.

"I have a passage for you aboard the *Armagh*—she's an old hooker that mostly carries freight, but there are a couple of staterooms and they'll rent you a deck chair if the weather is nice. You'll reach New York inside of ten days."

Vidocq took him down to the pier, and they shook hands very solemnly. They both knew there was a good deal that was going to have to remain unsaid because neither of them was the type for emotional displays and, besides, Steadman had no inclination to embarrass his friend and didn't as yet entirely trust himself to maintain the proper restraint. It had only been the day before that Vidocq had seen his way clear to telling him about Marañosa, so probably they were wise to play down the dockside farewells.

"Thanks for everything, Arsène. I couldn't . . ."

"Forget it. When you get back to all your millions, I plan to send you a highly inflated bill."

Vidocq grinned—he had always found the idea of David Steadman as a member of the oppressing classes very funny—and clapped his friend on the shoulder. A second later he was three quarters of the way down the gangplank. He never even looked back.

After a couple of minutes, Steadman went into his cabin, which contained nothing but a bunk, one chair, a set of dressers built into the wall, and a washstand, and began unpacking the cardboard suitcase Vidocq had put together for him. At the bottom, wrapped in a towel, he found a hunting knife with a five-inch blade in a stiff leather scabbard. There was also a small role of white cloth tape. It was a *bon voyage* present and a warning—he wasn't in New York yet.

Before he did another thing, Steadman took out his razor and shaved the upper half of his left calf and taped the knife into place upside down. He didn't leave his cabin until he could feel the ship moving.

By two in the afternoon they were just clearing St. George's Channel. In theory, he should have been able to stand on the stern deck and see Ireland to his right and England to his left, but a cold fog had settled over them almost the instant they left port and Steadman could hardly see to the end of his arm. It didn't promise to be a fun voyage.

The first time he had made the crossing it had been in the other direction. He had been with his mother; it had been 1920 and they were running away. As to the causes of his parents' divorce, Steadman didn't have a clue—all he knew was that one afternoon, when he was walking home from the fourth grade, a taxi pulled up beside him, the door opened, and there was his mother with three suitcases. They took the evening train to New York and were aboard the Queen Mary the following morning.

The second time had been after her death, when he returned to become his father's son again.

And now he was repeating the cycle. Having run away to war, he was coming home for a second time—only now his father was dead as well and America seemed an even stranger place in his imagination than it had in 1936.

He would deliver the letter—he had it back in his wallet now, safe as houses—but after that the future was merely a blank. He had no occupation now except that of warrior, but the prospects there didn't seem particularly bright—either side in what had been, up till then, his war would now quite happily have had him drawn and butchered. Probably he would never be able to go back to Europe again.

Well, maybe he could go join the guerrillas in China, or perhaps, even better, he could sit back on his money and learn to live like the idle rich. He could become a kind of Marxist cliché—take up polo and Havana cigars and spend part of every morning clipping his coupons and writing letters to the *New York Times* about how terrible the labor unions were getting. He could marry some Pittsburgh debutante and learn to hate her and the New Deal both. With a little luck he could develop into a genuine putrefying reactionary.

But for the moment he would settle for just being able to shut his mind off. Now that nobody was actively trying to kill him, all he seemed able to think about were the interrogation room at Strasbourg and Karen Windermere. He didn't know which was worse.

She had saved his life. She had thrown over everything, the code to which she had been raised, that was as much a part of her as her backbone, and all for him. *I love you. I'd do it all again. That's all that matters.* But it wasn't going to happen that way. She had had to give up too much to keep him from dying in some little basement room; she would never be able to forgive either one of them for that.

But she had saved his life.

Having made himself good and depressed, Steadman decided to look up the steward and find out what the drill was for dinner. With any luck at all, he would be seasick by then, but he thought he might just get the dining room located anyway. As it turned out, there didn't seem to be one.

"Seein' that we don't often carry more than the odd half-dozen or so passengers, we usually just set a couple o' tables in the main lounge."

The steward turned out to look for all the world like your standard St. Patrick's Day leprechaun, in his late thirties, probably, with a chubby, freckled face and a narrow circle of red beard going all the way round it like a hedgerow. He seemed to regard Steadman with considerable satisfaction, as if he looked upon him as his own personal property.

"This voyage, as it happens, we'll only have you and another gentleman—it's a good job I double as mechanic's mate, or I'd be out on the dock."

"Another gentleman?"

"Yes. He came on just before we sailed. You must've missed him."

Well, at least there would be some company for the nine days of the crossing. Thanks be for the minor mercies.

"And there's no one else?"

"No, sir." The little Irishman smiled, showing a row of mottled, uneven teeth. "It isn't the season when people travel just f'r their own amusement."

There was something to that—already you could look out toward the horizon, which was hardly more than an indistinct, arbitrary line where the gray fog met the slightly grayer sea, and watch it pitching up and down with the irregular, slightly startled rhythm of a child trying out the garden swing for the first time.

Steadman thanked the steward and inquired when dinner was to be served and then, out of ingrained habit and to keep his mind occupied, set out to tour the ship.

There wasn't much to see. The main deck ran all the way around, with a narrow open stairway up to the bridge on either side of the prow. What the steward had grandly referred to as the "main lounge" was in fact hardly large enough to accommodate four or five fair-sized chairs, incongruously made out of rattan, and a broken-down sofa covered with green burlap—there was no bar, so if you wanted a drink you pressed a little electric bell beside the door and hoped the steward wasn't down in the engine room with an ailing dynamo. None of the other rooms at deck level were open to passengers, but Steadman peeked inside anyway and found the kitchen, two utility closets, a passageway that seemed to lead down at least as far as the passengers' cabins on the second level, and a tiny pantry which, from the collection of magazines and empty coffee mugs that lay around on the one and only table, seemed to be the steward's private sanctuary.

The crew's quarters were on the third level, directly below the state-rooms, and below them, to the rear, was the engine room and, to the front, the vast cargo hold that seemed to take up most of the ship. The doors to both of these were, quite naturally, locked.

So the world, for the next nine days, had pretty well shrunk down to the lounge, Steadman's cabin, and the main deck; and the main deck, where the wet, gray fog clung to everything like moss, wasn't anywhere you wanted to spend a lot of your time.

But Steadman didn't mind. He wasn't in prison and he wasn't on the run. There were about seventy cheap edition novels on a shelf in the lounge, everything from *Mansfield Park* to *The Mystery of the Yellow Room*. It didn't seem likely he would be in too much danger of growing bored.

He dined alone that evening. The other passenger had let it be known that he hadn't found his sea legs yet, so the steward carried a tray of tea and digestible biscuits to his cabin. Steadman, on the other hand, dis-covered himself without a twinge of queasiness—perhaps he had simply exhausted his capacities for physical suffering—and by six-thirty was hungrier than he would have thought possible.

Dinner was surprisingly good and, perhaps because there was only one person to eat it, much more than Steadman found himself able to manage. There was a lamb stew with big chunks of potato, and that wonderful soda bread that only the Irish seem to know how to make, and trifle for dessert, served with real coffee, the first he had tasted in longer than he cared to think about.

"I could put a touch o' sweetener in that if you like, sir," the steward announced as he poured out a second cup. "In this weather a man needs a little somethin' to keep off the chill."

When Steadman didn't actively protest, the steward took away his cup and brought it back a second later topped up with heavy cream and about two ounces of Old Bushmill. By the time he was finished he could feel the comfortable, moist heat all the way down to the balls of his feet.

"You'll be on y'r way home then, sir," the steward said, more as a statement of fact than as a question. He smiled as he stood beside Stead-man's chair, whisking a few breadcrumbs off the tablecloth with his napkin—apparently he felt disposed to be conversational. "Been away long, have you?"

"About five years."

"That's a good long time."

The steward glanced down at Steadman's left hand, the fingertips of which were still covered with tiny white plasters to protect his injured nailbeds. He was frankly curious; he didn't make any bones about it. A man whose face and hands exhibit such a spectacular collection of bruises had no business being surprised or offended if people wondered how he came by them.

Steadman decided to take pity on the poor man.

"Makes buttoning your shirt a bit tricky," he said, holding up his hand with the fingers spread a few inches from the tablecloth. "I was in an automobile accident."

"Were you now, sir? It seems an odd way to get yourself mashed up in a car—I was just goin' to ask what the other fellow looked like."

The steward grinned. It was obvious he thought Steadman wasn't telling the truth, but he didn't seem to think any the less of him for that. He pulled back the chair when Steadman rose from the table, and it was quite as if a secret understanding had been established between them.

Steadman selected a book from the ship's tiny library and went back to his cabin to read it, but almost as soon as he lay down on the narrow bunk he realized he was too knocked up even for *The Innocence of Father Brown*. Apparently he was less recovered than he had imagined. An automobile accident indeed—he couldn't even make up a reasonably convincing lie. He tossed Father Brown across to the seat of his chair, closed his eyes, and tried not to dream.

The next morning, Steadman discovered that the fog had lifted. They were out of sight of land—even the sea birds had departed—and the water was a deep, opaque green, like jade. Steadman washed himself as well as he could in his cabin sink, suffered through the excruciatingly awkward business of trying to shave his battered and tender face, and put on the heavy tweed suit that Vidocq had picked up for him in Dublin. For the first time in weeks, the problems of getting through life seemed reduced to a manageable size.

He breakfasted alone, since once again the "other gentleman" didn't feel up to leaving his cabin. The sea was like glass; you could have played billiards in the lounge. But some people's constitutions, so it would seem, were marvelously delicate. Steadman wolfed down his oatmeal and tea, experiencing a certain smug satisfaction in the strength of his appetite.

By ten o'clock it had turned cold again, and he was tired of reading. The steward made him a brandy and soda. He drank it slowly, thinking how easy it would be to turn into a real barfly after a few more days of this. He would limit himself, he decided, to one cup of spiked coffee after dinner. There would be plenty of time later to go to seed.

Again for lunch the other side of the table was vacant. Steadman had just about made up his mind to be offended, but the steward's half-amused shrug of the shoulders managed to suggest that one had to expect such carryings on from a certain class of passenger.

"He's a foreign gentleman, you understand, sir," he said, putting the thing with all the delicacy at his command. "Which is to say, sir, a continental gentleman. We have him down in the purser's book as a Monsieur Boulloche"—he spelled the name—"but how much does that mean these days? The war's brought along a lot o' funny stuff with it, hasn't it, sir."

Steadman tried to manage a smile, but only to keep the chill he felt from showing in his face.

"Well, after all, we're both neutrals, aren't we?" He spread the huge white napkin over his knees as if he expected it to keep him from freezing to death. "It's not our problem, is it?"

"There's neutral and neutral, sir. Bein' Irish doesn't mean I have t' love 'em, now does it."

All during the remainder of the meal, Steadman had the distinct impression of being in disfavor. The steward returned to his pantry, not coming out again until it was time to clear away the dishes, and Steadman was left to drink his coffee in solitude.

When he was finished eating, he took a turn around the deck. He was like a guard on picket duty, looking for something to account for the anxiety he felt crawling around inside him like maggots in a dead cat. When he found nothing but empty deck chairs and the still, expectant sea, he went back to his cabin to lie down again. The book he had taken from the lounge lay neglected on the seat of his chair. He had lost interest in it, had forgotten its existence. He wasn't up to clever little mysteries with all the clues dealt out in the first two or three pages. He had problems enough of his own.

Finally, it was time for dinner. That was how things were aboard a ship—the meals were the only reality. Steadman washed his face, retied his tie, and slipped his arms into the sleeves of his jacket. When he returned to the lounge, he noticed that, for the first time, the table had two place settings. He sat down, plucking up his trouser legs and settling into his chair quite as if he expected to spend the rest of the voyage there.

Perhaps five minutes later, the other passenger arrived. He was tall and slender, and his dark brown hair was noticeably thinning. He glanced at Steadman and smiled.

And his name wasn't Boulloche. It was Weinschenk.

XXXIII

It was several seconds before David Steadman was conscious of a single lucid thought crossing his mind. He hardly even seemed able to move. It was only by the time Weinschenk had sat down across the table from him that he began to come back to himself.

"I wonder if it would be possible to arrange a drink before dinner," Weinschenk said finally, a weird smile playing on his lips. "Do you think it might be possible? Would you join me?"

"What the hell are you doing here, Weinschenk?"

But that was the moment the steward chose to make his appearance. In all his new dignity of manner, with a white napkin over his left arm, he approached the table in great state.

"We have lamb chops this evenin', gentlemen," he said. "And a choice of either salad or a mixed vegetable dish."

"I believe Monsieur Boulloche would like a drink first."

Steadman's voice was surprisingly calm—no one was more surprised than himself. He was looking at Weinschenk but without seeing him. All he could see was a damp gray wall in the interrogation room in Strasbourg.

Weinschenk must have said something, because the steward nodded and turned to Steadman.

"Anythin' for y'rself, sir?"

"No, nothing—thank you."

And then suddenly the two of them were alone again.

"What are you doing here, Weinschenk? How did you find me? Answer quick, or by God I'll . . ."

But Weinschenk waved his hand casually, dismissing the very possibility of anything like violence. The expression on his face suggested that even to imagine such a thing was in rather questionable taste.

"Come now—don't pretend to be dense," he said, picking up his napkin. "It was obvious, wasn't it? How else were you going to get out of England? All I had to do was to watch the shipping news and bribe a couple of ticket clerks. I've been waiting in Dublin for some word ever since Strasbourg. If you could get away from me, how much difficulty would you have with the British?"

"How did you know the British had me?"

"Who else?" Weinschenk's eyebrows rose and fell in a kind of attenuated shrug. "How many other players are there? Who else would go to the trouble. I suppose you know that this time you finally succeeded in killing poor Max."

"Good. I'm only sorry there wasn't time for you as well."

They stared across the table at each other as the steward set Weinschenk's drink down in the center of his plate. If he noticed anything he didn't show it—but, then, what business could it be of his if the two gentlemen hadn't hit it off?

It was only after he left that the amused curl returned to the corner of Weinschenk's mouth. He seemed to savor the situation for a moment, and then he took a long, slow pull on his whiskey and water.

"It seems forever since I've tasted one of these," he said, putting it down. "You shouldn't take these things so personally, Steadman. And you shouldn't be so unkind about a poor dumb brute like Max. I was rather attached to him, you know."

"You're really enjoying this, aren't you, you son of a bitch."

"Yes, actually. I am."

He took another sip of his drink, seemed ready to set the glass down again, but then thought better of it and polished off the whole in two or three swallows. By the time he was finished his eyes had taken on a wholly unnatural glitter.

"What do you want with me?"

"Oh, don't be so obtuse, Steadman." Weinschenk leaned a little forward in his chair, as if he wanted to take a better look. "What do you *think* I want with you? I've come to kill you, of course. As a matter of fact, I really don't have any choice in the matter."

He smiled and glanced up, just as the steward came back from the kitchen balancing a large metal tray between his two hands—the service was much more elaborate tonight; perhaps he felt that two diners constituted more of an occasion.

The whole interval of waiting for the lamb chops to be dished up and the vegetables to be arranged in an orderly little pile over one side of the plate, all of that was an agony for Steadman. He thought it would never end. Getting through it was like holding his breath. Weinschenk, on the other hand, seemed quite at his ease.

"You've made rather a mess for me," he said, after they were alone again. He cut a tiny piece from one of his two lamb chops and tasted it as if he were going to have to give his opinion under oath. "The SS doesn't like to be made to look foolish, and you've been doing that pretty regularly of late. So I'm afraid it's either your death or mine. They are quite explicit about that sort of thing."

Steadman's left hand dropped unobtrusively down into his lap, and within a second he was holding the knife he had been carrying taped to his calf. There hadn't been a sound or a sign, but Weinschenk of course knew all about the knife. He smiled, as if at the fears of a child.

"You won't need it now," he said, picking up with his fingertips his own rather flimsy little dinner knife and letting it drop back to the table again. "I don't plan to kill you now—I'm not even armed. It can wait for a few days, until we're well out to sea and our captain won't feel under any temptation to turn back. You didn't really think I'd do anything so obvious and self-defeating as that, did you?"

The smile had turned almost pitying. Steadman felt a strong temptation to see what Weinschenk would look like with his throat cut, but he satisfied himself with something less.

"We're on a neutral vessel," he said quietly, slipping the knife back into its scabbard. "The rules are different here—if you shoot me in the back of the head while I'm taking a nap, they'll call it murder. We're not in the Reich now, Weinschenk. And, besides, aren't you just a little worried that I might decide to take care of you first? You haven't got Max to watch your back anymore, you know."

"True. But even here I enjoy certain advantages."

Weinschenk cut another piece from his lamb chop, making a big production number out of the whole business. He could barely stand it, he was having such a marvelous time.

"You're a man with a mission," he went on, as if the thought had just occurred to him. "You've got the letter to deliver, and you can't do that if you're locked up in some prison awaiting trial for murder—who would believe you then? On the other hand, I don't give a damn about the letter, not anymore. All I want is the satisfaction of watching you die. That's one advantage."

"And I take it there's another?"

Weinschenk nodded.

"I'm traveling under a diplomatic passport, my friend." He was so pleased with himself that he abandoned even the pretext of continuing his meal. He was practically hopping up and down. "It was a last favor from our Lisbon office before they found out I was in disgrace—they've got drawers full of them. I can't be arrested. I can't even be detained. Unless someone actually sees me pulling the trigger, there isn't a thing anyone can do to stop me. I shouldn't be surprised if they would have to let me go even then. It's even a Vichy passport, so I won't be embarrassing the Foreign Office. So you see, I've got you."

There was more. Weinschenk had it all planned out. It even made some sense, if you happened to be half out of your mind. It might even work. The point, however, was that Weinschenk believed that it would work, and he was desperate enough, and crazy enough, to carry it through. Steadman gathered that certain parties back in Berlin weren't handing out many other options.

"In mid-Atlantic, there will be a submarine," he said—this seemed to be the part he liked best. "I'm a fugitive as well now; the Gestapo would have me shot almost as quickly as they would you, but it was a simple enough matter to arrange. I telephoned our Dublin embassy and explained everything to the head of security—who, needless to say, is one of our people. I gave him a message for Himmler. Himmler will understand. At a prearranged time, on a day and hour known only to myself, the submarine will come up right beside the *Armagh*'s port bow. Himmler will have sent them a coded radio message, and our route is public knowledge."

He paused for a moment and lit a cigarette, his fourth since the end of dinner. With the cigarette wedged between his fingers, he made an expansively casual gesture with his right hand.

"All I'll have to do is to jump off," he continued. "They'll pick me up. No one will think to stop me—no one will dare, not with a German submarine staring them in the face. Besides, this is an Irish ship, and the Irish are very scrupulous about their neutrality."

Steadman had his doubts about the submarine. The submarine struck him as going a bit far, even for the cowboys in the SS. What Weinschenk might have waiting for him—not out in the drink, but after the ship docked in New York—would be a message from a discreet source telling him that the Fatherland would appreciate it if he would save everybody a lot of trouble and hang himself in his prison cell. Either that, or a bullet in the face as he walked down the pier. No, Steadman didn't have a lot of faith in Weinschenk's submarine.

But Weinschenk did. He was playing long shots because they were all he had left. For him, the submarine was an article of faith.

"I really am going to kill you," he said, smiling that strange smile that told you as plain as words that he was pushed too far in his mind. "In a few days, when it suits my convenience, I'll walk in on you somewhere . . . The locks on this ship don't look very strong. What will stop me?"

"I might, since you've been kind enough to give me all this advance warning. Just why, by the way, are you being such a sport about it?"

They were walking around the deck together, just as if they had been friends all their lives.

Neither of them had brought a coat, and Weinschenk was trembling visibly. The fog was thick and clammy, so it might have been that, but Steadman didn't think so. Weinschenk, it seemed to him, was probably trembling with sheer mad excitement.

"Why shouldn't I? Wouldn't you have figured it out for yourself the moment you saw me? For how long could I have kept my presence here a secret from you?"

The glitter had never left his eyes. He was drunk, but not with anything that came in a bottle.

"And why shouldn't you suffer?" he went on, taking a deep breath and letting it out of his lungs slowly. "Why shouldn't you feel the noose around your neck? You've made me suffer, for years and years. I have this pleasure coming to me."

"I should have thought you'd have gotten all that out of your system in Strasbourg."

"No—in the end you even won that game from me."

Back in his cabin, with the door locked and barricaded, Steadman lay on his bunk, thinking the whole matter out. There was a lunatic loose who wanted to murder him, but, after all, they were out of the war zone now. The rules of civilized life applied, so there ought to be something he could do. He didn't have to just sit around and wait to be turned into fish food. Europe, it appeared, had forgotten all about the law—it was a universal amnesia; it had even spread to England—but they weren't in Europe anymore, not really. They were in transit from Ireland to the United States, and the law was something the captain only had to look up in the Maritime Regulations.

Through the bulkhead, he could hear Weinschenk moving around in his compartment. All the animals were restless this evening.

Steadman unlatched his door and stepped noiselessly out onto the deck. Even though the curtain was drawn, he could see light coming from Weinschenk's porthole window. He waited until it had snapped out, and then he started toward the staircase to the bridge.

"No, sir. The cap'n ain't on duty. He's an early riser, so he'll be bunked up by now."

The first mate, who sported iron-gray sideburns and was bundled up in a greatcoat and a huge muffler of the same dull blue, seemed to take as his first concern getting Steadman back below decks where he belonged. He was perfectly scandalized to have a civilian up on the bridge with him, as if it might be bad luck or something.

"If it's some complaint, sir, why do 'e not address y'rself to Mr. Boyne— that's the steward, sir."

"I'm not sure the steward would be of much help, and I really don't think it'll wait." Steadman smiled, perhaps not terribly convincingly, and then, drawing the first officer a little aside, began trying to explain to him about Weinschenk. The story wasn't much of a success.

"You say the gentleman is German, sir?"

"Yes. His name is Weinschenk, and he's a captain in the SS."

"Well, sir, I've seen 'is passport, and the gentleman's name is Boul-loche." The first mate pulled absent-mindedly at the tip of his sideburn, smiling at the odd French sound, which he pronounced *Bu*-lock. "I'm sure he doesn't mean you any harm, sir—it's prob'ly all just a misun-derstandin'."

"And you wouldn't be able to do much if he did, would you."

"No, sir, I wouldn't. Y' have me there—I wouldn't."

No, he wouldn't. The first mate had seen the passport and, like everyone else, he knew that a diplomat in transit cannot be interfered with. Not even if he commits murder.

Steadman started back down the staircase to the main deck, feeling like a proper chump. The story would be all over the ship tomorrow; every man aboard would have him down as a mental case.

"They weren't very receptive, were they."

Below him in the shadows, with his left hand balanced against the handrail, stood Weinschenk. His right hand was down at his side, almost lost in darkness, but it seemed to be holding something. Steadman could feel his entrails turning into ice water.

"Of course, they didn't believe you, but I suppose you felt obliged to try." Weinschenk took a half step back, so that the light from the bridge caught him a little better, and his hand came up to his mouth—he had had a cigarette cupped between his fingers. "I think you had better just accept that this must remain a matter between only the two of us."

Steadman decided to try breathing again and let out a long, ragged gasp—he didn't even care if Weinschenk knew he was afraid; he wasn't afflicted with that kind of vanity. Okay, he wasn't going to get it right here and now. There would be a little reprieve. Goody.

"But, as I told you, it won't be today, or even tomorrow." The smoke curled around Weinschenk's face and then disappeared into the darkness. "Perhaps not even the next day. Perhaps, when it actually does happen, you'll be almost glad. Perhaps it'll be a relief to have it over."

"You're going to regret this, Weinschenk. You're going to regret you ever put yourself back within my reach."

Weinschenk actually looked amused.

"Will I? You honestly think so?" He pressed the cigarette between thumb and middle finger and flicked it out over the rail—the tiny point of red light made an arch into the darkness and disappeared. "I suppose that's something we'll both find out, won't we, Steadman. Good night. See you at breakfast."

Steadman waited in the shadow of the stairway until long after the sound of Weinschenk's footsteps had faded into nothing. He looked toward the eastern horizon, wondering how long it would be before morning.

XXXIV

I'm not even armed.

And Weinschenk wasn't. If you know how to look, you can always pick out the telltale bulge of a pistol under somebody's jacket, and when Weinschenk came in to breakfast the next morning he was as clean as a whistle.

But he would have something. He would hardly be prepared to try killing an experienced man with his bare hands—and knives were Steadman's weapon of choice, not his. So it would be the obvious thing, a pistol. And if it wasn't on him, it would be back in his cabin. There wasn't a third choice.

Probably there would be more than one. There would be the one Steadman was meant to find—Weinschenk would take it for granted that sometime or other his room would be searched—and then there would be the other one. Weinschenk meant business, so he would have some backup.

But the one on public display was what interested Steadman just at the moment. He had to start building a case for himself.

After the breakfast dishes were cleared away, and Weinschenk had gone out for a stroll around the deck—everyone should have a good look at the harmless French diplomat; it would reassure them that the gentleman in Cabin B was an obvious paranoid—Steadman went in to confront the steward in his pantry. The poor little man looked up from his plate of scrambled eggs as if he expected to be attacked.

"Then you've heard the story about last night," Steadman announced, like a man accepting defeat. "You know all about my little chat with the mate?"

"Well now, sir, I . . ."

That he fell silent was simply a mark of his decent confusion. He didn't want to take sides—why should he? He glanced down at the table he had set for himself with all the longing of thwarted passion.

"I suppose you're entitled to think I'm a screwball." Steadman closed the pantry door behind him and crossed his arms harmlessly over his chest. He wasn't going to be any trouble to anybody. "I'm just wondering if you'd like to make yourself a nice, risk-free five pounds."

The note was held between the first and second fingers of his right hand, which he brought out from behind the other arm so that it was in plain view. It was British money—that was the only kind of currency Vidocq had been able to get for him in a hurry—but five pounds was still five pounds. Mr. Boyne didn't look as if he would turn up his nose at it.

"I never said I thought you wasn't all there, sir. I want you to bear that in mind." The steward, who was obviously a shrewd judge of character, grinned knowingly. "Now, what little service can I render to you, sir?"

"Mr. Boyne . . ."

"Call me Eamon."

"Eamon, when do you make up the cabins for the night?"

A worried glint came into the steward's smeary blue eyes. He didn't like this, it said. This might be getting in over five pounds' worth.

"Around three in the afternoon, sir—just before I start in on the dinner. Why would you be wantin' to know, sir?"

"And I'll bet that when you go into Monsieur Boulloche's quarters his suitcase is standing open on the luggage rack—am I right?"

"Right you are, sir. Where else would it be?"

"Do you suppose that this afternoon you could just let the door swing closed behind you and take a quick look if the gentleman has any bulky metal objects in his luggage?" Steadman held the five pounds almost at arm's length, as if he wanted the steward to admire its design. "You wouldn't have to remove it, or even touch it. I'd just like you to confirm for me that it's there."

Eamon Boyne hesitated, just for an instant, and then his hand closed around the note. You could hear it crackle inside his fist.

"I think I could manage that, sir. Any idea where the monsieur would be at that time?"

"Probably in the lounge with me." Steadman's mouth widened in a not-terribly-convincing rendition of a smile. "We find we have a lot to talk about. We've known each other for years."

At a quarter to three, Steadman was sitting in the lounge, reading an Agatha Christie novel—he had given up on Father Brown; he found he didn't want to be edified about sin and redemption. At ten to three the door from the main deck opened and Weinschenk stepped inside. The Hauptmann took a pack of playing cards from a drawer under the library shelves and held them up.

"Care for a game?" he asked. The two of them were alone in the room. Steadman shrugged his shoulders and laid his novel down on a small square coffee table beside him.

"Why not?" He moved the table out in front of him and waited for Weinschenk to draw up another chair. "I like having you straight across from me, where, if it comes to that, I can lunge out and spill your guts on the floor with my dying gasp."

"You could kill me now—right this minute. Why not? I couldn't defend myself, could I."

"No, you couldn't. It's something to think about."

For a long time after that they played in silence. The only game they both knew was gin rummy, and Weinschenk, possibly because it kept his hands occupied and visible when he wasn't dealing, kept score on the back of a menu. They were playing Hollywood, to two hundred and fifty points a game—they would be at it for at least an hour. After forty minutes, Steadman won the first game, but only by a single hand. It was still wide open.

"Have you had your little talk with the captain yet?" Weinschenk asked finally, picking up Steadman's discard and putting down a four of diamonds. Steadman picked up the four, laid down a three of spades, and spread out his hand on the table.

"Knock with two. No—I've decided it would be a waste of time. If the mate didn't believe me the captain won't either. Besides, there isn't anything they can do about it anyway. Can you make that?"

No, Weinschenk couldn't. He was caught with a pair of queens. It seemed to annoy him vastly as he entered the eighteen points in each of Steadman's two remaining columns.

"So. What are you going to do?" He kept his hands flat on the table as Steadman shuffled the deck. It was developing into a tense game.

"Well—it's a safe bet that just one of us is going to leave this ship alive. Can you guess the name of my candidate?"

Neither looked at the other as Steadman dealt out the cards. Weinschenk had the nervous habit of picking up each card as it came to him, arranging them in his hand as he went along.

"Have you recovered from Strasbourg?" he asked finally, there was just that uncertainty in his voice to cue you that the answer would mean something to him. Steadman swept up his cards all at once.

"I'm fresh as a daisy."

"And what about the British? Did they give you a bad time?"

"No." Steadman shook his head as he moved the cards around in his hand. "They had less than twenty-four hours and they were relying on drugs. I could sleep that off."

"You never cease to astonish me, my friend."

Weinschenk picked up the down card and replaced it with a five of hearts. For several plays they sat quietly, as if all they had to think about was the game.

It occurred to Steadman that the captain, should he happen to walk into the ship's lounge at just that moment, would receive a very odd impression. He had two passengers, one of whom had tried to have him awakened in the middle of the night with some story about the other one wanting to murder him, and here they were the following afternoon, playing rummy together like an old married couple. It also occurred to him to wonder what Weinschenk thought he was about being so decidedly chummy. Was it for the crew's benefit, or was this some sort of psychological gambit to maintain maximum pressure? Or did he just like to play cards?

"Have you searched my cabin yet?" Weinschenk asked suddenly. The question was so unexpected that Steadman nearly fumbled a card.

"No."

"Are you having the steward search for you?"

"I haven't got any allies aboard this ship," Steadman replied, not quite lying. He needed one more card to gin. He wished he'd get it, if for no other reason than to deflect Weinschenk's attention.

"Well, it doesn't matter." Weinschenk looked up over the tops of his cards and smiled pleasantly. "I didn't pack a spare uniform or something like that. You wouldn't find anything you could parade before the captain to prove that I'm not what I seem."

"Then why would I want to search your cabin?"

Steadman didn't get his gin card. In fact he lost that hand, and the next. By the time the steward passed through and stopped to ask if either of them would care for a drink, they were even at one game apiece. This would be the final hand.

Weinschenk ordered a whiskey and water, but Steadman decided to pass.

"Do you suppose he found anything?" Weinschenk asked as he twisted around in his chair to watch the steward retreat back into his pantry. The idea seemed to amuse him.

"I thought you said there wasn't anything to find."

"There isn't."

Steadman discarded an eight—he knew Weinschenk was collecting eights. When Weinschenk picked it up and laid down a four of clubs, Steadman spread his hand out on the table.

"Gin," he said, without any particular triumph. He took the four and fitted it into a club run. "My game, I think."

Weinschenk threw down his cards and proceeded to add up his losses. He didn't care. He knew which game they were playing, and it wasn't gin rummy.

"You win by four hundred points. Perhaps next time you won't be so lucky." He took a long swallow on his drink and then set it down on the table half finished as he rose stiffly out of his chair. They had been there a long time. "I'll go back to my cabin now and inspect the damage. I'm sure you and the steward have a lot to discuss."

Even as the door closed behind him, you could hear the laughter. He seemed to think it was all an exquisite joke.

When Steadman went into the pantry, he found Eamon Boyne sitting at his little table, his head resting between his hands and the hairs of his wiry red beard sticking out between his fingers. He didn't look particularly happy, and the expression on his face when he glanced up at Steadman was almost resentful.

"You neither one of you are exactly church deacons, are 'e, sir," he said. It wasn't a question. It was a reasoned conclusion.

"What did you find?"

He didn't look as if he wanted to say. His hands slid down from his face and locked together on top of the table. He appeared as if he were about to begin praying.

"You wouldn't think it to look at me, but I was in the Troubles. You know about the Troubles, sir?"

"I've heard the stories."

"Well, I was just a boy—I'd run errands and the like. But even a boy learns a thing or two runnin' around with them muggs." The hands came apart for a moment and then closed again like the jaws of a trap. "Your friend has a pistol in his suitcase. I recognized the type—lots of lads had 'em, sort of like souvenirs from the last war."

"A Luger."

"Yes, sir." Boyne nodded, looking not at Steadman but at the wall straight in front of him. "And that's not the end of it—I pried the clip out, just to have a look. He's drilled the points. In the old days, when the order came down for a killin', that's what the lads 'd do so the bullets would flatten out on contact and punch a hole through a man big enough to put y'r fist through. It wasn't pretty."

"No, it isn't. I've seen a few get it like that."

And then the little Irishman smiled. It would be all right now. He knew where he was.

"I had you spotted right off the mark, didn't I, sir." It seemed to please him when Steadman nodded in agreement—yes, he had. "The other gentleman, now, whose side would he be on?"

"Where he comes from, that pistol is standard issue."

"I figured that. And he plans to put y'r lights out, doesn't he. I don't think the cap'n 'd like that. Shall I tell 'm?"

Steadman only shook his head. "No. There's nothing he could do about it—it isn't against the rules for diplomatic personnel to carry a pistol. And my friend wouldn't take kindly to being interfered with. What I need from you is just a little help, and then I think it would be best all round if you stayed out of it."

After dinner, Steadman decided to take a turn around the deck. It would be the last fresh air he would be getting for a while, maybe ever, and he wanted to make the most of it. He also wanted a chance to collect himself, to get away from Weinschenk and decide if he wasn't making a vast mistake.

It won't be today, or even tomorrow, Weinschenk had said. Which meant, if one kept to the strictest interpretation, that the dispensation was up at midnight. After that, there were no more time-outs.

From where he was standing, Steadman could hear the hiss of the prow cutting through the dark water. If there was a moon, it was lost in fog. The only light came from the ship itself, and there was precious little of that. It was a cold, dank night, and Steadman found it a perfect match for the condition of his mind.

He hated pauses. It was all right when you were out of the wars, when you thought you were safe and would never have to go back. And you didn't mind it when people were actually trying to kill you because then there wasn't any time to think. But the hours in the trenches, waiting for the order to go out on patrol—those were the worst. The real horror in this life wasn't pain or death, it was fear. You only suffered when you had time to think.

Within the next several hours, Steadman knew, either he or Weinschenk was going to die, and Weinschenk was the one with both the initiative and the gun. It didn't look good.

He thought about going down to his cabin and writing a long letter to Karen, trying to explain himself. But if it were intercepted, which it probably would be, the end result could only be to get her into trouble, and he didn't have any idea how he could get down in words everything he wanted to say to her. Probably she wouldn't understand. People almost never did understand when you tried, really tried, to set out exactly how you felt.

So he wouldn't write anything. There would only be Hitler's letter—that would have to be explanation enough. It was still in his wallet, but his wallet was hidden inside a two-pound coffee can on a shelf in Eamon Boyne's pantry. It would stay there until New York, at which time, provided he lived, Steadman could retrieve it and go about his business. If Weinschenk was the survivor, then Boyne would place a telephone call to a certain number in Pittsburgh, Pennsylvania, and everything would be up to big brother Carl. What Carl Steadman could or would do with that interesting bequest was a matter for speculation. David the Black Sheep had no theories.

God, he felt awful. He had eaten too much at dinner, and there was nothing so bad as having indigestion and the funks, both at the same time.

Anyway, there was nothing to be gained by standing around waiting for people to kill you. If Weinschenk wanted a duel, that was fine. He could name the time if he wanted to, but he wasn't going to name the place as well.

Steadman felt around in his pocket for the key Boyne had given him, and when he had it between his fingers he started down the stairway to the lower decks.

"Be careful down there, sir," Boyne had said. "It's dark as the Pit, and there's not much room for a man to move around. I'll leave you a jug of water and some sandwiches inside the door."

The cargo hold was full of gigantic wooden crates, with just a few feet between them for the longshoremen to get in with their ropes. That much Steadman could see before he allowed the door to swing shut behind him and the darkness covered everything.

In the morning, Weinschenk would find a note under his door—it was all arranged with Boyne. If the Hauptmann wanted to kill Mr. Steadman, then he was going to have to come down here, into this black maze, to find him.

XXXV

It was a cold place. He was probably twenty feet below the waterline. There was nothing between him and the gray, winter-laden North Atlantic except these iron walls, trickling with damp. It was possible, since everything awaited the Hauptmann's convenience, that he would be down here for days.

Steadman felt around beside the door until he found the provisions that Boyne had left for him—at least he wouldn't starve. After about ten minutes his eyes had adjusted to the darkness and he was able to use the traces of light that found their way in here and there through the ceiling to feel a passage for himself among the cargo crates. Before morning he had to know every foot of this place. Every hole, every dead end, every avenue of escape. The mouse evades the cat because he knows the territory. At least, sometimes he evades the cat.

By tomorrow morning, the whole scheme would be in motion. Weinschenk would find an envelope lying on his stateroom carpet, telling him just exactly where to come if he still wanted his chance, and sometime in the course of the day, when it was discovered that one of the passengers had disappeared, the steward would go have a little chat with the captain.

Boyne had undertaken to secure the crew's neutrality. He would give the captain to understand that there were wiser things in this world than sending a couple of sailors down into the ship's hold after an armed man—if they docked in New York without incident, then everything would take care of itself. The wisest course had to be simply to stay out of this brawl.

Nobody was going to be screwball enough to interfere with Weinschenk. He was the man with the interesting gun and, after breakfast tomorrow, he would be carrying it.

Would Weinschenk come? Was it possible he could chicken out? It was comforting to think that he might have second thoughts about venturing down into a dark hole where a man with a knife was waiting just for him, but the odds were still heavily on his side and he too was wagering with his life. He had made that clear—there wasn't going to be a hero's welcome for him at home if he came back without David Steadman's scalp dangling from his belt. Weinschenk would come. He was evil, and very possibly crazy, but he wasn't the sort of coward who freezes up with panic.

As Steadman started moving around, he was astonished at how muffled the sounds of his footsteps were against the metal floor. The wooden crates probably acted as baffles. That was both good and bad.

The crates were stacked with considerable ingenuity, making tiers here and there so that you could scramble all the way up to the hatch opening—after all, people had to be able to move around in here or they would never get all this junk out. It was like the labyrinth inside a Pharaoh's tomb, except without the booby traps. And that could be remedied easily enough.

After about three hours of cautious exploration, Steadman felt as if he had mastered the basic design. He found himself a secure position about three quarters of the way up one of the tiers, blocked it off by moving a couple of crates around—they were lighter than he had imagined—and lay down to see if he could manage a few hours of sleep.

He was roused in the morning by the unpleasant expedient of a rat crawling over his chest. It went screeching away into the darkness the instant he moved, but the experience left him hopelessly awake. He reached down for the water bottle and the bag of sandwiches, which fortunately had remained tightly sealed, and had breakfast. By the time he had finished and had cracked open the crystal of his wristwatch so he could read the positions of the hands by touch, it was about a quarter past seven. In a very short time the fun should start.

Boyne, of course, had promised to put off telling the captain anything until the last possible moment. Even aboard a ship it is possible to miss a couple of meals without being listed as over the side, so it might reach into the middle of the afternoon before anyone had to think about taking any kind of official position concerning the fact that Mr. Lawrence—that was the name on his forged passport—was hiding down in the cargo hold with a knife. Weinschenk would have that long to make his play without having to worry that there would be a guard posted to keep everyone out of harm's reach. Submarine or no submarine, he would have to begin the revels by evening. Steadman had just exactly that long to get ready for him.

A pistol has a long reach—and with hollow-point bullets it doesn't have to command pinpoint accuracy to be lethal; you can hit someone in the hand and practically cut it off, which was the reason people went to the trouble. With a knife, however, there was no farting around. Steadman wasn't fool enough to try any fancy throws, not in the dark for Christ's sake. Even if you hit the bull's-eye—and most of the time the goddamned thing just bounced off—but even if you scored, one little puncture wound wasn't likely to kill anyone fast enough to keep him from killing you right back. The thing to do with a knife was to rip and tear, and for that you had to be right on top of the guy.

Weinschenk's advantage was his weapon, and Steadman's was his choice of the terrain. It was up to him to make the most of it.

By about eight-twenty, he was sweating and exhausted, but he was ready. Now the ship's hold, like Pharaoh's tomb, had its traps for the unwary. Steadman went back to his perch, where he had the best view, if that was the word, and sat down to await events.

The only sound was the low grinding of the ship's engine, and once in a great while the wind would pull tight the great canvas tarp over the loading hatch and it would snap like the noise of distant cannon fire. The darkness was nearly total. They must have been having a bit of weather up above, because sometimes he could feel a slight listing to port.

If there really was a submarine, and it decided, for whatever reason, to get belligerent, the torpedo would punch its way straight in here. There wouldn't be time to get out; the hold would fill up with water in less than a minute. He would drown in the darkness, which somehow made it even worse.

If there really was a submarine.

Weinschenk was whistling in the dark. They had told him a story and he had repeated it to himself so often that now he believed it. Weinschenk was probably a dead man no matter how things worked out down here in the hold. Not that that went very far toward solving Steadman's problems.

At a few minutes after ten o'clock, he thought he heard another rat scratching around on top of one of the crates. He was only half listening; he didn't like rats, but just at present the world held far worse terrors. And then he realized it wasn't a rat at all—down below, somebody was rattling away at the door.

Steadman was straining like crazy, trying to pick up every little sound. What the hell was going on down there? And then it occurred to him that the only person on board who didn't have easy access to a key was Egon Weinschenk. What he was hearing was somebody trying to force the lock.

Finally, after what seemed an unnaturally long time, the door sprang open and a rectangle of harsh, yellow light crept up the wall. He had been in the dark so long that Steadman found he wanted to turn his face away.

And then the rectangle collapsed and they were together in the sightless hold. Steadman was clinging like a lizard to the top of the largest pile of crates, far enough from the edge that he couldn't be seen. He had stopped breathing. He was ready to run in any direction.

"Steadman—you are here?"

Weinschenk had brought a flashlight; its thin beam played nervously over the walls and the edges of the crates. It was Weinschenk's first tactical blunder, because now Steadman would always know where to find him.

Steadman took the remaining sandwiches out of their paper bag, stuffed the bag in under his belt, and started crawling crablike toward the far end of the hold. When he reached it he crouched down and put his hand around the neck of the bag, squeezing it down into a ring with his thumb and first finger. It was a trick every schoolboy knows—when you have an opening no wider than the tip of your little finger, you put the bag to your lips and blow it up like a balloon.

"Steadman . . ."

The explosion was deafening—God knows what it must have sounded like to Weinschenk. He fired, and the bullet zinged off the iron bulkhead with an angry sound and then buried itself in one of the crates—Steadman heard the crack of splintering wood quite distinctly. He clambered back the way he had come, not caring how much noise he made; Weinschenk was obviously too edgy to be in a very discriminating frame of mind.

"You want me, Hauptmann? Then come and get me."

He laughed. He laughed and laughed, and the ugly sound echoed back and forth. He didn't feel the least little bit jolly.

"You made a bad mistake, Weinschenk. You have a lot to answer for, and I never was the forgiving sort."

The flashlight beam was still flicking here and there against the walls, like the tongue of some hungry insect, and then, abruptly, it went out. Weinschenk must finally have realized his mistake. That meant he was regaining his self-control.

"Steadman, it's almost time for me to go." He broke the last word into two syllables, singing them up and down. He knew with whom the odds lay. He wasn't fooled.

There was about eight feet of clearance between the top of the highest crate and the canvas dome that covered the cargo hatch. There was plenty of room for a man to stand up straight, but Steadman made his way along in a crouch, walking almost on all fours. He didn't want to be caught in Weinschenk's flashlight beam when he decided to turn it back on, and, besides, somehow he just felt less of a target.

It was possible to make one's way almost all the distance around three sides of the cargo. That was what Weinschenk was doing—he hadn't discovered the tiers yet. Steadman waited for him by one of the rear corners, trying to hear him as he crept along.

There was a box just there, not much bigger than a suitcase but heavy. It probably weighed close to two hundred pounds, and it was balanced to go over with the merest push. It would crush Weinschenk flat as a poker chip if he happened to be underneath when it went down. That was the idea.

Steadman crouched beside the edge, his hand against the side of the box. He tried not to breathe. If Weinschenk turned on his flashlight suddenly, and happened to get lucky about which way he pointed it, then he would have a clear shot. It was a gamble in both directions.

Weinschenk was coming around in the right direction—he could have been in his stocking feet and Steadman still would have heard him. It was like waiting with your fingers in a meat grinder.

Come on, sucker. Come on. Steadman willed him along. It seemed as if there were a rope stretched tight between them—all it would take was the merest pull . . .

Suddenly the flashlight went on. Weinschenk was directly below, almost as if he had felt every little tug, and in the blinding light Steadman could see that the pistol was pointed straight at him. He sprang away, pushing against the box to get himself out of the line of fire. It seemed that the hollow little bark of the pistol sounded almost in the same instant.

He rolled, listening to the box tumbling down. He didn't have any idea whether he had been hit or not. Then there was a sickening crash as the box smashed against the floor of the hold. As he turned his head, the first thing he noticed was the darkness—the flashlight was out.

Slowly, carefully, he crawled along, testing himself. If a bullet had caught him, he ought to be able to tell. Everything seemed to work. Weinschenk had missed. He must have been rattled.

Steadman crawled back into his hole and waited, listening. Weinschenk had missed, but had the box? Was he lying down there with his guts spread out like strawberry preserves, or was that gun still in his hand? It would be nice to know.

His heart was pounding—he could feel the throbbing in his hands. He tried counting. Thirty-five, forty . . . How long would that be? Less than half a minute, probably. All he could hear was the hum of the engines. Maybe Weinschenk was dead after all.

And then the flashlight went on again—okay, maybe he wasn't dead.

Steadman felt as if something inside him had begun to crumble. The light was feeling around the tops of the great stacks of crates as Weinschenk looked for more booby traps. So much for that idea.

But someone outside must have heard the crash, because all at once there was the sound of running steps down the iron gangway that reached to the door. The door flew open. A shot was fired—Steadman could see the flash as an orange glow reflected against the wall—and the door closed again with a shattering metallic crash.

Had Weinschenk hit anybody? Either way, they knew they had a maniac with a gun down here now—maybe they would have brains enough to stay the hell out of trouble.

But no. A few minutes later a strong triangular column of sunlight came straight down and buried itself in the stacks of packing cases, not fifteen feet from where Steadman was trying to hide himself. It was blinding. He felt as if it was burning the eyes right out of his head. They had lifted up a corner of the canvas over the hatch.

"Close that, dammit!" he shouted. "God dammit, do you want to get me killed?"

Weinschenk fired again—maybe he had seen something, or maybe he was only shooting at the sound of Steadman's voice. Steadman felt a spray of wooden splinters against the right side of his face, and almost the next second the canvas tarp fell back into place and the light vanished.

Steadman brushed his hand against the side of his face and discovered it was slippery with blood. He had to get out of there.

There was no choice now. He was running out of tricks, and every minute was another chance for Weinschenk to learn his way around. He was going to have to go down there and get him.

"Steadman—did I hit you?"

Steadman crawled back toward the edge. If Weinschenk wanted to broadcast his position, that was his business. He reached into his pocket and with the tip of his finger felt the edge of a coin; he didn't have the faintest idea what it was or where he had picked it up, but it was about the size of a half dollar. It would do. With a circular motion of his arm he pitched the coin into the darkness, ten or fifteen degrees away from where Weinschenk's voice had seemed to be coming from. It rang against the iron bulkhead like a dinner gong.

And Weinschenk bit. The flashlight went on for a moment, probed around a few seconds, and then snicked off.

Okay. We know where he is. Now the cheat is to get him moving in the right direction. Maybe he would spook. It didn't seem likely that he would fall for the coin trick many more times, though.

Which didn't mean that Steadman couldn't use it—there could be tricks within tricks, you know. The only problem was that he was running out of money.

He had two more coins: a milled coin about the size of a shilling and, with its flat-sided edge, what had to be a three-penny bit—as far as he knew, there wasn't another piece of change shaped like that in the world. They might be enough. What the hell, Weinschenk was a quick study.

He reached down under his trouser leg and pulled out the knife, taking the scabbard along for good measure and skittering it away across the tops of the crates and over the edge beyond—the more little noises Weinschenk had to think about the better. He held the knife blade between his teeth, the way the Indians had in all the movies he had watched as a kid, and began making his hand-to-hand way toward the closest of the tiers down to the cargo-hold floor.

The game was to induce Weinschenk to come to him. It would be nice to catch the Hauptmann running away, to frighten him into some dark corner where Steadman would be waiting to cut his throat, but Weinschenk hadn't come down here to run away. The best that could be hoped for was to let Weinschenk track him down and then bushwhack him along the way. Let him come, thinking all the time that Steadman was trying to con him into another direction. Let him get close enough that the advantage of having a pistol instead of a knife would melt down to almost none.

He worked his slow way down the tier of crates, staying close to the corners, where the wood should have least tendency to creak, and trying to distribute his weight as evenly as possible between his hands and feet. No matter how carefully he moved, he seemed to make an astonishing amount of noise. Weinschenk should have been able to hear him even with his head in a sack.

About halfway down, he took out the coin with the milled edge and threw it in a flat trajectory which he hoped would clear the boxes and strike against the bulkhead on the other side of the hold. It did—he could just make out the tinkling sound it made as it skimmed over the edge and dropped to the floor.

But Weinschenk didn't turn on his flashlight this time. Good. He had figured out that he was being conned.

When Steadman reached the last row of the tier, he was about five feet above the floor and hidden from sight. Weinschenk would have to be standing directly in front of him to know he was there. It was just as true, of course, that he would be trapped like a rat in a cage if Weinschenk did figure out where he was.

There was only the three-penny bit now. He pitched it almost straight up, so that it would land in the walkway almost right in front of him.

How long now had they been in here together? Steadman pressed his finger over the hands of his wristwatch. It was only ten-thirty.

How long had it taken Steadman to find the tiers? About half an hour, and he hadn't had a flashlight. But Weinschenk would be reluctant to come up—it was too easy to get ambushed that way. He had to assume that Steadman was still up there waiting for him, so he would prowl around the floor, waiting for a shot.

Steadman remained squatting at the rear of the lowest crate, where he would have something behind him from which to push off when the time came for his spring. He was cold, and his legs were getting tired. If it took much longer he might, instead of leaping out like a panther, simply fall flat on his face.

And then there was a smear of light against the bulkhead, disappearing almost at once. At long last, Weinschenk was coming back.

He had heard the coin. He was checking to make sure Steadman hadn't come down to that side of the floor, so now he would assume that he was still up on top, teasing him. He was waiting for some sign that Steadman had come back to the edge, where he could get a shot at him. He would be getting impatient.

Steadman, it's almost time for me to go, he had said. Now maybe the pressure was on him.

He could hear Weinschenk's footfalls now—he could hear his coat brushing against the wall, and the sound of his breathing. They were so close together now that it was almost painful. Steadman held the knife in his left hand, pointing straight ahead of him.

Weinschenk was coming from left to right, which meant that his right side would be to Steadman as he passed. Which meant that, rather than just tackling him against the wall, Steadman would have to go for the pistol. He would have to disarm Weinschenk—or at least pin his hand—because even a flesh wound with the kind of ammunition the Hauptmann was using was very likely to be fatal.

Steadman turned the knife in his hand so that the blade was flat, so it would have less chance of being deflected if it hit bone.

It was impossible to see—there was no light at all. It would all have to be done by feel.

Weinschenk was almost even with him now. There must have been some light from somewhere, because if he narrowed his eyes Steadman could just make out a kind of glimmer. It was probably the shiny metal casing of Weinschenk's flashlight.

Perhaps Weinschenk had heard something. The footfalls stopped for an instant, and then, at the worst possible time, the flashlight went on again. Weinschenk was standing right there in front of him.

The light was blinding. God, it was unbearable.

But somehow, by some miracle, Weinschenk hadn't seen him yet. He was merely there, apparently not sure what to do. That wouldn't last longer than an instant.

And then it happened. The expression on Weinschenk's face changed—or something changed; in that white glare it was impossible to tell with any certainty. But he knew now.

Steadman didn't wait. He just closed his eyes and sprang out, his right hand thrust forward, aimed at Weinschenk's arm.

The two men came together with a jolt, and the flashlight bounced away—Steadman knew that even with his eyes shut. Steadman closed his hand just below Weinschenk's elbow. He had him. The pistol went off—once, twice . . . Weinschenk tried to pull away, raising his arm, and Steadman struck out.

There was a sharp little scream, more of fear than of pain, and Steadman knew the knife had gone home. He let his right hand slide down Weinschenk's forearm, which had suddenly gone limp, and found that he was no longer holding the pistol. They both toppled to the floor.

Steadman forced himself to open his eyes. He could see the pistol now; it was lying down by Weinschenk's foot, a yard or so from the flashlight. The instant he glanced up at his face, he knew that Weinschenk was dying. He knew that even before he saw where the knife had entered, just at the base of the neck. Steadman could already feel the blood welling out over his fingers. He jerked the knife free and threw it away.

With a painful quickness, his eyes were adjusting to the light. He could see everything clearly now. He could see the way Weinschenk turned his face toward him. He thought perhaps he wanted to say something.

Steadman slipped his arm under Weinschenk's shoulders, cradling the back of his head and lifting him a few inches away from the floor. The man was going fast. In a few seconds he would have bled to death; now the struggle between them had ended.

Weinschenk turned his eyes up toward Steadman's face and smiled faintly. Then his lips moved, at first soundlessly as he gathered strength to speak.

"I shouldn't have waited, should I," he said in a hoarse whisper. Then he stopped for a moment and felt along his lower lip with the tip of his tongue. The operation, simple as it was, seemed to require all his attention and strength. "I should have known better. I should have let Max . . ."

The sentence died in a breath, and he was gone.

XXXVI

NOVEMBER 29, 1941

The waitress in the coffee shop where Steadman had breakfast his first morning in New York couldn't understand why he wouldn't settle for counter service.

"My legs are too long," he told her, smiling slyly. "I'm always banging my knees—you have more room at a table."

"No table service until after eight-thirty," she told him, just as if it were a law of nature. There was no shortage of tables and some of them were even set, but the waitress glared at him out of her heavy, puckered face, seemingly ready to fight him if he tried to drop his hat on one of the chairs.

"I'll take a table just the same. Make an exception."

He picked out a seat well in the back, with a clear view of the front window and the kitchen door only about twenty feet away if he needed an avenue of escape. It wasn't perfect, but it would do. At least he wasn't perched up there in profile like a target in a shooting gallery.

He was, of course, proceeding on the assumption that all the interested parties were aware he was in town. Doubtless they had people to watch the docks; he had to assume he had been spotted, although he wasn't aware of having picked up a tail. He would almost have felt better if he had—at least he would know how things stood. So far, it had all been just too god damned easy. It was difficult to fight down the comforting conclusion that everyone had simply lost interest and was letting him have a free ride home.

It was possible, of course. Maybe the SS had written Weinschenk off as an unprofitable lunatic and had decided to cut their losses all the way round.

Poor Weinschenk—there never had been any damn submarine.

Instead, there had been sailors armed with rifles waiting at the door to the hold. For some reason they had insisted on pointing them at Steadman when he stepped out across the threshold. It had seemed a silly thing to do, considering that he had given them plenty of warning that it was only him.

"Th' cap'n 'd like t' see you, sir," one of them had said—he was all of about twenty and doing his best to look very fierce.

"Sure—terrific. Any time."

Steadman had stood there, blinking like an owl in the strong light, hardly sure what was going on, when one of the men pushed past him into the hold with a lamp. He wasn't going to like what he found.

The captain was waiting up on the bridge. He was wearing a rain slicker, since the weather was still windy and wet—they had run into the tail end of a storm the night before, and it was still hanging on enough to make life in the open air thoroughly unpleasant—and his hands were clasped behind his back in a way that suggested he was standing very much on his authority. He was short and dark and solid-looking, not at all the type to take kindly to people settling private feuds in the hold of his ship.

"It's just possible, Mr. Lawrence, that we might owe you a bit of an apology."

He didn't smile, he didn't offer to take your hand, and the way he pronounced "Mr. Lawrence" somehow implied that he wasn't entirely convinced there was really any such person aboard. He was right about that, of course.

"It's also possible that I'll have to put you under arrest."

Steadman decided that this was not the moment to be conciliatory.

"Perhaps, if your first mate had taken me a little more seriously, all of this could have been avoided." He shrugged his shoulders and glanced around contemptuously at the young sailor with the rifle. "The man came aboard this ship to kill me. I informed you of that; I had a right to protection. As it turned out, I had to protect myself."

The captain nodded gravely and made a sign, a jerky movement with the first two fingers of his left hand, which sent Steadman's escort back down the companionway to the main deck.

"And would you have any idea, sir, as to the gentleman's real identity? I suppose he wasn't really a French diplomatic courier."

"I told your mate all that. His name was Weinschenk, Egon Weinschenk. He was a captain in the SS. He's about as French as Saint Patrick."

The captain smiled faintly, although Steadman hadn't really meant to be funny. He seemed to be considering all the different ways he could handle this rather delicate situation. He didn't look very happy.

The second sailor, the one who had gone prospecting in the hold, staggered to a halt just inside the threshold and saluted awkwardly.

"We brought the other man up to his cabin, sir," he said in a rapid, breathless voice. "He was stabbed in the neck, sir. It's a terrible mess down there in the hold, sir—blood all over."

For a few seconds, an interval that seemed to go on forever, no one said anything. The muscles under the captain's face gave the appearance of being ready to pull it in all kinds of different directions. And then, finally, he looked at Steadman, and his expression was one of impenetrable gravity.

"I take it, then, that we can assume that the gentleman committed suicide."

Five days later, they landed in New York.

He never did find out what happened to Weinschenk's body. Certainly there weren't any inquiries about it at dockside. Nobody questioned Steadman's papers at Passport Control, and half an hour later he had checked into the Waldorf under his own name. As soon as he could get rid of the bellboy, he dropped his room key into his pocket and went down to the lobby to find a public telephone. He made a collect call to an unlisted number in Pittsburgh, Pennsylvania.

It was only eight o'clock in the morning, so even Carl Steadman wouldn't be at the office quite yet.

"David? Where the hell are you?"

"I'm at the Waldorf in New York—can you be here by tomorrow morning? It's important, Carl."

"It's always important with you." His brother's voice was beginning to return to normal. If Little Davey was alive and at the Waldorf, it was safe to disapprove of him again. "But yes, I can probably be there tonight."

"Even better—then come tonight. And bring a couple of your bodyguards with you. And I'll need an appointment, a private appointment, with President Roosevelt for sometime tomorrow. Can you swing that?"

"Are you out of your mind, David?"

The waitress brought him his breakfast, practically dropping the plate into his lap, but who should care? There were fresh eggs and bacon and hash brown potatoes—Steadman hadn't had any hash browns in four years. America. He was home.

Then why didn't he feel safe? Nobody had come near him—were they waiting for something? Perhaps they were holding off until they were sure he had the letter back in his possession. Perhaps they weren't there at all.

Where in hell were the bad guys? Steadman shoveled the food into his mouth, hardly tasting it, maggoty with fear. He wasn't home yet, he kept telling himself. Not yet.

There was a wall calendar hanging behind the cashier's desk—today was Saturday, and the first week in December was only three days away.

They sat opposite each other in the railway compartment of which they were the only occupants—the compartments front and back were taken up by Carl Steadman's hired "detectives," so the two brothers had no worries about security. Even the blinds were drawn.

Carl Steadman was about forty and had not led a very active life. He looked rather prim in a three-piece charcoal business suit, and the mirrorlike shine of his black shoes gave them the appearance of never having made contact with a surface harder than the pile carpet in the board room of Steadman Tool and Die. His dark hair, which had only recently begun graying around the sideburns, was brushed back from his rather plump face. He was in every way a contrast to the son of his father's second wife and, in spite of the easiness that subsisted between the two men, which seemed the product not merely of affection but of near perfect communication, so it had been with them since childhood.

At the moment Carl was frowning at the German text of the letter he had just read in his brother's translation. The two sheets of paper were in his right hand, one behind the other, and he was holding them up to the light as if the truth of the matter might reveal itself to him that way.

"You mean to say this thing is genuine?" he asked, quite superfluously. "Where did you get it?"

"It's quite genuine. I stole it out of a diplomatic pouch in the German embassy in Stockholm four weeks ago."

"You *stole* it . . . ?"

Carl Steadman stared at his brother in genuine astonishment. Such things just didn't happen in his world—and certainly not to his own flesh and blood.

"Yes, I stole it. I've killed seven men with my own hands to get it this far—I don't even like to think how many other lives it's cost, but they probably run to at least that many again. As you might have guessed, nobody is taking this matter lightly."

"As I might have guessed . . ." Carl Steadman refolded the two sheets of paper and handed them back to David, evidently glad to be rid of them. "Well, obviously they have to be turned over to the proper authorities—I can see that plainly enough. But I'm damned if I can understand why everyone has been after you all this time. You really look a sight, David. You really do."

David Steadman nodded morosely. He no longer had to wear pieces of tape over his fingernails, and the bruises on his face had faded to yellowish smears; he looked as if he were recovering from jaundice. Still, anyone with eyes would have marked him down as a casualty. He had been through it, and it showed.

He merely shrugged his shoulders at his brother's remark, however. The British wanted to kill him because a Japanese attack on Hawaii would push America into the war, and the Germans wanted to kill him because they were squabbling among themselves over whether that would make any difference. It was all crazy, and Carl was perfectly sane and wouldn't understand a word.

"Did you get the appointment?" he asked, his eyes narrowing.

"No—not exactly." Carl Steadman shook his head. He wasn't apologizing so much as explaining the Facts of Life. "I contributed a hundred thousand dollars to Willkie's campaign fund, so you can imagine how popular I am with the current administration. That's how things are run, David. Besides, Roosevelt isn't even in Washington. He's down in Georgia, taking the waters. But I managed to threaten your way onto Harrison Walter's calendar for eight this evening—they can't just ignore me completely. He's a special assistant, if that's what they call them these days, and he's supposed to have Roosevelt's ear in foreign policy matters. His brother wants to run for congress from Harrisburg next year, if you take my meaning. I think he'll do for us."

The elder brother's face was as bland as milk, as if he saw nothing extraordinary about the fact that this little matter was going to cost him a good deal of money and, what was more important, some small share of his very considerable power in Pennsylvania politics. Little Davey was a Red, a romantic adventurer, and something of a criminal, but if Little Davey wanted an hour or so of undivided attention from one of the most influential men in the American government, so be it. If your name was Steadman, that seemed to be enough.

"What will you do when all this is finished?" he asked, taking off his glittering, gold-framed spectacles and polishing them with a handkerchief he kept in his vest pocket. It was a sign of embarrassment. "I don't suppose you can possibly go back to Europe."

David Steadman smiled. He knew exactly what his brother was thinking.

"No—you're right. I can't go back to Europe. I suppose we'll get into the war one time or another, though. I guess I'll wait for that."

"You know, pop didn't make good on his threat about disinheriting you. At least, not quite. A quarter of the company stock is still in your name, so if you want in . . ."

"Can you really feature me as a capitalist magnate, Carl?" The younger brother allowed his rather strained smile to broaden to a grin. "Can you really?"

"No. I suppose not."

The brothers Steadman had dinner together in David's room at the Madison Hotel. There were two goons out in the corridor to guard the door, and when the time came they would accompany him to the apartment building where he was to meet Harrison Walters.

"Is this where Walters lives? It doesn't sound like his sort of neighborhood."

"It isn't." Carl Steadman glanced nervously at the door, as if he expected armed stormtroopers to come bursting in from one minute to the next. "He lives in College Park—I had it checked. The apartment is leased in the name of George Bailey. I have the impression he meets his girlfriends there."

It was obvious from the way his voice dropped that he didn't approve. Carl had married right out of college, and his choice hadn't indicated much of a taste for fireworks. But it wasn't Harrison Walters' morals that had him worried.

"I don't like it," he went on finally, stirring his coffee with absentminded ferocity. "I don't trust any of that crowd around Roosevelt. Half of them are Bolsheviks and the others are working more for Churchill than they are for us. It was different with the last administration—Hoover at least was a gentleman, but these new men don't seem to believe in anything."

"I thought Hoover was a Bolshevik. Come on, Carl, when did Hoover stop being a Bolshevik?"

"You should have let me hold out for a meeting in his office," Carl announced suddenly, ignoring his brother's little joke. "At least there the fact of the meeting would be public property. He wouldn't be able to claim later that it never happened."

"There wasn't time—you know that."

"Yes, I know that."

Still, it was strange. The note had been waiting for them when they checked in: *Could we meet 276 Connecticut Avenue, Apt. #44? No third parties, please.* There hadn't even been a signature, but Walters was the only one who knew where they would be staying. Carl had phoned the White House and been told that Mr. Walters would be away for the rest of the day. It was a little out of the ordinary.

Walters didn't have the faintest notion of the subject of their meeting— or, at least, he wasn't supposed to have—but already he was handling the whole matter as gingerly as a hot coal. It made you wonder.

But David Steadman wasn't going to let any of that worry him. Perhaps Walters simply didn't care that anyone should have definite knowledge of his having had contact with someone about whom the intelligence services doubtless had all kinds of outlandish things in their files, or perhaps he was afraid of Carl—lots of people were afraid of Carl.

There was just no time to get picky. The first week of December was now only hours away, and Harrison Walters was close enough to Roosevelt that it hardly made any difference. Steadman kept telling himself that in an hour the letter would be off his hands.

Twenty minutes later, when the limousine Carl had rented pulled up in front of a rather squat brick building just north of the National Zoo, Steadman looked out at the sidewalk, empty and grayish yellow under the streetlamps, and wondered all over again if he wasn't committing a ghastly mistake. He had come a long way. He didn't want to get killed on the last yard.

"Why don't you guys cruise around a little," he told the two men sitting together on the front seat—during the entire trip neither of them had spoken or even turned his head; Steadman hardly remembered what they looked like. "Make sure things are clear for when I come back out."

The driver nodded slowly.

"Sure, Mr. Steadman. You want a heater to take with you?"

The pistol he offered over the backrest of the front seat was a huge military automatic. Steadman shook his head.

"Thanks, no."

No one tried to shoot him as he walked across the lobby, and the elevator didn't take him down to the basement to be set upon by thugs. Harrison Walters, when he opened the apartment door, couldn't have looked less like a desperado. Carl was an alarmist. Everything would be fine.

"Can I offer you a drink, Mr. Steadman?" Walters asked, stepping aside to let him pass over the threshold. Except that he was in better shape, and his hair was grayer, the man might have been a carbon copy of brother Carl—it could even have been the same suit. When Steadman declined, he was directed toward a chair with a courtly wave of the special assistant's well-tended hand. "Now. What can I do for you?"

Steadman reached inside his coat and passed across the small, uncluttered coffee table that separated them the two sheets of paper he had shown to his brother on the train. Walters glanced at the German text and a vexed expression passed over his face—apparently the adviser on foreign affairs was not a student of languages. He then read Steadman's translation. This time his face registered nothing at all.

"So?" He raised his eyebrows quizzically, folded the two sheets together, and slid them into his coat pocket. The action struck Steadman as significant. "What am I to make of these?"

"The German text is authentic. I imagine by now you must know the signature."

"These things are very easily forged."

"This one came out of the safe in the German embassy in Stockholm," Steadman said, tired of repeating himself. "I stole it at the behest of the British War Ministry."

He then told Walters the whole story, complete with names, dates, and places. He tried to leave nothing out—nothing, of course, except any mention of Arsène Vidocq and Company. Nothing except the merest suggestion that any such person as Lady Karen Windermere even existed. His audience took it all in with remarkable calm.

"And what do you expect us to do about all this?" Walters asked finally. Steadman was a little taken aback. It wasn't a question he had anticipated.

"I expect you to take measures to protect the Pacific Fleet. I expect you to take this warning seriously."

Walters squirmed uncomfortably in his seat. He didn't like any of this, but who would?

"That much, I suppose, we'll have to do."

He rose, pulling down the front of his vest to indicate that the interview had reached a close.

"I want to thank you, Mr. Steadman," he said, smiling thinly. "I appreciate the risks this affair has involved for you personally, and I want to assure you that the president will hear of the matter at once."

And that, it seemed, was that.

As he rode down in the elevator, David Steadman wondered why he felt so ill at ease. It wasn't his problem anymore, he told himself. The letter was in the hands for which it had been intended—or as good as—and he was out of business as a secret agent. The only decision he had to make was what he was going to do with the rest of the evening. He was now retired from the war.

The limousine wasn't parked outside, which was a little surprising, but perhaps they were still off on patrol. Steadman had reached the sidewalk before he noticed that there was a taxi parked on the other side of the street with its interior lights on. The guy seemed to be reading something.

Half of them are Bolsheviks and the others are working for Churchill, Carl had said. You hardly had to ask which way it went with Harrison Walters—with a suddenness that virtually amounted to paralysis, Steadman realized that he had been set up.

There was a screech of tires and the low growl of an engine as the taxi started angling across the street toward him. He knew it was time to run—what else was there to do?—but somehow he couldn't. He stood there fascinated.

And then he understood why. It was so funny he almost laughed. Weinschenk hadn't been the only one to anticipate his next several moves. The man behind the wheel was Major Brian Horton. That was why he had the interior light on—he wanted Steadman to know.

By the time he could bring himself to move he knew it was already too late. He managed to turn around and actually started running. It didn't matter—there was nowhere to run to. As the noise from the accelerating taxi grew loud enough to blot out everything else, he just had time to wonder, in a spirit of disinterested inquiry, if the impact was likely to kill him.

XXXVII

MARCH 21, 1942

The weather was frightful that March. People said it was supposed to be the longest period of sustained cold in centuries. No one ever seemed to smile anymore. It was as if they had come to the end of their strength.

Karen Windermere had left the War Ministry in January. No one wished her luck or said good-bye; it was as if they all knew that she had betrayed them. Brian Horton hadn't even been in the office on her last day. She had taken a job resettling the children of people who had been killed in the Blitz, and she found that very much more to her taste. The only side she cared to take any more in this war was that of the victims.

She had never heard what happened to David. Vidocq might have known, but she hadn't wanted to risk contacting him—sometimes she had the feeling that she was being watched. Besides, she was reasonably sure that David was dead.

On December 7, the Japanese had attacked Pearl Harbor, just as he had said they would. If he had lived to deliver his warning, then how could such a thing have happened? David had been so prepared to die, so how could he possibly be alive? So they had stopped him somehow after all.

And that had been over three months ago, and in all that time there hadn't been a word from him. He would have sent some message.

Gradually, like the children for whom she tried finding foster parents or, when that was possible, family members who were prepared to take them in, she had come to accept the fact, as a fact, that no one was coming home. It was like being widowed all over again and, this time, not in easy stages.

It had been bitterly hard. There was no one to whom she could talk about it, no one who knew, no one who would have understood. When Bertie had come unstuck on her, there had been David there to help her over the worst of it, but there was no David this time.

The worst of this was they had never really had a chance to love each other. There was no store of happy memories, nothing but the future that had never happened. She felt empty. It was only after she had come to accept that he was dead that she really understood how much she had cared about him, how much he could have meant to her if the chance had been given to them. There was a great void in her life that he had been meant to fill, and now she couldn't even fill it with his ghost.

She filled her time with other people's problems and, like other people who lived alone, closed off the vacant rooms in her heart. It was like being dead.

But today was Saturday. She only worked a half day on Saturdays, and they were the worst. Yesterday it had been exactly four months since the last time she had seen David. Four months ago today he had sailed. She honestly didn't know how she was going to get through it.

As usual, the bus let her off on the Cromwell Road, and as she stepped out onto the sidewalk her breath formed a dazzling white plume in the air. Everyone looked acutely miserable and walked along with quick little steps, as if they couldn't wait until they were back inside. The frost in the corners of shopwindows gave the appearance of having been there since the beginning of time.

There was no fruit to be had, not even tinned, and the few available greens looked wilted and flabby. Karen used the last of her meat points to purchase a quarter pound of boiled ham. She had an apple at home, and that suggested possibilities. If things got any worse, she would have to break down and go visit her mother in the country, where the neighbors were making a fortune selling vegetables out of their private garden plots, but that was absolutely a last resort.

As she made her way back toward Bulls Garden, the wind bit at the backs of her legs and she could feel the cold settling in the joints of her feet and toes. The pavement was like ice. She felt so low that the sheer physical misery was almost a relief.

The elevator in her building remained patriotically off. By the time she reached her door she was as numb as a pack animal. She hardly even knew where she was.

When she opened the door, and switched on the light, the first thing she saw was a pair of khaki trouser legs sticking out toward the cold fireplace.

She experienced a flash of memory, followed by nothing except despair. She didn't know who it was or what he wanted, and she hardly cared. This was simply too much.

Then, with the slow movement that seemed to involve the management of a cane, he stood up. He was smiling at her. It was David. She felt her heart breaking within her as hope competed with a stunned, astonished dread.

"David," she whispered. "Is it really you?"

A second later, in his arms, where she could feel the solid reality of him, the tears racked her in great, helpless spasms.

Suddenly she pulled away from him, holding him by the arms as she stared into his face. Her eyes were wide with fright.

"How did you get in?" she asked excitedly. "You didn't . . ."

"No, I didn't. I bribed your landlady, and she let me in with a key. I hoped you wouldn't mind, but my days as a cat burglar are over."

Then she remembered the cane.

"I was hit by a taxi," he said, swaying back into his chair and hooking the cane over the arm. "I remember the impact, and bouncing over the roof, but I don't remember hitting the pavement. I woke up in the hospital ten days later with a broken hip. I'll never run any four-minute miles, but eventually, they tell me, if I keep it exercised, I should be nearly as good as new."

He smiled at her. He looked fine—rested and healthy. He was wearing a tan greatcoat of unfamiliar military cut. It was with something of a shock that Karen realized she was looking at a soldier.

After a few minutes, when the heat from the gas fireplace began to make itself noticed, he took off the greatcoat and she could see that he was wearing a pair of silver bars on each shoulder.

"I wasn't sure what kind of a reception I'd get." The smile, which had never left his face, began to look a trifle strained as she knelt down beside his chair and he covered her hand with his own. "I wouldn't blame you a bit if you kicked me out this minute."

"I love you, David."

"That makes it convenient," he said, taking her fingers up to his lips.

"But how did you get into the army? I mean, if your hip . . ."

"It was my price." He leaned forward and kissed her on the temple, almost as if he intended to whisper something in her ear. "For keeping silence."

He had been in a private sanitarium in Baltimore for two and a half months, under armed guard.

"My brother wouldn't let anyone near me," he told her. "He was afraid they might try again."

"Who might try again?"

"For one, your good friend Brian Horton. He had help, of course; we never established very clearly who. But let me tell you this—there's a fellow named Harrison Walters who will never work in government again. That was my brother's price."

They were sitting in the kitchen, eating tinned peaches that hadn't been on the shelves in London in longer than Karen could remember. As usual, David had brought a knapsack full of unimaginable delicacies with him, enough to light life up for the rest of the month.

"But this is the end of it," he warned, wiping a drop of syrup from his chin—he was as greedy as a child. "I've sworn off being rich for the duration."

It was a joke. He dropped the spoon back into his empty dish, where it rang like a chime, and slid down in the kitchen chair, resting his hands on his stomach with the air of an overfed cat.

"They spoiled me in that place," he went on. "They had everything but dancing girls. They even had a glassed-in sunroom up on the roof— how do you like my tan?"

"But how did you ever get clear?"

"Oh—that. My brother took care of that. He went to see Roosevelt, practically pushed his way into the Oval Office. 'You hooligans think you can get away with anything! Try to murder my brother, will you? I'll have this all over the front page of every newspaper in the country!' I don't think Roosevelt had an inkling what he was talking about, but the message got through fast enough. It was a week after Pearl Harbor, and they didn't need that kind of trouble. Four thousand killed or wounded, did you know that? The fleet shot to pieces, then Singapore, Malaya . . . The Japs have already got most of the Philippines. It's a proper mess."

The muscles in his jaw were working as if they had a life of their own as he sat staring out the kitchen window. Karen didn't know what to say, so she said nothing. He hardly seemed to realize she was there anyway.

He snapped back to life, smiling and getting up from his chair, using the back of it for support as he rummaged around through the cabinets over her sink.

"I could use a cup of tea. Is there any tea left in this country, or are they using it all for airplane fuel?"

It was at moments like this, when he was at his brightest, that she saw most clearly the intensity of his pain. It seemed to have nothing to do with guilt, or a sense of lost opportunities, or anything so crudely personal. It was as if the world had forfeited its innocence.

"They won their point, you know." Just as quickly as it had come, his animation left him. He stood there, with his hand on the back of a chair, apparently not even remembering why he had troubled to stand up. "Your boss never had a thing to worry about. Nobody wanted to hear any warnings—nobody was listening."

"It wasn't your fault, David."

For a moment he seemed not to have heard, and then he looked at her with his peculiar, strained smile, as if she had made a joke.

"I know it isn't my fault," he said softly, like someone acknowledging the innocence of some third person. "What difference does that make? I don't have to shoot myself—fine. I can go on with my life as if nothing had happened. In the meantime, thousands of men are dead and thousands more are going to be because it was decided that it was okay to throw them away. They're acceptable losses. It was worth it to get the United States into the war. Maybe it even was, but they're just as dead for all that."

He shrugged his shoulders and smiled again and started opening the little square tins that were lined up in a row in the cupboard directly over the sink. Finally he found one that seemed to have something in it; he sniffed the contents and his eyes widened with pleasure.

"Formosa Oolong—it'll be a while before we see any of that again. We won't even have to use milk."

Karen took the tin from his hand and started heating up some water. She got out her best teapot, since it seemed to be something of an occasion, and for a while they were able to escape again into their little private party.

"Anyway, by the time I came around we were at war." He reached across the table and took both of Karen's hands in his own as she decided that she was probably going to have to get used to these abrupt transitions. "My poor chump of a brother had actually thought it was just an ordinary, garden-variety traffic accident. His bodyguards—*my* bodyguards—had been decoyed away. It was all very skillfully done. Then I woke up and told him how the taxi had been parked there, with a driver straight out of my nightmares. But by then, of course, it was too late to do anything. What were we supposed to do? Announce to the country while they were waiting for the Japanese to land in California that their president was surrounded by traitors? It wouldn't wash."

"So you did—nothing?"

She hadn't meant for it to sound so . . . well, disdainful. It wasn't that she didn't understand. After all, what were the choices?

Still, it didn't sound like David.

He squeezed her hands, as if to make her understand that he wouldn't hold it against her if she didn't believe he was perfect.

"I had a lot of time to think," he said, releasing his grasp, seeming to wait for her to withdraw herself from his touch. When she didn't, when she brought her thumb up, the tip resting against his, it seemed once more to balance things between them, and he let his fingers curl around the sides of her hands.

"I had weeks and weeks with my leg up in traction, with Carl's goons parked on the other side of the door—so I didn't even have to worry about getting shot in the head by a passing orderly, and after a while it came to me that nobody was going to believe a story like that anyway. I didn't even have the letter anymore and, besides, what good would it do? Even Carl saw that eventually."

"Carl is your brother?"

"Yes. You'll like Carl—he's the last righteous man. He thinks I should become vice-president in charge of ball bearings."

"And instead you became a soldier."

"That's right—the president himself ordered my commission. I'm a captain, assigned to Intelligence. I think my posting over here so fast is Roosevelt's idea of a joke on the British, a little reminder that he knows about the family skeleton."

"But—" She shook her head. It was all coming too quickly. "What about Brian and all that? Is it safe, David?"

"Safe as houses." He smiled again, and this time without the confusing overlay of sadness. "That was the first thing I did when I got off the plane yesterday. I arranged a little meeting—I can do that sort of thing now; you'd be surprised at the drag I've got—and you should have seen his face when I walked in through his office door."

He raised his left hand, spreading the fingers, which somehow managed to convey an impression of speechless surprise. Yes, she could imagine precisely what Brian had looked like.

"I laid it out for him," he went on, bringing his hand back to cover hers. "There's a letter being held by my lawyer in the States. I'm the forgiving type, but if I die in a bombing accident or get hit by a bolt of lightning or fall down from a heart attack in the middle of Bond Street, my little memoir of life on the Continent goes straight to the *New York Times*. And there are to be no reprisals against my friends, if he ever figures out who they are. His secret is safe, provided he doesn't get too ambitious. I had to make sure of that before I could come here."

"I never thought I'd see you again." She stretched her arms across the table, touching his face with both hands. The tears were springing up in her eyes, but she didn't care. "Oh, David, I never thought I'd see you again."

"Neither did I. I never thought I'd be able to come back."

He reached around for his cane, which was hooked over the back of his chair, and, possibly as much out of pure embarrassment as anything else, rose and took his teacup into the other room.

"I don't mean because of Horton," he went on, talking over his shoulder as he struggled with the delicate business of keeping his tea from spilling. His limp was really very pronounced. "I mean because of what I'd made you do. I said to myself, 'She's turned herself inside-out to keep me alive. Is that what she's going to remember every time she looks at me?' And then all of our grand sacrifices came to exactly nothing. They went ahead and let Hawaii get bombed anyway. There weren't any sterling characters anymore, and both of us had gotten diddled. You by Horton and his crew, and me by the special assistant for foreign affairs. Don't ask me why that made the difference, but it did."

He frowned, setting down the cup on the table where Bertie's old numbers of *Horse and Hound* used to lay, and lowered himself into the chair where Bertie used to sit reading them. His eyes were fixed on Karen's face as she stood with her back to the kitchen door; he almost seemed to be daring her to look away.

"It's not really my war now, sweetheart," he said, shaking his head as if at some distasteful recollection. "I'll sit at a desk and write memos about the Berlin-Madrid cable traffic. It's just as well—I couldn't even catch a bus now—but I'm out of it. I'll work City hours and shop at Selfridge's for knitted ties to send home to my brother. And the worst part of it is I don't seem to care. I seem to have lost my taste for causes."

He paused for a moment, just as if he planned to say something else, and then suddenly he took a deep, gulping breath and his lower jaw began working in a peculiar way. It wasn't until she saw the tears coursing down his face that she realized what was happening. She started to move toward him when the sound of his voice stopped her.

"Oh, God, baby," he cried, almost choking on the words. "Oh, God, what have they made us do? What have they done to us?"

When his tea had grown cold she brought him another cup, and they sat together in the tiny parlor of her flat for a long time, neither of them speaking. Gradually he began to come out of it.

And then a thought struck her, a practical consideration.

"You don't have to live in barracks, do you?" she asked. "Do you suppose we could just keep on in this place?"

"That was what I had in mind."